CW00548930

THE GENIUS KILLER

ORLA
KELLY
PUBLISHING

Mark Robson

Copyright © 2023 by Mark Robson

978-1-915502-21-6

All rights reserved. No parts of this publication may be reproduced, stored in a retrieval system or transmitted in any form or by any means, without the prior written permission of the author, nor be otherwise circulated in any form of binding or cover other than that in which it is published.

This book is intended for your personal use only and is a work of fiction.

Any resemblance to actual persons, living or dead, or actual events is purely coincidental. Published in Ireland by Orla Kelly Publishing. Cover design by TSL Designs.

Orla Kelly Publishing
27 Kilbrody,
Mount Oval,
Rochestown,
Cork,
Ireland.

ACKNOWLEDGEMENTS

My thanks go to many inspirational influences. I was originally given encouragement to write 'The Genius Killer' by one of Northern Ireland's legendary journalists Deric Henderson. Deric wrote 'Let This Be Our Secret' - a story of love and double murder which later appeared as a hugely successful mini-series as 'The Secret' on ITV and Netflix with James Nesbitt and Genevieve O'Reilly in the main roles. Later I was given fabulous advice by Michael McLoughlin from Penguin Ireland and Patsy Horton of Blackstaff Press.

I worked with the Inkwell Group publishing consultancy in Ireland through Vanessa O'Loughlin, founder of Ireland's International Crime Festival, who has written a compendium of successful novels under the pseudonym Sam Blake. I had two 'Reader's Reports' through Inkwell by Mary Stanley, author of 'The Lost Garden', and Adrian White, author of 'An Accident Waiting To Happen'. I grafted many of their incredibly helpful suggestions into my rewrites which got me to this novel - the final product.

I'd also like to thank my former girlfriend Petra for giving me the kick I needed to start this book. Petra read the very first tentative draft, offered great advice, and patiently monitored my troubled and grumpy relationship with punctuation. Petra's Mum Helen played a huge role too. Then there was Dorothy Jones, Katie Sparham and her daughter Aoibh, and journalist Rebecca Root who all took the time to read various drafts and give me essential feedback. Many great women have helped me. As you'll have confirmed in 'The Genius Killer' they are the more important gender of the human species.

Then there was Graham Simmons, the finest journalist I have ever worked with, who painstakingly reviewed the first manuscript and came back to me with a forensic analysis. Graham, I think, is almost addicted to good writing and collects first editions – he knows what he's talking about. My good old Dad read an early version too and hand wrote pages of helpful notes. Cheers Dad. Also a nod to my chums Andy Brennan and Les Conn who gave me nods of approval. And young James Skelton who gave me vital feedback on character development.

And thanks to Alan Mains who investigated a large number of murders during his long service with the RUC. Alan was involved in the solving of the horrific Soham Murders in 2002 when two 10-year-old girls, Holly Wells and Jessica Chapman, were killed by local school caretaker Ian Huntley. Alan, having read the final rewrite, kindly gave me the quote that you see on the front cover.

And finally to my wonderful publisher Orla Kelly of Orla Kelly Publishing. On our first Zoom call I could feel her warm and enthusiastic energy. Without Orla you wouldn't be reading this.

PART ONE

CHAPTER ONE

A crunchy canopy lay under naked branches. Like spider's legs they whipped in the wind. It was a late autumn day on the flatlands close to the western fells of the Cumbrian mountains. Karl Jackson parked his 1972 Saturn Yellow Volkswagen Beetle under the copse of trees in the north corner of the Royal Burlington Hospital car park. He stepped out of the classic car and flicked a look, as he always did, at the roof which had faded over time to a shade that was more school dinner custard. Karl was hit by a blast as cold as his soul and flipped up the wide collars of his favourite camel hair coat. His breath steamed like a freshly boiled kettle. The fur on Karl's old trapper hat rippled like waves in a squall. The flaps resembled the wings of a hovering hawk as they thrashed in a frenzy. Karl Jackson, the chemistry teacher at the local boys school, Rimpton High, struggled to gather the leather thong beneath his chin but, after several grasps, Karl caught it and tied it. The easterly gale was relentless. It was Cumbria's coldest November day for thirty-three years. Men in mittens and duffle coats had shovelled salt over the potholed tarmac, reducing the glazed car park surface to a creamy mush. It was hard to tell what was icier, the Siberian airflow or Karl's intent. He paddled and crunched his way to the main entrance, and took the lift to ward 6C.

The day before, Karl's mother, Valerie, phoned him. Social services had told her that her long-time ex-husband Harry had suffered a heart attack. Karl held the mobile to his ear and listened and sizzled. At times like this, he could almost taste the change in his body chemistry as if the excitement was actually seeping from his skin. Karl's gentle tremble was just about the only physical give away when his darker side kicked in, and he struggled to quieten the noise that swirled like a starling storm inside his head.

***

Karl hated his father more than any other man alive and now, at last, he had the kind of access he had been craving. He needed to

3

slow down his thinking. As his Mum talked in her classic clipped style Karl closed his eyes and sucked air over his tongue. It was a form of tantric relaxation, something he'd picked up from a book on Buddhist meditative breathing. The black mass of starlings began to thin, and Karl could see the sky again. This was where Karl, in his own mind, was at his best when he could slide from frenzy to fantasy to formulation to final solution. He crafted a plan, and the planning was just as much fun as the execution. Karl was often overwhelmed by his genius and needed all those meditation techniques to corral his impulsiveness.

Karl would have preferred a Texas Chainsaw Massacre-style attack on Harry. He smiled as he walked to the ward. He imagined himself crashing off the hospital walls and howling out a Cherokee wail while on a deer hunt for his Father. But that wouldn't have been cool. Best to make sure that the lock on that particular padlock stayed rusty, and in any case, the not-so-humble Karl genuinely believed that, in terms of ingenuity, he was probably in the top five killers on the planet. However, it had been some years since he'd committed murder.

It was visiting time. The nurse at reception cradled her chin between her flowering palms; head tilted as if she had a lead weight in one earlobe. If eyes could sing, hers did. 'The Magnet', as Karl had been nicknamed at university, was standing in front of her. Karl inhaled a coagulation of disinfectant and rose petals as he smoothed his way into the nurse's personal space. Her spherical face reminded Karl of a beach ball, but he knew that women could be pliant in his presence.

"Hi there… Ruth?" Karl had snatched a look at her name badge. Ruth was becoming more malleable with each skipping heartbeat. "Oh that's a lovely perfume," Karl drizzled. Ruth weakened before the Amazonian gaze. Karl's face creased into irresistibility, "I know it's only meant to be an hour, but I haven't seen my Father for many years. And I've heard that he is desperately ill. There might not be many more days like this." Karl telling the truth was rare but here it came, "I love him so much."

By now, Ruth was pouting like the female lead in an amateur dramatics romcom. If she'd flirted for much longer, she would have melted completely and ended up as a puddle on the floor. Karl picked his moment perfectly, "I know it's only meant to be an hour, but could I possibly stay a little longer? I have so much I want to talk to him about. This might be the last time." Ruth had stripped Karl naked and was scanning him, "Take as long as you want, as long as you come and say hello before you go."

Karl walked into Harry's private room. The hulking brick that Karl remembered from his boyhood had turned into a fleshy mound. At first sight, the blob on his dad's shoulders didn't look like a head. Harry's best friend, Jack Daniels, had clearly used a meat tenderiser to create a masterpiece of pudge and blotches all connected by prominent veins. The snorting, slurring mass that had haunted the lives of his family now lay vulnerable and exposed. Harry was slumped and dozy. He looked like the exhausted, drunken, post-apocalyptic beast who would crash on 'Dad's Chair' while mum cooled the hysteria of bruises that made a pastel board across her body.

Karl and his brother Nathan often had lumps of their own to look after. What feelings did the sight of his father bring back? Seething, boiling, bubbling hate! Karl wanted to rip out the multitude of tubes and wires attached to Harry's prone and vulnerable frame. But Karl knew that he wouldn't have to. Instead, he felt a soothing warmth; his plan was in place.

Through his groggy fog, Harry recoiled, slowly disappearing into the bubble of pillows. A rasp replaced his even breathing. Harry appeared to be attempting to make his escape by reversing through the wall. How many times Karl had dreamt of a day like this. But he was not at the Royal Burlington Hospital for malicious reasons. Well, he was, but not yet. That could wait. Right now, he was genuinely interested in his father's health and fascinated to learn about the finer details of his treatment from the cardiac specialists. And sure wasn't this a great time to show his brutal father that he could forgive. Karl was very much in the moment and thinking happy thoughts, "This is my time. Let the pantomime begin."

Karl settled into the moulded chair beside his father's bed, "Hi Dad." "Hello... son." Harry's voice had a soupçon of vibrato running through it. "Sorry Dad. It's been a while. I think you can work out the reasons. Do I need to tell you? I mean, really, do I?" Harry stared, veins now flushing with a dangerous density. Karl continued, "You and Mum, you know, splitting up was difficult for all of us but Mum told me you were ill so I just wanted to see how you were. Doing a son's duty. Simple as that really."

Harry was having flashbacks. A combination of painkillers and genuine fear. He remembered the day when the teenage Karl had first fought back. The day when Harry had gone for the usual backhanded swipe but instead of skull a forearm had met him and a voice, more gravelly now. Karl's acidic eyes were angled up to meet his father's look of bleary shock, "Fuck off Dad. You fucking drunken bastard. Someday I'm going to fucking kill you. You don't scare me anymore."

Harry would never have made the lithe and athletic club, but if there'd been a fat rhino look-a-like competition, he would have been consistently on top of the podium. As time passed, the rhino morphed into a hippo while Karl's soft tissue hardened simultaneously. Harry's torso began to expand into a cantilever of blubber while Karl's ascension into vine-muscled demi-god gathered pace.

No surprise then when Harry felt himself stiffen at the sight of his now fully mature son. Karl was smiling, the callous charm treacling out. Harry threw lizard-like looks around the room, smelling his own heat. He was as vulnerable as a kettled whale. Harry tried to think himself into a calmer state, *"There is little danger here. This is a hospital. He wouldn't do anything would he? Not in full sight? He's not that stupid. Is he?"*

Eyes liquid and bulging, Harry was remembering more. He had been threatened by Karl many times towards the end of his marriage to Valerie and, on separate occasions, by Nathan too. He had witnessed both of his sons' rage first hand. That fury had come as no surprise to Harry, after all it was in the Jackson DNA.

Harry didn't know that he had only ever witnessed Karl's contained 'Red Rage'. The 'Red Rage' was a verbal rage. Violence was often threatened by Karl in that state but never truly forthcoming. It was the Arctic 'White Rage' that Harry needed to be worried about. Right now Karl was in his ice-cool white zone. That space where he could engage in an apparently empathetic way while thinking completely differently. Harry was in no danger at all. Karl was all olive eyes and glistening grin - the mask was on. He was slowly gaining his father's trust but deep within the landscape was a little different. Karl was on full tingling alert, periscoping his surroundings and taking in every detail. He could sense that quasi-sexual feeling. This was the foreplay and how much Karl loved foreplay, especially when it came to murder.

Harry had suffered a serious cardiac arrhythmia brought on by his hard-living, boozing years. And those years were still happening. He'd been drinking on the day he'd been admitted to hospital. Harry saw this inconvenient cocooning as an interruption to a hobby he'd loved much more than his family. The main issue for Harry, while in hospital, was that he had no access to alcohol. Harry could feel the start of the 'DT's'- Delirium Tremens. Though right now, as he watched his son, he wasn't sure if the shakes were completely alcohol-related.

Harry was in the Cardiac Care Unit. As in all CCUs, and Intensive Care Units in general, it was staffed around the clock by highly trained physicians, and the staff-to-patient ratio was higher than that in a typical hospital unit. The patients were monitored closely and constantly. This was a hindrance to Karl, but it was also a glorious challenge.

Harry was on a cardiac monitor, which analysed each beat of his hard heart. The staff would be alerted automatically if his arrhythmia kicked in. Harry also had, amongst other pieces of complicated-looking equipment, a catheter in a wrist artery to monitor his blood pressure with another connected to his bladder. Specialists came and went in sporadic flurries of green gowns and white coats. Karl small talked with his father while forensically studying the staff's every movement and time spent on each task.

"Have they given you a prognosis Dad?" Karl didn't care. He was happy to warble on for as long as was necessary as he multi-tasked. When it was time to go, Harry, the old tyrant, who had stuttered and stumbled for the best part of an hour, saying nothing of consequence, was almost relaxed despite the discomfort of his medical trauma and the presence of his son. "Will you be back? I know we've had troubles in the past Karl, but it's been good to see you." Karl thought, *"Maybe age has mellowed the chubby, pickled, vicious old bastard."*

"Yes I'll be back," said Karl, who felt slight nausea as he snaked out the words, "Seeing you ill has given me a sense of the importance of family." He said a lot of things he didn't mean. The morally ambiguous Karl told many multitudes of untruths, but this was his own personal propaganda. Throw in a bit of gaslighting, and he had a powerful combo. Karl wanted the man he despised more than any other to be at ease. At least for now.

"I'll come back next week," said Karl. Harry leaned across and whispered, "Will you do me a favour son? Could you bring me a wee nip of whiskey? I'm desperate for a drink here. It's against the regulations, but it would give me something to look forward to." Karl was delighted. Ecstatic in fact. "Of course, Dad, of course."

***

The Dark Web was a useful place and Karl was an expert navigator. He knew exactly what he needed. The dungeons of the internet were such a marvellous playground for the malevolent. Karl returned to the hospital nine days later - on full predatory alert. He noted that, on this particular day, fewer medics were on duty.

Ruth was in the hallway of the Cardiac Unit and caught a glimpse of her superman gliding across the mop-streaked tiles. Ruth ghosted like a banshee, and Karl instinctively jolted when the staff nurse, as if by magic, appeared in his face. "Hello Karl." The ear still had the invisible weight attached. "Ah! Ruth. I've been thinking about you. How are you?" Ruth did a full body swoon, and for a moment, Karl thought he might be dragged into one of the consultation rooms to be consumed by Ruth amongst a wash of bodily fluids. "Your Dad is doing very well Karl. He's talked about you. This visit. He has definitely been excited about it."

The smell of disinfectant and rose petals was worse than the last time. "You're still wearing that lovely perfume," said Karl, fully aware that Harry was excited about the thought of alcohol and most definitely not excited about the idea of seeing his son. Karl moved closer and pressed his presence into Ruth's personal space. "Ruth," the melting process had started again, "Can I have some more special time with Dad? My visits will be limited. I really want to make the most of it." He moved in closer and whispered, "Ruth, I'll make it up to you." Ruth broke under Karl's brutal interrogation. Now he had all the time he needed. When Karl walked in, Harry was sitting up in bed, looking less rubbery than the slumped carcass of before. However, he was still a shade of magnolia and slivers of saliva hung like stalactites from his lower lip. "*Excellent,*" Karl thought. Too much of an improvement in his father's condition would have been no good at all. Might have aroused more suspicion than necessary.

As he developed through youth and into adulthood, Karl's creative, if unhealthy thinking, had sprouted slowly at first. Over time he assembled the crucial building blocks. Then, as his imagination gathered pace, it took off like a pandemic. Karl had already dispatched two human beings who deserved his attention. Over the years, he had gathered a selection of foolproof methods, which he stored on his internal hard drive and in his notebooks. Now the time had come to transfer the contents of his handwritten textbooks from ink to evil.

During his stone-hearted studies, Karl was often dismissive. He couldn't determine why so many killers could kill with such skill but then make a schoolboy error and get caught. This pulled Karl into many hours of rumination.

"Why don't they plan more? Surely the idea is to kill and get away with it. Most serial killers seem to follow predictable patterns - their 'Modus Operandi'. I thought Ted Bundy's method was clever; an

estimated 36 kills, that's a good return. Bundy would approach women while feigning an injury, often wearing a cast, and ask them to carry his books. A clever ruse.

Drove a yellow Volkswagen too - good taste. Not sure if it was Saturn though. Post-mortem killers often have a 'Signature' like leaving a stamp on a body or 'posing' a corpse into a particular position. In my view, that's too idiosyncratic. It's a fault line that increases the chances of getting caught.``

Karl understood the reasons for a 'Modus Operandi' and why killers preferred to have their own particular 'Signature'. 'Modus Operandi' being the way killers felt they had to carry out a murder to feel maximum satisfaction. In Karl's view, this simply exposed them as weak and ill-disciplined. Discipline was essential. Much more chance of achieving one's goal and sliding away unnoticed. Then multiple successes could be achieved without any investigation team linking murders together. Karl was a perfectionist; for him, the kill had to go precisely the way he had planned, or he didn't quite achieve full satisfaction. "*My climax,*" he called it. Karl's journals were exercise books really. Neatly compiled and filed - some hardback, some not. Highlighter pens illuminated favoured passages, those that gave him that glistening thrill of almost electric intensity. Was journaling his signature? Karl didn't think so. After all, he wasn't removing a memento like a necklace or a body part, and he didn't perform any ritual at a murder site unless he was trying to frame someone else. And in any case, regarding the journals, Karl planned to destroy them all when the time was right.

Karl wanted each murder to be unique. The question here was this: could Karl carry out what he needed to do without leaving any cause for suspicion? When he arrived at the hospital for the second time, he was certain that he had the skill set to achieve this goal. Harry was primed for departure. Old man Jackson watched his son glide from the door of his room to his bedside. The sedatives that had helped Harry sleep the previous night were beginning to wear off. He was still a little slow but the sight of Karl helped to jog Harry out of his sloth-like state.

Harry could be engaging when it suited him, but his motives were generally predictable. A man of a shrunken soul with few feelings for others. However, he did have an addiction.

Harry's feelings of enthusiasm when he saw Karl were not because his own flesh and blood had returned to see him, it was much more to do with his anticipation of the whiskey. Karl carried a small rucksack, and Harry's cold malfunctioning heart jumped at the thought. To Harry, Karl was nothing more than a mule. "Did you manage to bring me that wee nip son?" Karl recognised that slippery and crooked smile. He'd often seen it on his father's face as he stood over his mum in a moment of violent reflection.

Karl looked around and checked carefully that none of the staff were near the doorway. He then pulled a small plastic bottle from the side zip pocket of his mini rucksack. Harry spied the golden liquid that had helped to ruin his own life and, by default, that of the rest of his family. Karl noted later.

"I handed the bottle to Dad, at mattress level, and he slid it beneath the sheets. I watched Dad take a quick scout of the room and then unscrew the cap. He took great care not to spill the 'priceless' contents. Dad held the bottle to his lips. He closed his eyes. Dad seemed ecstatic as the fluid slid slowly down his throat. Fortunately for me Dad couldn't taste the crushed valium I'd powdered into the whiskey. Step One completed. I knew that the drink wouldn't last long. Dad was too desperate for the alcohol. I watched him cherish every drop." From there, it didn't take long."Son, maybe I'm not used to the alcohol," Harry said, "But that's hit me already. I've missed that feeling. Missed the taste. Thanks son."

Harry's eyes closed as he drifted into a sedated state. Karl was fully tuned in and hyper-vigilant. No medics or nurses were in the room, but the window of opportunity wouldn't last long. Karl walked to the door and scanned the corridor. The white coats and green smocks scurried about, absorbed in their business. Ruth was touching up her lipstick. Karl, from his first visit, reckoned he had two minutes maximum.

Karl had learned during his detailed reconnaissance that an autopsy rarely followed a hospital death if the patient died from the illness for which they had been admitted. This was what Karl was banking on. He had bought what he needed on the Dark Web. Another example of the lengths Karl would go to.

"I wanted to be as certain as possible that the purchase couldn't be traced. I had to fly to Amsterdam to collect the package. Initially, I wasn't sure why the stuff had to go to Holland, but that was the deal. I learned early that you didn't ask too many questions when working in the grubby underworld of the Dark Web. You got what you wanted and got out. Sometimes there were conditions to meet. Fine. After all, you were working with criminals. They dictated the terms - not me. The package had been left in a wild area of sand dunes close to Zandvoort on the Dutch North Sea coast. They'd sent an encrypted message with an eight-figure grid reference where I was told I would find a small ventilation shaft. I did a bit of Googling and found out this had been built as part of an Allied Forces camp during the Second World War. The area was heavily overgrown with seagrass, and the shaft took a little finding. Inside the package was a size 20 FR Catheter. I didn't need to go to the Dark Web to get a catheter, but it was exactly where I needed to go to get cyanide. I don't normally get nervous, but there was a little fear on the way home on the boat, although I was fairly sure that any kind of search was unlikely."

At Harry's bedside, Karl felt exceptionally calm. Everything was in place, and Karl simply had to complete a job he had looked forward to for many years. He removed the FR18 catheter attached via a tube to his father's bladder and replaced it with the FR20, which was slightly bigger. Karl needed the width for the carefully measured length of the wire coat hanger, which he transferred from his rucksack to the catheter. He slid it with calculated purpose into Harry's internal organs. The wire punctured Harry's bladder and perforated his intestines just enough to produce the required internal bleeding.

"With a hypodermic syringe, I injected the contents of a small vial of cyanide through the catheter. Dad didn't flinch. The whiskey and valium had done their job. I removed the wire, being ultra careful that not one drop of blood or body fluid fell onto any bedding. I wiped the syringe with a tissue and slipped all the incriminating items into a plastic bag. I switched the catheters again, put the FR20 alongside the wire and tissue inside the bag and then into the pocket on my rucksack, and zipped it up. Perfect."

About a minute later, Ruth came into the room."Still a bit dozy is he?" she said."Yes," said Karl."I got a few whispered words out of him but then he drifted off. Is it ok if I stay for a bit in case he wakes up?" In her head, Ruth was already planning dinner for two - and bed. Karl got permission to stay, and he sat staring at his father's face. He felt hatred and contentment at the same time.

Karl left the hospital knowing that Harry would die quite quickly due to internal bleeding. Toxic shock and a massive cardiac arrest would follow fast. The cyanide would hasten the procedure. Karl didn't want Harry to come round and cry out. Karl was covering his bases. Meticulous. The only slight disappointment for Karl was that Harry would die relatively peacefully and that he wouldn't be there to witness his father's final breath. After all that Harry had done, Karl felt his old man deserved a more brutal death. But this was about performing a task. It was all about revenge. The method had to be clean and leave a minimal chance of discovery. Karl, despite his self-belief, doubted that any murder could be fool proof, but his only concern here was an autopsy. A good pathologist would notice the small internal puncture wound that had led to the bleeding. A pathologist understanding biochemistry would notice the tell tale aroma of bitter almonds, a dead give away in the presence of cyanide. Karl minimised the risks, but they were still risks. Karl's technique for killing his father Harry had been inspired by the original 'Angel of Death' Donald Harvey.

Harvey had murdered an estimated eighty-seven people while working in hospitals in America. Harvey mostly killed cardiac sufferers, and Donald Harvey was one of Karl Jackson's dark-hearted heroes. Like Harvey, Karl, on this occasion, had used coat hangers and cyanide. Karl had wanted to kill his dad. Simple. That was the goal. Karl felt an intoxicating mix of power and control. His own addiction. As he had expected, there was no autopsy.

The death certificate read, "Natural Causes." Job done.

CHAPTER TWO

A sprinkling of reluctant mourners hunched themselves forward, exposed flesh nipped by icy fingers, the elements wrestling with black umbrellas. Leaves crackled under polished brogues. The hill looked like a half-buried bowling ball, and the crematorium clung with deathly determination to the summit, the converted church looking like an old crow when silhouetted against the salt and pepper sky. The building could be seen from the villages it serviced, a stairway to heaven for those who believed in such post-mortem delights. The grimy stained glass windows streamed, and each drop of rain landed with a gelatinous splat. Harry Jackson's coffin sat on a plinth. A forgettable hymn played through the speakers as the casket began its short journey across the rollers. The cheap gold curtains parted, and Harry was gone, descending slowly to the furnace below. Random echoing coughs were marinated with the melancholia of a drudging hymn. The crematorium had a distinctive aroma, dank and waxy, like a fusty bible. The smell had the kind of heaviness that permeated clothing.

Karl was pretty sure that the relations who had bothered to turn up were attending out of a sense of duty. Mourning wasn't a necessary emotion at this particular funeral.

Forty-two-year-old Karl Jackson sat in the front row, to the right of his brother Nathan and their mother, Valerie. Karl didn't have much in common with Nathan. The closest they ever got was the nine months they had spent face-to-face in their Mother's womb. To Karl's right was his wife of twenty-one years, Patricia, and their only child, nineteen-year-old son Kerry, who was thinking about abnormal behavioural patterns as he contemplated a subject for his psychology thesis.

To Kerry's right was Harry's brother Charlie who had flown in from Thailand - Charlie had always liked the Far East. Karl wanted to kill two of the people in that front row. He had his reasons. Too many members of the old church's gathering checked their watches. There wasn't one tear from any member of the sprinkling of gathered nearest and dearest.

Harry's ex-wife Valerie had felt a lot safer when the marriage ended, a marriage made in the place where Harry was hopefully going to spend perpetuity. *"When Harry met Satan,"* Karl mused a tight grin, the only evidence of his malevolent thoughts.

Valerie's emotions were relief, verging on happiness. She had a heron-like appearance and seemed to be in a permanently submissive pose. Her body was slightly curved, the shape of a woman preparing herself for an attack. Her complexion was milky, with prominent trench-like lines running in erratic patterns across her face. Valerie preferred to communicate through nods and short phrases, all delivered with a haunted whisper.

Throughout her marriage, Valerie learned that any attempt at authority ended with a beating at the hands of her husband. Valerie's belly warmed at the thought of Harry slowly incinerating somewhere in the bowels of the crematorium. The death of her husband felt like the gift of a second life for Valerie. The tyrant had finally gone.

Karl was daydreaming, imagining that his father was still alive in his tomb. Harry Jackson's heart thrashing inside the walnut coffin. The old bastard still breathing, hearing the initial ferocious fiery blast wrapping his wooden box in its hell fire embrace. Karl, when excited, could be remarkably poetic.

"Dad, I can see you. Your eyes are throbbing, full of fear. You are writhing like a demented contortionist, inhaling the seeping plumes of smoke and listening to the engine blasts of the burners reaching their crescendo. Can you hear the splits and cracks in the walnut? Dad, you're the burger on the barbecue," Karl was smiling. He'd read that the human body was 75% water. *"Dad, do you steam like broccoli on the boil? The skin would wax first, wouldn't it? Then burst into fist-sized blisters with your charred muscle extending and flexing?"* Karl's senses stirred. The feeling was almost sexual. *"The skull Dad, does it blow like a microwaved potato? Do you feel the pickled pink mush*

inside expanding before the bloody explosion? At what point is the pain at its most excruciating?"

The thought of his conscious father toasting made Karl buzz, enjoying the thought of Harry's final humiliation when the wire-bristled broom brushed out the five pounds of grey charcoal ash. Ball bearings would reduce the remains to a gravel of bone.

Karl was smiling, *"A gruesome human smoothie."*

The Jackson family thought God was nothing more than a swear word. A truly caring omnipotent being would have turned up for them by now. They'd hired a cheap rent-a-death vicar to conduct the ceremony. Clearly he'd never encountered a low-calorie diet. This man of the cloth resembled a walrus in a dog collar. Karl remembered that gluttony was a sin. If it was, wouldn't it mean that this flabby man of God would be consigned to Hell with his dad? The vicar ran his gaze along the line of closest relatives in the front pew of the crematorium. Valerie's mannequin stiffness was corpse-like. In a dark brown trouser suit, Patricia seemed to have melted into the oak pew behind her. Nathan nibbled at nail stumps.

Kerry had the raven's eyes of his father, and they darted occasionally. It seemed to be the only part of his body that moved. Charlie's every movement said slime, and he had the build of a man with a phobia for food. Charlie reminded Karl of a small giraffe, and he often wondered how Charlie's neck supported itself without scaffolding.

A very bored Karl was sneering at the vicar with a dismissive glaze on his face. *"Patronising prick. Look at him. Fat pig. He'd burn well in hell, sizzling like the meat on a kebab spike. I wonder how many hundreds of grieving relatives he's fixed with that look of faux sympathy. Pathetic."*

The vicar, who'd been standing respectfully to one side, waited for the canned hymn to reach its solemn conclusion and waddled back over to the pulpit to give the standard closing eulogy. A hackneyed, pre-prepared little sermon, perfect for the quasi atheists like the Jackson's. It had come straight from the book of insincerity. Karl imagined little gaps where the vicar added, in pencil, of course, the name of this funeral's particular unfortunate - to be rubbed out and replaced by the name of the next corpse on his list for the day.

A distracted Karl half heard a bit of it. Something about Harry Jackson joining the angels. Hells Angels, Karl would agree there, but by now, the vicar's words were a background wash. Karl had shifted into his dark world, fantasising again, this time about the various fun ways he could use a crematorium.

"Wouldn't it be great if you could do it? What a way to get your own back. A bit of road rage with some tailgating idiot. Drug him. Bundle him into the boot. Get to the crematorium.

Distract the funeral directors. Pull the dead body in the hearse out of the coffin and topple in the tailgating ass hole. Then you join the congregation. They're all tears and tissues, thinking they're giving a loved one the big send off. Meanwhile, tailgate boy is being barbecued alive in someone else's carefully chosen top-of-the-range cherrywood coffin."

The reverend dabbed at his fleshy brow, reddening a shade more with every passing minute. Karl had already given him a nickname, 'The Black Buzzard', and was sure the vicar had spotted his smirks. Karl didn't care, as he was enjoying his malignant inner space far too much. After all, Karl had killed before. He'd started quite early and had already murdered twice by the time he'd left his teens. Once while playing close to the family house in Satterscale, one of many sombre villages that lay in the shadow of the hill. The second kill came during his college gap year in Australia. Karl's first two murders hadn't been on his special list, but this one very much had been. Karl had waited a long time for Harry to become vulnerable and it had been the most sensual killing so far. To Karl, fantasising about killing was just fun, and he was quite happy to kill anyone or anything just to stay sharp.

Thinking of murder was a brain game for this master of the craft. The murder of Harry marked the end of Karl's relatively long dormant phase.

When the service was over, Karl was forced to do the old grip and grin drill. White teeth trapped behind his freeze-frame smile. He was now copying the vicar's well-practised simulated grief routine. Karl grasped the hands of those mourners he despised just a little tighter, holding on until discomfort and mild alarm set in, the eyes of the victim widening. The small litter of relatives quickly disbanded and headed for the exit. Harry's creepy work associate, Muriel, slithered over to Karl, "I know he wasn't the easiest man to be around, but I'm sorry for your loss." Muriel had bulging eyeballs. It was a condition known as proptosis. Karl wanted to lance them with a hot needle and squeeze out the contents, the way a teenager might do with a puss-filled pimple. Karl listened to several shallow comments of condolence. A little bit of Karl - actually quite a big bit of him - had wanted to hijack the vicar's address to the congregation, jostle him out of the pulpit, and preach his own rather more accurate eulogy.

The night before the funeral, in front of the bathroom mirror, Karl had practised what he might have said. Karl knew it would sound cringing and naff, but he wanted it to. Watching people squirm at his words would have been a large part of the satisfaction.

"We are here to celebrate the death, not the life of Harry Jackson. I'll apologise for my pretentiousness in advance. If I could borrow from Shakespeare, and 'Julius Caesar.' I have come here to bury Harry Jackson, not to praise him. The evil that men do is remembered after their deaths." Yes, celebrate Harry Jackson's death. Karl suspected that the rest of the family might have celebrated with him. The word that came into Karl's mind was closure. He shut his eyes and painted a final luscious picture of Harry's final moments in his pizza oven for one.

19

CHAPTER THREE

Every morning, Theodore Deacon felt okay for the first few seconds when he woke, but only for a few seconds. Then he remembered why there was a space beside him. A year earlier Theodore's wife Susan had contracted a rare liver disease. When a fungal infection was followed by sepsis, the specialists told Theodore that hope had gone. The palliative care nurses did all they could. Susan kept her fingers hovering over the morphine driver but no chemicals could save her. Theodore was there when the life support was switched off. Susan Deacon was 47.

Theo's movements had slowed, and he shuffled through life, sometimes wondering why his legs bothered to move at all. Through his job, he was allowed six sessions with a grief counsellor. She was Mrs. Smethwick, her hawthorn hedge of hair was held in a Quaker's bun, a vulture's nose the perfect perch for her half glasses. Theo had noticed that she rarely looked through her spectacles but over them, with knees clamped and hands clasped. He was sure he could detect a slightly stagnant aroma when Mrs. Smethwick moved. She was a vision of melancholia.

"Mr. Deacon, I'm very sorry for your loss. It must be traumatic for you. Let's start with your feelings, and we'll take it from there."

"*That's a mantra,*" thought Theo, "*My name? Delete and insert where appropriate. Deacon, Duncan, Deadman. How many times has she done this? Rinse and repeat. This is box ticking.*"

Theo didn't want to talk to anyone, but Barbara Bracewell, the Chief Constable of the Rimpton force and DCI Deacon's boss, had told him that that's what he had to do. Theo attempted to open up to Smethwick, who'd worked with many senior police officers. "There's no escape. I feel leaden," said Theo, "The weight crushes me. In bed I bury myself under the duvet. It's the warmth. Sometimes I think I can smell Susan. I know I can't, well, I don't think I can. My head burns with pain. I pull my knees to my chest. I'm like a sack of sand. Getting out of that bed takes so much effort. There's a numbness that's hard to describe, as if pins and needles are trying to creep into every crack in my body. It's difficult, Mrs Smethwick." "Call me Audrey, Mr Deacon." She looked concerned when Theo talked, but this could well have been a practised professional expression. Audrey Smethwick kept scribbled notes in a hand almost as wiry as her hair. She looked up occasionally as if automated, head tilted. You could see the blood in Theo's fingertips as he squeezed his hands together.

Despite what people he loved and trusted said, Theo was certain that he would never get over Susan's death. He was alone now, properly alone. No kids to support and help when they too felt the pain that consumed his soul. Theo and Susan had tried repeated rounds of IVF treatment. They were frustrating and extremely emotional. Theo's guilt simmered. He often wondered if Susan's devastation led in any way to the eventual breakdown of her immune system.

There was vast support from a fantastic group of family, friends and work colleagues. Theo Deacon had spent twenty-four years in the police force, and now, two years short of his fiftieth birthday, he had built a reputation for being an exceptional professional. Until he could somehow dredge himself from this abyss, Theo would have to rely on his experience and natural aptitude for the job. It was about clocking in, clocking out, and doing his best while trying to navigate a way through the cloying fog.

Everyone in the Rimpton Hollway Constabulary knew Theo. He had a warmth about his presence, a softness in his eyes. There was a trained bulk to his upper torso. Theo's buzz cut was a thicket of wire wool, making him look like a special forces instructor. Theo had been a feared middleweight in the police championships, winning three of the six finals in which he had appeared.

Theo had a nickname. For two reasons, his colleagues called him 'Tex'. His obsession with FBI techniques and his wild west gunslinger gait. A walk Ennio Morricone could have written a score for. Tex's physique had softened while his focus had been on Susan's illness. However, his frame was naturally athletic. With the gift of exceptional genes, you could see that Tex wouldn't take a lot of work to return to his physical peak.

As an officer, Detective Chief Inspector Deacon was revered. Tex's greatest strengths were his almost psychic ability to see what no one else could and carry out his duties in often frenzied environments while appearing to remain completely calm.

Tex was known for his genuine benevolence, patience, good grace and gently caustic sense of humour. A raised voice from Tex Deacon was rare indeed. Tex had his moments, and he generally presented himself as a sensitive and empathetic man. But it wasn't the whole truth. When the darkness came, he felt himself slipping into what felt like an oily lagoon, his soul pooling in the apparently bottomless abyss. Maybe Tex had seen too much. As time passed, the flashes became more intense, the nightmares more detailed.

They were always memories of horrific death sites. There was a suicide. White shards of bone attached to something soft which was glued on the cheap flock wallpaper behind the victim. The gun barrels resting where the chin used to be, a naked toe still on the shotgun's trigger. There were random terrifying dreams of mangled flesh, bloodied hair matted, and waxwork shapes lying coiled and frozen in death. The sooty gunk around an entry wound. The trellis of defensive slashes on the hands and arms of murder victims. People in white spacesuits picked through the trauma, with tweezered hands hunting for something that might catch a killer. Tex dreamt about the smell. How long was it since a victim's last breath? He could guess by the strength of the stench.

He'd had these nightmares before Susan's illness, but now the emotional tsunami elicited by her death had amplified the white noise. Maybe that's why Tex Deacon was so well-equipped to hunt down those who lived in the shadowy corners of various personality disorders. Tex had snared some of Britain's most notorious killers. When struggling with a case, other forces in the United Kingdom often brought Tex in as a troubleshooter. In that respect, Tex Deacon was a legend.

Deacon's superiors could see that his focus had slipped. Tex had taken compassionate leave, but he didn't want any more. Tex wanted to work, but that would be Barbara Bracewell's decision. The Chief Constable had a brain as sharp as her hawkish features.

Bracewell was trusted and respected, and she had a certain charisma that colleagues could sense before she entered a room. A big advantage in a world that men still dominated.

Running down a criminal wasn't a problem either. Bracewell had previously represented the force in the four and eight hundred metres at several Police and Fire Academy Games. Chief Constable Bracewell was fully aware of the bandwidth Tex Deacon brought to his detective work, but there was some crackle on the line.

Bracewell, from a deep pool of straight-talking Lancastrians, was possibly the straightest-talking Lancastrian of them all. The two were close friends and had known each other since their time in cadet school. Bracewell hoped that Tex's static would eventually die down with the right approach, aided by the grief counselling. She thought a shift in schedule might help Tex rediscover his vigour.

***

The Rimpton Hollway division, with Bracewell, as the driving force, had been re-shaping their cadet training programme. In fact, the forward-thinking and original ideas had been getting great praise from HQ. Barbara was all business.

"Tex. As part of your rehabilitation, I want you to work part-time with the enforcement agency recruits. In terms of instructor potential, you have all the ingredients. I'm confident that, with your reputation, the cadets will embrace you as a kind of guru figure."

Tex reddened, a flush moving through his body. Praise made Tex feel uneasy, and Barbara knew that a self-deprecating riposte wasn't far away.

"Good God Barbara. A guru? What, like the Dalai Lama? Show them how to combat suffering. Take them on a journey towards the goal of nirvana. Develop mind and character on the path to enlightenment? Will I have to milk any Yaks?" Barbara inhaled the heavy sarcasm as Tex rolled onto his heels, pressed his palms together, and offered a salutation to the heavens. Bracewell arched an eyebrow and countered with a tight-lipped no-nonsense response.

"As you well know Tex, operational specifics in the cadet training programme are only carried out by retired detectives who have been through the compulsory qualification programme. Would you like me to retire you Tex? That's an option."

Tex drew an imaginary weapon and performed his best Clint Eastwood grimace, "Feeling lucky, punk?" Tex felt that tiny ping of pleasure that humour brought, and inside he was relieved to know that he could still feel that way at all. Since Susan's death, a smoky cloud had consumed Tex. For a few seconds, he could almost see through it. Bracewell jerked back in faux terror.

"Don't shoot me! I won't retire you." Barbara didn't really know why her comeback had been accompanied by a slight, and crap, American accent. It had felt funny, but a simultaneous cringe made them both baulk.

"Ok Tex. Look. I'll pull a few strings. I really want you to do this. Honestly, I think it'll do you good. Help to put you on the right path. This means we can move forward gently. I want you back on the force, but I want the fit and completely healthy Tex Deacon. I'll work with you. If you're not happy, we can tweak a few things or even take a fresh look. Start again.

Are you with me Tex?" Tex's head appeared glued to his shoulders, which looked hunched and cramped, but after a few seconds, he nodded.

"Ok. Good. Here we go. Don't interrupt." said Barbara. "I want you to take some lectures on the training programme for the greenhorns. Help you to focus on something else for a while. You'll still be on the force. You'll still be on full pay, but we're going to go at a different pace. Can you trust me?" Tex looked between his feet and found a knot in the floorboards; an anxious ripple squirmed through him.

"Lectures? Bloody hell, Barbara I'm not qualified. I've had no training whatsoever. Never done that before. I'm a dirt-digging foot soldier. Not bloody Billy Graham." Barbara smiled. This was one of

Tex's attractive characteristics. Very often, no matter how tense the situation, Tex could snap out a punch line.

"I know Tex, I know. Look, I need you to buy into this. A three-pronged approach. This plus the grief counsellor, and you're also going to see our police psychologist." Tex jolted, "Psychologist? Where's this come from? Is sadness a mental illness?"

Barbara Bracewell did phlegmatic very well. "He's very good. David Braithwaite is his name. Braithwaite told me that without specialist treatment, it'll take considerably longer for you to improve enough to work effectively. So it's Smethwick, Braithwaite and the cadets, and I'm going to dilute the load of direct police work. Making you take more compassionate leave isn't the answer. The timing is right. You're between investigations. Tex, look at it as a massage for the mind."

Tex's head sagged towards his sternum. He was crestfallen, but he also knew that his old friend was right. Grief had emptied him, his strength spiralling away. Despite the fact that a coma-stricken Susan couldn't respond, he'd spent long days at her bedside, sometimes sitting with her through the night. The soft clicks and gurgles of the machines were the only noise. The whole thing had crippled and exhausted him. But Tex still wanted to work - and do proper work - killer hunting work. He knew he had no choice right now though. The Chief Constable had spoken, and she was about to speak again.

"You know that 'Great Lancastrians Festival' that's coming up? As you're very well aware, a Bury man established the Metropolitan Police. Good news, you're going to host something the force wants us to promote, 'The Sir Robert Peel Lecture'. Are you good to go?"

Tex looked up a lot more quickly than he'd looked down. "WHAT!!!" Bracewell's hands flapped. She looked like she'd just surrendered to an arrest. "Don't panic Tex, you'll be great. I want you to have something totally different to think about. And I want that something to challenge you. Get the brain fizzing in a different direction. It'll get a bit of adrenalin into those veins of yours." Tex was shaking his head, lips tight. Barbara continued.

"And it won't be a totally scripted format anyway. There'll be a significant question-and-answer component. Just a wee chat from you at the top, and then we'll open it up to the floor. And if that goes well, we'll use the same format on the cadets' training programme. The kids will love you. You can 'guest' lecture on that without having to sit the qualification paper. I'm excited. Tex Deacon, the very first host of 'The Sir Robert Peel Lecture'. You'll be fantastic. Now go and think of a subject. Let me guess what you'll talk about?" Barbara Bracewell's face crinkled. Tex couldn't hide a sarcastic grimace.

Three weeks later DCI Theodore 'Tex' Deacon stood at a lectern in the Rimpton Conference Centre. An expectant murmur rumbled around, and chit-chat echoed off the high ceiling.

Wide-eyed and wedged in was an audience of four hundred people. There were a few amateur fanatics who waited by the letterbox for their monthly fix of 'True Detective,' but one thing was for certain - everyone there had heard of DCI Deacon. Tex, who avoided bright lights with the enthusiasm of a vampire, wasn't fully aware of his own reputation. Not just within the force but in the public domain. Deacon had helped to bring several of the United Kingdom's worst serial killers to justice.

An energy sizzled across the hall. Entry was free, and there was a strong body of curious police cadets mixed among members of the public. The trainees knew all about Tex Deacon and were looking forward to his instructive guidance and ripping yarns. A chance for the slightly awestruck students to drink in the advice proffered by this quiet legend of the force. The lecture title was 'The Art of Catching a Killer'.

There was no doubt that Tex Deacon's life story was bursting with incredible tales. Tex had learned so much, more than most, and now that he was actually standing at the lectern, the old pro took over. Tex was wearing a dark suit and a white shirt underneath it. Unseen but attached to his trousers were a set of blue braces. The colours of the football team he had supported since childhood, Clitheroe FC. He'd been at their home ground Shawbridge when they'd won their last trophy. The 2004 North-West League.

Tex knew a fair bit about football, but this was all about his profession, and he was here to make sure that he transferred the fullness of his knowledge. He had thought long and hard about his opening address. He wanted to make an impact.

**

"Hunting a killer is just like seduction. You want them so badly. You dream about them at night. When you eventually connect and arrest them, you can feel as if you've just betrayed your lover. It's like a soul connection. After a while, you'll know them that well, but only if you do your background work properly. Occasionally killers will hide in plain sight. They'll know that you're onto them. Then the game starts. It's a kind of romance. 'You know, and I know", but they rely on the belief that you haven't got enough evidence to convict them.

Otherwise, you'd have arrested them already - wouldn't you? Killers, especially psychopaths, can be very confident, often aloof. Frequently this is justified. From a mental perspective, they can be hugely challenging opponents. From my personal encounters, if I manage to make contact with a suspect, I try to develop that relationship with them. Just like lovers.

Gaining trust can be so important. It can help you get inside their heads and take you to your goal: their incarceration. Contact can be, for example, online. They'll place cryptic posts in newspapers or maybe send letters to the police. Sometimes it can be face-to-face. There's a brand of a murderer that gets off on this. Ending up in the killer's web is not good. Tangled in the sticky strands. Psychologically you're their prey. Killers love to create a power trap, and some will lure you into it if they can."

Tex held the room, and the eyes of all were transfixed on him. He pressed his hands against the sides of the mahogany podium. "The intelligent ones make fewer mistakes. They'll try and manipulate those hunting them down. I don't rely too much on whims. Some might lead you somewhere, but usually this will play into the killer's hands. That kind of thinking can take people like me off track. That's where they want me to be. Dining on red herrings. I have to be very careful how I think. Follow the trail and collect the evidence. If I have enough information, I build a profile, but I don't make assumptions or take quantum leaps based on a hunch. That's dangerous territory. Instinct coupled with experience is good, but the thought, 'I have a feeling', is usually bad."

The audience were encouraged to ask questions from the floor. Simultaneously dozens of hands shot skywards but only one person stood up. Tex was drawn to this tall, good-looking man in the middle of the hall. He had an aura. The man flashed a smile.

"Detective Deacon. My name is Karl Jackson. Thanks for taking my question. You've talked about the mind of the hunted and the hunter's approach. Is there a preferred mindset for the chasers? Specifically, I mean, do you have any particular philosophy you use to help you catch psychopaths?"

The detective nodded approvingly. "That's an excellent question. I'm glad you mentioned philosophy. I would take a mainly stoic approach. I've read a fair bit of Epictetus and the letters of Marcus Aurelius." Tex smiled and went on. "Mr. Jackson, I don't mean to sound pretentious. The teachings of the great Stoic philosophers transfer beautifully to police work. That might sound grandiose, but hopefully I'll be able to convince you."

In his own teenage years, Tex had gone to a talk on 'The Nature of Stoicism' at the local hall. There, he'd listened to a rather bohemian-looking character talk passionately about the subject. Tex thought the man wouldn't have looked out of place at the Last Supper. His sandals flipped and flopped as he walked across the stage and spoke for an hour about how stoicism had changed his life. Tex was sure that he wasn't about to have his own evangelical awakening, however, he did develop a fascination for the Stoic school of thought. In particular, Tex liked a central stoic belief that optimists were inclined to die first in some survival situations. Tex dropped his next nugget of information.

"The realists live longest. The psychologist and writer Viktor Frankl recorded this during his incarceration at Auschwitz. It's the main theme of his book, 'Man's Search For Meaning'.

Those who survived the longest in the Nazi death camps were the realists. Anyone who had an 'It'll be over by Xmas' mentality didn't usually last very long. They rarely got past Boxing Day. In a murder hunt, if you only had optimism, that wasn't much to go on. During my career, I have tried to remain realistic at all times. Optimists make too many guesses. The realist remains objective, approaching the challenge forensically from all available angles." Tex looked directly at the man who had asked the question. Jackson felt the luxurious soft wave that washed over him whenever he was the centre of attention. Karl drifted smoothly into calculation mode, feeding off every word that Tex said. He knew that he could glean valuable information. Karl liked that Stoic realist line. A man with a plan, just like him. Karl sensed his own sharpness and revelled in his superiority.

"If only Deacon knew. The sanctimonious prick hasn't a clue. Here I am, a Master craftsman. Deacon should be grovelling in my presence. He thinks he understands murder and thinks he understands people like me."

Karl's eyes were locked on the podium, and he listened intently, waiting for a word or phrase that might help him. "Mr. Jackson, the Stoics had a fairly straightforward approach. Here's a good mantra for you. 'See clearly, act correctly' If you want to read more on the Stoics, can I suggest Ryan Holliday's, 'The Obstacle is The Way'. You'll face a lot of obstacles when you are trying to solve a crime. Embrace them all. Don't think about the end and the satisfaction of arrest and capture. Think about the process and stay present. Learn to tolerate failure and keep moving forward. Do your research. Facts are gold dust. I continually ask myself the question: what am I missing? Sometimes I'll get too close to some aspects, so I try to keep the bigger picture in mind. I'm prepared to shift my perspective and start again totally."

Tex inhaled deeply, and Karl Jackson took his chance, politely interjecting with his even-toned voice sifting gently through the high-walled hall. "I must say I'd never thought that Greek Philosophy would be part of detective training."

Tex smiled again. "The Stoics can teach us valuable lessons. Detectives shouldn't allow themselves to be provoked. My advice is to try and avoid impulsivity. Stay calm and rational. Perception is important too. We are each inclined to perceive things differently. Listen to others and work with your team."

Karl Jackson nodded vigorously, his enthusiasm was clear. *"I'm enjoying this,"* he thought, *"Karl Jackson soaking first-hand advice from inside the mind of a man who had helped to incarcerate multiple serial killers. Advice that will keep me free and free to kill."*

As soon as Tex finished his answer, another forest of hands shot up. After careful consideration, Tex scanned the crowd and pointed to a young woman sitting close to the front of the hall. "Good evening. My name is Deborah Pilkington. I'm a reporter from the Rimpton Chronicle. Detective Deacon, could you talk us through a case where the processes you've talked about actually transferred effectively to the field?"

Tex had read some of Pilkington's newspaper reports. He'd been impressed. She looked cool, but Debbie's stomach was twisting. Unlike Jackson, the thought of being a central figure, if only briefly, brought cool sweat to the back of her neck. Debbie knew that she was an ambivert. A personality type somewhere between an introvert and an extrovert. However, Debbie had decided long ago that she would conquer any nervous disposition. After all, she had already mapped out a career path, and a little cold sweat wasn't going to stop her. She wanted to be a crime correspondent for a national newspaper. Debbie hoped that the Rimpton Chronicle would be her springboard.

Behind the lectern, Tex felt relaxed. He had been planning on recounting a case history. Debbie's question was well-placed. Tex related a notorious quadruple murder he had helped to crack. Everyone along the mountainous spine of England knew about it. It was a massive story at the time. Tex didn't need any notes.

"A family had rented a country lodge in Cornwall. A week's retreat to a place of peace and solitude during a long hot summer.

Perfectly for the killer, the lodge was set at the end of a long winding lane nestled between two hills at the far end of a small valley. The family certainly had peace and solitude. For a couple of days anyway. I have with me the concluding paragraph of the official police report. It succinctly described the horror of what happened to the family on what was, significantly, a hot and humid night at Black Bridge Lodge:

'The killer, Thomas Jacobsen, entered the house by using a glass cutter on the rear porch door. He was ultra-efficient. His gun had a silencer. After firing one bullet each to the heads of the mother and father, he moved to the number two-bedroom. There he followed the same process to dispatch the two children. Jacobsen was in the house for no more than five minutes. The press called the killer 'The Black Bridge Lodge Assassin.'

Tex continued. "It had been a clean murder scene. There was a blood splash but no struggle. It looked on the surface like a contract killing. The KGB would have been very proud. The murderer was high on structure and low on effort. The detectives initially assigned to the case reached a dead end. There was no forensic evidence that they could find. No fibres left, and as these had been such quick and apparently non-personal kills there was no flesh beneath the fingernails. None of the victims had time to fight back. There was nothing else of an obviously incriminating nature. After a few months of blind alleys, even the police were beginning to believe the rumours of a Russian connection."

Tex looked down on his audience. All eyes were zeroed in on the detective. The only noise was the gentle bee-like buzz from the strip lighting. "I visited the scene. The lodge had been boarded up for quite a long time. I wasn't looking for physical evidence. Forensics had done all that. I was trying to penetrate the mind of the killer. Why was there no engagement with the victims? There were no obvious signs of outward anger. No bruising. No sexual assault or fetish-like behaviours. The killer didn't appear to have taken any mementoes, such as strands of hair, rings or articles of clothing. No signature. If it hadn't been a contract killing, whatever fury there was had simmered deep within. This had been an ice-cold execution."

Tex hadn't heard so much as a cough for several minutes. The onlookers were silent, like refugees in a basement, waiting for the sound of boots on the floor above.

"In terms of leaving no trace, the killer had been extremely meticulous. Obsessively so. The silencer? It was clear to me that the murderer had used that attachment so he could kill without wakening the ones he still had to kill. The murders did have the hallmarks of a contract killing. I've also brought with me my personal recording of the words I taped that day on my cassette player. I talked as I walked through the lodge."

The atmosphere in the audience was of pin-drop variety. Tex played the scratchy tape while holding his old cassette player close to the lectern microphone.

"The killer is most likely male. Outside of the gunshots no signs of violence. No sexual assault. He wanted to kill, and that was all - just kill. No additional physical damage to the victims which suggests that the killer has an emotional link to the family. He didn't want to hurt them in the traditional sense. So very likely to be a family member. The efficiency suggests he's highly skilled and has killed before - multiple times. He's probably used this method in the past. There are no marks on the glass door. To avoid leaving any evidence or contaminating himself with blood spatter or fibres, the killer may have been wearing a full body cover of some kind. Murderers of this experience think of everything. Well, almost everything."

The DCI's taped voice came in hushed tones. "It would have taken many years to build this level of expertise. My guess is that he is quite mature. There was minimal exertion as the killer moved around the house. Deliberate and purposeful, he wanted to conserve energy in the extreme heat. There were no car or vehicle tracks so the killer probably walked some distance to the lodge. The weather was very steamy. The rural lodge had no air conditioning. If a protective suit covered the killer's body, he would have perspired profusely. For DNA purposes, the carpets should be rechecked, notably where he positioned his feet for each kill. Sweat may have leaked from the elasticated cuffs around his ankles. The blood splatter gives us the angle of each shot and the rough position of the shooter."

Tex switched off the cassette. "We made an arrest soon afterwards. The father of the murdered mother was the killer. He had worked for decades for Government agencies. They had his DNA on file. That DNA was on the dried sweat marks on the lodge carpet. While there was no proof that he had assassinated anyone while in the line of duty, there were plenty of rumours. The man was in his early sixties and had worked in the shadier corners of the intelligence networks."

Debbie was making notes. Jackson was mentally absorbing every word. Tex went on. "His daughter had, through forgery, illegally acquired Power of Attorney over her father. In conspiracy with her husband, they had attempted to get her father diagnosed with early-onset Alzheimer's disease. They had bribed a neurologist. There was a substantial will and various insurance policies. If they hadn't had their brains blown out, the now-deceased couple would have benefited considerably from the killer's death. Had the father decided it was kill or be killed? I've often wondered how the man dealt with murdering his own daughter and grandchildren. Even though there was no outright evidence that the dead adults were planning to kill the father, the police suspected that they were. The old boy had found out about the forgery and had probably worked out that his victims were planning to seize his estate fraudulently. The dad was angry. You really don't want to irritate pathologically unstable retired contract killers - if that's what he was. It doesn't usually end well."

Tex had been talking for ninety minutes. He got a nod from the Superintendent at the back of the room. This was his cue to wrap up. Tex came to a considered conclusion. "One of the problems with killers is that they can be very hard to catch. You may think that's stating the bleeding obvious but remember, murderers rarely set out hoping to get caught. They will go to bewildering lengths to stay free. There are stupid killers, and there are clever killers. Also, there are what I call genius killers. There aren't too many of those. Yes, you come across some murderers who possess considerable brainpower, but very few have the IQ of an intellectual. So be prepared for anything. Assume nothing."

Tex Deacon received an appreciative response from the audience. A genius killer was amongst those standing and applauding.

CHAPTER FOUR

Karl Jackson was on top of the world. After all, one of the country's top detectives had told him, admittedly indirectly, that he was a genius killer. Karl loved that little phrase and grinned every time he thought about it. Falling out with genius killers was not to be recommended. Unless you wanted a tag on your toe, a sheet over your head, and a spell in the regulated chill of a mortuary.

Karl's life had followed a successful, if rather fortunate trajectory. He had been very proud, though not surprised, when, at the age of just twenty-six, he had been appointed as Head of Chemistry and Technology at the Rimpton Hollway Senior School. For sixteen years, he had held that job. Even a man of his inherent arrogance would admit it was a bit of a result considering what had gone before.

Karl had a supreme ability to compartmentalise all of his activities. One action, when completed, was just that - an action completed. No matter how heinous it was, it never affected his ability to focus on the next task. It was like a switch. On/Off. On/Off. Complete concentration on whatever it was that needed to be done and then move on. Karl never saw this as strange behaviour. It was just the way he was. He could do the most dastardly things and then, with a beaming smile and words of sympathy, slip coins into a charity box a few minutes later.

Karl had a vicious childhood and had been brought up in a tough house. His dad Harry was a chain-smoking labourer, hulking and brick-like. His belt buckle strained against decades of excess, and he looked like old road kill. Harry's daily homecomings were to be feared. Tools bounced around his rusted truck as it rattled over the rough track up to the old gate. The family always froze when they heard the rusted hinges squeak. The house seemed to shrink. The smell then followed. It reminded Karl of rotting seaweed, and he wouldn't have been surprised if maggots had oozed through the seams of his father's ragged lumberjack shirt.

The family only ever saw Harry sober at breakfast, and when the construction site hooter sounded, he always headed to the same place, a place he loved more than any other. By the time he left his face had puffed through alcohol, the red veins had returned, and Harry was transformed into a tornado of rage.

A cold chill consumed Karl and Nathan as Harry swayed and belched. A leather strap was his implement of choice. Harry's boys moved like rats in their attempt to escape the relentless stings as he cascaded wildly around the house, howling profanities and threatening death. The twins knew when a lash was imminent. Harry's sour and whiskey'd breath was the stench that preceded pain. How often Karl wished he could stop his father from breathing.

In the family house, the strap was just a glimpse of the bigger picture. Harry's favourite target was Valerie. Karl was sure he'd never seen his Mum pull herself to her full height. Cowed and trembling, she spent many harrowing years receiving Harry's special attention. Harry would lumber towards her, a washed-up heavyweight, spittle frothing on his lips. When his work was done, he would slump into his armchair, a jellyfish of perspiring blubber, and demand to be fed. Exhausting work. Harry felt that no one really appreciated that.

"Your fault you pathetic bitch. Sort this fucking house out. Sort your fucking children out. If you were better people, I'd never touch you." It was almost a catchphrase. Harry was always flushed when the violence stopped. "Why do you make me do this, you stupid woman? This is going to give me a heart attack." With his warped sense of justice, he used to say things like this all the time - it was Harry's game.

Almost all of Valerie's exposed flesh was red, yellow or green, with patches of skin in various stages of recovery. Ribs were cracked or calcified, her breathing shallow, her movement crippled. She slid her slippers across the floor, her feet barely leaving the carpet.

According to Harry, it was all her fault. This didn't make much sense to Karl purely from a rational point of view, but he did admire how his mum seemed to take her beatings with such good grace.

Valerie knew that a whimper would bring another hammer blow. If she weakened, the wrath would intensify, so she suffered in silence.

Harry's house was not a great environment for Karl's early development. Nature or nurture and all that. Karl might have turned out to be okay, but years of vicious beatings, the memories of his mother's muted sufferings, and his father's insistence that Karl was one level up from pond life moulded an already faulty personality into a seriously dangerous one. If you damage the hard drive, you might release hidden darkness.

Karl found his head was often filled with strange, hard-to-define noise. A bizarre but regular experience, where negative thoughts and morbid fantasies would spin like candy floss. Plenty of fractured ideas which were graphically doom-laden, but, as a child, there was no clear structure to them. The coherence would come later as Karl matured. In the meantime, schoolwork was a distraction, and the sciences were the only subjects that enthused Karl. He distilled that down to chemistry and gadgetry, things that involved detail and moving parts. When Karl was focused, the internal noise seemed to dampen down. Karl struggled to make friends, and he enjoyed being alone. He loved capturing frogs at the lake beside a copse a mile or so from the house in his spare time. He made little notes, recording the euphoria he felt.

"I attached these firecrackers to the little fuckers and giggled when they exploded. I had bets with myself. Would the frog be hopping or on the ground when its ugly body would burst, spraying a slimy crackling display of green and red gunge over what was usually a satisfyingly long distance."

Karl always felt an intoxicating jag of excitement when one of his unfortunate little beasts blew up, turning to blancmange and heading for that Big Pond in the Sky. Nathan came with Karl once, "What are we going to do?" Karl's lips fluttered, making a noise like a whoopee cushion, "Have some fun bro, have some fun, you know, fun. Fun, fun, fun."

Nathan's face knotted, "Fun with you isn't fun." Nathan was tense and would crawl inside, looking for that safe space. Now and again, his breathing stopped. Nathan's instinctive reaction when he didn't want to be heard. Why did he feel this way when he was alone with his brother?

A temperate breeze tousled with the twins' straw curls which had been bleached out by the summer sun. Ahead of them the water's surface tinkled. There was a shoosh as the zephyr tickled the leaves of the beeches that stooped over the bank of the shining lagoon. There were also multiple throaty, froggy burps. This was Karl's special place, and Nathan knew of the dark shroud that consumed his brother there.

A maze of tangled strings and fuses stretched Karl's denim dungaree pockets. He was well armed for this afternoon of 'fun'. The dozy burpers only moved when it was too late. Karl's homemade frog trapper was a wide-mouthed confusion of cane and netting resembling the fishnet stockings on a fat-thighed hooker. Karl swooped frogs into his glory hole and the burps blended into a cacophonous jumping mess. He had over twenty to play with. The sight of the panicking green globs was enough for Nathan, and off he would run. Karl's hammed-up snigger followed Nathan as he scampered through the waving wheatgrass. "You're such a wimp Nathan. Wait till you see what happens to them. Imagine if I put a bomb in your paint tray. It's like that. Honestly, you'll piss yourself. It's a laugh. Trust me bro." Karl held up his box of long matches and shook it with a violent rattle.

Karl was strapping tiny rucksacks of gunpowder to the disgruntled band of croakers using baler twine to lash the cargo to their backs, cutting into their flesh as he twisted. Nathan was shinning upwards and grasping branches in a smooth, methodical order. The thick rubber on his cheap gutties was ideal for a dry day like this. Within a minute, he had reached his look out post in the ancient oak tree. Thick bark prickled his back, and the limb was worn yellow by the constant twitching of Nathan's feet. They sandpapered the wood when he sat in the foetal position, his arms wrapped hard across his kneecaps.

Nathan could hear a combination of cracks and laughter, followed always by a splash. After a while, the croaking stopped. He saw Karl at the base of his tree, "Come down, you prick. The show's over. We're going home." Nathan knew Karl could see him, but still he froze, praying for invisibility. Karl's movements were slower, and he didn't have Nathan's trapeze-like dexterity. Karl's breath deepened as he climbed Nathan's tree, but it didn't stop him from shouting,

"Nathan is a wimp, Nathan is a wimp, Nathan is a wimp. Scared by the froggies, scared by the froggies." Nathan heard but didn't see, his head buried into his legs, damp speckles streaking his khaki shorts.

"YOU'RE PATHETIC, NATHAN!" He could feel a misty spray of warm saliva on the side of his face, and then it came. Nathan felt a pounding thud to his right shoulder, and suddenly he was tumbling, bouncing through the greenery, soft brushes and then sharp pokes as branches stabbed his cascading body.

Then there was another noise. This time like a gunshot as Nathan's right leg hit the sun-hardened ground under the eves of the beech. Nathan heard a guldering scream. It terrified him, then he realised it was his own.

Karl shimmied down the tree with an angular lack of grace, placing each foot carefully and ensuring he didn't descend quite as fast as his brother. Expressionless, Karl surveyed the scene. Two red and white sticks pronged through the skin of Nathan's leg. Around it, a dark pool was forming, spreading across the impenetrable mud.

"Fuck," Karl was calculating after his icy observation of the situation, "I could be in the shit here." Nathan's cries irritated Karl, *"How could such a tiny body make so much noise."* He thought these might have been like the squeals Piggy made during his torture in 'Lord of the Flies'. Karl had no idea what to do, so after his tight-lipped scrutiny of Nathan's plight, he simply turned and jogged back to the house. Nathan's long piercing shrieks began to drift away.

Karl wandered up to the brick terrace and round the back to find his mum, sleeves rolled up, scratching at ancient pots in the grubby sink, "Nathan has hurt himself, the prat. He fell out of his special tree." Karl scrunched his face, attempting to feign a sort of concerned innocence. Nathan had almost bled out by the time the emergency services reached him, lying in his maroon puddle, face like puce, low husky breaths escaping intermittently through his caked and splitting lips. It took four surgeries to put his leg back together. He had five months in hospital and two years of a partially successful rehab. Nathan had almost died but never mentioned the push. Karl was just relieved that he hadn't taken the blame.

Nathan wasn't the only boy to suffer when Karl was around. The little lad slipped off the bank while fishing at the river near the lake and drowned. An accident? Well that's what everyone thought. Karl enjoyed that one. He had done his best to save the kid. Hadn't he? The story he told about what had happened that day was extremely convincing. Karl cherished the sympathy and attention he got from those who consoled him.

Regarding the boy, people told Karl how horrific it must have been to witness something like that. They'd put their arm around him, offering words of consolation. Sometimes they offered him sweets. It was almost as if the child's death was secondary to Karl's apparent personal hell. Karl, as usual, couldn't understand the emotional backdrop that enveloped the saga.

He somehow became the focus, and of course, he enjoyed that immensely. Karl knew what Karl knew, and he would spend hours replaying the boy's death over and over in his mind.

That gave him so much pleasure.

CHAPTER FIVE

Harry Jackson had spent most of his money on the demon drink so there wasn't much left for the kids. Butter-coloured skin sucked at their bones like an over stretched canvas. They'd claw at food when they got it and mashed it quickly past dry lips. When Harry got pound notes into his hand, they usually ended up drowning in alcohol. The ghostly twins got used to the smell of each other, but in truth, they stank like rotten fruit. Passers-by would recoil when they encountered the boys down in the village.

When Valerie finally found the courage to report the domestic abuse and break away from Harry's evil grip, life improved a little. The various government benefits certainly brought in more cash than Harry's meagre contribution to the crumbling household. From fleshless beginnings, Karl grew into a healthy specimen. His mother's Italian genes were a gift. He had eyes like black pearls and a Romany complexion with cheekbones sharp enough to slice through the defences of any woman. The light hair of youth darkened with age, and Karl created a body of olive marble through a combination of gym and steroids. Sometimes he had to duck to avoid a door jamb. The blend of natural and chemical pleased Karl and appealed to his narcissistic tendencies. Karl slept around with astonishing vigour. He detested people in general, but Karl was smart and found that he was able to massage his limited emotional spectrum to create a powerful charm.

Sex was an outlet and definitely fun, but Karl felt nothing for the females who lay beneath his magnificence. Karl would stare into their eyes and feign all sorts of emotions with astonishing effectiveness. He'd wonder what the girls felt. They could feel a lot of things that he couldn't.

Karl understood some emotions better than others, however, depth of emotion was a mystery to him. Empathy, for example. Karl simply couldn't see why you would need that feeling. He preferred emotions with a harder edge. Ruthlessness. Revenge. Now revenge was thrilling and worth waiting for, and much better than sex.

Karl could be very restrained when it came to getting his own back. He could wait for many years with chilling patience. His ability to park a perceived slight was another remarkable quality. When the moment of vengeance arrived, Karl would feel a sensual heat flow through his body. A penile orgasm - even a very good one - would only last five or six seconds. The orgasmic ripple that came with a kill, or even the memory of a kill, could last for many minutes. Definitely worth the wait, but rather addictive.

CHAPTER SIX

Life changed for the family when Harry was forced out, thanks to assistance from social services. A restraining order was issued, but a lot of damage had already been done. When he was fourteen, the behaviour of Karl brought him to the attention of the local mental health team. He had detached himself from the rest of the family, and, while always a loner, he'd become dissociative.

In Cumbria, the leader in this type of juvenile disorder was Dr. Agniezka Kowalczyk. She was based in a small terraced house in Keswick. The Doctor had a small nameplate in bronze, and every time he looked at it, Karl imagined someone vomiting the alphabet over her door. He attended consistently until he was almost sixteen, after which the good Doc was ready to present her report. Valerie was summoned.

"Your boy has a combination of problems Mrs. Jackson," Agniezka Kowalczyk spoke in staccato with a strange accent that somehow combined a splash of Cumbrian and Polish with the subtlest hint of a lisp. Karl found it quite hypnotic. He sat in his usual chair before her but found the whole exchange rather bizarre.

"Karl doesn't appear to have any real sense of empathy or guilt, Mrs. Jackson. It's just two of several red flags which suggest a severe personality disorder." Karl squinted at the Doctor, staggered that throughout her synopsis, she looked at his mum and never once at him. It was as if he was invisible. Karl ruminated angrily while the Doc blabbered.

"Bloody hell, that's quite a statement," he thought, *"She's never said that before. All those sessions with Mrs. Nicey Polish Prat smiling away, trying to get me to trust her. All those hot chocolates. Come on, Karl, just tell me exactly what you're thinking. What a load of bollocks. Fucking turncoat. Now she's basically screaming, 'Get the strait jacket, he's a nutter' For fuck sake!"*

Karl had noticed how strange his psychologist's presentation had been. He felt like a dog at the vet, with Kowalczyk as the vet telling

the owner that the dog should be destroyed. Karl also noted that
his 'owner', mum, who was wedged into a corner of the room, was
hunched like a nun at prayer. The only thing missing was a habit.
Karl was used to seeing his mother adhere to the vow of silence
when Harry was around, but now he needed her to speak. Karl, the
equivalent of a rabid dog according to Kowalczyk, widened those
irresistible eyes, slid forward in his seat, got as close to the specialist
as he could, and snapped back.

"You'll have to explain the proper meaning of guilt to me. Why
would I even bother with that? Don't get me wrong Doc, I can see
the 'sense' in guilt, but how do I feel it? Do you ever feel it? Like right
now? Or remorse? That seems to me like guilt watered down.

Surely remorse is something you use only when you're caught
doing something you shouldn't do. I do remorse only to make others
think I'm sorry. That's what people do, isn't it? I mean, it's an act, isn't
it? What confuses me is that other people can't see that. They actually
think that people mean this remorse thing. They do, don't they?"

Dr. Kowalczyk basically ignored Karl and, after a desultory flash
in his general direction, carried on. "Your son has a particular skill
Mrs. Jackson." Karl noted the lead weight of sarcasm and placed his
elbows on his knees, trying to intimidate her with a crazy-eyed stare,
but the Doctor simply thundered on. "It's a fabrication. An uncanny
ability to remember his complicated maze of lies and how they
connect together. A useful talent for some things, I suppose." She
fired a caustic glance in his direction.

"My diagnosis of that particular condition is 'Pseudologia
Fantastica'. Have you heard of that, Mrs. Jackson?" Mum the nun,
remained true to her vows. Karl couldn't hold back anymore and
burst out. "Of course, she's never fucking heard of it. Pseudo what?
You're the psychologist. Mum's spent her life bobbing and weaving
away from the fistic flurries of an alcoholic, not studying fucking
neuroscience."

The ice woman continued. "This is a condition that defines
someone who, once they've told a lie, then believes it to be the truth."
Kowalczyk was into her flow. She looked stern and announced more

perceived character faults and 'issues'. The Doctor suggested that maybe this or that tablet or course of therapy might work. Baffling for Karl because he saw every single one of these so-called 'issues' as strengths. Psychiatrists were always looking for answers. In his own way, Karl did his best to help but, right now, he wasn't going to play the well-behaved house pet.

"I do know the difference between right and wrong. I know I have a choice. I can't work out why everyone doesn't see it my way. Doesn't everyone crave control? Surely it's all about survival... I mean isn't that what Darwin said? Natural selection. Getting rid of the weak strengthens the species. Isn't that what Darwin was all about? That's how evolution works isn't it? Thank you, but I'll follow the science."

In the opinion of the specialists, the teenage Karl had clearly defined behavioural problems, which they tried to treat with Cognitive Therapy and various drugs, including anti-psychotics. Karl knew that the latter was often prescribed as a chemical cosh. He'd read about their heavy use in places like Broadmoor. Antipsychotics kept the really disturbed criminals quiet - Criminals like Peter Sutcliffe.

***

Karl developed an early fascination for the works of the criminally insane and spent long hours during his teenage years reading up on those he thought to be great practitioners. Even in his formative years, Karl made copious notes detailing the intricate aspects of the methods he most admired.

As a boy, there was one serial killer who, from a psychological aspect, particularly fascinated the young Karl, and he wrote about him with a morbid zeal. Carl Panzram. Karl saw himself as the next Jo Nesbo, the only crime writer he truly respected. He was sure he'd write a series of crime thrillers about himself someday. But for now, it was about building a library.

"Carl Panzram: Intelligent, witty, and clinical. Another Karl, but Karl spelt with a capital 'C'. However, it didn't start or finish well for Carl Panzram, a relentless killer from East Grand Forks in Minnesota. He finished life in a noose, with a black bag over his head, on the

5th of September 1930. On the gallows, Carl with a 'C' was asked if he had any 'last words' He spat in the executioner's face and loudly proclaimed, "Hurry up. I could kill a dozen men while you're screwing around". I loved that! When I analyse Carl, I can see certain parallels between his life and mine. A brutal childhood is one. The psychiatrist who treated Panzram said that he, quote, "Probably wasn't born as a killing machine. It was the horrific abuse that had oiled the cogs."

Of course, lots of kids, like Karl and Carl, get knocked about, but very few kill once, let alone multiple times. For Panzram, part of his problem may have been abuse, and part may have been genetic, but he was certainly damaged. It's additional damage in some form, according to Karl's reading, that can be enough to turn a troubled boy into a career psychopath. Carl Panzram ended up killing twenty-one males using varying levels of barbarity.

"Panzram had been a mischievous teenager and went from burglar to church arsonist to killer. Panzram, like me, had those Latin looks and panther-like physique. He drifted around the USA, living the life of a hobo by stowing away in box cars and committing murder as he went."

At the turn of the last century, there weren't too many literate drifters in America, but Panzram had an education. That's what attracted Karl the most. Panzram was super smart. Unfortunately, his schooling came with pain. He'd taken many vicious beatings at the Lutheran Christian establishments he was forced to attend. That's why Panzram burned churches. Revenge.

Panzram put his albeit brutal education to good use. He worked the system effectively during stays at seven different prisons, including the notorious Sing. But there was another ingredient of the Panzram story that really fascinated Karl, and he wrote.

"Very few serial killers write an autobiography, but Panzram did. "Killer: A Journal of Murder" It was a fantastic read. Eventually, once my work is done, I think I'll write my own. Panzram described himself as 'rage personified'. Ha Ha. We sync so well. Two documentaries were made about Carl Panzram, "Carl Panzram: The Spirit of Hatred and Vengeance" and "Carl Panzram: Too Evil to Live". The book was made

into a Hollywood movie. The actor James Woods played Panzram. I hope my story makes the big screen but who would play me? Maybe Jason Statham, or Russell Crowe. Or, if he was alive, Robert Mitchum. He was brilliant in Cape Fear. Mitchum would be the man. Very good looking and similar eyebrows. LOL. The blockbuster about me will be called, "Karl Jackson: The Killer They Couldn't Catch".

Karl had paid homage to his obsession with serial killers by getting a tattoo on the back of his right calf. It was a quote from the original Hannibal Lecter character from the Thomas Harris books, as played by Brian Cox in the 1986 movie 'Manhunter'. The tattoo was inked in Edwardian script style, "If one does what God does enough times, one will become as God is."

On the treatment front, Karl never took any of the drugs the professionals had prescribed for him. Instead, he stockpiled them in his mum's old tea chest. After all, he was perfectly fine, and in truth, Karl found the therapy sessions extremely irritating. One thing they did prove to Karl was that he had a 'very low boredom threshold'. He once watched Kowalczyk make a note of that.

Karl's multiple visits to see Kowalczyk in her creepy office that smelt of must and shadows took place intermittently during those teenage years. The smarter members of his coterie of probation officers and social workers would detail their concerns about his 'potential capability'. Karl had killed a small boy when he was first directed to mental health professionals. At that stage, the young lad, and the dead amphibians, were just Karl's dirty little secrets. Over time more carnage would follow.

As Karl noted during his early scribbles. *"I know I have a craft to sharpen. It feels a little like a sportsman's warm-up routine, and I want killing to be my sport. Why? I can't answer that yet. It feels like a calling. There's a lot of homework to be done, but I've all the time in the world."*

The smugness of Karl Jackson, like the smell from a slurry pit, was all-enveloping.

CHAPTER SEVEN

When Karl was eighteen, he got a summer job at a newsagents in Kendal. He wanted to take a gap year from his chemistry and technology studies at Lancaster University and spend it in Australia. But he had to earn some money first, so he worked at Hampton's on the High Street, not far from the castle. The Hamptons had lived above the shop since it opened in the last century. Like many of the buildings in the town, it was crafted from ancient limestone and looked as if it had been sprayed with cigarette ash. Hampton's was a small purveyor of newspapers, tobacco, lighters, batteries and other basic essentials. It was a family business and had been open for several decades. It was run by Billy Hampton, grandson of ninety-one-year-old Samuel, who lived in the flat above. Karl caught the occasional glimpse of the prehistoric old man. *"He looks like he was laid down at about the same time as the Precambrian rock they used to build his shop."*

Karl endured long shifts, and the 0500 alarm call came as a hellish cacophony to his lazy bones. He would swear to himself as he rolled out of bed, showing all the enthusiasm of a tranquilised sloth. Karl started at first light, and his first job was to slash with a Stanley knife. He used it to remove the webbing that held the bundles of newspapers together. It was one of the few things that Karl enjoyed about the job. His day finished when the last nicotine addict left at around eleven at night.

In classic Karl style, he dodged the tough stuff, like shelf stacking, and spent most of his time at the till. Part of the fun of the job was fantasising about how he'd murder the customers who irritated him. One man came in last thing each night to order a packet of twenty Marlboro, the brand Harry had smoked.

Karl's inner world quickly developed an angry pulse at the sight of the familiar packaging. He didn't know the man's name, but he wondered if this unshaven, sallow-eyed gent who smelt a bit like

Harry, smoked exactly twenty every day. Anyway, Karl didn't like him. The man never looked at Karl and would point at what he wanted and grumble demands in a gruff, aggressive and dismissive manner. Karl was polite enough to the man's face, but he knew exactly what he really wanted to do to this rudest of customers.

"Twenty Marlboro." "Certainly Sir"

"Hopefully the lung cancer is taking hold, you old bastard."

"Gimme some matches." "Of course."

"I'd love to inject acid into your testicles"

"Hurry up boy, I haven't got all night." "Going as fast as I can, sir."

"Ever had your legs broken by a tyre iron, you fuckwit?"

After three months, Karl had enough cash for his dream trip. In Australia, he built a conglomerate of skills, honing the dexterity of his thinking, but Karl also swallowed industrial quantities of the amber nectar. He'd hook up with unknown locals and most nights ended the same way. Karl, drunk and trying to pick a fight with the hardest-looking bloke in the pub.

"Come on you sheep shagging wanker. Let's see what you've got. One punch Karl they call me. King of the World. 'Rocky Jackson' Fancy a piece of that?"

Quite often, unfortunately for Karl, the hardest-looking man in the pub usually did fancy a piece of that, and Karl was definitely true to his self-appointed nickname. One punch usually did it, but not one that he threw. The result, consistently, was Karl being booted out of the bar in a semi conscious state with blood oozing from one of the slashes on his face. Despite these painful setbacks, Karl loved building his bush whacker vagabond persona. When sober, he absorbed any characteristic that might be to his advantage. Karl the chameleon was in Oz and on the loose.

On an exercise book, covered by a sticky-backed plastic image of the Sydney Harbour Bridge, Karl often lost himself in his highly individual inner sanctum. 'Down Under' was pencilled on the cover.

"I arrived at Sydney Airport with a backpack and not much else. The plan was to cruise the East Coast student hot spots, take in the sun,

pick up a few ad hoc jobs, grab a few shags. Maybe bar work, perhaps some labouring. I've heard plenty of money men in the construction industry are looking for strong, cheap students. Muscle for hire? Maybe I'll do that. Head up the East Coast and then inland. Might earn some cash on the harvest circuit. Citrus fruits and garlic, lots of opportunities there."

All good intent, but Karl binned most of those ideas when he realised that it might involve seriously hard work in the heat, something he was determined to avoid. Karl, in the end, didn't do any of the usual backpacker gigs.

"It's the Blue Mountains first for me. They're just a couple of hours West of Sydney. I'm sure I can hitchhike it up to the hills."

***

This stunning place was described as blue for a very particular reason. Dust particles and water vapour combined with oil droplets from the Eucalyptus forests, scattering short wavelength rays of light which irradiated a predominantly blue tinge. The heat was oppressive, and it sat on the shoulders like a freshly smelted iron girder. You didn't need to move to sweat. It was a constant companion and rolled across exposed skin like rain down a window pane. Clothing was permanently hot and wet. It was as if you'd just walked out of a washing machine's boil cycle. The sweet smell from the Eucalyptus hung in the air, and if you closed your eyes, you could imagine yourself in a hot bath full of particularly fragrant essential oil.

Karl used his self-proclaimed escalating magnetism to sell himself to the Blue Mountain Tourist Centre's manager, Brad Stackpole. Karl basically gatecrashed Stackpole's office. Karl took a quick glance at the nameplate on the door and, after one hard knock and before Stackpole could clear his throat to respond, Karl had opened the door. He launched straight into his pre-prepared patter.

"Mr. Stackpole, my name is Karl Jackson, and I'm so excited to be here. I'm on a gap year. I've had this fantasy since childhood of seeing the Blue Mountains. I've worked along England's fabulous mountainous spine - The Lake District. I worked part-time as a trainee for their Mountain Rescue team. I was their youngest-ever recruit. I designed a specialist trail map for the local mountain region. One specifically crafted to help first-time and inexperienced walkers. Oh my God, it would mean so much to me if you allowed me to help in this amazing place. I'm a good navigator. I'm great with people. Do you have a spot? Is there anything I can do? Clear the trails of rubbish? Anything at all. You won't even have to pay me."

Brad Stackpole was a dull man with a deadpan delivery. It was as if any semblance of personality had been scrubbed away with wire wool. Brad had rocked onto the back legs of his chair as if he'd been catapulted there by the sheer force of Karl's rapid-fire address. He'd already forgotten about Karl's rude entrance and was, instead, impressed by the teenager's sheer enthusiasm, which had, remarkably, pierced Brad's monochrome persona.

"Eh, what did you say your name was?"

"Karl Jackson. Karl Jackson - the mountain guide you've always dreamed of."

Karl beamed. Brad's face had cracked from a rigid grimace into a rarely utilised smile. He was captured by the energy of the young man standing in front of him. Karl had a broad grin that Brad thought might split the corners of his mouth.

"Karl. Okay, Karl, well, I'm not going to make you a mountain guide before I see you in action, but you're in luck. We need bodies for the season and have used plenty of gap-year students. They're usually smart, and you, young man, sure as hell don't lack spirit. Let's see how you go taking small parties out on the short easy 'Green Trails'. They're between three and five miles long. If you do a good job and keep the customers happy, well, you never know. No promises, but I'll give you a two-week trial, and I WILL pay you."

"Thank you Mr.Stackpole," Karl offered in a well-worked humble tone. Brad's speckled fat face was covered in red wine blotches that made him look like a sunburned racoon.

"The money isn't much, but it'll buy you a beer or two in Bullaburra. Go speak to Johnny Marsh at the reception desk. He'll run you through the basics. I'll ask him to take you out tomorrow, show you a few trails, and point out the sights and lunch spots. Johnny knows the drill inside out. No better teacher, but it doesn't sound like you'll need much teaching."

It had worked. Karl deployed his own brand of honeyed charm whenever he could, and once again, sweet and persuasive words dribbled from his lips in sugary torrents. The outcome? A positive result.

"I'd already worked out that conning people was all about the delivery. By now, I was embellishing with ease. It was coming naturally. Every time I do it, the next lie comes more easily. Now I'm just smoothing off the edges."

The Blue Mountains were a series of connected plateaus highlighted by plunging cliffs that plummeted down to a canyon floor. They were covered with canopies of those heavily perfumed Eucalyptus trees. The heat would sink onto the plateaus. It seemed to slide down the vertical cliff faces, building to melting point as it rolled towards the tree-covered flatlands below. This was a dangerous place, and you had to know exactly what you were doing. It was generally fine if you took a guide and were able to stick to the network of fire trails, but wandering off line could be lethal. Karl's homework had been productive.

"There was so much potential to get nightmarishly lost. Once in amongst the thickets of Eucalyptus, unless you were a seriously adept navigator or possessed exceptional bush craft, there was a high chance of a poor outcome."

There was also the alarming possibility of being consumed in a fire; there were more of those. The ogre of climate change was now on the agenda at the government level.

Sometimes fires were lit on purpose or accidentally by an inattentive hiker, flicking away a smouldering butt, or by some ignorant Neanderthal tipping ash from his 'barby'. The Eucalyptus burned spectacularly well, with the flames sucking up, and, using as fuel, the tree's naturally thick and flammable oil.

The fires could move remarkably, like a horse from hell galloping at full speed, spewing flames from its mane as it destroyed anything flammable in its path. And then there were the snakes. In particular, the Eastern Brown and the Red-Bellied Black, indigenous to this area. Karl knew all about them. It had been the most exciting part of his research, and he was fascinated by the chemistry of their venoms.

"The Eastern Brown is fast-moving and small-fanged, and it's reckoned to be the world's second most poisonous snake. A reptilian serial killer, it accounts for around sixty percent of lethal bites in Australia. Nasty bugger. Fortunately, it's a little more docile in the winter. It hibernates then."

Karl was fascinated by any detail that might build his bush craft. In the Blue Mountains, he could feel himself germinating in the way he had hoped. In his mind, deadly snakes were to be cherished, not avoided.

"Eastern Brown bites are inflicted on slow walkers who encounter male snakes on cloudy, windy days. Those conditions dull their senses, and the Eastern Brown doesn't 'feel' you until you are almost on top of it. Startled, it strikes. I like its style. You don't want to disturb a male around September time. When he's in the mood for shagging, like most men, the Eastern Brown gets very grumpy. But this was June, and it was sleepy time. I'd made a map of some of their favourite spots. Once bitten by an Eastern Brown, the symptoms come on fast, with clotting occurring within thirty minutes. Death can come shortly after, often through cardiac arrest. An Eastern Brown would be a perfect pet for me."

***

A few years later, when doing his chemistry teacher job interview at Rimpton Hollway, Karl had said that he had studied the snake's neurotoxins, a major component in the effectiveness of the venom, while on a research scholarship in Melbourne. Karl, of course, had never been anywhere near a research scholarship in Melbourne. However, he had learned a fair bit about snake venom in Australia and visited Melbourne. He had gambled in the casino. Once.

"The Red Bellied Black snake has characteristic orange flanks and a pink belly. Best to look out for that! It usually slithers away when a person comes close, but it can attack when provoked. While much less deadly than the Eastern Brown, you don't want to be left too long after a bite. Significant illness is guaranteed, and necrosis sets in fast. This is putrid, and the victim may need an amputation if left long enough. Death would likely follow if someone got bitten and spent a night alone and abandoned on a canyon floor."

Karl was ambitious to succeed in his guiding role because it was an easy job for him. Even though he was still a teenager, Karl had by then clocked up plenty of mountain miles at home in the Lake District and had plenty of mountain craft in his arsenal. He had taken up orienteering when he was nine. Karl took part in the Keswick mini-series and built up a compendium of navigating skills. Growing up, he spent any free time he could either orienteering in the foothills with the other kids or venturing higher up the mountains towards Bleaberry Fell and High Seat. He was obsessed with the fine detail and perception required to be a top-class navigator. When Karl got to the Blue Mountains, it felt like it was his patch. In more ways than one.

"This is great. Plenty of benefits, I've heard. The tips are excellent, especially from the rich Chinese clients, who are supposedly polite and generous. Loads of extra cash. All I have to do is smile, nod, laugh at their jokes, and ensure they have a good lunch spot."

There was a nook beside the cascading bellow of the Katoomba Falls below the Three Sisters at Echo Point. Karl usually stopped there. It was hot work. The steaming punters would gulp with noisy slurps straight from the river and munch with ferocity at their packed lunches. The hiking was hard work for the clientèle, with rivers of perspiration to mop and swarms of flying insects to swat away - and you had to be careful where you stood. Checking under the toilet seat for spiders was a good idea too. Australia had a lot of nasties that could cause serious problems - even kill you.

Karl lived at a hostel in Bullaburra, a small town not far from the Mountain Centre. Sometimes he would take his tent and camp out, becoming familiar with the network of paths away from the tourist trails. Within a few months, Karl was able to navigate this terrain at night.

Fully equipped, he would head off, the strong beam of the head torch bouncing off the jumbled terrain and monstrous shadows of the Eucalyptus. Karl would stumble amongst the roots and, with every fall, half expected to feel the fangs of one of his slithering chums pierce his skin. Every exploration ended with Karl dank and stained with pungent sweat. With his face matted with bush insects, he looked like flypaper. The focus it took to learn the labyrinth of trails brought on headaches of migraine intensity.

There were very few 'handrails' on the flat expansive ground beneath the cliffs. No lakes, or rivers, or walls, just an amorphous sweep of twisted Eucalyptus groves. Locals and tourists had died down there. They got lost or were sometimes bitten by snakes or spiders.

"I made friends with another guide. Carlos, a young Brazilian lad who was also on a gap year. Carlos didn't have my experience of this kind of environment, but the clients engaged with him fast. I stayed close to Carlos. I knew I could learn a lot."

Karl already had his own learned charm, but he always felt it had an unnatural hard edge. Carlos was the opposite. Every facial movement seemed so natural, and he had a mouthful of sparklers - what a smile. Could Karl imitate 'natural'? He started by practising the Brazilian's alluring grin in front of the mirror. Nicole Kidman did this while playing a psychopath in the movie 'Malice'. To the rest of the crew, Karl and Carlos, or KK as they were called, were blood brothers.

"I hate it when they call us KK. Two reasons. First Carlos doesn't begin with a K, and second, I don't like that wee bastard Carlos."

It was jealousy, and the Brazilian wasn't much more than a puppet to Karl, who only wanted to absorb specific aspects of his personality. Karl wanted the smoothness. Carlos was open, unforced, and a natural communicator.

"It took me about two months to stitch his patterns into my mind. I watched Carlos closely. How he carried himself, the way the hikers seemed to gravitate towards him instantly. Why were people able to feel his warmth? It was clever how he would march up to customers and immediately be tactile. Hand shakes, a forearm gripped, a friendly patted welcome. It was actually quite easy to copy. Faking while appearing warm turned out to be a question of diligent practice."

Karl mirrored Carlos until there was no reflection left. *"Carlos gave me everything he could,"* were the words scratched on the last page of the *'Blue Mountains'* section of the exercise book.

Karl and Carlos would go camping reasonably regularly as Carlos was keen to learn some of his fellow guide's bush skills. The overnights helped Karl save money and avoid forking out for nights at the hostel. One late afternoon, after their guiding shifts had finished, the two apparently kindred spirits set off with their tent and supplies for a night in the wilds. No problem, they'd done this many times before in their months working at the Mountain Centre. This time they didn't come back at the scheduled time. The search began on the third morning, but Karl had only left a rough sketch of their intended route and potential camp site. Finding them would be difficult. The terrain was a wiry mass of thicket and bush, with hundreds of indistinguishable paths shooting away in all directions. Hikers often said they'd felt they were in the world's most complicated maze. In places, the light only managed to tickle its way through the canopy to the canyon floor, creating a perpetual semi-dusk.

It felt like being in an enormous wok, with apparently infinite plains, eventually finding a resting place at the base of the sheer red cliffs.

Most of the space had been conquered by the twisting, invasive trunks of the Eucalyptus. A bleak and beautiful graveyard. On the morning of the fourth day, a shrivelled and dishevelled Karl, his mouth as dry as his emotional spectrum, reached the bottom of the steep steps west of the Three Sisters. Another guide found him. Karl was on his own. He had a story, a convincing one, which seemed to check out.

At the mountain centre, Karl guzzled water with crazed intent and stuffed down anything that the staff set in front of him, chewing and swallowing with the devotion of the starved. As they say in Australia, he smelled like a 'Dead Dingo'. It had been tough for Karl, hiding for that long, purposely depriving himself of any sustenance, but it was worth it. With hollowed cheeks, fissured lips, and jump scare eyes, he explained to Brad Stackpole what had happened. Johnny Marsh was listening too.

"Everything went well on the first day. We had a great time. The weather was perfect. We went to the aboriginal caves, you know, the ones with the hand stencils. Then we took a route below a hanging swamp to the west. I thought my navigation was good, and we went into a gorge beneath one of the ridge lines. We walked a long way and, as darkness fell, pitched the tent in a tiny clearing. We had a good feed and a laugh. Carlos is great company. There were no clouds and the stars were above us, piercing through the canopy. Perfect really."

Brad and Johnny didn't know that Karl had gone to one of the Eastern Brown's winter hiding places and lifted one of the dopy snakes with a stick. He'd bought a syringe at the Bullacurra chemist, sedated the snake with a handmade codeine syrup, and slipped it into his rucksack. Karl's main concern was that the Eastern Brown would stir from its drugged state before they reached their camping spot. Walking with Carlos, Karl stayed light footed; he needed the Eastern Brown to remain in its winter coma. Of course, Brad and Johnny were oblivious, but Karl's notebook revealed the truth.

"Carlos dropped into a deep sleep. I eased the snake into his sleeping bag. I hoped that his body warmth would rouse my reptilian chum. Carlos woke with a sudden jerk. He thrashed about, still in the bag. His arms stretched out, flailing, reaching for help. Our eyes met, his wide and swimming with fear. The look of a pleading, dying man. It was wonderful to watch, but it didn't take long. Strange, I thought, that he didn't scream, in fact, the only noise he made was these weird tortured gasps. Did it feel like a nightmare to Carlos? Who knows. One thing I did know was exactly how long it would take for the toxin of the Eastern Brown to take effect."

Karl's head dropped in Brad's office and his voice became a whisper. "I woke just after dawn. Carlos was still asleep. Well, I thought he was. We were in no rush, so I lay there for a while, very relaxed. Carlos didn't stir though, so I rolled over, still in my sleeping bag, and nudged him." Karl put his head in his hands; the blubbering was theatrical. Karl was much better now at being 'natural' after his practice sessions, but, now and again, he displayed the kind of woodenness that Brad, in particular, should have spotted easily after decades of watching 'Neighbours'.

"I couldn't wake him. I pushed him, shoved him, shouted at him. Nothing. I grabbed Carlos under the armpits and started to yank him so I could do CPR. Then it flashed past me, out of his sleeping bag. An Eastern Brown, a bloody Eastern Brown. Carlos was dead. He was dead."

"Jesus Christ, Karl." said Brad, reaching out and clutching Karl by the forearm. Then Brad pulled him into his chest. Karl had dissolved in his crocodile tears, chest heaving through stuttering sharp breaths. An eyebrow of a good detective would have risen, spotting that Karl's silences were a little too long.

"What could I do? I wrapped him up in the sleeping bag, whispered a few words and left. I was panic-stricken. My mobile battery was flat. I got disorientated on the way back. I should have been able to navigate out … but… I don't know, maybe I was in shock. I got horribly lost. For a while, I didn't think I'd ever make it to the mountain centre."

Brad's face showed nothing but sympathy. He was horrified for Karl and devastated at the death of Carlos, who had been a hugely popular staff member. "Don't blame yourself, Karl, there was nothing you could have done. Snakebites kill hundreds in this country. Australia's full of deadly animals. Carlos was just incredibly unlucky. You were lucky not to be bitten too."

Karl's story was very believable, and getting lost was quite common. That particular area of the Blue Mountains was notorious for it. Karl gave the search party all the clues he could, and the following day the team found the pair's tent with Carlos still half in and half out of his sleeping bag. He was very dead. The autopsy revealed a pair of needled lances on the left calf of Carlos. Around it was the bleed of bruising and tell tale signs of clotting. The pathologist declared that an Eastern Brown had bitten Carlos. 'Death by Poisoning' read the coroner's report. If he'd had access to Karl's exercise book, the coroner might have written something else.

In his mind, Karl had his reasons for killing Carlos. He'd drained out all he needed from the Brazilian. Through the use of his blood-sucking essence Karl had another version of himself to call on when required, and again the dark side had triumphed magnificently. One major mistake that Carlos made was to be more popular than Karl - otherwise, he might have allowed him to live.

"That made him a dead man walking, or, in this case, hiking. The tourists had been posting loads of stuff on social media sites, and Carlos was getting stacks of five-star reviews. So new clients, who had read the reviews, had started to request Carlos personally. Now the smiling, effervescent Brazilian brat was getting more work and bigger tips. I'd had enough. He'd outlived his usefulness." The disappearance was recorded, with diligence, as a tragedy. It had been useful schooling for Karl.

CHAPTER EIGHT

Not long after the Brazilian's death, Karl left his job in the Blue Mountains. In the opinion of Brad Stackpole, and quite a few other staff members, including Johnny Marsh, Karl had changed. No one was surprised as they suspected he'd suffered mentally from the Carlos incident. Everyone gave Karl time and space but internally, he wasn't suffering any reaction at all. Karl was, quite simply, bored. Understandably, other people at the centre had been deeply affected by the whole affair. Carlos had been a very popular member of the team. It was such a sad story, and the staff at the centre felt all of the emotion Karl couldn't. Now he wanted to do something else.

Karl had become impatient with the tourists. *"Soporific predictable chit chat, and most of them aren't fit. Bloody irritating, puffing and panting up the climbs. They're slowing me down and lengthening the time taken on the hikes. As a knock-on effect, this increases the gaps between tips. And the tips are up since I killed Carlos. The customers seem to like me more.*

My hard work has paid off, but Carlos's departure should be increasing my income much more than it is."

The tips were all that Karl cared about now as the grind of the hikes on the same trails, day after day, drove Karl into a torpor. One Friday, Karl collected his retainer from Stackpole, offered not a word or a backward glance, and was gone.

"I wanted to explore the outback and headed towards Alice Springs below the tropics in The Northern Territory close to the MacDonnell Ranges. The dry heat was fabulous, with an average summer temperature of 36 degrees Celsius. I got a new job fixing fences near Dundoo at the huge Larapinta cattle station about 100 kilometres north of the Springs. The owner was an old-school Aussie called Greg Cuthbertson, whose family had arrived from the Scottish Borders. He looked as if he might have played in the second row for Scotland, but his shoulders had rolled, and it looked as if the relentless heat had

dissolved away the muscularity of his rugby-playing youth. If that's what breaking your ass in the outback does for you, I'll give it a pass."

Greg had a small army of part-time backpackers doing odd jobs, and he worked the fence crew hard, which was not what Karl had hoped for. Karl had expected to be left to his own devices and had planned to tinker away at fence posts, at his own pace, between long naps in the shade. However, Cuthbertson had plenty of staff rumbling about in a fleet of old quad bikes checking up on the work rate.

Each worker was given a designated length of fence to fix each day, and the money paid was determined by how much of it you completed. There was a bonus if you completed your section and Cuthbertson knew how to motivate poor and thirsty students. In the outback, the skin-bubbling heat from a sun that felt a lot closer than 92 million miles away came with a consistent breeze. This oscillated between light and almost gale force, sometimes bombarding the fence fixers with a shrapnel of sand, which ripped at exposed flesh like a cheese grater.

Cuthbertson had a bizarre accent, a combo of Borders and Australian. The students called him Bruce-The-Noo, "Aye yee lazy boogers, do yay shift, and there'll be free beer for the lotta yee. Alright mate?"

Never once did Karl finish the job. At the 'Rustler's Rest' every night, while the bulk of the gang got pissed for nothing, Karl had to reach for those Blue Mountain tips. His reduced pay packet didn't cover his teenage capacity for alcohol. There were also regular visits to the town's sole hardware shop, which doubled as a chemist, to buy bandages to repair the damage following his latest fracas with the local hard man.

Cuthbertson had other jobs. For one of them, he needed someone who could confidently and accurately fire a gun. Not many foreigners of student age could handle a weapon, but of course, Karl could - or, to be more accurate, said he could.

"Mr. Cuthbertson, I'm a top-class marksman. I was a member of the Kendal Shooting Club back in the Lake District. We shot at targets on the range, rabbits, and small vermin in the fells. I know what I'm doing. Trust me." Karl had used a gun once in his life, as a 15-year-old, when clay pigeon shooting with Harry. In a full afternoon, Karl had clipped two clays. Not exactly an expert, but a half-truth to most was a full truth to Karl.

Cuthberston seemed happy to take the young Englishman at face value. He could have tested him out by lining up a few old bottles on a fence, but didn't. "Aye, right oh sonny boy. The test for you will be in the product. Dingo deaths are what I want. You're on your own, you shoot a dingo, cut off its tail and take the tails to any of the ranger staging posts. It's five dollars a tail. The ranger will give you a signed receipt, you bring it to me, and I give your cut of the cash. You get 60%… 20% for me, and the other 20% covers costs for your food and fuel."

Karl was in full-bore bluffing mode, "No problem. Can't wait, sounds exciting, great to be self-sufficient."

It was fortunate for Karl that old man Cuthbertson didn't ask too many questions, and, when he did, very few people understood him anyway. But the third-generation Scotsman just needed a volunteer; if that volunteer was useless or shot himself, he'd get another one.

Cuthbertson wanted a warm body to shoot those wild dogs.

Overnight Karl had gone from 'Fence Fixer' to 'Dingo Hunter', which he felt was a significant upgrade. He took his final briefing from the crusty rancher. Karl managed to battle through Cuthbertson's address without a translator.

"Look mate, here's the deal. Dingo's are a pest out here. They prey on all sorts of mammals, including sheep and cattle. They'll even take a Red Kangaroo… if they can catch the booger. They take my stock, and I need them culled."

Karl was handed a rifle, a serrated knife which glinted with menace, and the keys to one of the rustier jeeps parked in the hard pack yard of the ranch. There was a bit of a catch though, as Cuthbertson explained.

"You'll make your own money, mate. And where there's money, there are people wanting to steal it. Be on your guard." Cuthbertson talked with a low sandpapered growl. Karl was already fantasising about some OK Corral-style shoot out with wandering bandits. Karl could map read, which was a help. He'd be spending his days gazing over the sun-baked shimmers of the outback. Karl struggled to drive the jeep, never mind firing the rifle. Of course, Karl's natural arrogance helped him, and he was sure he'd get the hang of the gun after a bit of practice. Karl was on a fast learning curve.

"Fuck me. I couldn't believe how many dingoes there were. Packs of dogs loitering, lounging, and sniffing on the raised bluffs. Chewing at chunks of stinking who knows what. Old Man Cuthbertson had given me a mountain of ammunition in the back of the jeep, and I spent the first day firing wildly in the general direction of the dingoes."

Karl didn't hit one or even come close, and the only thing he had at the end of the day was a massive blister on his trigger finger and a savagely bruised shoulder. As dusk fell and the temperature plummeted from oven to freezer, Karl threw his tarpaulin over the back of the jeep and crawled, exhausted and aching, into his sleeping bag.

According to the map, there was a ranger station eighty kilometres away. Karl didn't have a dingo tail to his name, but he drove to the station anyway as he needed a few supplies and some water. As he closed in on the ranger's hut, he noticed two jeeps parked outside. In the back of each jeep was a medium-sized hessian sack. Karl topped up his water bottles and had a closer look.

***

"I took a risk. The two bags. I just went for it. Did they have dingo tails in them? I grabbed them and drove off. I was, I suppose, technically, on the run. There was a certain glamour to this. I was barrelling across the outback with a loaded gun in a jeep heaving with contraband. I was now a murderer AND a thief. I felt like Ned Kelly."

Karl made his getaway, and after an hour, when he'd found a secluded spot, he opened the bags and found stumpy tufts of hair and blood inside. Karl bolted upright when the hot stench smashed into his face. "BINGO!" Karl muffled through the bandana that was now wrapped around his nose. There were plenty of tails in each sack. They had probably been piled up over a period of days. *"They were defo beginning to decompose. But a tail is a tail."*

Karl checked his map and put a red ring round another ranger station. Not the nearest one, he wasn't that stupid, one about one hundred kilometres away. Karl was hoping that no one had communicated the missing tails to the ranger he was heading towards. He set off, the jeep bouncing through the holes in the barely recognisable tracks, like a baby on a bouncy castle. Karl, even usually calm Karl, was nervous when he reached the hut's hatch. He was greeted warmly by a dust-encrusted ranger. "G'Day, Whadya got mate? Tails?"

Karl breathed out a laconic reply, "Yep, been out a few days, good haul."

There were dozens of ranger stations and cattle stations in this area. Karl's prayer was that the station he'd pilfered tails from wouldn't connect with the ranger station he got the receipt from - or Cuthbertson. Karl was lucky, and Cuthbertson was mightily impressed.

"Fuck me mate. Forty-three tails in three days? Aye you're some lad. Better than twelve herrings and a set of bagpipes." Karl stared, and his mouth opened wide, further cracking his already sun-split lips. *"Twelve herrings and a set of bagpipes? What the fuck!"*

"There's two hundred and fifteen dollars here for you laddie. You're either bum and parsley oor the best shot in the outback. I like you son. Better tae bust oot than rust oot." Which, when translated from Scots/Oz, means 'Live every moment of life to the fullest before you die.' Karl certainly intended to do that, but instead of trying to work out what Cuthbertson meant, he stuffed the money into his backpack. The next day Karl packed in the job, much to Cuthbertson's dismay. The craggy Scot thought he had a skilled dingo assassin on his team. Karl took the regular student jeep run to the bus station, and headed South to Melbourne. Karl had cut and run again, but he was getting used to this successful lifestyle. The adrenaline rush of the Carlos kill and the dingo hunt had made it much more exciting.

After blowing most of his fraudulently obtained dingo hunting cash on the roulette wheel at the Melbourne Casino, Karl flew home from Australia on his pre-paid economy ticket. He was soon telling his friends tall tales of his time in Oz. According to Karl's recollection, it wasn't dingoes that he had tracked down; it had been flesh-ripping reptiles.

"I was hunting Crocs in the Talbragar River in New South Wales. They called me 'Crocodile Dundoo' Great nickname, yes?" That was Karl, making up stories about relatively unimportant events. It gave him a small hit, a tiny buzz. For Karl, lies were the truth. He just didn't care and up to this point, he was getting away with it.

On the flight back, Karl added to the notes he had made about his adventures, paying particular attention to his time in the Blue Mountains. He made sure to hide the notebooks when an air hostess passed by.

Back in Oz, the curious case of Carlos had been filed in a State of Victoria Police folder: "Carlos Ferreira: Accidental Death. Snake Bite". No one came after him for the theft of the forty-three dingo tails. Still a kid, Karl was already convinced that he was invincible.

CHAPTER NINE

When he returned home, Karl completed his chemistry and technology studies at Lancaster University, still determined to teach chemistry locally. Just after finishing Uni, when Karl was twenty-one, he met a girl, Patricia, and their romance developed fast. Patricia, poor Patricia, had flown into the web of a narcissistic psychopath. The wooing by Karl was spectacularly romantic, but the emotions were vacuous. Sadly, Patricia missed the red flags, like the suspicious immediate declarations. "Patricia, I can't believe how lucky I am to have met you. The Universe has thrown us together. It's magical. We're soul mates. It's so obvious like this was always meant to be." Patricia was sucked into the sticky abyss, "I think I can feel it too Karl. It's a special bond, isn't it? I've never been made to feel this way."

Karl's good looks and flair for the insincere soon captured his target. He made Patricia feel very special indeed, the way narcissists do, and she was hooked. Settling down and getting a job was all part of the life tapestry Karl had planned to knit together, and Patricia was his perfect stooge. Attractive, fit and pliable.

As Karl drifted through his twenties, Tex Deacon was building his career in the police force. Initially the progress was slow, but as the years passed, his reputation grew as an effective and thoroughly professional Cumbrian detective. Then came the massive breakthrough that would enhance Tex's reputation and put his career path onto a sharp upward curve. He had just turned forty, he'd recently married Susan, and his work, as a relatively young detective, had helped the Cumbrian force to capture Arnold Nutley, or 'The Jester', to give him his media-inspired moniker.

Nutley had murdered romancing couples who had pulled up in remote isolation at various beauty spots in the mountains of the Lake District. Bodies had been found in small car parks on the eastern shores of Derwent Water. The couples were always killed in the gathering gloom when distracted by heavy petting or other light sexual engagements. They brought their picnics of fast food, alcohol, skunk and cocaine. After yanking open the driver's door, the killer always shot the male first and then, almost in the same movement, shot the female before she could react. Each double killing took no more than one minute.

'The Jester' would pull the male out onto the tarmac. Then the rituals began. The killer, bizarrely, injected both victims with bleach, probably to ensure death. He would sever a finger from the hand of the male and then rip the victim's shirt open and write a joke with a permanent red marker on his chest. One of 'The Jester's' jokes read: "What do you call a hard to 'catch' riverside killer? Eeeee-Fish-Ent. TEE HEE."

He also applied lipstick in thick smears to the mouth of the dead male. The colour was 'Maybelline Killer Red' - what else would it be? The killer butchered four couples over a period of eight years.

Tex was known as a decisive and intuitive detective with a knack for lateral thought. At this point eight people were dead, and the 'Jester' was still on the loose. The investigating team on 'Operation Lakeside' were not getting very far - a decade had passed since the first killings with no arrest and very few leads. Tex wasn't on this case but, while working elsewhere, had been impressing his seniors and asked his Superintendent if he could draw up a profile of the 'Jester'. Tex studied the evidence with diligence.

"The killer is, most likely, local. He knows the lakes and river systems well. He probably lives very close to the banks, most likely in secluded accommodation. There were never any additional fresh tyre tracks at or near the kill site. This suggests that the murderer accessed via Derwent Water or the feeder rivers of Ashness Gill or Cat Gill. This also gave him the element of surprise. He is fanatical about cleanliness and peace and quiet. He may murder these couples simply because they leave a mess in HIS domain and don't respect HIS environment. He'll be upset by loose morals and drug taking. The lipstick and the jokes? This killer could be a woman or even a cross-dresser," Tex then added wryly, *"With a poorly evolved sense of humour".*

It turned out that DCI Deacon had got a lot right in his profile of Arnold Nutley. He was indeed a cross-dresser - Nutley was a failed touring drag queen. He had gone under the stage name of 'Ginger Snap' and never lasted more than a fortnight at any of the clubs during his travels. Bizarrely, Nutley's public persona was a mighty contrast. He was an Evangelical Christian, and a Biblical Literalist, and Nutley had done quite a bit of preaching in the area. The Puritan in him objected to the morally limp, and he did detest what they did at night in their cars and the damage they did to God's earth. Nutley would rant through the megaphone at his evangelical preachings about the 'Sexual Sins of Man.'

Nutley was also a part-time volunteer park ranger and wildlife campaigner and hated the build-ups of rubbish. He was known for trawling the lake shores and remote rivers on foot and in his small boat and filling bin bags with litter (and condoms) dumped by visitors. Except for Sundays, when he put on an old priest's cassock for his public addresses. Then Nutley looked and dressed like an old hippy. Baggy jeans and shirts with beads round his neck and a long ponytail.

Nutley lived deep in the woods in a decrepit fixed caravan between Walla Crag and Great Wood not too far south of Keswick. A steep escarpment sheltered him to the east, which ran north to south within view of Blaeberry Hill. When he was eventually arrested, four male fingers were found mounted in a frame, buried in a small wooden chest under the crawl space of his caravan, alongside a lock of hair from each of the women. Below the frame was the murder weapon. The police, almost literally, had a smoking gun. Tex interviewed Nutley after his arrest and asked him why he had killed. The accused had a strangely effeminate, granular voice and denied everything with a deranged frenzy.

"I'm on this endangered earth to help the scum that pollutes it. They drain the planet's soul. But I didn't kill anyone. God says, 'Thou shalt not kill.' I pray for the sinners. I preach for them." Verbally Nutley put up a ferocious defence, but then, after all, Nutley was a practised performer, whether in drag or in a cassock. Tex noticed that when the killer was ranting, he would morph into his alternate character. This was detailed in Tex's case file.

"Nutley started behaving like a pantomime dame, all screeches and flailing arms. This was probably connected to his sexuality and maybe helped Nutley to feel more comfortable. With the role play came sudden exaggerated histrionics. Learnings? The theatrics were a conscious or subconscious device designed to distract from the lies. Look out for role-playing from a suspect under pressure." Arnold Nutley was convicted of the eight murders and sentenced to life, without parole.

The coverage was intense. It had been a while since Cumbria had been the killing field for a serial killer. It was believed that Fred West may have murdered while lodging in the county for several months during the long hot summer of 1976. West, in harness with his wife Rose, had butchered many young girls, and the notorious husband and wife team were most definitely guilty. However, in the Nutley case, there had been a mistake. The wrong man had been convicted - Arnold Nutley was innocent. Every Sunday, at eleven o'clock in the morning, Nutley had preached for two hours from a raised boardwalk beside the River Rothay. His spittle fuelled and fervent delivery, reminiscent of a young Ian Paisley, always drew a small but inquisitive crowd.

"And the Lord said thou shalt be brought down into an eternity of fire if you fail to take Jesus into your hearts. Fear the Lord and ask him for forgiveness. You are a sinner, and for eternal sinners, there is only Hell." Nutley would rant, almost without breath, while punching the air with his right hand and pointing to where he thought God was.

A man attended every Nutley sermon for several months and watched him intently but impassively. This man needed someone to frame before he could kill. Man before murder was the philosophy. Nutley fitted that profile with absolute perfection. The sermons started at eleven and always ran for at least two hours. This gave the true killer the window of time he required. The man had staked out Nutley, lying flat, like a sniper, on the high ground above Nutley's caravan, binoculars in hand, spying on his every move. He trailed him through the village, staying well back, his baseball cap and hoodie keeping him incognito. He listened to the locals when Nutley left a shop. They talked about the weird eccentric who lived in the woods.

On the Sunday morning after each double murder, the killer, wearing a forensics-style bodysuit, would visit the caravan. It was placed on a rare flattish spot on an otherwise steep slope, with the downhill half of the caravan built up on wooden blocks. A spirit level would have revealed that this home was a little like the leaning Tower of Pisa, or, to put it another way, if you'd put a snooker table inside the caravan, all the balls would have rolled against one cushion. The killer wondered how the caravan got there and imagined it had landed like the Tardis or been dropped in by a helicopter. Nutley's home was also within a short hiking distance of five Lake District car parks, which were often used in the early hours of the morning by hormonally charged couples. Young lovers and those indulging in clandestine hook ups and affairs. All of the bodies had been found in those particular car parks.

On arrival at Nutley's precarious site, the killer would remove one of the protective boards that ran from Nutley's caravan wheel base to the turf, and then snake belly to the small pit he had dug and covered up. In the pit was a small chest the size of a child's music box, and the killer would carefully place a finger and a lock of hair inside a purpose-built frame. After the killing of the fourth couple, the murder weapon was placed under the frame. Nutley was damned, but it was DCI Deacon's profile that had helped them to trace Nutley in the first place. Tex was a local hero.

It was a shame that the investigating officers hadn't removed the rear right hinge on the chest. Under the bottom flap of the hinge, between the two screw holes, they would have found another little something the smug killer had left for them but was sure they wouldn't find. It was right there, carved in almost microscopic letters - the initials K.J.

The real 'Jester', Karl Jackson, had murdered the first couple in his mid-twenties. He had paced himself nicely, quite content to practise his art while he waited for the next person on his special list to come into perfect focus. Like Denis Rader, the infamous and grizzly BTK killer (Bind, Torture, Kill) , Jackson was never concerned by long dormant periods between murders. For Karl, apart from the 'Jester' practice sessions, it was about who he killed, not when he killed them.

PART TWO

CHAPTER TEN

Tex was eleven months away from his fiftieth birthday. Everyone thought that, so far, he'd enjoyed a virtually unblemished career. Tex had just received rave reviews for his keynote address at the inaugural Sir Robert Peel Lecture. Jim Thorpecroft, the editor of the Rimpton Chronicle, wanted to send the newspaper's young star, Debbie Pilkington, on a mission.

Debbie, a relative rookie at just twenty-two, embraced challenges like anacondas embrace prey. There was the day when she doorstepped the Government's Minister for the Environment, who was on a flesh-pressing PR visit to Cumbria. He was only supposed to meet neutral, fragrant folk with lippy smiles and fawning insincerity. These are the kind you see on TV that almost pass out when offered the Queen's hand. The accredited journalists had been carefully selected. This was to be a trouble-free zone because the shiny suited, chinless Minister didn't want to have to react to the shit show caused by an overnight raw sewage spillage into the Sourmilk Gill tributary. Debbie was relatively young, but had already developed a piranha's zeal for blood and had built quite a reputation as a journalist with the Rimpton Chronicle. Debbie's request for accreditation had been filtered out, so she had to shout from behind a retaining barrier.

"Minister, what do you have to say to the residents of Rosthwaite who have woken to the sight and stench of raw excrement on their land?" Debbie was shouting with a piercing determination. "Or the fisheries on that stretch who now face financial ruin. The early fish kill estimate is five thousand. MINISTER!"

It seemed that the Rt Honourable Tim Ramsgate had lost his sense of hearing. The man with the over-slick parting was doing his best Tory Boy impression. He continued with a relentless crab-like motion along the long line of sycophants, mouthing platitudes as he went.

"Would you care to comment, Minister? The people here want answers, and they want action. What have you got to say?" Debbie was folded over like a collapsing deckchair, the pressure of the rail painful against her midriff. She didn't need any clichéd content from the Minister, indeed it was better for her story if he said nothing. She had masses of quotes from the locals down around Rosthwaite, and the front page lead was already formed in her head. The lead story strapline read:

"MINSTER IGNORES PLIGHT OF STRICKEN PEOPLE OF ROSTHWAITE"

Underneath it was a photo of a distraught fisherman holding a keep net hanging heavy with dead fish, and a snap of a Rosthwaite resident hosing excrement away from the laneway that ran into the stream, her scrunched-up nose adding extra impact to the image. The story filled most of the Chronicle's cover page. Debbie's report began:

"Tim Ramsgate, the Government's Minister for the Environment, arrived in Cumbria yesterday for a pre-planned charm offensive but refused to acknowledge the tonnes of offensive raw sludge that had been pumped out into the River Derwent's Sourmilk tributary. The catastrophic overflow has potentially caused thousands of pounds of damage to local property, denying the local fishermen their livelihood. The environmental disaster cannot be measured in pounds and pence. It could be years before the river recovers. Instead of reacting and offering the Government's support, the Minister helped himself to tea and scones with a carefully selected group of unthreatening dignitaries."

Debbie revelled in the nickname she'd been given in the office, 'The Rimpton Rottweiler'. She was turbo powered and spiky. A fitness fanatic who ran down stories until her journalistic instincts bled. She, like Karl, had been in the audience at Tex Deacon's 'Sir Robert Peel Lecture'. Debbie had always felt that there were strong links between the processes of a journalist and those of a good detective. In fact, she felt she'd have made a good cop herself. Journalists and detectives hunted for the truth, or they were supposed to. Debbie came straight out of college and into an interview for a trainee post at the local paper. The Editor, Jim Thorpecroft, had asked her, "What makes a good story?"

Debbie's quick response was concise and accurate. "A strong narrative with a powerful top line and punchy climax." Thorpecroft pursed his lips, impressed with the answer and Debbie's bubbling confidence. A good detective had to make sense of the narrative of a crime, and a good story for them finished with a punchy climax too, and, in their case, capture and conviction.

Hunting local news stories had been Debbie's beat in the first few years. She knew she was close to a full reporter's job. A huge boost came when Thorpecroft handed Debbie her first feature. He wanted her to do a middle page spread on DCI Theodore Deacon. The 'Sir Robert Peel Lecture' was the hook, but Jim wanted an in-depth piece.

"Find me the man behind the man, Debbie. I've heard that he's complicated and that there's a little bit more to the Deacon shtick than a hard-nosed detective. Get to the next layer." He paused for effect, " I want Deacon ... raw."

It always made Debbie smile when Thorpecroft used phrases like that. Something you'd expect the Editor of the Sun, in Union Jack braces, to scream across the newsroom floor. As a budding hack, Jim had dreamed of Fleet Street. He'd seen himself as more of a red-top baron than a copy cutter with the local rag, but his hair was cigar ash now, and the jowls had long since dropped. However, he took pride in the progress of his protégé and, for Debbie, this was a big break.

"Thanks Jim. I'm honoured that you've trusted me with this feature." Thorpecroft smiled while nonchalantly teasing some green vegetation from between his front teeth. "Jim, it's the feature stories that I love. The hard news chases? They are fabulous fun too, but I'm glad you're allowing me to develop my skills." Thorpecroft inspected what looked like a sliver of damp lettuce and rubbed it between thumb and forefinger before flicking it into the waste bin. "Debbie, I know you've got the instinct of a hardcore newshound. You can sniff out and hunt down the kind of stories I want, but this is a different style of journalism. The feature writing will give you the opportunity to develop your writing in a different arena. Go read the feature writers you admire. Study their methods closely. Pick up tips but find your own style."

"I'm on it Jim. I won't let you down. Tex Deacon? I've already read a lot about him. Hotshot detective. I was at the 'Robert Peel Lecture', Deacon was very impressive."

"Well, let's see if you can be too Debbie. I've heard Deacon is quite reserved. You'll have to be able to persuade him to talk first." Thorpecroft pulled a massive ham and cheese doorstop sandwich out of his top drawer and, while unwrapping the cling film, ushered Debbie out of his office with a wave of his left hand. "Go get him Debbie."

Debbie already had several tag lines in mind. 'Tex Deacon: Psycho Hunter' was one. It had been a long time since Tex had helped to send the innocent Arnold Nutley to prison for life. Technically Tex had nothing to do with the actual arrest, but he had provided the profile. That profile helped lead detectives to the ramshackle retreat of Nutley's. When Tex received reports of the mementoes found in the crawlspace, he was certain they'd nailed the right man.

Also, in terms of results, Tex most certainly had a reputation that demanded respect. During the years that followed the wrongful conviction of the still incarcerated Nutley, the profiling and lateral appreciation of cases had helped to convict two serial killers, Colin Nedbank and Gary Bloomberg. On those occasions, Tex had been one hundred percent right in his profiling; the killers convicted were the guilty men. Tex had travelled extensively, often being called in as a troubleshooter to heat up cold cases or to unravel tangles of evidence that had stymied forces elsewhere.

However, Tex didn't quite make the short list of 'Fifty Great Lancastrians'. The Chronicle were running features on the automatics. Like John Lennon, Emily Pankhurst, Eric Morecambe, Gracie Fields, Alistair Cooke and Victoria Wood. Debbie had mentioned in an aside to Jim that it might make good copy to do parallel pieces on those whose achievements sat outside that framework. Lancashire's Knighted, the MBE's, the OBE's and maybe one of the most famous police minds in England.

"It'll add a real feel, Jim. A human touch. It'll show that the Rimpton Chronicle is here to trumpet the achievements of the local heroes. Might sell a few more copies," Debbie threw that line in quite a lot, knowing that Jim was obsessed with figures and was always chasing sales. Debbie had her brief from Thorpecroft. This would be a no fluff and flannel feature, "What a great guy, and what a great lecture." No, none of that stuff; she wanted that double spread 'staple section,' and she wanted it in the top-selling Saturday edition.

Debbie had already taken a deep dive into the darker corners of the Deacon story. She had contacts all over Cumbria; she knew the advantages of networking and had met one, to be unnamed, of course, to find out more. An unlikely source, to be fair, as this was no bent copper or some ex-con. No, this was an arthritic lady with varicose veins, her speckled hair in a tight bun, knitting needles jammed through it. She had baggy stockings, a loose tongue and had known Tex for decades. He'd helped out Maureen Battersby before, notably when she suspected her husband had been murdered. There were no suspicious circumstances but Tex had worked hard to put her paranoia at rest. Maureen was a honey pot for a journalist. A gossip. Debbie sat in Maureen's Portinscale retirement village, the old-fashioned teapot spilling over and the slightly burnt tray bakes sitting on a plate. Through her cottage window, shadowed Lake District summits perched on the horizon.

"I've heard Tex was very depressed following his wife's death," said Debbie, her tones hushed and her eyes darting as if she expected to see a CIA agent hiding behind the cushions. Maureen couldn't wait to get her tongue wagging.

"A terrible illness, you know, out of nowhere, and how the poor woman suffered. It drained Mr.Deacon terribly, I'm told. They say he didn't sleep for weeks, attentive to the end, either at home, in the hospital or at the hospice. And then there were the infertility problems." The fire crackled, drowning out the gentle whirring noise of Debbie's tape recorder.

"I've also heard that Tex was doing that lecture as part of an unofficial therapy." And, Maureen added, almost poetically, "The poor man needs to steam clean his troubled soul." Debbie had heard from elsewhere that this had been the idea of Barbara Bracewell. The Chief Constable wanted the old, sharp, incisive version of Tex Deacon back on her front line. Most of the other stuff that Debbie needed for her feature was in the public domain. Deacon, the serial killer chaser, would be the skeleton of the piece and, around it, the kind of 'raw' that Thorpecroft and the public loved to feast on. The more heartstrings Debbie could get a note out of, the better. Requests for one-on-one newspaper interviews with detectives had to go through the Chief Constable, especially ones like these that weren't directly connected to an active case, but Barbara Bracewell was enthusiastic. She thought it might help her friend Tex find a way out of himself.

Also, Bracewell was keen to promote her brainchild, 'The Sir Robert Peel Lecture', and the restructured police cadet training programme. Debbie was very keen to talk to Tex about both of those, but she didn't mention the personal angles during her request. Quiet man Tex was initially reluctant, but eventually agreed to do the interview, mainly to help out the Chief Constable, but the quick mind of Tex Deacon was already whirring ahead. Tex and Debbie met in an empty and grubby police restroom at the station - she threw a broad smile.

"Very nice to meet you officially, DCI Deacon. I'm Deborah, or Debbie, Pilkington. Call me Debbie. Hopefully, soon to be the Senior News and Feature writer for the Rimpton Chronicle. You can help there can't you?" Tex offered a thin smile to Debbie's icebreaker, "I asked a question at the 'Sir Robert Peel Lecture'. You might remember, you might not?"

Tex was well-mannered and polite, "Oh yes. You were at the front. A good question too, from memory. I thought I recognised your name. I've read quite a few of your stories. There's always a copy of the Chronicle at the front desk. Good stuff. You've aptitude I'd say. Very thorough. A bit of colour. I've heard that Thorpecroft rates you?"

Debbie's head dropped slightly as she blushed and fiddled with her pencil. The flattery was nice, but she knew to hold her guard.

She'd already sensed a particular sharpness about Tex. He felt that he knew just a little more than he liked to reveal. Of course, this was the razor's edge that others knew so well. A recognised part of his DNA, but there was a protective shield there too. He had the incisive mind of a brilliant detective, but Tex knew his way around journalists. He'd read more than 'quite a few' of Pilkington's features. Tex knew her type. Fortunately for Debbie, she was the kind of journalist that Tex respected. "I like thorough, and I like lateral," said Tex, "I reckon that if you'd covered the sinking of the Titanic, yes, there'd have been lots of stuff about deckchairs and lifeboats, but your report might have included a lot more. Like a detailed analysis of the precise mental state of Captain Edward Smith at the very second the big boat hit the iceberg." Yes, Debbie did detail and back story, but today Tex had no intention of giving away either.

"What do you want to talk about, Debbie?" They faced each other, both sitting in frayed armchairs, the patterns long since worn into submission, the armrests made threadbare by thousands of copper's elbows. Debbie leant forwards, closing the distance between her and Tex. "I was in the conference hall for your lecture and thought it was fabulous. And, of course, I've read up on all of your successful manhunts. To tie in with the festival, I'm doing a series on Lancastrians who are outside the official list. Those that are currently making a significant contribution to our society." Tex said nothing, but he cleared his throat. It sounded like he'd done it on purpose. He also pressed his lightly stubbled chin with a closed fist.

Debbie pushed on, "Well yes, there's more of course. I need to put some flesh on the bones." Tex smiled, "That's the difference between us, Debbie. You look for bones to put flesh on; I hunt for fleshless bones." It was more cringe than humour, but it was very 'Tex'. There was a nervous nod from Debbie, who had clamped her legs together and set her hands on her kneecaps. "Detective Deacon, look, I have my contacts. You know I can't reveal them, but I know quite a bit about your depression, your wife's death, and the problems with fertility. I know about the Chief Constable's plan for your recovery. It's a great story. I'll wrap it all around your incredible career. The lecture and your future role at the cadet training school. Build you up as a great Lancastrian. A double spread in the middle pages." Debbie had potential, but she had yet to learn the finer arts of subtlety. Tex raised his eyebrows and feigned indignity by shaping his lips into a tight curve.

"Good effort. Fishing for my ego and my broken heart? Or both? To be fair, you've done your homework. I would very much like a chat with your source. Maybe I'll hunt that person down. Look Debbie, I actually think your writing is exceptional. I can see that you think the way a decent detective might do. There's a lot of research, loads of detail. Thanks to your, it would appear, morally destitute 'source', I suppose you can write your story without me saying a word and hope that it's all true. Feels a bit like a sting. If I give you the quotes, you'll get the truth out there. You need my quotes to validate it, but either way, you run it. Am I right Debbie?"

Tex would have been surprised to hear that the dastardly source was currently knitting a cardigan, but this was Debbie's test. Tex's rump hung on the edge of his scuffed armchair. He had her dark eyes in close-up. Debbie knew that she had to select her response carefully.

Debbie's next few words depended on any prospect the journalist and the detective had of fostering a proper relationship.

"Detective Deacon. I'm a journalist, and some journalists apply different principles to others. I have a lot of information and, it seems, the details from this source are accurate because you haven't denied or contradicted any of them. It would be hugely frustrating for me, but I'm not going to use the story in any form unless I get your permission and your quotes. I don't work that way."

Tex settled back into the chair. "Well you're not getting any quotes. But you've told me exactly what I wanted to hear, and now I think we can work together." Debbie was confused or, to be more precise, she was shocked. "Work together? But I'm not getting my story. How do we work together?"

"At the moment, I'm not exactly sure," said Tex, "But I have a problem, and you might be able to help me. Barbara Bracewell is a great boss, and she's really trying to help me. I enjoyed doing the lecture, and I know I'll enjoy working with the cadet recruits. Yes, off the record, you're right about Susan and my depression and the other stuff. It's affected me, but I get my burn, my high, from working on cases. Murder cases, preferably. Catching killers; that's my fuel. The Chief Constable won't let me into the heart of any investigations until, as she says, I get my sharpness back, but my boat only floats when I'm at the fulcrum of an investigation."

Debbie had listened intently but still couldn't work out exactly what Tex wanted from her, "So where do I come in?" Tex lowered his voice, which he didn't need to do because, apart from them, the room was empty. "At the moment Debbie, nothing. You talked about your source, the one who gave you the background stuff on me. Well, I have my sources, and I get information and tip-offs, but as it stands, I won't be able to follow any of them up. If I switch on a computer here, start accessing files or doing anything on the street, there's a chance word would get straight back to the Chief Constable, and I'd be in the shit. It's simple. If I hear something, I want you to start doing the digging for me and feed it back. That's all. You're a very good journalist. Enthusiastic. Ambitious. I think you'd have no problem getting into the nooks and crannies. Then, if I get onto something significant, I'm sure Bracewell will let me out of solitary and back into the wild."

Debbie, neck muscles stiffening, surprised herself with her sarcastic response. "So we've had this meeting. I get no story on DCI Deacon. Now, just to cushion the blow, you want me to do all of your dirty work, which is, as yet, non-existent and unspecified."

Tex was undeterred, "This Lancastrian Festival. It runs for twelve months. They have quite a few people to pay tribute to. Including, I'm told, George Formby. Why? Have you ever looked at Formby's lyrics? Dodgy at the very least, probably offensive. Have a read of the words of 'When I'm Cleaning Windows.' It's a song about a perverted peeping Tom. You could argue Formby gives the ukulele and Lancashire a bad name."

Then Tex returned to the immediate business. "So here's the deal. I've read your work, in some areas, your contacts are almost as good as mine. If anything comes up that might be of interest, you tell me, and vice versa. Then you do the background research, with my unofficial guidance, of course. Everything goes through you. If I, or of course it will now be 'we' get a firm lead, and I mean a firm lead, then I know, well, I 'think' Bracewell will put me on the case. She knows what I'm like when I smell blood. I think there's a budding detective in you anyway, Debbie. Your hard news stuff? It reminds me of the way I think." Tex rocked back into the baggy softness, "And here's the deal. Whether or not any leads turn up in six months, I'll give you your 'Tex Deacon' story. The Lancastrian Festival will be in full swing by then. And I'll give you every emotion I have, every detail. And not just the stuff on me you already have some knowledge of. There's more, which might need another page. Probably the front one. Of course, we might hit upon something much bigger between us and then the Tex Deacon story won't seem so important, will it?"

Debbie was flattered, flustered and frustrated all at the same time, "So I've to wait patiently for this 'hold the front page' lead, and in the meantime, let me get this right, I'm your unpaid apprentice?"

Tex smiled again, "You've got it, but as an extra sweetener, if I hear anything this end on some of the other current cases, I'll push the info your way. It can't be sensitive stuff, but I'm now another source for you, so we both win. If you can trust me."

CHAPTER ELEVEN

Karl loved quiet time in the house when his wife Patricia and Kerry were out. Mozart, from his beloved surround sound, would fill the room. He'd plunge a super strong Columbian grain in his cafetiere, settle back in his tartan high back, sip his coffee, and reminisce about the macabre side of his double life. Karl often thought about his first kill. He'd only been a kid but he still admonished himself, *"I was stupid. Clumsy. Took a big risk that day. Could easily have been caught. Why didn't anyone join the dots? How could the boy slide down the river bank on his own? Yeah, I got away with that."*

No one had linked the then nine-year-old Karl to the death of the boy or picked up on anything as being suspicious. Karl was a lot happier with his second murder, *"Yep. The gap year put another brick in the wall. Australia was great. Slightly better weather than Cumbria, and that dumb fuck to practise on. And Arnold Nutley. Jeez that was the best of the lot. How fucking funny was that. An evangelical Christian rotting away in prison, knowing he's innocent but accepting in his prayers that this must be part of God's great plan. Some sort of learning. God, the imaginary friend. You can explain anything away if you believe in that crap. Arnold HAD met God. Sadly for him, it was ME!"*

Karl cackled as he pulled the coffee cup to his lips. Serial killers often have a 'cooling off' period before they strike again and the length of this dormant phase can vary greatly. Days, weeks but sometimes years, like Denis Rader the BTK killer. Bind Torture Kill. Ten murders across two decades. A respectable family man, a church leader - of course he was. After the Nutley framing Karl was dormant. Not on purpose though, he was waiting for the right opportunity. When it came, several years after the last murder assigned to Nutley, Karl pounced and killed his father. *"Harry, that was well structured,"* had been Karl's summation, *"Straight to 'death certificate'. Harry, and the kid on the riverbank. It was funny. At both funerals I ended up getting sympathy for murders I committed."*

Karl inhaled deeply through his nose, the satisfying coffee aftertaste rolled across his tastebuds. He was content, for now, and his satisfaction was enhanced by his recent incognito engagement with the so called great detective, Tex Deacon, at the 'Robert Peel Lecture' in Rimpton. Karl moved his head in tune to the Mozart symphony that circled in melodic spirals around the room. Karl was, in the moment, pleased with progress, but the undercurrent of his thinking always included an element of caution. Getting caught was a familiar concern for a serial killer,

***

"I've still got much to learn. The victim escaping, or raising the alarm, poor body disposal. I must have a foolproof method. Think it all through Karl, leave nothing that could expose damning leads. No clues man, no forensic material. Clean-ups must be thorough."

The other half of the double life, for Karl, was his job and his family, Patricia and Kerry, who was nineteen but looked quite a bit older. Possibly because of the dark half moon that seemed to live permanently on his face. His mates joked that he'd been born with a five o'clock shadow, and mocked. "Did the midwife slap you first, or shave you?"

At home, Karl came first. In his mind it was up to Patricia and Kerry to make sure that everything moved smoothly. This was no easy task because, from Karl's perspective, the rest of his family never did much right. He had a poor relationship with Kerry, who didn't feel that his dad understood the mechanics of fatherhood. There was no warmth, no displays of love or affection. Growing up with a psychopath as his old man had been a tough school for Kerry.

The learning curve had been sharp and steep. Karl's inability to integrate caused huge strain between him, Kerry and Patricia. Most conversations were perfunctory and Karl's control freakery and snarling demeanour created a leaden atmosphere.

Naturally some of Karl's DNA had been downloaded to Kerry. Physically they were doppelgängers. Kerry had a little filling out to do, but he was blessed with the familiar Jackson genes. He walked like a Queen's guard, and all that was missing was the Bearskin cap. His body was wire and steel and the looks were there too. Eyes of soft toffee melted into his swarthy and symmetrical face. His hair was a scrambled dark thicket. Mentally, Kerry was sharper than a Las Vegas poker pro and, like his Dad, he was a bit of a loner. Kerry was more library than nightclub, and ghosted his way through life, living, it seemed, inside some sort of protective coating, giving off an aura that said 'approach with caution.' Kerry also shared his dad's love of the sciences and, in particular, psychology. Kerry was coming towards the end of his first-year model at Lancaster University. The subject was morphine to his veins.

Probably from living under the tyranny of his Father's rule he developed a particular interest in personality disorders. Kerry was drawn to great exponents of the criminal psychologists sub culture of profiling. People like John Douglas and Robert Ressler. A look at the books on the small shelf in Kerry's bedroom reflected that. Several volumes written by Douglas and Ressler. His particular favourites were, "Mindhunter: Inside the FBI"; "Journey Into Darkness"; and "The Killer Across The Table". All by Douglas.

From Ressler, "Whoever Fights Monsters". Kerry read "Mindhunter" four times. Deep down Kerry knew exactly why he found this strange and addictive philosophy of profiling so mesmerising. Kerry always had suspicions based on his lived experience and, as he learned about the mind, especially unstable ones, he began to see more and more psychopathic traits in his father. If he was honest, Kerry could see a few in himself too. Kerry had also read, "Without Conscience: The Disturbing World of the Psychopaths Among Us", by Robert D. Hare PHD. For Kerry, the introduction to the book summarised psychopaths well and he would read what was his favourite passage over and over again.

"Serial killers are among the most dramatic examples of the psychopath. Individuals with this personality disorder are fully aware of the consequences of their actions. They know the difference between right and wrong, yet they are terrifyingly self-centred.

Perhaps most frightening of all, they often seem completely normal to unsuspecting targets."

Based on 25 years of deep dive research, Dr Robert D. Hare graphically described this apparently parallel world of con artists, hustlers, rapists and other predators who charmed, lied and manipulated their way through life. This book provided Kerry with the solid information and surprising insights he needed to understand this devastating 'condition' - and people like his Dad.

Hare had drawn up the famed "Hare PCL-R Psychopath Check-list". There were 20 lifestyle and personality indicators, and it was part of one model in Kerry's Uni course. Kerry was on study leave and his Professor, the memorably named Ignatius Carstairs, wanted the Hare Check-list completed, "You can do it yourself, or you can ask someone else to do it. It's purely an exercise and the results are not going to be marked or published."

Kerry rated his Professor highly, but thought he had the personality of an iceberg, and was probably just as cold to the touch, *"Carstairs looks like he'd be the man fixing the electrodes to your temples for electro convulsive therapy."* Kerry definitely shared his Father's caustic approach to humour. Kerry wanted his dad to do the test, to find out where his father was on the psychopathic scale. There was a problem. Karl wasn't the most approachable, and could lash out when criticised. Indeed Karl's reaction to almost anything could be unpredictable and, not surprisingly, Kerry was nervous about broaching the subject, so he took a safer route. "Mum?" Patricia, as usual, was marooned in the kitchen, "In here, Kerry."

"Mum, I've a project to do, and I know the ideal person to help me, but I'm rather worried that an approach to this particular bloke might trigger Hiroshima -The Sequel!"

"What's it about?" said Patricia.

"Mum, it's part of my psychology model. It's a test they give to see how psychopathic a particular individual is."

"Oh Jesus!" said Patricia, "You want to ask your Dad? Wear full body armour is my advice." The spectre of Karl hovered over the family like a vampire but, through it all, mother and son retained a sense of humour as black as bitumen, "Kerry, you better hope he's in one of his rare approachable moods. You know what he's like. If he's cuddly Karl, you've got a chance, but you know how narrow that window is?"

With cheeks full, Kerry looked like a puffer fish, and let out a slow breath.

"Yeah I know. What's the worst that can happen? One of his stupid little tantrums. He doesn't touch me now. Knows what he'd get back."

"Well on that assumption," said Patricia, "And I'd never assume anything with him ... go ahead but it's your call. I'll have 999 on speed dial just in case." That was a line that could have drawn a laugh, but in this house, it was a number they'd come close to calling several times before. Instead Kerry and Patricia stared at each other. Karl was upstairs in his office. Kerry snorted air through his nose and knuckled the door of his father's den twice. "WHAT!" Karl always shouted the first word with the frustration of a man who'd just been woken in the middle of a wet dream. "Dad. It's just a quick word." Karl shut the flap on his desk top and was swivelling round as Kerry came in.

"Dad, Professor Carstairs has given me a project. Could you help me with it?"

"Can you not do it yourself Kerry? You know, you could try independence sometime instead of expecting me to do everything." This was an interesting comment from someone who did virtually nothing for anyone.

"It's a test, Dad. It's called the Psychopath Test. Easy really. Box ticking with maybe a comment or two. I'm sure very little of it will apply to you." Kerry's forced expression made him look like a ventriloquist's dummy.

"The Psychopath Test? Really?" Karl was instantly fully engaged and enthusiastic, much to Kerry's surprise. Karl sensed a challenge. It was also an opportunity. A chance to show himself how well he understood the inner sanctums of his own mind. And, of course, Karl had spent large chunks of his younger years listening carefully to so-called mental health experts. Now he could compare his knowledge to theirs. "Let me see it son."

"It's on my tablet Dad, I'll forward it to you. Thanks, I really appreciate this."

Kerry closed the office door. It wouldn't have been an exaggeration to say he'd been somewhat staggered by his father's enthusiasm. Kerry popped the attachment to Karl, who immediately studied the checklist on his screen. He wasn't good at honesty, but on this occasion, he decided to be truthful. Karl, the experienced killer, flexed his fingers, relishing the task. He attacked the keyboard like a mad pianist.

CHAPTER TWELVE

Karl read the line on top of the page, "The Hare Psychopathy Checklist – by Bob Hare (1980)" and got started.

Item One: Glibness/Superficial Charm

Glib. I looked up the definition. "Insincere and shallow". Maybe other people would see me this way, but I'm not really sure. I suppose I don't have much concern for what anyone else is doing, or their emotions, unless they have an effect on my life, but I think I hide it well.

Sometimes I have tried hard to immerse myself in another person's issues, but I find that my mind drifts very quickly. My attention span is short. The life of someone else is for that person to sort out. Isn't it? Superficial Charm. That's an interesting one. I do work hard on being charming, but is that superficial? I suppose it is an act in a way, because I can switch it on and off. In my view, charm is there to be utilized when required. Anyway, what is the difference between superficial and real charm? Does real charm actually exist? I suppose I am inclined to fake interest. I know that my eyes and my smile can work a little magic. But I'm a good-looking bloke. My technique would be to get people to talk about themselves and pretend to listen intently to what they say. Flood them with questions, "Gosh that's fascinating; tell me more about that." I do this while holding their gaze and nodding slowly at all the right moments. It's a Socratic technique. Psychiatrists use it. It's incredibly effective. Women certainly mistake it for charm. Ok, it's a big green tick for "Superficial Charm".

***

Item Two: Grandiose sense of self-worth

There's nothing grandiose about it. Of course I value myself highly. I have huge self-worth. I mean, look at me. Tall, handsome, humorous, and massively intelligent. Lateral thinker.

What do you have if you don't think a lot of yourself? Maybe that's what depression is. A poor self-image. I've never understood mental illness. I think it's a weakness. Darwinian principles should apply to people like that. Natural selection - get rid of them. I see myself as superior because I am superior. How does that make me a psychopath? Item two is irritating.

***

Item Three: Need for stimulation/proneness to boredom
Good God. I thought item two was annoying. Who doesn't need stimulation? Who isn't prone to boredom? I used to tease frogs when I was a child. Nothing to do at home. To be fair, I have yet to meet anyone who I don't get irritated with very quickly. I suppose I am inclined to move rapidly from one project to another. The only area of my life where I feel "settled" is when I'm planning to do something exciting. Or engaging in something thrilling. Certain pursuits are more exhilarating than others. I enjoyed base jumping. It was like having adrenalin on an intravenous drip. Throughout my life, I've become obsessed with a lot of sports. Rugby, skiing, golf, cycling, rock climbing, bodybuilding, fell running, base jumping, parachuting. Every single one has been dropped, and every single time I've lost complete interest in a matter of seconds. That's not an exaggeration. I remember playing golf. I had one particularly bad round. It was one particularly bad shot ... smashed my club into the bag, breaking the shaft, and I knew I'd never hit another ball.

Same with skiing. Gliding down a slope in France one day, knowing that I wasn't going to get any better, and saying to myself that this was my last day on skis. And it was. Are those signs of boredom, or impulsive thinking, or something else? Again not sure. Actually, I'm getting bored with Item Three. Time to tick it and move on.

***

Item 4: Pathological Lying.
Yes, but what's pathological about it? It's done to gain an advantage in any given situation. Nothing wrong with that. Politicians do it all the time. So do young children.

***

Item 5: Cunning/Manipulative.
Yes, but isn't this simply being smart? I'm only 5 items in, and it looks like the brilliant Dr. Hare is profiling a supremely intelligent being. So far, I can't see too much that's psychopathic about any of these so-called behaviours. I don't see any problem without-manoeuvring another person to gain personal advantage. I win... they lose. That's life, or death. A triumphant tick.

***

Item 6: Lack of remorse or guilt.
Now, I've never understood the concept of guilt. Neither did the Dalai Lama. Apparently, he had to have it explained to him. According to the great Buddhist leader, guilt was destructive, so what was the point? Re-visiting something and feeling bad about it. What a complete waste of time. You do something, and you move on. Remorse. Is that the same thing? Did I ever feel remorseful for something that I did?
I never felt any emotional pain for anything.
Nothing ever cut me up. I would see others struggling with some incident or other from their past. Sometimes they'd want to talk about it. Bloody Hell. Why? It's done. Learn from it, yes, but that's different. I could understand regret though. I'm going to say that I do occasionally feel regret. To be more precise, I think that, at times, I could have taken a different path.
Maybe I'm not a psychopath after all. Box un-ticked. LOL!

***

Item 7: Shallow Affect.
Once again, I've had to look that up. The APA Dictionary of Psychology states, "Shallow Affect: Significant reduction in appropriate emotional responses to situations and events." Well, I suppose I do flat line a bit. Fear, sadness, joy, disgust, surprise – they all feel the same to me really. I've never jumped during a so-called scary movie. Pennywise makes me laugh! It's a running theme, but in general, I don't see the point of most feelings. Fear, sadness, joy and disgust are just words. Anger is different. I can feel anger. Bone deep, all consuming rage. My "Crazy Horse" state. Red is uncontrolled, which is bad – white is controlled, which is good. Anger is definitely in me, although I've never actually hit anyone, but why are most of the other ones absent? I'm a bit confused here because I'm very good at one of these emotions, while the rest are all vanilla. As if they've been dampened down. I won't tick this box either. Maybe I'm normal.

***

Item 8: Callous/Lack of Empathy. Tick. Maybe I'm not normal. LOL!

***

Item 9: Parasitic lifestyle.
No. I'm extremely independent. A loner. I'm selfish, I suppose, and I would sometimes exploit others, but does that make me a parasite? That sounds like someone who clings to another and takes something from them. Like a vampire, but that's a bit different. A vampire is more aggressive. A parasite can work away quietly, doing subtle damage. Dracula is rather full-on. Blood everywhere. I do hook into people who have something I need or want. But who doesn't? Nothing better than sinking fangs into a juicy carotid artery and slurping my fill. LOL..! Actually if I do this at all, I do it in a passive way. People who have the knowledge I need can quickly become my best friend and then be dropped as soon as I have what I want. If you can replace a parasite with a vampire, this box is a tick. LOL. But it says parasite, so I'll be disciplined. There's a difference between the two. So Item 9 is un-ticked. Sliding back towards normality. HA HA!

***

Item 10: Poor behavioural controls.
On the contrary. I'm brilliant at controlling behaviour when I'm at my best and in the zone. If you are not in control, you can make mistakes. Box un-ticked.

***

Item 11: Promiscuous sexual behaviour.
I'm not answering this. Patricia might read it! LOL.

***

Item 12: Early behaviour problems.
Does teasing frogs count? I have read that in childhood, psychopaths sometimes hurt animals, start fires and are persistent bed wetters. I did burn down the neighbour's barn once. I always felt that was harmless enough though. I was just a kid who wanted some excitement. Seeing the fire engines scream along the dirt track was great, and who doesn't love a huge blaze!
Warm memories. The fire crackling, and the panicked gutturals from the old cattle in the barn. I'd just ignited the world's biggest barbeque. The herd of Charolais was very well done indeed. (HA HA Kerry, I made that all up. LOL). I did wet the bed a few times, but any child would with a man like Harry around. (He was my dad). Tick.

***

Item 13: Lack of realistic long term goals
No. Always wanted to be a teacher. It had nothing to do with educating kids though; I just liked the look of the long holidays. LOL! Bit of a mistake though. Teaching was much harder work than I'd hoped it would be. I'm quite lazy, except when I'm focused. Then my zealous attention to detail can consume me completely. I'm very focused at Rimpton Hollway (Wrote that in case the Board of Governors read this. LOL) Sorry, can't tick this one.

***

Item 14: Impulsivity
Most of the things I do aren't impulsive at all. I like to plan fully for anything that is important. Exact execution is crucial. Nothing happens until everything is in place. No tick.

***

Item 15: Irresponsibility
Irresponsibility is subjective. 50/50 on this one. Half a tick.

***

Item 16: Failure to accept responsibility for own actions
No. I have absolutely accepted responsibility for all of my actions. I have always had a choice, and it's not as if I don't know what is right and wrong. Everything I've done has involved a decision or a series of decisions I made. No tick.

***

Item 17: Many short-term marital relationships
Once married. Long term. Must be doing something right!

***

Item 18: Juvenile delinquency
Is this not the same as "Early behavioural problems"? I did have a few fights as a teenager, but that's hardly unique. Never arrested. Too smart for that. One time, I had a scuffle with a boy down at the lake. A fight over a fishing rod. He had one, and I wanted it. I held his head under the water briefly, then I let him up. He gasped. He looked startled, but that's just kids' play. I kept the fishing rod. That was a one-off though. I'm not sure that categorises you as a delinquent. No tick.

***

Item 19: Revocation of conditional release.
Again I had to look this up. It means failing to comply with the conditions of some form of early release from a correctional facility. Well I refer you to a previous answer. Never arrested. Never served time. Too clever. No tick.

***

Item 20: Criminal versatility
Do you have to be caught to be a criminal? Let us assume that the answer is no, but in terms of a literal translation, the answer to Item 20 is yes. I do have the gift of versatility. But surely, this is something to be proud of. Without versatility, I might not have my independence. One of my greatest skills is bobbing and weaving my way out of trouble. "Agile of action, persuasive of tongue". I read that phrase somewhere, and I had it pinned to my fridge behind a magnet for a while.

***

SUMMARY
"I didn't tick as many boxes as I thought I would. But surely the ticked ones show character strengths, not weaknesses? Mind you, I've read enough on psychopaths to know what the red flags are, and I suppose I've ticked quite a few of the categories. All right, Ignatius Carstairs, I hold my hands up. I'm probably a psychopath. LOL!"

Once Karl had finished the psychopath test, Kerry was summoned to his father's office. On the mahogany desk, he saw a screen full of bunched sentences and LOL's, then a blank as Karl pressed "Select All" and "Delete".

Karl snapped round, looking smug, eyes of a crow. "Changed my mind buddy. Ask your Mum to do it." Kerry chewed on his lip and resisted the temptation to somersault through the air like Bruce Lee and fly-kick his father on the side of the head. "By doing that, Dad you've proved what I already thought. Grandiose, manipulative, shallow and callous. That's you.

And no feelings of guilt either. I'm so lucky to have you as a Father."

CHAPTER THIRTEEN

Tex sat in the waiting room, tapping his right foot anxiously and thinking about his fiftieth birthday. It wasn't far away, and he'd heard rumours about some sort of party. Apparently, Barbara Bracewell had mentioned it to someone. Tex's stomach squirmed at the idea. His throat dried as the dreaded thought of being the centre of social attention consumed him. He'd rather discover a superating cadaver than host his own landmark knees up.

The first thing Tex noticed when he walked into the psychologist's therapy room was that the 'quack', David Braithwaite, had by some margin the more comfortable seat. It was a butterfly-winged armchair with overstuffed cushions. Tex didn't think much of the yellow-green pastel fabric, which reminded him of dried vomit. Tex's chair looked angular, like the ones they used when questioning in the police interview rooms. *"The backs of some of those had been over-pronated so that, after a while, it would put pressure on the lumbar region and cause mild back pain."* This encouraged those being interviewed to talk more freely so they could get relief from the growing cramps. *"One of our clever cop tricks. I wonder if Braithwaite does it too?"*

Braithwaite, a private psychologist, had conducted police trauma work for many years. He had chimpish movements, his arms flailing around like a monkey falling from a tree. Braithwaite also had an apologetic manner. Words flew out - it was a stream of consciousness but fired from the barrels of a machine gun. Braithwaite bumbled around the room, closing blinds and stuffing papers from previous clients' notes into his antique cherry wood Davenport desk.

Braithwaite was old school in nature and was hard to age. Tex figured he was about sixty. Braithwaite never quite finished a word, moving onto the next one just when the final consonant was just around the corner.

"Take a seat detective Deacon, I'll be with you in a moment. Busy, busy, busy." The words whizzed around the room like a tornado looking for an escape route. Braithwaite came across as genuine but slightly scatty. He mentioned something about this being his therapeutic space. Tex thought that the word eccentric might have been invented for this man. Braithwaite wore a waistcoat and a butterfly bow tie. Tex didn't like that combination. They reminded him of a murderer he'd arrested. After his warp-speed episode of tidying, Braithwaite sat down.

Fortunately, the word rate dropped from warp speed mode as he settled into his Victorian chair. As he did so, a shaft of sunlight settled on a head that resembled a polished snooker ball.

"Detective Deacon. Very nice to meet you. Do I call you Theo or Tex?" "Tex is good."

"Your superiors have given me some briefing notes, so I know about your wife Susan. Please accept my condolences. Now, how can I help you?"

Tex thought it remarkable how quickly Braithwaite switched from dervish to sympathetic psychologist. Tex had prepared himself for this moment, but he immediately sensed pins and needles in his feet and felt the desire to bolt for the door. Tex thought that what he needed to move on from Susan's death, if only incrementally, was time. Tex was sure that he could sort out his own mind, but Tex had promised Barbara Bracewell that he would go through this process. Well, at least the start of it.

"Dr. Braithwaite. I think that Susan's death is something only I can only work through. It's grief. We've had grief since man first walked the earth. They didn't have psychologists a million years ago. They just got on with it. I'm actually wondering what it is you can do for me? Do I just talk? Unburden myself, get better and move on?"

"Tex, we have therapies and treatment programmes. CBT and EMDR for example. At the end of our session, I'll give you some reading material. We have had some very good results with both, especially EMDR. Before we look at any particular programme, which will be styled to suit you, I need to know exactly how you are feeling mentally. I know this can be very difficult to express, but I can only help you if you help me. And that's with honesty." Honesty.

Now there was a word. If Dr. Braithwaite wanted honesty, Tex would give it to him. "Have you ever seen a murdered child close up Dr. Braithwaite? Have you ever turned up at a crime scene to be met by the sight of a butchered family, their blood sprayed across the walls? Have you ever seen a face with eyeballs removed? Have you ever recoiled from a cadaver, the acidic stench like ammonia in your nostrils? A human decomposition creates a particular odour. One you will never forget."

Dr. Braithwaite was resting the top of his pen between his lips.

"Tex, I have a lot of experience with policemen like you. Men who have seen terrible things and suffered great mental anguish. My profession has been able to aid recovery. We learn in psychology that everyone has their tipping point. Perhaps you have reached yours. The sad passing of your wife, coupled with those horrific sights and the memories they leave. PTSD appears likely. That would be an instant diagnosis, but we'd need to talk a lot more."

Tex was shuffling and twisting. "The issue I have with psychologists in this type of situation is this. You'll tell me what you've learned in psychology, but I've actually seen these things. I've been there. You haven't. You get all your treatments from a book. Your learnings from a lecture theatre. I've been in the field feeling it. Inhaling it. Immersed in it. How can you fix me? I've lived the nightmares. Experienced the horror."

Braithwaite tapped the pen on his teeth. "Tex, police psychologists, army psychologists - those of us who work in this field - have developed a variety of techniques that have been proven to help people like you. War veterans who have seen the most harrowing things and survived indescribably awful injuries. We've seen remarkable improvements. I suspect that you may have buried away your experiences which can put things on hold for a while. The death of your wife may have pushed you beyond your tolerance level. I hope you'll let me work with you."

Tex's belly was filling with fire. He was about to tell Braithwaite something he had never told anyone before.

"Ok Dr. Braithwaite. I think you're right. Susan's death has pushed me over the edge, but I'd like you to help me with this first."

Braithwaite pressed himself into the wings of the chair as Tex spoke. "Twenty years ago, I was called to this particular murder scene. A man had been tied to a chair in a basement, tortured and then killed. The man was a relentless career paedophile, and his killer was one of the boys he had repeatedly raped. The boy, a very patient boy, had waited many decades to snare his abuser. The boy – mature now - took a very long time to kill this paedophile. We reckoned it took about five days. I'll never forget the smell as we entered the murder scene. A horrifying cocktail of excrement, urine, blood and the sourness of fear. A windowless shadowed tomb, mould weeping on the walls. The victim was rigid, restrained, and hogtied. The ropes were red soaked where they'd cut into the skin. I'll never forget his face. It was like a relief map. Eyes sitting proud as if inflated, the engorged face the colour of mustard and moss. Dried scarlet streaks criss crossed his face, thin, neat slices suggested the cut of a Stanley knife."

Braithwaite was scribbling in a doctor's scrawl. "Dr. Braithwaite. Try and imagine the scene. The man was naked. The flesh was rancid and blackened, the skin that was left was like bubble wrap. You could see bone at the bottom of multiple wormholes. The killer had used a blowtorch. Something had been inserted into his feet. Turned out to be meat skewers. The gums were pulped, the mouth toothless. Dried blood where the finger and toe nails should have been. His joints had been drilled, and flakes of bone dust were everywhere. The abused had taken his stiletto knife to various parts of the man's body, engraving 'pervert' on the paedophile's chest. His testicles and penis were in his throat. All of these injuries, and that's just a selection, were pre-mortem. Cause of death? A cheese wire had sliced through his throat to his spine. So quickly done that the head had stayed upright. In a way, that was beautiful, like a magic trick. What do you think of that, Dr. Braithwaite?"

Even the veteran psychologist looked horrified. "Oh my God, Detective Deacon, that must have been indescribably difficult to deal with."

Tex took a long breath. "Well, here's the issue Dr. Braithwaite. I wasn't as horrified as maybe I should have been. I think I could have watched that live and not wanted to stop it. Is that normal? Does that make me disturbed? You see, I despise certain types of criminals, some more than others, and paedophiles are at the very top of my list. I think this man deserved what he got. Don't get me wrong; I couldn't actually do anything like that myself but let's put it this way, I don't lose sleep over the death of a paedophile. What do you think, Dr. Braithwaite? Should I be in therapy for that?"

"Detective Deacon. What I can say to you is that I think I could help you manage those thoughts."

The hour with Dr. Braithwaite chugged to its conclusion. Tex did not intend to return. He hoped that the fact he'd gone to the psychologist would keep Chief Constable Bracewell happy. The session revealed to Tex the depth of his pain, but he decided to focus on his Stoic mantras and beliefs. Tex had a post-it on his fridge,

"Stoics talk about the importance of discipline when confronting the most brutal facts of a current reality. They say we all have our Inner Citadel: The fortress inside us that no external adversity can ever break down."

For Tex it was about acknowledging the pain while doing his best to move forward. Did he have the resilience? Only time would tell. Now, feeling ice cold inside, Tex walked away from Brathwaite's office.

CHAPTER FOURTEEN

Karl did a lot of his planning in the mountains of the Lake District. He loved the striking rises and plunges. The hills nuzzled close to the Irish Sea on the western flanks of Cumbria, sprawling close to his Satterscale home. Sometimes the peaks were blasted by magnificent storms and occasionally touched by heaven on blue sky days when the sun turned the necks of a thousand hikers crimson. From a distance, the peaks looked like a printout from a failed lie detector test. The skyline was highlighted by precipitous slopes that led to pyramid summits. The lower hills looked like egg boxes. They ran around and between the bigger mountains, which were blotched by the wondrous lakes that gave this area its name.

The range was well known for a microclimate that brought rapid changes to the weather with the low and high-pressure systems generally sweeping in from the Irish Sea. When Mountain Rescue went on a call, the most popular opening line from a salvaged walker caught out in a raging monsoon: "It was sunny when we left the car park." It was important that you knew what you were doing. Navigation skills were essential, as was appropriate clothing for every eventuality. Even on sun-drenched days, the mountain men and women who knew the vagaries of this microclimate always carried their waterproofs.

Karl loved climbing the Lake District's peaks like Helvellyn, Skiddaw, Scafell Pike and Great Gable. His favourite patch was a relatively small mountain range area on the Eastern side. They included mountains like Bonscale Pike, Leadpot Hill, Wether Hill, The Nab and Steel Knots.

The lowland area between these hills was called Martindale. In the fifteenth century, this spot had been named, by superstitious locals, as 'The Devil's Cradle'. The peaks themselves had been given alternative names by the mediaeval inhabitants. One was called 'Beelzebub', and below that sat a small well-known rock climbers pitch called 'Baby Beelzebub'.

Witchcraft had been practised in these mountains during the Middle Ages and, according to legend, human sacrifices were carried out on a regular basis. Apparently, there were covens galore. Local mythology had it that some of the infamous Cumbrian and Lancashire Witch Trials had taken place in these mountains. One story recounted how the witch Alizon Device, found guilty at Lancaster Castle, was hanged close to 'Beelzebub'.

A stone cross to the North was raised proud, a sentinel against the rapidly changing skies. The cross towered over a stained and gnarled granite slab. That was where, as the fables said, a possessed local priest had martyred children as a pacifying gift for his master Satan. The lakeland had a dwindling network of storytellers. Once very popular, they had now been usurped by the advance of technology.

The internet had taken away their trade. This vaguely eccentric breed camped themselves at the summer fairs and would charge a few pounds to churn out their stories. The goggle-eyed tourists loved it. Bill Carltondale was a classic Cumbrian character, a gritty retired hill farmer with features that had survived a thousand storms. He used his pliable features to shape a panoply of emotions. Bill's poetic way with words gripped all who listened, and there was a natural chill in his crusty Cumbrian tones. The one about the child martyrs was Bill's favourite.

"The story goes like this," Bill would lean forward, looking as if his next move might be to bite the nearest listener. "Hundreds of years ago, a priest, originally a bible-slamming evangelist, performed exorcisms on troubled souls. He said he could sense any demonic energy by placing his hands on their heads, which then raced lava-like through his shuddering body. It was quite a sight, apparently, with the priest writhing and spewing words in foreign tongues. Green flem would bubble out from his nose and ears."

That opening stanza would always pull the punters in. Bill placed his tent a little further back from the others at the country shows so that the wind would flap at the folds of his wigwam. It was even better when Cumbria's black rain hammered at the canvas, sounding like it was coming from a nail gun. Bill's voice could have sent a chill down a robot's spine.

"The priest would end up on the floor prostrating himself while uttering terrifying yelps and spitting out passages from the Bible. Then he would rise, collar drenched in sweat, ectoplasm on his lips and proclaim in 'The name of the glory of God' that the demon had been sent scurrying back to the hell fire below."

Bill's audience, by now, was always bug-eyed. A few trembled, and some crabbed out of the wigwam, unable to take any more. Bill was well used to tingling spines, and on he would go. "But the power-crazed priest went too far, and dealt once too often with the powers of darkness. He took to haunting the streets at full moon, a Transylvanian cape wielded with a flamboyant whisk. Terrified locals stampeded into their smoky bricked, two up, two downs. Babies began disappearing, stolen from their cribs. A charred cross was left on the bed, smouldering on the sheets, with one spot of blood on the tip of each timber. The infants were never seen alive again. The tale told us that, years later, little bones were found buried below the stained granite slab, hidden in a tangled copse high up in the storm-lashed hills. Martyred for the Devil. A Murder of crows hooked their saw-sharp claws on the trees. They screeched with malevolence, as if standing guard, when tear-stained parents came to pray."

It seemed that 'The Devil's Cradle' was an appropriate alternate title for the area. Many of the hills, saddles and pathways had their official names and their 'real' names as determined by folklore. There were summits with flamboyant demon-themed designations. 'Lucifer's Leap', 'Great Demon', 'Old Serpent'. There was a deep narrow canyon known as 'The Abyss'. A triumvirate of small mountains named 'The Goblins', a waterfall called 'Fallen Angels' and a jagged outcrop christened 'The Vampires'. Admittedly Dracula isn't specifically a child of Satan, but what else would you call sharp-toothed rocky barbs in a place like this? Poetic licence in the naming and, of course, the story of the possessed priest wasn't the only creepy tale. There were dozens of those. Very few people went anywhere near 'The Goblins' when the so-called Ghost Fog descended. Many had disappeared in an instant, so they said, after being engulfed by the fast-forming mist. On the wilder nights, you could hear whistling screams rasping through the basalt tors.

As a kid, Karl dived into folklore. He'd heard most of the stories. He never knew where he might pick up an important tip. He also loved to run in the mountains. Even psychopaths need a brain wash.

He'd started out with orienteering, and now in his forties, Karl was still jogging around the Lake District peaks. He preferred to be on his own, immersing himself in the sound and feel of the capricious winds. They could sooth or punch, depending on their force, ripping at his pertex top, and, when combined with needled rain, his face could take on the appearance of a spicy plum.

During the arctic days, the cleats on his specialised fell running shoes were challenged by frozen turf and treacherous rocks and slabs, sometimes glazed under inches of ice. Karl had twisted many an ankle in pursuit of his sport and spilt blood too. The days when the gales were so fierce that running into one was like fighting a wind tunnel. Karl had crawled the final metres to the summit of many mountains. If he'd stood up, the invisible howl might have lifted him off his feet, threatening to forklift him over some forbidding death drop.

Then there was serenity. Usually summer days when wafting breezes warmed his skin, cobalt blue skies pockmarked by the jagged profile of distant peaks, as the sun baked his exposed flesh. The sneaky nips from the midges and horse flies were his only annoyance, otherwise, it was bliss. Karl cherished the boiling sweat that steamed his body. He guzzled vast quantities from sparkling rivers, sometimes finishing his runs with a skinny dip under one of the many thundering waterfalls. You had to know how to find them. Easy for Karl, the expert navigator. Very few people knew the nooks and crannies of the lesser-known areas of the Lake District better than Karl Jackson.

This was also where Karl did most of his devious thinking. Hatching schemes. No better place for demonic thoughts than places with mediaeval names like 'Lucifer's Leap'. The darkness of Karl's soul perfectly matched the fabled sinister past of the grey-flanked peaks. He had walked and hiked here since childhood, but during the last ten years or so, mountain fell running had become a passion. The obsession had truly begun during the Nutley framing. Karl knew that if he was to carry out his plan successfully, he would have to know every inch and access point. Running speeded up the process, and he was hooked.

Karl began running the fells competitively. He joined a club and started with some small local races. Karl wasn't social, but he was hyper-competitive and couldn't see the point of all that training if he didn't have people to beat at the end of it. He enjoyed all that came with mountain running. His thighs pulsed, eyes locked on a peak, lactic acid flooding, sucking air into lungs that never felt big enough. On the downhill, the agony could be worse. His joints crunched when he hurled himself with total abandon down steep and slippery bouldered slopes. The dynamic terrain demanded incredible balance. Karl hopped on the turf and over rocks as if he was trying to negotiate the coals on some huge fire pit. His limbs danced with a particular madness. He looked like a marionette having a seizure. Karl's rubber soles made flash contact with the obstacles as he bounced towards the finish line.

Physical and mental toughness came easily to him. Five and six-hour training jaunts in all weathers and all seasons were no problem. Karl dealt with his own pain by planning how to inflict it on others. There was plenty of room in his black heart for creativity. Karl began his serious fell running in his early thirties and kept meticulous records of his training runs and races.

"Finished fourth today. It was the 'Old Serpent Seven' Sixteen miles, seven summits. Felt good. First five summits; no problem, then fatigue. Pushed hard on the final two climbs. Good on the downhill. Body burning. Great feeling. Made up four places in the last three miles. Caught Jimmy Spence at the last cairn. My nemesis, but not this time. I couldn't help a sneer as I cruised past him. His face was purple, and I think he was on the verge of throwing up. He had nothing

left. I got him. Finishing time five hours fourteen minutes. Only twelve minutes behind my personal best. Conditions were tough though. There was lots of rain overnight, so really boggy underfoot and a buffeting wind, which was into us on four climbs. Happy enough, and I used the thinking time well."

***

Karl relaxed as he ran, retreating into his fantasy world, his imagination vivid. It took his mind off the bursting blisters and the pain that rippled through his body.

"Am I a lion? Select a weak zebra, then sink my teeth into its neck. Three minutes maximum from the chase to death, and they can't touch you for it. But of course, I don't hunt for food. I'll leave all that to the crazy men like that mad cannibal Jeffrey Dahmer. There wasn't one thing that I admired about Dahmer. The trial was interesting though. Great TV. They won't catch me, but if they did, I wonder how my trial would look on the box? Maybe I'd do my own defence, like Ted Bundy. I imagine there'd be loads of screaming women outside the court for someone like me. Bundy was a bloody sex symbol even to women who knew he'd butchered thirty-something females. What the fuck is that about? Lunatics. Anyway, Dahmer. Not my thing. Leaving the heads of your victims in the fridge is just asking for trouble. There was nothing of use for me in the Dahmer M.O. Too careless. Lust-motivated killers take too many chances. I wonder why? Maybe that chemically driven desperation leads to schoolboy errors. Note to self. Lust is to be avoided."

Karl was building into his usual routine of combining his ideas with other killers' procedures. He needed to cocoon his next target which was often the most difficult bit. Karl preferred to kill with a motive, and that's why he had his list. The last person who deserved to die was Harry. Karl had been patient since he'd killed his father and was content in his dormant phase, but another opportunity was about to come his way.

CHAPTER FIFTEEN

Karl burned vast quantities of adrenalin in the mountains. He loved those solo runs, but once in a while, he would buddy up with a club colleague, Bart McGoldrick. Karl wasn't too fussed about fellow members of his own species unless he was killing them, but running in pairs or groups for safety reasons was encouraged in the mountains. If you'd burned Bart alive, there wouldn't have been one spark of sizzling fat. All bones, his skin appeared to have been sprayed over his skeleton - Bart was a matrix of sinews. Karl wondered where he got the energy to run. Maybe from the only area of mass on his body, the explosion of grey on top of his head where the strands of hair shot off at peculiar angles. Karl thought he looked like Doc Brown from 'Back to the Future'. They worked well together on the fells, both good navigators, and Bart ran at roughly the same pace.

Bart was not only a member of Karl's running club, he was also a volunteer with the Keswick Mountain Rescue Team. Had been for over 20 years, and Karl enjoyed listening to Bart's myriad of mountain stories, which were more reliable than Bill Carltondale's, the man of chilling myths. For Bart had seen remarkable rescues, grisly injuries and body recoveries.

On one drizzly March morning, Karl and Bart were jogging a crumbling trail between the summits of Seat Sandal, Dollywagon Pike, Nethermost Pike and Helvellyn before a drop-down to the car park at Thirlmere. A throwaway line from Bart spiked Karl's attention to full alert. "You know... the mountains. It's the perfect place to commit murder." "What?" said Karl. He wasn't sure if he'd picked Bart up correctly through the gusting breeze.

Karl shouted, "Perfect place for what?"

"A murder," Bart confirmed. Karl had never been more interested in a conversation in his life. In his two decades with Mountain Rescue, Bart had picked quite a few dead bodies off the hills. According to police reports, they were all accidental deaths. He pushed Bart for more detail.

"The deceased included hill walkers, quite a few ageing farmers and one Outdoor Pursuits Instructor who, brilliantly, while out with a bunch of teenagers, had slipped and fallen into a river which was in spate and had been swept away. One of the kids dialled 999, and my party was first on the scene, but it was too late. We picked up the body in a pool a couple of miles downstream."

Karl smirked, "666 would have been a much better emergency number. You were trying to save a man from a raging torrent below a mountain the locals called 'Great Demon.'"

Bart was talking through a mouthful of protein and carbohydrate as he chomped on an energy bar.

"In twenty years or so, I think I've collected maybe thirty bodies from the hills. On average, that's one and a bit bodies a year. Sometimes animals got there first." Karl smiled as he pictured Bart hiking for hours with his team to pick up a chewed, decomposing leg full of maggots. Karl snorted between deep lungfuls of air, "Sounds like great fun Bart."

"It's never easy. In fact it's brutal." Bart said, "Usually the deceased is in a group, and a party member has had a cardiac arrest or something. Less often, they are on their own. Three times it's been suicide. Cutting hanging men down in the lower forests. Harrowing. I knew one of them personally. And there's no mental health support for us. We're volunteers, and some of us have a form of Post Traumatic Stress Disorder. It's hard to deal with ... death."

Karl's lips pursed. Bart continued, "Twice I was absolutely certain it was murder. Both times it looked like accidental death, and that's how it was recorded. Hunting down evidence in the wilderness isn't easy, and it's a lot of work for the police."

Karl wasn't interrupting this; his senses were as acute as a bat's sonar system. "For those two incidents the investigators would have had to walk for many miles through tough terrain to get to a potential murder scene. A detective once told me that it was really hard to prove that a death in the mountains was murder. One reason is that there is simply too much potential to make it look like an accident.

Push someone off a crag and claim they stumbled. How do you prove otherwise? There's no CCTV in the mountains."

Karl suspected Bart had used this line before. No doubt he and his Mountain Rescue chums had told their anecdotes of murder before while huddled over flasks of tea waiting for a call out.

"And then there's the paperwork." Bart was rolling into a rhythm, "There's a lot of it for a suspected murder when you can quite simply chalk it down as 'accidental' and move on. A lot of the detectives I've encountered are lazy." Karl wanted to know as much as possible about the murders - and lazy detectives. Bart closed in on the detail, "Well one was more mysterious than the other. I'll get to the weird one in a minute. But at the outset, the first possible murder we saw looked like just another 'fell off a crag' death. At the time, it very definitely looked accidental. And it was recorded as such."

By now, Karl and Bart were negotiating a lesser-known bog-strewn route. With mud-splashed legs, they focused on their dance routines, skipping from limb to limb and forging towards 'The Goblins'. The area was covered with patches of soaked sphagnum moss at saturation point after the recent rains. They were the trapdoors of vegetation. Many sheep, and a few human beings, had perished when sucked into the rich liquid of drenched ground below. You had to watch where you placed your feet, especially away from the worn tracks.

They reached a stile. The wind was bellowing now, and an ominous black blanket was rumbling in from the sea. It appeared to be suffocating the horizon, and even the lower peaks could no longer puncture the clouds. Bart stopped talking as the two men clambered over the wire-grilled wooden steps that arched across the dry stone wall. They dropped back into their comfortable pace, and Bart's breathing regained its even rhythm.

"We got a mobile phone call from a hysterical woman. Said her husband had lost his footing on the edge of the 'Witches Ledge' cliffs and fallen a hundred metres onto the shattered boulders below. We got there - six of us with all the gear - and this lady was curled up on the ground sobbing. She was almost hypothermic. Through the tears, she stumbled out an explanation. It was their wedding anniversary. Traditionally, on this date, they'd always walk this ridge. They'd been close to the precipice but not too close, and then a freak gust of wind had funnelled through the gully and caught them. She said it threw her husband off balance, and he fell, sliding feet first and fast off the edge. It was dark by the time we collected the body. As we got to him, the police arrived, guided to the grid reference by another Rescue Team member. The usual procedure. Absolutely no way of defining the death in any other way than accidental. No evidence of any kind, and none of us suspected anything. Just another unfortunate incident. We've seen so many."

Karl had to move right into Bart's personal space, otherwise, his words would have been whisked away by the gathering storm. Now they were so close that their waterproof tops rustled together. Karl spoke, "So when did you suspect murder?"

Bart hurdled over a rock in the middle of the trail without breaking stride. "It kind of started on the night itself really. It took us a couple of hours to get the lady off the mountain because they'd walked quite a way from the car park. Emotionally she seemed to recover quite well, maybe too well. From experience, that was not abnormal, as when people go into shock, they can display a range of things. Wail and shout. Go still and quiet. Start to shiver. You never know really."

Bart and Karl hit a rocky ramp, and the two men were soon gasping in tandem. Karl's lungs felt like they'd filled with acid, and he couldn't have spoken even if he'd wanted to. And he didn't want to speak in case he threw Bart off kilter. Karl kept his lips tight and ears open.

When they were back on the flat, and recovered, Bart, having rasped out a few croaked and illegible words on the ramp returned to his flow. "By the time we got her to our Land Rover, she seemed to be on a sort of high. Again your first thought is shock. The police took her away to get a few details and to comfort her really. To make sure she was okay. She was taken to a relative. But on the way back to base, a few of us remarked on those emotions. We hadn't seen that exact pattern before. The couple had come from Shapshear, a small town ten miles from the Eastern edge of the mountains. Rumours had been rolling around, and apparently, the woman had been having an affair. Turned out her now deceased husband had been a cruel partner, not much liked by the neighbours. Of course, when we heard this, there were more than just knowing looks and nudges from my mates in Mountain Rescue. The rumours gathered momentum. The Police did come out and interview the woman for a second time. Yes there was a possible motive, but it was flimsy."

Karl wished he'd been able to take notes but had to rely on memory, while praying that the whipping wind didn't steal away any important information. Bart went on.

"Not every woman who is having an affair kills her husband. The woman stuck to her story. Strong gust of wind. He slipped and slid. Or was her lover hiding in a gully, waiting to pounce? That's actually where we first used the line, 'Shame there's no CCTV in the mountains.' We wish there had been. Would have cleared things up. There wasn't much the police could do, and to be honest, she could have been completely innocent. But there was a problem. Well we thought so."

Karl almost cricked his neck, trying to jog while keeping his ear as close as possible to Bart's mouth.

"A few of us walked back up to where the 'accident' had occurred. Robbie Benson, who's been with Rescue longer than me, said, 'It would take one hell of a gust and one hell of a slide to go off the cliffs from this point. A wee shove would definitely help.' We told the police. They listened to us, but it was all hugely circumstantial, with no physical evidence. To this day, there are suspicions in Shapshear, but there were never any charges. Police reckoned the chances of a conviction were incredibly slim. But by now, we were pretty sure the woman was lying. And there were the woman's strange emotions that night. She went from hysterics to being bright-eyed and almost manic. Was it shock, or maybe she just felt she'd got away with murder."

CHAPTER SIXTEEN

In silence, Bart and Karl ran on towards Thirlmere, but Karl's brain was fizzing like an effervescent tablet in a glass of water. The dark clouds were scampering closer - in the distance, the sky cracked and roared. Karl Jackson and Bart McGoldrick pushed hard. Getting caught in the mountains when there was lightning about wasn't a great life insurance plan.

Bart, the old man of the hills, estimated thirty minutes until the storm hit with full force. He continued with his stories, talking now between heaving rasps.

"But there was an even stranger incident," said Bart. " One warm summer's day, we got a call out for an incident on the southern fringes. A walker had found a body lying at the bottom of the cliffs at 'Baby Beelzebub'. That small remote hill below the main 'Beelzebub' mountain. Do you know it?" Karl's head was buried in the hood of his gortex top, so instead of nodding, he gave Bart a thumbs up and said.

"Yes, that's the smaller bluff below the main hill. Has a series of crags on one side and is rounded and bouldered on the other. Perfect for solo climbing."

"That's it", said Bart, his own voice loudening as the buffeting increased. "The body belonged to a man called Bob Crabtree, a well-known local rock climber. He'd been using a sling as a top rope."

Karl knew enough about rock climbing. A sling was a loop of webbing, often nylon, that could be wrapped around a rock and used as an anchor. Karl had always been a climber and was a decent exponent. He felt no fear, which helped. Perhaps Karl took a few too many risks. Initially, as a kid, he had gone to the indoor wall at the Mountain Centre with his dad, but Harry's brother Charlie was the best climber in the family. The Jackson family all loved the outdoors. Charlie spent his summers in the Alps and had climbed the Matterhorn. He'd completed some serious routes in the French climbing Mecca of Chamonix. Karl hated Uncle Charlie and had very good reason.

Bart continued, "Crabtree was just lying there surrounded by a crumpled stack of ropes and climbing gear, including his sling. Dead. While four members of the team tended to the corpse, two of us scrambled round the crags to the flat top above the cliffs. There was a secure point that climbers had used without incident for many years. A spike of rock.

Crabtree must have put his own sling over that anchor, as a lot of climbers had done previously. It was the only place for it."

Karl remembered some of the details of the aftermath as reported in the local 'Rimpton Chronicle'. One of Debbie's early stories for the paper. The police had been called, and the apparent reason for the fall was that the sling must have independently jolted its way up the spike. Crabtree must have been quite a way up the cliff face when the sling came free. His injuries were spectacular. Crabtree's head had exploded on contact with the broken ground. It was as if someone had hit a coconut with a sledgehammer. A reddish pink goo was spread far and stained the rock-strewn turf.

Crabtree's body had buckled on impact, bones splintering. He lay there in ghoulish twists, like a crash test dummy after a particularly hard day at the office. Crabtree also had a broken neck. The coroner determined that this had been caused when the deceased arched backwards during the end of his fall. Crucially, there was no evidence of foul play."

Bart broke off to negotiate a short steep rise and then finished the story. Karl just kept on listening. "The police spent two days on-site. It was possible that Crabtree hadn't slid the sling far enough down the spike, but he surely had too much experience to make a mistake like that. Plenty of highly qualified people had their suspicions, including us, but when there's nothing to go on, there's nothing to go on. The police looked into Crabtree's background, including his marital status, searching for clues or a motive, but they couldn't lock into any incriminating evidence. Crabtree could have been guilty of shoddy workmanship when he set up the sling. In the absence of forensics or leads of any kind, 'Accidental Death' was recorded, and everyone moved on."

Karl consumed it all with the relish of a starving dog, "So you had your suspicions? Was that all they were? Suspicions?" Bart's breath was now spraying through pea-sized drops of rain, and he'd been wrong about the half-hour window. Armageddon had arrived. Karl found Bart almost impossible to hear through the pounding and roaring, but he was picking up more than enough useful and usable background noise.

"For years, yes, but the death and the nature of it never went away. A year after the accident, two of Crabtree's close chums were convicted of fraud. Crabtree was linked to an attempted blackmail. It turned out that he had an overseas account. Lots of cash in it. He never seemed to be working much but Crabtree was never afraid to spend money. A low-level local drugs operation was busted. There are quite a few small-time criminals around here."

Bart's words were being blasted out of earshot, so Karl pulled him behind a sheltered crag, tugging Bart into a crouch. Bart wasn't too enamoured with the rough treatment, but at the same time, he was glad of a break from the typhoon.

Karl needed to hear Bart's finale clearly.

"In terms of the crime links, the police found Crabtree's name on a list in an envelope, but that was it. That loosely connected him to the drugs gang, but nothing was damning.

However, that was enough for our bunch of amateur sleuths at Mountain Rescue. We've good imaginations! Maybe Crabtree had upset someone? A few of us, including Robbie, went back to 'Baby Beelzebub' and did a Crimewatch-style reenactment. We put a sling on the rock anchor and a man on the end of it. We spent all day experimenting. We tried the sling at various heights on the anchor and the climber at various heights on the cliff face. Up and down. Up and down."

Bart gesticulated, acting out the movements, looking like a window cleaner shifting his extension ladder. "Even if Crabtree had placed the sling halfway up the rock spike, we couldn't see how it would slip off on its own. Remember, there was a man, Crabtree, on the other end of the nylon webbing, creating tension. The sling hadn't snapped. It had somehow worked loose."

Karl was ahead of Bart and, at last, interrupted. "I think I know where you're going. You think someone slid the sling off the spike?" ..."Yes," said Bart. "But how?" said Karl, "As you said, there would have been too much tension on the sling holding it taught. How could you edge it up the rock in those circumstances? Even if you did, how would you be able to do it without damaging the sling? I mean, that would be evidence of interference, there would be fraying on the sling. And if there was a killer, surely they would have left scratches on the rock where they worked the sling loose?"

Karl looked hard at Bart, his eyes just visible below his dripping hood. "We'd thought of that Karl, you're right. There was no damage of any kind to the sling. Not sure how the killer, if there was one, managed that. But Crabtree wasn't the fittest. Bob was carrying a little excess weight and that route on 'Baby Beelzebub' is difficult and exhausting. It's rated as Elite E8 on the GB rock climbing grade system. Locally, that route is called 'Satan's Chamber'. There are a number of tiny ledges on the climb. If there was a murderer, he would have needed a good knowledge of climbing in general and that route in particular. Robbie was our guinea pig on the 'Crimewatch' climb. Every time he stopped for a breather and put a toe on a ledge, the sling briefly went slack. There are seven ledges. We worked out that with fast hands and a suitable lever, a clever, well-researched killer would have had just enough opportunities to slip Crabtree's sling up and over the spike."

Karl had found that, when it came to murder, one of the most difficult things was positioning the person where you needed them to be. Sometimes it takes a lot of patience. He had almost unlimited supplies of that, and he'd waited from childhood for the moment that was about to arrive. Harry had been ticked off Karl's list. Another of the targets was about to appear in his viewfinder. Charlie Jackson.

CHAPTER SEVENTEEN

After Harry's recent funeral, Karl's Uncle Charlie rushed back to his home in the Far East. He couldn't get to Heathrow quickly enough. Charlie had come to his brother's funeral purely out of a sense of duty. He knew how much he was despised by Harry's sons, Karl and Nathan.

Uncle Charlie spent almost all of his time overseas. Karl was in his twenties when Charlie had initially left the country and often wondered how he got his kicks in places like Thailand and Cambodia. Karl had his suspicions because even now, he would wake scrunched up and terrified in his damp duvet, remembering Charlie's impact on his childhood. Karl's notes of his nightmares held the horrors.

"I'm in my bed waiting for the noise of footsteps. I look through the gloom of the bedroom and see the door opening while it creaks with a slow squeal. On the far wall, buried in shadow, I can see the shape of Uncle Charlie's neck. It looks like it's been stretched out on a rack. My body stiffens and now it's frozen. Uncle Charlie is drifting towards my bed like some sort of ghoul. This isn't happening. This isn't happening. This isn't happening. Charlie spoke, saying what he always said, "Hiya buddy. I'm here to help you sleep." His hand slips into my pyjama bottoms. He is searching, feeling, squeezing, and pulling. I can see him grabbing at his jeans. His other hand is jerking up and down. A low groan and then warm liquid spurts over my pyjama top. What is it? What is it? What is it? Sticky. It's disgusting, but at least I know it's over. "Say nothing kiddo; one word, and you're dead." Then I see him cross back to the door, it squeals again as it closes. I feel another stickiness but tears this time. They are mine, and rolling down my cheeks."

***

Charlie was back in Satterscale a matter of months after Harry's death to see the few friends that he had been unable to see at the funeral, and, in that arrogant Jackson way, he thought he might be able to

118

rebuild burnt family bridges. Karl was very keen to see Charlie too. While Charlie was near the local mountains, he wanted to tackle a few crags. Uncle Charlie wasn't as fit as he used to be. In fact, like poor old Bob, he was a little paunchy but still keen to climb. Karl suggested a solo route and provided Charlie with all the gear. Karl knew exactly what he had to do. In his mind, he'd rehearsed it so many times.

Karl and Charlie walked across the fells to 'Baby Beelzebub', chatting as they went. Small talk mostly, the kind Karl hated. It amazed Karl how nonchalantly his Uncle, when confronted, had dismissed the evils of his past.

Karl, when younger, had faced him down before, getting close, breaths mingling. Charlie waved it away as, "A bit of horseplay. An uncle and his nephew mucking about. Fun. Nothing more than that. Maybe you even learnt something." A relaxed Charlie genuinely believed that his actions could be dismissed as easily as that. Karl thought differently, and would hold Charlie's gaze, daring his uncle to look away. Karl would simply stand and stare, hoping deep in his dark soul that someday he would get his revenge.

Charlie knew what he was doing and didn't need much help to set up his sling over the rock spike. Karl watched his uncle drop the long rope down the cliff face that led away from the summit of what was more of a hill than a mountain. They walked round the cut-out path down to the base of the climb. The sun was out, and the conditions were good. "How long will you be, Charlie?" asked Karl.

"Give me three hours, and then I'll buy you a pint." Karl put his top lip under his top row of teeth and squeezed hard, causing a jag of pain, "No problem Charlie. I'm going to hike a few peaks. I'll be back in plenty of time." Karl watched and waited until Charlie had set up his gear, including harness, rock shoes, carabiners, helmet, and the essentials. With his top rope on the spike, Charlie was good to go, and so was Karl. Instead of conquering summits, he arced back to the top of the cliff face, well concealed from Charlie behind the rock. Then Karl, each time the weight on the rope slackened for a second, edged the rope up the spike with a small chisel. The moment when the loop of rope cleared the top of the rock, Karl felt an orgasmic explosion inside, maybe like the ones Uncle Charlie enjoyed when he had ejaculated over his nephew. There was a scream that no one but Karl could hear and then a thud. Bart McGoldrick had been Karl's unwitting instructor.

That evening Charlie's body was found at the base of the 'Satan's Chamber' route. The apparent accident had happened close to the stained granite slab made famous by Bill Carltondale's story of the priest and the missing children, 'Martyred for the Devil.' Appropriate indeed. Karl had enjoyed his very own family fun time.

CHAPTER EIGHTEEN

Debbie Pilkington was given the job of writing up the report of the horrific rock climbing accident. It was her first front-page lead. At last, she had been given some real responsibility by Jim Thorpecroft, the Editor of the Rimpton Chronicle.

The headline read, 'TRAGIC DEATH IN LAKE DISTRICT BLACK SPOT', beneath it was printed, "Climber plummets to death in horror accident" and then, 'Debbie Pilkington reports.'

"Yesterday morning, Lake District Mountain Rescue discovered the body of Charlie Jackson at the base of what the locals call 'Baby Beelzebub'. The deceased had fallen while solo rock climbing a 'Satan's Chamber' route and suffered fatal injuries. A police investigation revealed that Jackson had placed a sling as a top rope over a rocky outcrop at the top of the cliffs. The sling had apparently slipped up and over the granite spike, propelling Charlie Jackson down the precipitous slabs to his death. This incident was a carbon copy of one that had occurred in exactly the same place several years previously to a man called Bob Crabtree. An intriguing coincidence."

A patchwork of colour photos was wrapped around Debbie's lead. A scenic view of the Lake District peaks, a close-up of the spike on the summit of 'Baby Beelzebub' and the rope that had fallen with Charlie Jackson attached. It lay in a loose coil on a patch of dark grass. Without the body, the blood stain looked like an oil leak.

But something didn't sit right with Debbie. Like the talented newspaper reporter she was, Debbie had based her article on the information she had to hand. The facts might have said one thing, but her journalistic instincts were telling Debbie something else.

CHAPTER NINETEEN

Another family death and another family funeral so soon after the first. Harry, and now his brother Charlie. What were the chances? It gave Karl an opportunity to talk to his twin, Nathan. They hadn't conversed too much at their father's funeral, as there were too many family duties to attend to. The boys hadn't had a proper get-together for a very long time, mainly because their relationship had fallen apart. To put it mildly, this had not been a mutually amicable split, and there was a palpable tension between them. A chat over tea and buns at Charlie's funeral had been their first attempt at a decent conversation in many years. "Nathan," Karl said, "We can't let this opportunity go to waste. We are brothers, Nathan, twin brothers. I know our relationship has been difficult, but I've matured."

Nathan was a little perturbed. He'd experienced enough of Karl's malicious nature for this behaviour to make him itch. Being pushed out of a tree by Karl and suffering permanent damage to his leg wasn't easy to forget. But Karl, not for the first time in his life, was very convincing. "There's so much we can do together. We've drifted apart Nathan, but it's not too late."

But Nathan really didn't expect the phone call when it came. Karl's name flashed up on Nathan's mobile, "Fuck, what does he want?" Nathan let the phone buzz, and his body tightened, but he eventually pressed the green button. Nathan didn't get a chance to say hello. "Nathan, Nathan, is that you?" "Well, it is my mobile Karl" the frost flashed between the phones. "What do you want, Karl?" "Nathan, look, the funeral, both funerals, you know, tough days, a tough time for all of us." Nathan had rarely been fooled by his hard-hearted twin, "Nathan, look, Harry was Harry, and we were all glad to see him sizzle. Charlie was no angel either." Nathan's lower jaw jutted. He hated Karl's pantomime language, "But I should have made a date with you there and then, you know, a get-together. Now Harry has gone, and Mum has a chance to properly reboot, and Charlie won't be causing any more problems, so maybe it's time we made a proper effort to get back on track."

For Nathan, the old days were one long saga of brutality from his father with an added soupçon of bullying from his brother. Nathan had taken slashes from a double-edged sword wielded by the other two men in the household.

"Karl, to be honest, I'm quite happy with where we're at. What's the point of a catch-up? So we can put on pretend smiles and make out as if we actually like each other. The past stings Karl, it always will, and I've moved on and want to keep on going in a forward direction." Karl, for a change, hadn't interrupted, "I get all that Nathan, but I want a chance. Will you give me that? I think it's different now, or rather, I think it can be different now. You know, with Harry gone and now Charlie gone. What about a fresh start?" Karl grimaced as he delivered that final phrase. What a cliché.

Karl was going to suggest a coffee, lunch, and a walk. Something, anything, but he changed tack. A match flamed in his mind, "Okay Nathan, there's something I want to tell you about. It's been hanging on me. It's about Dad. There's something you need to know about him.

Something that happened at the very end."

Now Nathan was interested, "What was it Karl? What was it?"

Karl sighed hard, "It's not the sort of thing I can talk about on the phone, and it's a complicated story. It needs to be just you and me."

Karl was talking and thinking. Of course, he relished the fact that no one knew how Harry had actually departed, and it fired the vigorous fantasy side of his brain. Karl thought he should have climbed into the pulpit, and told them the whole story about the coat hanger and the cyanide – instead of his original plan to quote Shakespeare.

Nathan persisted, "Tell me Karl, just tell me."

Karl was cool, "Look Nathan I'll tell you about the whole thing face to face. Let's meet on the old pontoon. I'll bring a flask. Nice and early, watch the sun come up. Like we did as kids. We can talk in detail then." Reluctantly Nathan agreed; not for the first time in his life he'd succumbed to Karl's recognized sales technique.

As kids, the boys had spent many days enjoying the sanctuary of the lake. They would get up before sunrise, that way they could avoid dad and his raging hangover. Karl, of course, knew his next play.

CHAPTER TWENTY

A few days after his head-to-head with Nathan, Karl phoned Peter Ferris. Ferris had been assigned years previously to a teenage Nathan by social services when he'd got into a bit of trouble. "Hello Mr. Ferris. It's Karl Jackson here. You might not remember me. I'm the brother of Nathan Jackson. You were incredibly helpful to Nathan when he was a kid. A troubled teenager. I think he'll always be grateful to you."

The snake in Karl was hissing. "Oh yes", said Ferris, "You're his brother aren't you? I remember. Identical twin. I hope I did my best with Nathan. You had a seriously abusive father, if I remember correctly. What's the problem?"

Karl controlled his breathing. He was good at that. "Look, I really want to talk to you about Nathan. He's done something bad, very bad. No one knows about it but me. I'd really like to talk to you privately and in person. Somewhere quiet, you see, it's horrendous stuff, and I can't risk Nathan finding out that I've told anyone. It needs to be confidential."

Peter's instinct and training was to suggest to Karl that he go to the police. "Mr Jackson, the Nathan Jackson misdemeanour case I handled is long closed. There are professional principles in my department." But Peter Ferris had a significant ego, and Karl knew that.

Ferris's demeanour when visiting Jackson's house gave that aspect of his personality away. He was arrogant and bombastic, and Karl's reckoning was that Ferris wouldn't be able to resist the offer of some big-time, career-advancing discovery. A possible breakthrough moment for an egotistical man, and Ferris thought he deserved a promotion. "Mr Jackson, regarding Nathan, why have you come to me in particular?"

Karl pounced, "Because I know he trusted you, and if he trusted you, then I know I can trust you. No one knows better than you how Nathan ticks, and you seemed to understand his mental processes. I honestly think you are the only person in the world who can point me… point us in the right direction and tell me what to do next. If you can help, I'll make sure that the powers that be know all about it."

CHAPTER TWENTY-ONE

The young Nathan's path towards social services had been a much travelled one and stereotypical in many ways. Behaviours as a teenager, like smoking weed, eventually led him into Peter Ferris's care. Maybe it was the troubled upbringing that drove Nathan to chase relief. At the age of twelve, he was doing small drug deals, but nothing major, a few grams of Cannabis. He took some himself, sometimes skunk. This was minor criminal activity, and Nathan, personality-wise, didn't have the bitumen blackness of his brother. Nathan just wasn't built like that, lacking the versatility of thinking required to operate at Karl's psychopathic level. However, this small-time stuff was leading Nathan down a rocky path. Nathan had been out on his bicycle the first time he was caught, and felt his face greying when he saw a flash of blue in the oversized mirror on his handlebars. The siren burst out one whoop-whoop blast and Nathan braked with a screech, his clammy palms gripping hard. He didn't look around but heard the policeman close the squad car door. Would he walk straight past him to deal with something much more heinous than a boy carrying a negligible amount of cannabis resin in his bicycle saddlebag?

"Young Jackson?" Nathan recognized the voice. It was Constable Palmer, the officer who had called to talk to him and his mum when Nathan had been caught smoking a joint behind the Crabtree pub. Then it had been a ticking off and a warning, but nothing more. Palmer stood looking at the profile of Nathan's face who still hadn't turned to face his fate. For a moment, Nathan thought his neck had locked. "What are you up to, Nathan? Training for the Tour De France?" Palmer, a man with a rich Cumbrian accent, was known for his sarcasm, "It's just that I have never seen a professional cyclist with a saddle bag."

Nathan's skin prickled, and blood rushed from nowhere to everywhere else. He appeared to have lost the power of speech on top of suffering from a psychosomatic spinal seizure. Nathan felt as if he needed some oil on his vertebrae. Fear had frozen him, but somehow, he managed to get a noise out of a mouth that felt as if it was made of parchment and sawdust. Looking straight ahead, Nathan said, "Oh, hi Officer Palmer. Yep, just cycling home." Still sitting on his bike, Nathan somehow managed to turn to Palmer to hear the policeman's reply.

"Isn't your house in the other direction?" Nathan let out a noise, which sounded like an owl hooting. He had hoped for words, but none came. "Nathan, do you mind if I take a peek inside your saddle bag? We wouldn't want to catch a professional cyclist like you carrying some illegal stimulant. You know, like EPO, something to get you up Rattlefork Hill."

Palmer had been tipped off. An anonymous call to the front desk. Nathan thought he might urinate when Palmer unzipped the saddle bag and pulled out a bag of solid resin. "Looks like your Pro cycling days are over, buddy." Nathan spent some time in a Young Offenders Centre, and during this spell he met his Probation Officer. His name was Peter Ferris, and he was supposed to provide support and practical advice making sure that Nathan attended appointments and his specialised group programmes. In other words, monitoring Nathan and keeping him on a straight path. Nathan didn't see it that way, and he felt eternally harassed. To Nathan, Ferris was an arrogant bully.

Karl observed his brother's distress with his usual detachment, and, not surprisingly, he found it entertaining. Nathan, compared to Karl, was relatively docile, but he could, occasionally, be explosive. The Jackson temper was in there somewhere. Ferris called to the house at appointed times when he would chat to Nathan, check his movements, and update his notes. Ferris's hand shook as he wrote, the early onset arthritis had gnarled his joints into a claw.

But, after some early setbacks, Ferris felt he had made significant progress with Nathan. "Well, that should be my final visit," said Ferris as he stabbed a full stop onto the page and then stared at Nathan. He closed the manila file with a slap, "Unless you cause any more issues Nathan, I won't be seeing you again. You've done nothing wrong during your probation period. You've ticked the boxes, but there is one major red flag for me. Your tone has been arrogant and your attitude dismissive. It'll be in the headline paragraph of my report."

The Harry genes in Nathan stirred, the trigger had been pressed. "Arrogant? If anyone has been arrogant, it's you. You called me a juvenile delinquent at our first meeting. Every time you come here you talk to me like a child. Chastising and patronising. Now a fucking red flag? Arrogant tone? Is that your level? Verbally bullying children?" Nathan's voice was beginning to rumble. "Where do you want to be Peter? Working with the heroin traffickers? Or maybe you're not good enough for the big stuff. Harassing kids, is that it? Is that all you're cut out for? Where do I go to complain about YOU?"

By now, Nathan had opened up and was well past the point of caring. "I've a few choice words for a headline paragraph of my own. Does the kid not get his say, so I can tell the social services what a dick you are?"

Ferris appeared stuck to his seat, his pen frozen in his swollen grasp. "I'm afraid I'll have to include that outburst in my report," Nathan glowered, resembling a sprinter on the blocks, about to spring for the man's throat. Ferris intercepted the potential of an attack by jumping to his feet and heading for the door. "Somebody from my department will be in touch", he said, half of the sentence delivered from inside the house and half of it from the driveway. Nathan never forgot his exchanges with Ferris and would sometimes mutter, mostly to his mother, and in detail, exactly what he was going to do to this irritant. But there wasn't a man, boy, girl or child who thought for one moment that Nathan would go after him. He wasn't capable of killing Peter Ferris, was he?

CHAPTER TWENTY-TWO

Karl had a murderous plan, but he needed Nathan and Peter Ferris to play lead roles. This was why he had contacted his brother and Nathan's former social worker, and now Karl had Ferris where he wanted him. Karl needed to set up a meeting with Ferris at the right place at the right time. Now Karl had Peter Ferris on the phone, and it was time to make his play. Karl took a languid nasal breath, "Peter, I've seen you walking at the lake early mornings often. I never bothered you; after all I'd only met you briefly once or twice at my house. But, if you'd agree to meet me, I think that would be the perfect spot. Early would suit me if it suits you. There's never anyone there. We'd have that peace and quiet that we need."

Karl hoped he would benefit from researching the morning habits of Ferris. His black heart missed a beat as Ferris replied, "We could meet at the pontoon. I go there to watch the sunrise. It's the best vantage point. There's a gap in the trees, which gives you a direct eye-line to the horizon. 0530 tomorrow?" Karl replied, "0530. That's perfect."

The following morning Ferris stood at the end of the small pontoon. The sun, which had peaked its brow above the yellow grass of the distant fields was already forming a heat haze across the lake, forming silver shadows. A haphazard smattering of trees circled the lake, their branches waving with a hypnotic synergy as if absorbed in some mysterious dance.

Karl, in no rush, walked towards Ferris, taking the long route round the boat house. Ferris, relaxed and vulnerable, turned and held out his hand. Karl took it, but instead of shaking it, he used it as a pivot. Karl pulled hard and fast, and Ferris spun round on his heels.

Karl pressed the chloroform-soaked cloth over Ferris's mouth. To minimise what he knew would be a brief struggle, Karl pulled his free arm across the man's chest. Ferris blew a muffled cry through the drenched rag. Resistance drained quickly and Karl was in complete control. He positioned the unconscious victim face up on the pontoon and then slid out a stiletto knife he'd concealed in his sleeve. Half light from the early sun bounced off the blade and the rippling water. Karl slid the stiletto between Peter Ferris's ribs. There was a barely audible murmur and in a heartbeat it was over.

Earlier that morning, Karl had rowed across the lake, a lake he knew so well. This was where he had enjoyed so much fun blowing up those hopping amphibians. It wasn't far from the Satterscale village between the towns of Rimpton and Hollway and the site of Jackson's old house. Karl had placed two heavy dumb bells on the struts below the waterline underneath the pontoon. Now, after the kill, Karl used cable ties to attach the dumb bells to the floppy corpse of Ferris. Karl rolled him over the side of the pontoon. He sank fast, the weight helping Ferris on his final journey, and he would soon be buried in the lake's deep soft silt.

Ferris disappeared below the water as a few geese lifted from the water, disturbed by the gentle splash. It was such a peaceful disposal.

With Ferris dead, Karl pulled the rowing boat from the weeds nearby. He coasted for about a hundred metres along the bank, then he got out and doubled back to the pontoon. He took a very particular pre-planned route, as he had on his way to the murder site. But this time, the route was different. Karl cut out the small marina to make sure that, this time, he avoided the CCTV camera at the boat house.

The timing had to be absolutely spot on, and it was. So far, Karl had been an efficient but also a lucky killer. He saw Nathan strolling down a path from the other end of the lake, dressed neutrally as usual, his joggers and sweatshirt the colour of the ravens that sat on the high branches nearby. Nathan still dragged his left leg, with the foot pronated, it was as if the limb was full of pins and needles. This was the remnant from the damage caused when Karl pushed him out of the tree, very close to this spot, all those years ago. It was also where Karl had mercilessly teased Nathan, mimicking his brother's limp while crying, "Quasimodo, Quasimodo, the bells, the bells," and then laughing with inappropriate glee.

Nathan had arranged to meet Karl on the pontoon at six. Nathan was always on time. Karl had banked on that. The psychopath was calm as if the murder of Ferris had been nothing more than the casual dumping of a garbage bag. There was a fumbling embrace, lightweight, without meaning. "Hey bro," said Karl. "Hi Karl," said Nathan. Nathan was nervous. His face flecked in the confusion of the early half-light. He forced out the words, "Good to see you." Karl moved to embrace Nathan again, but Nathan pulled back. For a few moments, neither spoke. A ray of light stabbed through the branches, the beginnings of morning birdsong were floating in the stillness. "Come on Karl, what is it with Dad? What's the story?" Karl stared at his running shoe laces while the first warmings of the day pressed on his neck. "Nathan, Dad didn't die of a heart attack." Nathan stiffened and clenched his fists. "Nathan, I think Dad was murdered. But I'm not completely sure. I have some loose ends to tie up, but I wanted you to know."

Nathan pulled at the shirt, now sticking to his matted chest, "Murdered?" Karl nodded his head, "Murdered, Nathan. I grant you, no great loss to the Universe, but I'm very close to finding out the why and the who. That's what I mean about the loose ends. I need to chase a few things, but it's between us in the meantime, okay?" Nathan was still hushed but whispered with urgency now. "If it's a suspected murder, then we must go to the police. Do you have enough evidence? I mean, his death was officially recorded as natural causes, wasn't it?"

"Yes it was Nathan, but here's the problem." Karl left as long a gap as he dared, "I think Mum might have killed him." Nathan's face was one of pure horror. With an automatic motion, the twins moved close and held each other again, much firmer now. So far, Karl's plan had worked to perfection. Here they were, 'Just like the old days,' standing on the pontoon beside the lake. Below them lay the freshly submerged body of Peter Ferris, weighted down by Nathan's dumb bells. Karl, despite having just murdered a man, was floating on his own magic carpet of persuasive charm. Nathan, of course, had witnessed this type of behaviour many times before and was on guard, but the circumstances were different this time. "Karl, Mum killed Dad? Is this one of your lies? Jesus Christ Karl, you cannot run around accusing anyone of murder unless you are absolutely certain, and, my God, you're talking about our mother here." Karl did his perplexed look. "Nathan I swear to the Almighty, I'm right on the cusp of getting the proof. I need a little more time. I'll call you when I have the evidence, and we'll do what we always did when it was worse than hell at home. Go to the mountains, and that'll give me the time and space to tell you the whole story. If I'm right, and I'm sure I am, we will need each other more than ever." Nathan, feeling tension in his jaw, looked hard at his twin. "Okay Karl, but you better not be fucking me about here."

Naturally, people soon came looking for Peter Ferris, the social worker who had gone for his morning stroll to the lake and never come home. The last person Ferris had spoken to was his wife Gillian and the last words he had said were uttered in bed the night before his disappearance, "I'll sneak out early, try not to wake you. Just a lap of the lake, usual routine. I'll be back for breakfast." Police divers searched the water but uncovered nothing. Of course, at this early stage, no one knew for certain if Ferris was dead or alive.

CHAPTER TWENTY-THREE

The reasons for many of the malfunctions in the twins' behaviours could be traced back to their brutal childhood. Karl had murdered Harry Jackson for a good reason. He had been a savage gargoyle of a man and beat both boys, but seemed to save the more vicious beatings for Karl. The blows would spin in with the persistence of a windmill's blades. Harry's arms swung with barely contained madness. Karl's resistance made it worse, and Harry would use his feet like pumping rods as his son writhed on the floor. Karl threw himself between chubby fists and his mother's blood-orange bruises, absorbing the fury that came with the drunken lunges. Karl took most of the 'friendly fire', leaving his own body throbbing. Nathan would observe limp and subservient, arms wrapped around his chest, tears reaching his quivering lips. Karl seethed at Nathan's passive stance. He thought of his brother as a wimp.

They were both intelligent kids, but while Karl would have crushed the brain of an injured bird, Nathan would have nursed it. Like a thundercloud Nathan could burst but his emotional spectrum didn't include the lightning flashes that exposed the extremity of Karl's rage.

Nathan was naturally more engaging. You could see it in the people they met. Their faces opened and instinctively they gravitated towards Nathan as a freezing man might to an open fire. Karl generated about as much heat as the outer edges of the solar system, but then Karl was more of an invention than a man, practical and relentlessly paranoid. Compared to his twin brother, Nathan was enthusiastically free-spirited.

Karl had survived abuse from Harry and Charlie. Karl didn't know if Uncle Charlie, operating in his own perverted shadow land, had groomed Nathan too. He'd never asked, but he hoped Charlie had done to Nathan what he had done to him.

It may have been Karl's paranoia, but he was sure Nathan received preferential treatment from Harry. One evening he arrived home with the predictable stench hanging from his dirty clothes, which were embedded with that Marlboro smell. Harry's whiskey breath enhanced the disgusting aroma. Earlier, Nathan, while attempting to complete Harry's unending list of chores, had managed to sever the electric cable on the lawn mower. The boys knew this would probably trigger an explosion. Harry led a terrifying inquiry, slurring and frothing through an intoxicated haze. Dad was determined to identify the guilty party. Usually, in situations like this, the brothers held firm and shared the blame and a beating.

But this time, Nathan snitched and blamed his sibling. Harry charged bull-like at the accused with a vigorous fury. Karl ended up in A+E, blood seeping through a tea towel, his knuckles white trying to staunch the flow. The doctor had pulled the sticky cotton mass away to reveal a bright red trench behind his right ear, a trench that was shaped like a tiny canoe. Karl could still remember how the Doc yanked at the stitching to tighten it. Karl never forgave Nathan; inside, his resentment boiled like a bubbling broth.

CHAPTER TWENTY-FOUR

Nathan persistently phoned Karl in the days following their meeting at the pontoon, and the conversation became repetitive. "Any proof yet Karl?" "Not yet Nathan, but I'm getting closer. Any day now." Just when Nathan was losing patience and about to blow his brother out, Karl called. "I've got it, the missing piece of evidence. Oh fuck Nathan, this is so sad. We both love Mum, just look at what she's been through. Can we really blame her for killing Dad? There were many days when we thought about it. Didn't we?" Nathan's stomach churned as he listened, he could feel acid building in the back of his throat. Naturally, he wanted the full story there and then, but Karl told him that the intricacies of the affair and its background were extremely complicated. "Nathan, trust me bro, I'll go through every single detail with you when we meet. Mum was bloody clever, and then, when we BOTH have the information, we'll have to decide what to do with it. That's another massive call. Commit a crime by withholding evidence or condemn our own Mum, potentially, to life in prison?" Nathan swallowed hard and feared the acid might burn its way through his Adam's apple. He felt as if shivers were oscillating through every molecule of his body. Nathan felt the bile building, dropped the phone, spun on his heels, ran fast and reached the bathroom just in time. The vomit came in choked waves. He stared at the yellow mess floating in the bowl, as he tried to consume the contents of the conversation he'd had with his brother.

Two days later, Karl and Nathan met just before first light in the car park near Swinside, beside Derwentwater. Karl had planned an excursion to take them well away from the madding summer crowds that buzzed around the Lake District's honeypot routes. Nathan, twitching with tension, stepped into discomfort from the iced air-conditioned confines of his SUV. There were the details of a cold-blooded murder to discuss, but the conditions the twins were about to face were anything but cool. A tropical high had locked over the whole of England, setting temperatures that were breaking all sorts of records. Even at this time of the morning, perspiration came fast.

Nathan was pulling a tarpaulin and poles from his SUV, pots and pans clattering amongst the chaos. Karl was truffling around too, looking for his extra large backpack bladder, with his head half buried in a haystack of mountain gear. It was half an hour before Karl eventually threw the rucksack over his muscular back. Nathan spoke as they made their first steps towards the mountains and the long slow climb to Catbells. "And what about Dad then? That's why we're here right? What happened? I need to know."

Karl was trying to find the tip of the bladder tube, which had slipped out of its webbing, "Not here, Nathan. Are you serious? Look at the car park. There's already another car here. I can see the lights of more. There's a huge amount of stuff to go through. I want to do it when we settle at our campsite, not while we're hiking and busting our balls. The campsite will give us all the time we need. Peace, quiet, food, drink and a story you won't believe."

Nathan reluctantly agreed. They carried tents as a fail-safe. Karl had shown his brother a remote mountain hut for their overnight on his Harvey's Map. They set off on a wide path which soon became a ribbon. Their rucksacks were caked to their backs, salt-stained, and in the heatwave the usual water sources were mere trickles, the high watermarks standing out on the exposed river banks. The trails crunched beneath their boiling, blistering feet. They had three litres of water each but with five hours of hiking behind them there was just a drizzle of liquid left in their bladders. Karl knew that the next point of hydration would be the shack he'd shown Nathan on the map. "There's an old well outside it, bro. We've got our iodine tablets, and there's bound to be water in it. I've heard there's an old blue plastic barrel outside it as well. The water might be a bit manky, but another extra iodine tablet should make it drinkable."

Karl had done his usual forensic research for this particular trip. He was the better navigator of the two and definitely had much more mountain craft than Nathan. Karl's intense recce, which had taken place weeks before, had proved to be fruitful. The shack was nothing more than a small black dot on his mountain map and hard for lesser navigators to find. To scale, the collapsing shack was hard to see, squeezed as it was between two contour lines. A black dot beside a scree field about three miles from the nearest road. The building, if you could call it that, had merged into the surrounding mixture of scrub land and tangled briers. The brown corrugated iron roof was more like a colander. Wrist-thick vines curled through the holes. There was a single Trip Advisor report that mentioned the shack. A camper had posted it. "The view from the floor is an interesting combination of rust and stars. The place looks like it hasn't seen a human being for decades." But all the twins wanted was shelter, and Karl needed the shack to be as desolate as possible.

As kids, the two boys had often camped in the open air bringing nothing more than low tog sleeping bags, a few sandwiches and a flask. For Nathan, this day out had rekindled memories of those mellow summer days. Mind you, they had never been in the blood brother category. Nathan craved acceptance from the rather distant Karl, but he never got it. From a very young age Karl had felt a casual resentment for Nathan. Probably because, in his judgement, Nathan was his father's favourite, although the definition of favourite was relative in the Jackson household, and Nathan was no saint.

Karl's recce of the mountain shack had been thorough. He had left a few things he knew he'd need behind a pile of firewood, where the flaking bark was wrapped in cobwebs. The stack looked like something from the set of 'Arachnophobia' and stood in the corner of one of two small dusty rooms. All moisture had evaporated during the heatwave, expanding cracks in the pine walls. The roof appeared to have been struck by a cluster bomb. Karl wasn't quite sure how it hadn't collapsed completely, as there seemed to be more holes than metal. There was a square wooden table in the middle of the larger room, the legs of which stood on a floor covered with a combination of dried and rotting foliage - another spiders' theme park. Beside it were two chairs, which Karl tested for robustness. He had all he needed.

The two men were exhausted by the time they reached the shack. They had walked in a rare lakeland furnace for six hours, dodging and weaving, finding shaded sanctuary when they could. They chewed on the teats of their rucksack bladders, sucking moisture now, their spines cramped under the weight of the overnight essentials. As the vegetation in their way increased, the paths decreased in width, and for the last two hours Karl and Nathan lumbered on in single file.

Eventually, they felt the furnace door of the blazing day closing, replaced by the ecstasy of a cooling evening mist. Nathan had tried to cross-examine his brother many times, especially early in the walk, before his body decided that breathing was all it could do.

"Come on Karl, tell me about Dad. There's no-one for miles." Karl's reply was repetitive, like an echo. "Nathan. It's all in my notebook. The evidence laid out stage by stage. I'll read it to you in full at the shack."

Nathan felt the loom of darkness, and now every twig was a tripwire. Just as Nathan said, for the twelfth time, "Are you sure you know where this fucking place is?" They rounded a track bend and caught a gloomy silhouette. The lowering fog gave the impression that they were walking into a mirage.

At last, the shack. Fortunately, there was enough water in the barrel to quench their thirsts, but it was brown, stewing in god knows what. Their tongues lolled out as they watched the iodine tablets dissolve. Nathan emptied an entire blister pack into the dark brew. Despite the brackish colour, the first mighty quaff of liquid had tasted like maple syrup. Their clothes, previously drenched in steaming sweat, had cooled as the chilling mist rolled in. Nathan felt the first tickles of a shiver.

Karl pulled wood from the top of the stack, built a little pyramid, and then skilfully lit the fire with one match. The smoke had multiple choices and filtered out through various escape routes. Nathan set up a stove, the gas-fired flames flickered around the old stained pot. They had hot water for tea, and to hydrate, their freeze-dried 'Macaroni and Beef Ragout' followed by 'Apple Pie and Vanilla Custard'. They ate these delights straight from their foil bags. 'Pour in and stir, then wait eight minutes', it said on the packs. Thirst and hunger engulfed them and they wolfed down most of what they had carried. This was exactly what they'd done as kids. Nathan was fed, watered and relaxed. "It's got to be the time now, Karl?"

"Yes Nathan it is; let me get the notebook. It's at the bottom of my rucksack." As Karl rummaged, Nathan reflected that Karl had answered only one of his intermittent questions on their trek across the mountains. "Why did you go and see Harry in the hospital? You hated him. We both did."

"Not sure really," said Karl, "I suppose I wanted to enjoy his illness. I mean, I wasn't there with a bunch of grapes and a get well soon card." Nathan's belly burned. He had always recoiled at Karl's crass darkness. No subject was safe from the tentacles of Karl's death cult humour. After the hard day in the hills Nathan's back muscles were cramping. He lay back to ease the lumbar pain, stretching his arms behind his head. Nathan looked at the hole-filled, rusted roof and then closed his eyes waiting for Karl to start reading from the notebook that would expose his own mother as a killer. Karl pulled a hypodermic syringe from a dry yellow bag; and then moved with a neat swiftness. He slid over to his brother and injected him in the neck with a sedative. A dose of liquid valium with some added etorphine.

Nathan recoiled wide-eyed and let out a strangled yelp, "What the fuck Karl?" But within seconds, his desperate cries were slurred as he fought blackout. While the drug took effect, Karl reached behind the firewood. There he had left thin strips of towel and blacked-out goggles. The rims inside the goggles had been lined with soft sponge. Karl didn't want to leave any bruises or signs of restraint. It was a bit of a struggle lifting Nathan's unconscious dead weight. With some effort, he hoisted Nathan onto a chair and bound him to it with the towelling strips. Karl fixed the goggles in place and used another piece of towel as a gag.

Nathan slept on, and, for a while, Karl wondered if he'd overdone the drugs. Etorphine had famously been used by the serial killer

Dexter in the long-running American TV series. Karl admired the methods of killers, both real and fictional. Eventually, Nathan surfaced from his stupor, and Karl listened to the mumbled alarm. The chair almost toppled as Nathan writhed, blind and confused. Karl held him, gripping Nathan's shoulders, and watched his brother's saliva seep into the cloth. Karl moved close, his breath warming Nathan's ear. "Bro. My Harry mystery? The murder? Well, guess who did it?"

Nathan, of course, despite the fog that was scrambling his brain, knew the answer now and wriggled with manic desperation. Karl strengthened his hold. "Nathan. A psychiatrist used to talk to me about my worrying compulsions, and I agree, I don't think they are very healthy. I killed Harry, but do you want to know something? He wasn't the first. Remember the accident with the kid at the lake? That was my warm-up routine. And that snake bite that killed the lad in Australia. I set that up. Magnificent plan, like this one."

Sweat flew in spirals from Nathan's brow as he tried to free himself. "And Peter Ferris? About fifteen minutes before I met you, I put a knife through his heart. I weighted him down with your dumb bells. Guess who'll get the blame for that Nathan? And I'll be off. Again. Happy and free." This felt like therapy to Karl and a form of confessional, too, a very safe confessional. Karl watched his brother writhe, a jellied mass.

"Look Nathan", said Karl, "I'm not an animal. This is simply something I have to do, and I'm going to give you a choice. Well... not yet. I'll explain later, but I don't want you to suffer more than is necessary. After all, you are my brother." Karl reminded Nathan of the day he had snitched. Talked him through the lawnmower incident, showing him the long canoe-shaped scar on his head. "I've still got the red weals to show for it. Do you remember that? When the buckle from Dad's belt sliced into my scalp? You've brought this on yourself Nathan. Deep down, I hope you will appreciate that you are responsible."

Karl was excited at the thought of what was coming next. Inside the notebook he'd removed from his rucksack were Karl's preparatory notes for this very situation, and he read them in silence as Nathan struggled beside him.

"I can't wait to see if this technique will work. I binge-watched that drama series 'Wormwood'. Bloody hell, it was good. It was based on the brainwashing techniques developed for the CIA by a Scottish Psychiatrist called Donald Ewen Cameron. He was a former President of the World Psychiatric Association. Imagine giving a man like him a job like that? Cameron's methods had been used for what he called 'enhanced interrogation' of inmates at Guantanamo Bay. Methods they said could break the most determined terrorist. The project was known as MK Ultra. I also watched about five times, a documentary on Cameron's work called 'Eminent Monsters'. I absolutely loved it. Prisoners would be put for hours into coffin-like boxes. They endured agonising cramps. Their heads would be clamped and a gun pressed against the temple. The chamber was empty when the trigger was pulled, but the recipient didn't know that. Russian Roulette. The idea was to undermine the basic instincts of survival. As the CIA would say, "If the detainee dies, you're doing it wrong. Prisoners don't talk if they are dead." What a quote. I might get the last bit of that tattooed somewhere."

There was great enthusiasm in Karl's writing. *"Part of the Cameron technique was to place a subject in solitary confinement and then deny them any form of sensory stimulus. Keep them in pitch black and deprive them of sleep. Pump in loud white noise. The decline into madness is often 'rapid and deep', as they put it. Cameron discovered that humans could withstand quite a bit of physical torture, but they quickly develop an overwhelming fear of anything vague and persistent. A learned helplessness. Death becomes preferential. It was an Orwellian use of psychology. Jesus. How good is that?"*

Karl had one song on the power banked mini red iPod in the top flap of his rucksack. It was 'Let The Bodies Hit The Floor,' by the band Drowning Pool from the 2001 album 'Sinner'. The track was on repeat and set at full volume. Karl moved close to Nathan's ear. "Enjoy the music. I'll be back before you know it." Karl slipped the padded headphones onto Nathan's head. The blacked out goggles were in place and a repetitive cacophony blasted Nathan's ear drums. Karl quickly packed his rucksack and left the shack to continue his hiking.

When Karl returned to the shack twenty hours later, he jolted. He squinted at a distance through the fractured shards in the window. Nathan had gone, at least that's how it looked at first. Karl crept closer, crouching like a member of a SWAT squad. The chair had toppled over and Karl could only see the bottom of the chair legs, but as he inched round the building, he could see that his twin was still attached to the seat. Karl's first concern was that Nathan might have sustained an injury while falling. The last thing he needed as that might have given officers evidence of foul play. Nathan was lying still, a stream of tiny bubbles dribbling from his mouth.

Karl was a yard away, but he could hear the rumbling of, 'Let The Bodies Hit The Floor' streaming through the headphones. Karl had worked out that Nathan would have by now listened to the song approximately 840 times without sleep. Karl struggled, but he managed to haul the chair upright. Nathan's eyes were open, but his pin-sized pupils told Karl that he was in some sort of a trance. Karl switched off the iPod. Good timing, as the battery was down to the final bar. Karl gently removed the headphones and the goggles as he didn't want to leave any incriminating marks.

Nathan's eyes were pink-rimmed, the pupils dilated. He looked utterly broken as if he had already passed the point of madness. "Nathan. Listen to me. As I said, I'll give you a choice. This horror can all be over in a matter of minutes. You take these tablets. I'll get you some water. Help you swallow them. You'll quietly and peacefully slip away. If you don't, this is the option."

Karl pulled another three iPods from his rucksack, one pink, one black and one blue. Each one had a fully powered battery. "Just your favourite song Nathan. Do you know the words yet? 'Let The Bodies Hit The Floor'. Rock N' Roll? Or the tablets?"

As they said in the CIA, 'Death becomes preferential'. Nathan's parched tongue stretched out towards the tablets, grasping, greedy now, praying for an end to his torture. Karl, with care, tipped water into Nathan's mouth to help him swallow a quick path to death. This time Karl was able to enjoy the added pleasure of watching his brother die. Such a satisfying feeling. Karl bathed in the glory of the moment. The staring dots in Nathan's head began to dull and his eyelids flickered, once, twice. His breathing had been short and rapid at first, but soon it slowed. Nathan's final exhalation came with a soft rush against Karl's face. It had been a long road for a slow kill.

Now Karl moved fast. He removed the goggles, the towelling, headphones, and Ipod. Anything incriminating was thrust into the dry bag. The remnants of the fire were fine. Nathan had carried all the cooking gear; after all, he could have allowed himself a last meal.

Karl left Nathan face up on top of his sleeping bag and slipped a note into his brother's pocket. The note Karl had printed on Nathan's own computer.

"I'm so sorry. This was the best solution. I killed Peter Ferris. I hated the bastard. He deserved it. He's under the pontoon at the lake. I love you Mum."

Karl took as much time as he needed to clear any evidence of his presence. He had used excessive padding to make sure he didn't leave any pressure marks on Nathan's head and was particularly careful to remove any loose fibres. Then Karl hiked back to the trail, walking hard and fast to the car park. It took six hours to get there.

Karl had a plan. He always had a plan. Karl made sure that the battery on his mobile was flat. This was why he couldn't call for help from the hills. It was the brother's third day in the mountains, and Karl knew that a flat battery was to be expected. He charged his phone when he got to his car, he'd make sure there was only one bar on it when help arrived. He then phoned the police and asked to be put through to Keswick Mountain Rescue. Karl, of course, knew most of the team, and it was Robbie, faithful old Robbie, who picked up the phone.

"Hi Robbie. It's Karl Jackson here. Look, it's probably nothing to panic about. I've been out in the mountains. Hiking and wild camping with my brother Nathan. At dusk last night the mist came down. You know what it's like, we couldn't see more than 20 yards. I was in front, and we came to the end of a trail. I went west, certain that Nathan was close behind. I'll admit I probably wasn't concentrating. I was chatting away and then realised that Nathan wasn't talking back, so I turned around and there was no sign of him. He must have taken the east fork."

Robbie was very well used to this kind of call, and experience told him that it wasn't a particularly alarming one. Some of the terrain in the area Karl had detailed was complicated. With the mountains relatively close to the sea, thick fast-forming mist was a regular issue.

Robbie also knew that Karl was an experienced mountain man and wasn't surprised when he read out an eight-figure grid reference for the trail fork.

Karl continued, "Look, Robbie I'm pretty sure he wandered east. I went back up and hunted for a while, but Nathan could have gone quite a distance while I was pacing about and shouting out. I could see nothing, and it was getting dark. I screamed, but you know what it's like, Robbie? How quickly your voice carries away on the wind. I thought the best thing to do was to stay out, set up camp and try again in the morning. I was up at first light but those eastern trails quickly split into a labyrinth of paths, and I couldn't find him. I'm pretty sure Nathan's done what I did and hunkered down."

Robbie hoped this would be a fairly straightforward search and detailed a team of four. But three days later, and with no sign of Nathan, Robbie was forced to deploy a dog team. They were searching about half a mile from the trail fork through the overgrown ground and difficult territory. One of the border collies sniffed a scent close to a ramshackle cabin.

Decomposition and putrefaction had begun. Nathan's face was badly disfigured, tinged green and grotesquely bloated. His eyes and tongue were protruding. Insects and animals had begun their morbid feast. The foul odour of death was overwhelming.

CHAPTER TWENTY-FIVE

The news of the discovery of Nathan's body and the incriminating suicide letter raced its way to the relevant authorities. Tex had spent much of his furlough time trawling through active investigations and had been drawn to one in particular, 'Missing Person - Peter Ferris'. He'd jolted when he read the overnight addition to the case notes. Nathan's suicide and admission of guilt appeared to be the missing link. When Tex first read the report on the disappearance he felt that it had an Agatha Christie feel to it, 'The Mystery at Moonlight Lake.' Tex enjoyed dreaming up titles for this imaginary Queen of Crime blockbuster and wondered how many twists lay within the tapestry of the storyline. The obsessive side of Tex, who was desperately missing the buzz of hands-on involvement, buried into the intricacies of the Ferris conundrum. Now it looked as if the jigsaw was complete. "*This is the bit when Hercule Poirot gathers everyone together in the drawing room and, to gasps of horror, reveals the name of the killer.*"

Tex, even though he wasn't much more than a nosy neighbour when it came to this case, still took great pride in his ability to process and solve a crime. His first concern when this 'smoking gun' arrived was whether he had been as professional as he could have been. He wasn't sure. Tex wasn't long into therapy when the Ferris case was opened, and his brain had been a ball of mush. It's not easy to think straight when you've frogspawn between your ears. Tex worked his way through the evidence as it stood before the discovery of Nathan and his note. Peter Ferris had gone missing somewhere between his home and who knows where. His wife had told the police that her husband said he was going to the lake for a dawn walk. The lake was a mile from his house. The initial investigation covered a wide area, but the detectives failed to uncover anything significant.

The police team on the Ferris case couldn't rule out the possibility that he had faked his own death and was now living in some Peruvian hacienda. A bit like the fraudster John Darwin, who, facing financial ruin, set off in his canoe and never returned. It was all part of an insurance scam and the missing, presumed-dead, Darwin reappeared in Panama years later. Of course, the Ferris case shifted dramatically following the discovery of Nathan's corpse. Potentially there was now a killer, but they still didn't have a body. Yes, there had been a perfunctory sweep of the lake by the diving team, but it was a large stretch of water. Now, the police had a precise search position.

Tex went through the initial case notes for the umpteenth time and spotted a mistake. Easy to pick up in hindsight but there was a basic task that hadn't been completed, a box that hadn't been ticked. Tex could see how it had happened, but it was a poor miss. No one had considered that there might be CCTV at such a remote lakeside location, maybe because, before Nathan's note, there was no clear suspicion of murder. Ferris could have taken a train and committed suicide in an abandoned croft in the Shetlands, or just decided that he'd had enough of the wife and bunked off with a new woman to that Peruvian hacienda. There are many reasons why a man might go missing.

Due to the edict from the Chief Constable, Tex couldn't become directly involved, but he spoke to the investigating officer. It turned out there was CCTV, one rusted camera which hung at a steep angle from the corner of the guttering at the north end of the small boat yard at the lake's marina. Remarkably the camera was working and was running on the morning Ferris went AWOL.

The grainy and smudged black-and-white footage tracked a man walking toward the pontoon. To no one's surprise, even as a ghostly silhouette, it looked like Nathan. He had a distinct identifying limp, a perennial reminder of the tree incident, and this disability was confirmed by his mother when she viewed the footage. Her howl of, "Oh my God, Nathan. No Nathan. A murderer, not my Nathan," was pretty convincing stuff.

This time the police carried out a deep dredge of the area around the pontoon, as specified in Nathan's suicide note. Peter Ferris's bloated, bound and weighted body was found buried deep in the soft silt. The Probation Officer's arms and legs were cable-tied to Nathan's dumb bells. As determined by the pathologist's report, the time of death helped seal the deal. Later the investigators found a poorly cleaned stiletto knife among Nathan's possessions while searching Nathan's bedroom. Just where Karl had placed it. Everything fitted together, as Karl knew it would. He had made sure that the segments slotted neatly.

CHAPTER TWENTY-SIX

The theme from Jaws rang out. Tex cut off his ringtone when he swiped the screen upwards and clamped the mobile to his ear. He shuffled, in his tartan slippers over to his tartan chair. "Hello Tex. It's Debbie."

"Yes I know. Your name came up on my phone, Debbie-Reporter-Slash-Detective." Debbie's eyes screwed, "Does it really say that?"

"No," said Tex, "But I'll add the last bit if you give me something to get my detective juices flowing." Debbie was still adjusting to Tex's sense of humour, "Look, it's not new news, if you know what I mean. It's about that Nathan Jackson suicide and Peter Ferris murder." The story of the deaths had made the national press. Tex shifted against the cushions that supported his twinging back. He winced and then whistled through his teeth, "Kind of done and dusted Debbie."

"I know that", said Debbie, "I'm writing another piece on that right now. Doing a back story on Nathan Jackson and building into it the death of his Uncle Charlie. You know, Tex, the 'cursed family' angle, triggered by the death of the patriarch, Harry. Hardly groundbreaking journalism, but at the Rimpton Chronicle, it's sassy enough to sell a few more copies. The locals love the gossip. I've been going back and checking all my notes. There are a few bits and pieces that I thought might be of interest, and you might be able to go somewhere with them. I can allude to certain suspicions in the article, but that's all I can do. The notes, in full, might be more useful to you." Tex hoped he hadn't put too much faith in a young journalist with zero detective work experience.

"Tex. Nathan Jackson's Uncle Charlie died in the Lake District. Nathan died in the same range of mountains, and Ferris died within screaming distance of the hills. Three deaths that link one family! A story that is definitely worth some journalistic speculation, don't you think? The Charlie Jackson death was my first front-page lead. That was recorded as accidental. Charlie fell off a rock face." Tex rocked his head back and said, "Yeah I know, I'm aware of the case, and I read your article."

"Thanks Tex, I'm glad you're an avid reader of the Rimpton Chronicle. Would you like me to sign you up for a subscription? Anyway, regarding the Charlie Jackson incident, there were rumours. When I was doing my background trawl, I talked to Mountain Rescue and a guy called Robbie Benson. He said it was a carbon copy of an accident in the same place years earlier. In the Charlie Jackson version, Robbie believed someone might have worked some webbing free. Webbing for what rock climbers call a sling. It secures the rope around the rock, and Robbie said he looked at the anchor point. If you had the right implement, you could slide the sling off. Robbie wouldn't let me quote him; they only had suspicions and zero proof. I know this is a bit wild, but Nathan had a motive to kill Ferris. It was a grudge killing, and I wonder did Nathan also have a grudge against his Uncle?"

Tex had his legs crossed at the ankles and was stretched out, waiting for a gotcha moment from Debbie. It sounded to him like Debbie was trying far too hard to be Agatha. "Debbie. The first time this thing happened with the sling, what did Mountain Rescue do then?"

"They reported their suspicions to the police, suspicions based on an instinct gained from decades in the mountains. There was nothing but a 'feeling' that the sling couldn't have moved on its own. But that's not all, Tex. I was searching the Chronicle's old microfilm library and put JACKSON into the search box. There are loads of articles filed that haven't been downloaded to the computer yet, they're still in cardboard boxes. All the copy is logged on the computer though, with a sketch of each story. One popped up, and it pulled me in like a magnet. The headline: "BOY DIES IN HORROR LAKESIDE ACCIDENT". A seven-year-old boy had drowned. The tragedy was on the Rimpton Chronicle front page. A few other boys were playing close to the river, the nearby lake, and the woods. Some of them were interviewed by the police, and the paper used the quotes. Two of the boys were the Jackson brothers, Nathan and Karl."

While Debbie was talking, Tex had flopped off his slippers and right sock and was picking dirt from his toenails. On hearing Debbie's final sentence, he stopped his disgusting habit.

He was a little more interested now, he remembered the death of the boy, and admired Debbie's determination. This was a part of Debbie's character that reminded him of his wife. Susan's relentless pursuit of anything important was one of the things that attracted him to the woman he'd loved, and Susan had fought her illness with the same grit. Tex's body was now stiff and right-angled on the chair.

"Tex," Debbie continued, "Isn't it quite a coincidence that Nathan Jackson, a self-confessed killer, was so close to that little boy's death? The kid had drowned and no one could properly explain how he'd slipped down a dry, gently sloping bank. And isn't it strange that Nathan's uncle died in what Mountain Rescue believed were rather suspicious circumstances? Nathan, it seems, has killed once, could he have killed more than once? I'm not saying he definitely did, but isn't it worth chasing?"

Tex wished he had a cup of industrial-strength black coffee in his hand - His drug of choice when he needed to think. Instead, all Tex had were a few flecks of dirt from his foot, which he rubbed between his fingers. "Debbie, we'd be surfing through heaps of paperwork from ancient solved cases. Extremely time-consuming, it could lead nowhere, and anyway, as you well know, I have no official remit to chase anything." Tex swallowed hard as he finished speaking, knowing that he was being, at the very least, slightly hypocritical.

"Tex, is it worth talking to Nathan's brother Karl? He might have some information buried away that could help you link this all together. You might, and I repeat, might be looking at multiple murders. Does that sound crazy?"

A light had gone on but, despite that, Tex was still dubious. "Debbie there's absolutely no way I'll get this past Barbara. I have a better chance of selling a skeleton to a cannibal. There's no hard evidence, yes some circumstantial links but not enough of a story for the Chief Constable to open up old files. And even if Bracewell did, would she let me chase it?" There were a few seconds of silence, then Debbie chirped back. "Tex, I don't know you very well, but if MY instinct is right, I'll bet you're itching to go after this. I know this would make you a very naughty boy but, you know Tex, go rogue. Nobody will find out. I always sniff around stuff like this and get away with it."

"Yeah, Debbie, I can imagine. Part of your warm-up routine for that Crime Correspondent job at the Washington Post. Debbie, this isn't a remake of 'All The President's Men'.

Debbie laughed. "I see us more as Cagney and Lacey, not Bob Woodward and Carl Bernstein, or maybe Bonnie and Clyde would be better. Yes. Bonnie and Clyde, that's us."

Tex puffed out a laugh, "They get shot in the end, in a hail of gunfire." Debbie chuckled with him, and then waited. "Okay Debbie, ring Valerie Jackson. That's Nathan and Karl's mum. Tell her you're doing a follow up piece on the murder/suicide. She'll either tell you to piss off or she'll talk – a mother's grief can last a lifetime, and sometimes they want to get things off their chest."

Debbie could feel a pleasant light sting in her heart, "If Valerie agrees, I'll tell her I just want some basic information on the atmosphere in the house. What childhood was like to see if I can find out how the various relationships worked. We might get something."

Tex did his teeth whistling thing again, "That's all grand Debbie, but Valerie will want to know why. These cases are like your Chronicle microfilm, all buried away in sealed dusty boxes, and Valerie might want to keep some things buried too. But if she says yes, then go ahead and talk to her, but tread softly, please!"

Tex ended the call and sat back. "Bonnie and Clyde, or maybe Thelma and Louise? Is that a better title for our combo?" He remembered the climax of the movie when the two girls drove, hollering to their doom, over the edge of a cliff. Tex and Debbie were clinging to a precipice, and he certainly didn't want their clandestine activities uncovered. But then, this is what Tex wanted Debbie to do in the first place, and now was no time for second thoughts.

They'd either hit the rocks or land soft. Time would tell. Even as he agreed to buy into Debbie's plan, Tex was thinking ahead. He knew that if they were to push this forward, he'd have to speak to Karl Jackson. Just a general chat, and, as Tex was currently badge-less, it would have to be unofficial. He could tell Karl that he was just wrapping up a loose end in Nathan's case.

With the permission of Tex given, Debbie approached Valerie. To her surprise, Mrs. Jackson invited her round. "Tomorrow?" said Valerie in a weak and wavering voice. "I'll see you then," said Debbie, eyebrows raised in disbelief.

At eleven o'clock the following morning, Debbie knocked on the door of a house that had entered a rather flaky old age. The white paint on the wooden framed windows was cracked and peeling. A rampant ivy had spread like a pandemic and was digging its way into the old cement, between red bricks that were blackening on the edges. It took Valerie three tugs to open the bottle-green front door - the tugs needed to overpower the warping that had helped the Victorian-style panelled structure to cling to the warped floorboards. The whole tenor and atmosphere in the Jackson family's home was one of misery and was matched by Valerie's face. Debbie was drawn to the sagging flesh below Valerie's washed-out grey eyes. Two puffy bags were flanked by thick lines that didn't look as if they'd been put there by laughter. Valerie's thin smile seemed to take a lot of effort, and a weak, spindly grip took Debbie's hand. And then she inhaled a powerful waft which sent Debbie's senses floating back to the bakery she used to visit as a child. It was the smell of freshly baked bread and the intense sugary aroma of pastry that had just been pulled from the oven. It may have horrified Valerie's neighbours but she served only Yorkshire tea here in Lancashire.

"It's the best, dear. Do you like it strong? It's the only way. Doesn't taste like tea otherwise." Despite everything that had happened to her, Valerie's words danced with unexpected energy. They felt unreal coming as they did from the small, hunched body and whipped features of Harry Jackson's ex-wife. Debbie was listening to the voice of a survivor.

"How can I help you Debbie?" Valerie said as she fussed around, placing a plate of warm shortbread and a pot of strong hot tea onto a table that wobbled slightly and then, somehow, stabilised like a drunk regaining balance. Valerie's smile looked forced, hiding a lifetime of painful memories, but she seemed keen to help. Debbie had a long list of inquisitive questions. Valerie talked with an unexpected candidness, releasing family secrets between sips of the thick Yorkshire brew. Debbie felt like an unchained maverick and loved every second of it.

CHAPTER TWENTY-SEVEN

Karl Jackson's unremarkable detached house blended in with most of the others in his leafy but hardly ostentatious neighbourhood. It had a red brick chimney at each end, with three matching sash windows on each floor. An imposing oak door was the centrepiece, framed around an old-fashioned brass knocker which glinted in the morning light. The building was partly hidden behind a row of mature poplar trees which flanked a driveway covered in gravel that looked like popcorn. His custard-coloured classic Volkswagen Beetle was wedged between the house and the hedge. The German factory called this particular shade of yellow 'Saturn'.

Karl was sitting in his maple-panelled office, a bookshelf lining the entirety of the far wall. It was stacked with manuals on the art of teaching chemistry and a number of books that indicated a wider range of interests. There was "Snakes in Suits: How Sociopaths Operate in the Workplace" and "Helter Skelter", the story of cult leader Charles Manson. Both were global best sellers.

Karl was at his computer, his fingers tip-tapping with a smooth rhythm. Soon the pupils would return from the holidays so he added the final touches to his lesson schedule. His wife Patricia was out and had been away for several hours longer than she said she'd be. Karl had made a mental note of that.

His son Kerry was in the house too, nodding to the beat blasting from his Sennheiser Momentum earbuds. He was studying for his psychology module and had big exams coming up. Kerry had buried himself in the attic room that sat against the west chimney. Kerry was unaware of his own odour, which might have made a mortician recoil. He definitely had that stereotypical student aroma, a combination of all sorts of fluids, mainly alcohol and sweat.

Patricia, purely by smell, had calculated that her only child was showering maybe once a week.

Kerry was hard to spot amongst the bundles scattered across the room, a crazy paving of fabric. He had yet to learn the art of folding.

Shirts, hoodies and various types of pants were scattered all around and looked as if they'd been cast from a passing tornado. On the floor, bottles and cans formed an unlikely obstacle course. The walls were covered with a quilt work of posters advertising heavy metal bands and concerts. There was an incongruous print of Paddington Bear above his bed. Kerry surfaced only for his mother's cooking. Once or twice his father had threatened to kill him if he didn't tidy up his room. Kerry assumed that his Dad was kidding.

Cocooned in his room and with the constant thump-thump-thump in his ears, Kerry couldn't hear the other noises in the house. Like the shouts and screams that were inclined to rattle around the building when Karl and Patricia were at home together.

Karl's scanner was permanently in the on position, searching for faults and changes in his wife's behaviour. Paranoia heightened his senses, and he had considered fixing a tracking device to his wife's car. There was nothing that couldn't be blamed on Patricia, who had spent several long stretches back in her old bedroom with her parents in Scotland. Karl and Patricia's relationship simmered, but now and again, Karl would light it up with a volcanic blaze. Unlike Harry, he didn't need alcohol to push him into an eruption.

Karl would get easily distracted from formulating his school timetable, his mind swimming triumphantly at regular intervals to the crystal clear memories of the morning with Ferris. There was the sweet smell of summer flowers that permeated the air at the shores of the lake along with the sensory tingle he had felt when he heard the footsteps of Ferris bouncing lightly on the planks of the old pontoon. Karl recalled the caustic burn that nipped when he had inhaled a wisp of chloroform. He also recalled the muffled squeals of a man struggling to live and that sensation of power when the knife cut through skin, slicing smoothly and easing past a rib, the point seeking out its target. When Karl released the body into the water, he did it with the loving care of a fisherman returning a marlin to the sea. Like all of Karl's kills, the whole episode appeared in 3D in his mind, like a hologram.

Then there were the days in the mountains when Karl had ruminated for hours over the finer details of every stage of his masterful plan. He gloried in his magnificence and often wondered if there was anyone anywhere with a more devious intelligence. There had been the sensual sound of Charlie's body hitting the hard ground below the cliff face. Karl had felt like God himself when he injected the cyanide into Harry's catheter. He thought he could almost taste the delicious fear that poured from Nathan when his brother realised his hopeless position. Karl glanced at a pile of vinyl stacked on the cream carpet and reminded himself to dispose of the record sitting on top, but it didn't stop him from singing the lines from the track that had hastened Nathan's demise.

"Let the bodies hit the floor, Let the bodies hit the floor, Let the bodies hit the floor, Can't take much more. Let the bodies hit the floor, Let the bodies hit the floor, Let the bodies hit the floor.

Skin against skin, blood and bone.

You're all by yourself, but you're not alone. You wanted in, and now you're here. Driven by hate, consumed by fear,

Let the bodies hit the floor, Let the bodies hit the floor, Let the bodies hit the floor."

Karl had a flat, contented expression and a dark smile, "There's only one person who knows those lyrics better than me."

Once Nathan had been buried, Karl quickly settled back into his routine. The life of a chemistry teacher, a rather charming one, who would have caused carnage at a girl's school. Karl knew that the temptation would have overwhelmed him. Teaching in a boy's school was safer, and right now, Karl, in terms of killing, was dormant again. The rumblings of a fresh project were beginning to stir, but Karl needed more evidence before he could proceed. A few things about Patricia's movements, and her explanations of them, were beginning to trouble him.

He needed proof of infidelity, and if he could get it, Karl had decided to make a move.

CHAPTER TWENTY-EIGHT

Karl was in his crimson dressing gown when the phone rang. "Good morning. Is that Karl Jackson?"

"This is him," said Karl.

"This is Detective Chief Inspector Tex Deacon from Rimpton Hollway CID." Karl recognised the voice before Tex had identified himself. It was the host of the 'Sir Robert Peel Lecture'. *"One of the force's big boys,"* Karl thought. Karl had got a kick from the police's belief that the Ferris/Jackson case was a straightforward murder/suicide. Tex spoke, "We're tying up a few loose ends here, and in the process, we seem to have unravelled some more. I'd like to talk to you."

Karl's thoughts bumped around but he had control of the pinball. He was still confident that he hadn't made any mistakes. Karl had closely followed the analysis of his brother's death in the local papers and on the news. Tex went on, "I'd like to come and see you. Quick chat. Shouldn't take long."

Karl was still cool. "I presume this is about my brother's suicide and the Ferris murder?" Deacon drew in a long breath, "Well. Yes and no. There are a few more things too. As I said, loose ends Mr. Jackson, loose ends."

As it was still the school holiday break, Karl easily created some space for the following morning. He explained to Patricia the reason for the visit from the police and told her that he'd like to be on his own when he met the DCI, but Patricia didn't need an excuse these days to head out. It was usually shopping or long coffee catch-ups with friends, or so she said.

DCI Deacon crunched across the popcorn driveway and lifted the polished knocker. He stood on the lower step. Two echoing raps later and Karl Jackson was at the door and staring at the policeman. Jackson's tooth-filled greeting almost outshone the brass. Deacon scanned Karl's face with practised precision. The photograph Tex had seen of Karl, which he'd accessed through the driving licence data bank, had shown him a face that looked familiar. He was, of course, the double of his twin Nathan, but the features on the boatyard CCTV had been very blurred. Tex was sure he'd seen Karl somewhere else but couldn't quite place him.

Karl made an exaggerated sweep to welcome Deacon in, like a matador with a cape. Karl had switched to his automated charm mode, which sometimes became too lavish, like right now. *"Too much,"* he thought. This kind of thing wasn't easy for the sociopath, as most emotions were acted out. *"Be bland Karl, be bland. Remember bland Karl?"* He didn't want to trigger the truffling instincts of a sleuth with a reputation like Deacon's. Jackson had a fair idea what he was up against. At the 'How to Catch a Killer' lecture Karl had been mightily impressed by the processes Deacon had used to help solve the 'Black Lodge Assassin' case. Karl also knew that he'd already outsmarted Deacon once before, and he wallowed in the memory. *"Poor old Arnold Nutley. I can see him now, stuck in his cell, maybe wearing his ginger wig with his preacher's dog collar, and asking God why he had been punished for something he hadn't done."*

Jackson guided Deacon into the lounge. It was the summer, but the central heating was on in the room, and the excessive warmth had Tex reaching for the top buttons of his shirt. He took off his jacket, and Karl took it and tossed it accurately, without looking, onto the sofa. Tex thought that the huge marble fireplace looked out of place in a house built for the middle classes of Cumbria. Cold ashes lay in the grate, a mahogany coffee table sat in front of the fireplace, and two plush velvet-covered armchairs sat on either side of it. Deacon reckoned that wasn't their usual spot in this room and thought they'd been placed that way just for him. "Please accept my condolences Mr. Jackson. Tragic business with your brother and his social worker. It must be difficult for you and the family." Deacon watched Karl's eyes as if trying to see behind them.

Karl had settled into one of the soft, easy chairs. "Over the years, we've had a lot of tragedy," said Karl, who clamped his lips together to look forlorn. Feigning sadness and distress had always been difficult for Karl, "It's hard to believe, Detective Deacon, it really is." Karl knew that, in situations like these, it was best to keep the comments short. Less chance of saying anything inappropriate or incriminating.

Tex drew a snorting breath through his nose and exhaled it with a soft rush. "Yes, I had a good look at your family history. I helped with some background on the Ferris case and contributed to the work that mopped up Nathan's suicide," Deacon faltered, "Sorry, 'mopped up' isn't very appropriate, that's kind of police jargon. I mean, helped the investigation team to reach its conclusion." Karl tried to maintain the look of a man in mourning and nodded as he clasped his fingers together and pinned them under his chin.

"Mr. Jackson, your father died a while ago. I believe a heart attack while in hospital, and then there was your Uncle Charlie. A horrible accident, but then rock climbing is dangerous, isn't it Mr. Jackson?" There's an old fable that says psychopaths don't sweat, but Karl could feel his palms becoming clammy and kept them squeezed together. Jackson knew that someone like Deacon didn't do house visits to offer condolences. Karl's face broke into a wooden smile.

"Inspector Deacon, the Jacksons have had about as much luck as the Kennedy Clan." Deacon wasn't in the mood for a witty riposte. "Mr. Jackson. We'll get to your uncle's death in a moment, but first, there's something else I want to talk to you about. Something that I'm struggling to make sense of." Deacon leaned forward, his knees touching the edge of the coffee table. "Mr. Jackson. I want to ask you about another death. It happened a long time ago. Peter Ferris was killed at the pontoon, that's been established, but not far from there, decades ago, where the river runs into the lake, a seven-year-old boy died."

Karl still felt confident, but the stickiness of his palms intensified. He squeezed his fingers into his knuckles and then quickly released them as he noticed Deacon watching his hands. "Mr. Jackson. Do you think Nathan could have killed that young boy? Do you think Nathan could have killed your uncle?"

Karl had an impulse to jump in the air and shout Hallelujah! His thoughts raced. *"Christ, how fucking stupid. This guy thinks he's*

Super-Duper Sherlock Deacon, and he's as thick as the rest of them. Arnold Nutley and now Nathan? Is this all this prick does? Convict innocent men?"

Karl was not a man to miss an opportunity. He was sure that his tactic of hiding almost, but not quite in plain sight would work to his long-term advantage. "Detective Deacon, to be honest, I've never even thought that way. Yes, the family did think that Uncle Charlie's death was strange but the police assured us that it was a climbing accident. I mean, it wasn't the first death there. There'd been a bloke years ago who'd fallen at the exact same place. Bart McGoldrick from Mountain Rescue told me all about it. We used to run together and I've often thought they should ban top roping from the rock spike on that climb. Far too dangerous. But a murder? Nathan? Surely not?"

Deacon had been staring at Jackson's lips. "We looked back at that case and spoke to Mountain Rescue. We also spoke briefly to your mother."

Karl jumped in. "She told me about that. A girl came to her house. Said her name was Debbie. Who is she?" Deacon answered without losing momentum, "Debbie is a colleague. Valerie told us that you both had issues with your uncle and she said he was a bully like his brother. To quote your mum, she said your dad Harry was a 'brute'. They sound quite similar, Harry and Charlie."

Karl was into his stride, "Uncle Charlie was a bully, yes, and so was dad. But you wouldn't kill someone just because they gave you the odd slap, would you?"

Deacon had straightened up, "Generally speaking, no, it's not a good reason for murder, but then, as we know from the Peter Ferris killing, Nathan had a poor tolerance threshold. Your brother clearly had bottled some rage. His probation files suggest it. Maybe Nathan had the capacity to hold a grudge. If he could kill Ferris, he could possibly have killed Charlie?"

Karl was very eager to please; all he had to do was couple his verbal dexterity to Deacon's thinking and convince the Detective that he was on the right track. "What did Mountain Rescue say, Detective Deacon? Did mum say anything else?"

Deacon went on. "Your mum told us about the discipline handed out to you and Nathan. Maybe there was more than discipline from Charlie's hands? It sounded like the family lived in terror. Is that true?"

"Yes, all that is true, as are mum's suspicions," said Karl. "Uncle Charlie would look after us when we were young boys. He would volunteer to babysit, and, yes, there was more than discipline. Charlie would interfere with me during his childminding duties, but I don't know about Nathan. I knew he hit him, but anything more tactile, I'm not sure, but if he was abusing me, why not my brother too? But now that you've told me your suspicions about Nathan, I suppose it makes a little more sense. If he could kill Peter Ferris for being an arsehole, I suppose he could kill a man who abused him."

Deacon logged the allegations of abuse and stayed on track, "Mountain Rescue told us more about that apparent accident below the cliff face. They believed someone could have worked the webbing sling off the spike. Robbie from the team went to look at the anchor point, and he reckoned someone with the right implement could have slid the sling up and over. I was wondering if Nathan had ever mentioned anything about that day?"

Right implement? Karl was relieved that he'd put a rubber sheath around the chisel he had used to slide the webbing free. No suspicious deep scratches. The good news was that Detective Chief Inspector Deacon seemed to have decided, with total conviction, that all of the killing had been done by Nathan.

Karl wanted to push his advantage home, "Nathan didn't talk about it voluntarily, but funnily enough, he was inclined to change the subject when I brought Charlie's death up. Now that you have put all that stuff to me Detective Deacon I suppose it might have happened that way. It's hard for me to believe that my brother could have killed more than once."

Now Tex wanted to discuss the seven-year-old kid. Karl didn't know exactly where Deacon was going with this one. Of course, Karl knew the truth and often reminisced about that sunny afternoon. Deacon began to talk in detail about the information that they'd gleaned from that incident, but Karl drifted away, and Tex's words were a shadow in the background. Karl was watching, half interested, at the moving lips of the detective, but he was lost in thought.

"What a day that was. Choking the bloody frogs, too many people around to blow them up. Not as much fun and the slimy wee bastards kept on slipping through my hands. So boring.

And then the boy. Strangling frogs was probably more difficult to do than killing the kid. I was young but even then, wondering what it might take to kill a human and what it would feel like to watch a human fighting for life. To see if the last breath would give me a better kick than the one I got from killing helpless amphibians."

The boy, who would soon be dead, had been sitting on the parched and steep mud bank with his fishing rod. He was staring at the burbling water, watching his tiny float. There was no one else around when Karl slipped in behind him, moving like a cat across the short grass. The rod dropped when Karl grabbed the boy's elbows and put his foot in the middle of his spine. With one sharp move, Karl drove him down the bank. The boy tumbled, gathering pace, grasping at a thin patch of reeds. The reeds were greasy, and he slipped into the water, bobbing up and down, sometimes below and sometimes above the water line. Karl remembered wondering why the boy hadn't tried to swim. Maybe he couldn't. He was gasping and choking, swallowing and spitting, looking at Karl with pleading eyes.

There was an explosion of fear and confusion on the boy's face. Karl watched with rapt intensity. He was so excited he wanted to clap his hands. The noise of the splashing soon stopped, and the boy rolled over, face down and bobbing like his fishing float. From thrashing to death - in five minutes. It was the most fun young Karl had ever had.

"So what about the boy?" asked Deacon, clipping Jackson out of his distant daze. He repeated the words to the distracted Jackson. Inside, Karl was fizzing, but of course he had to maintain that external calm. Karl knew where this was going and was happy to flow with the theme. Deacon continued, "It was reported as an accident, and the coroner agreed. But in the light of the murder of Peter Ferris and suspicions about your Uncle Charlie, we can't rule out murder. Your brother Nathan could have been a serial killer, and it's well-known that serial killers can start very early in life. Building their skill set and getting a feel for what killing is like."

Karl heard himself muttering something about how horrific that all sounded and inanities like, "How could anyone think like that," but inside, Karl was ebullient. Deacon concluded, "According to the accident report from the police records, Nathan was there that day, wasn't he? You were both interviewed, weren't you?" Karl stared at Deacon, doing a great job of mastering a quizzical look. "I was. We both were. We both told the police the same thing. The lake was a regular haunt for us especially in the summer. We just thought we were helping the police do their job."

Deacon looked at the serial killer in the big chair, "Thank you Mr. Jackson. I appreciate your patience. I imagine that what I've told you today has been a bit of a shock. Just one other thing. I think I've seen you before today. In the flesh? Maybe not."

Karl beamed, "Oh you have indeed, Detective Deacon. I asked you a question at the 'Sir Robert Peel Lecture.' I thought you were brilliant. I've always been fascinated by police procedure. Who doesn't enjoy a good murder or two ... unless, of course, it's your own brother carrying them out."

Tex churned at the inappropriate comment. It stirred something deep inside, but Tex remained composed, "Indeed Mr. Jackson, indeed. If you think of anything that might help us, please get in touch. We may talk further."

CHAPTER TWENTY-NINE

A day that had started in glorious sunshine had broken, and wipers flicked across his view as he drove home. Tex's fingers drummed as he accelerated. He was attempting to connect a myriad of dots. Some of those dots he could see, some he could not. Right now, the crucial ones were on the periphery of his vision. He had that feeling, one he'd had many times before, that something just wasn't right. A Dolly Parton classic 'Nine to Five' clattered around the car's upholstery, but to Tex, it was just background fuzz.

Tex's thinking was a spaghetti of confusion. He was pondering his discussion with Karl, trying to read things into it that may not have been there, while, somewhere else in his head Tex was attempting to prepare some content for his next lecture with the cadets. Tex was enjoying working with the recruits, and their enthusiasm gave him a lift - the Chief Constable had been right.

Alone in his car, Tex felt the temple throb that usually preceded a migraine and tried to focus on the happier aspects of his current existence. He increased the wipers' speed to match the rain's persistence. *"The cadets stuff. It has kinda freshened me up I think. It's not quite the kick I got from the 'Sir Robert Peel Lecture', but maybe training the kids is my thing after all. I've had enough of these bloody migraines."*

Enthusiasm was something Tex had been lacking since Susan had passed away. He felt as if he was living a claustrophobic life now, like a mariner inside a diving suit, and that the real world operated outside of his own consciousness. This artificial zone was full of frenzied thoughts and dark corners.

Tex felt persistently heavy and eternally anxious. His usual clarity and sharpness was a soup of negative static, trains of thought jumbled and incoherent. When on his own, he spent too much time blinking away the wetness while shrouded in an imaginary dark blanket. The memories of Susan were persistent, and Tex found himself in an oily pit from which there appeared to be no escape. Despite his mental health frustrations, he still found being sidelined by Barbara Bracewell incredibly frustrating. Deacon appreciated the good sense behind the decision, but a little bit of him thought that a free fall into the depths of something like a murder case might magically set him back on course.

Back home, the work on the cadet seminars continued, but the hunter's mind in Tex continually spun back to the Jackson conundrum. His instinct was to burrow, like he used to do when colleagues had compared him to a crazed gopher. Tex was one hundred percent aware of the fury that would be unleashed if Barbara Bracewell found out that he was 'doing the double'. The official cadet work and the not-so-official graft on the evil workings that appeared to be part of the matrix of the Jackson family's psychology. Tex was working without licence and if caught, he knew the consequences. His ponderings were brought to a halt when his mobile buzzed. "Hi Tex. Debbie here. Look I'm sorry, but I had to ring you. How'd it go with Karl Jackson?"

"Yeah fine," said Tex, "You might be onto something there. I didn't get anything concrete from Karl, but it looks like he's as suspicious as you about Nathan. He was certainly able to give me a little bit more that might ultimately help us to link Nathan to the other two killings. Nothing though that helps us to solve the riddle. And, of course, nothing on record. Nothing admissible. I still feel like a man who's been asked to eliminate an outbreak of bubonic plague with a packet of wet wipes."

Tex listened to a distant crackle and wondered if Debbie had been cut off. He looked at the dashboard of his Audi A4, but the Bluetooth connection was still 'live'. Then Tex heard Debbie's breath, a breath that was quickening, "Tex. I might be the next murder victim." Tex stiffened, "What? What are you talking about?"

"Tex, when I tell you what I'm about to, YOU might want to kill me yourself. I can already hear you saying, "Why did I let that Pilkington girl get involved in all of this?"

"Oh Jeez Debbie, give me strength. What is it?""Tex, all that theory about Nathan being a multiple murderer. It might be all wrong. I know you said at your lecture "Don't take quantum leaps based on a hunch." Well, I've just taken a quantum leap based on a hunch. It careered me off in another direction." Tex wished he'd taken that extra compassionate leave, but stayed patient and listened hard.

"Tex. I kept the Charlie Jackson article from the paper, you know, cut it out for my scrapbook. I kept a lot of my stuff and was going to store it when I noticed a photo on the flip side of the page. It was of some kid from Rimpton Hollway School being given an award for chemistry. The boy was shaking hands with his chemistry teacher. It was Karl Jackson, and what a smile. I think any woman would find that bloke attractive. Swarthy, very fit. He'd make a career heterosexual think twice."

Tex sighed, "Stop lusting and get to the point." He heard a distracted giggle, "Sorry Tex. I know it's all a bit of a 'stream of consciousness', but I'll get there. Pour yourself a drink." "Not easy Debbie, I'm driving." Debbie wasn't really listening to Tex. She had too much to say, "Beside the photo of the chemistry award, there's a little biography of the prize winner and the teacher who had inspired him, who was, of course - Karl Jackson."

"Jackson had quoted his interests: 'Fell running, rock climbing, avoiding my family and the joy of toxins.' Sarcasm, I suspect, Jackson's idiosyncratic humour. He's a chemistry teacher, so he'd know a lot about toxins, but he'd made that joke about the family a day after his uncle had been killed in a rock-climbing accident. Then that smile was like he didn't care. Tex, I just thought that there was something very, very, creepy about all that. The sort of things a normal person wouldn't do. So I had what I call 'a deep ferret' into Karl Jackson. I just wanted to see where it would take me... and I think I've got something."

Deborah had grabbed Deacon's full attention. Tex wished he could have poured that drink and felt his guts pang for the amber liquid. Instead, he tightened his grasp on the steering wheel. "Right", said Deborah, "Our computer at the Rimpton Chronicle. We have a global press database on it that's linked to every other registered newspaper in the world. So I put the name Karl Jackson into the search box. Tex, our Karl Jackson, your Karl Jackson was involved in, and I'm air quoting here, an 'accident' in the Blue Mountains in Australia during his college gap year. It was in the Sydney Morning Herald. A Brazilian called Carlos was sharing a tent with Karl when an Eastern Brown snake fatally bit him. Reported as an accident and recorded as an accident. A toxin, okay it's a snake bite, but Karl loves his toxins, doesn't he?"

"This is still very loose Debbie, and so circumstantial it's not even circumstantial. This is patchy stuff, there isn't enough substance here. I hope you've more than that?"

Debbie barrelled on, half listening to the response from Tex. "And how did Nathan die, Tex?" Tex was imagining a second glug of his favourite Bushmills, but his only option was a Werther's Original he found in the box between the front seats.

"Valium, Debbie, Diazepam to give it a brand name, plus the effects of etorphine. It was a huge overdose."

Debbie was in again, "More chemicals though, more toxic substances. Another, air quotes again, 'unfortunate incident' when Karl Jackson was present." Tex interjected, he'd seen the toxins report, "And why take the etorphine as well, and where did he get it? Because of Nathan's note, the detectives didn't read anything into that, mainly because there were only minute traces. Etorphine is a thousand times more potent than morphine and would certainly finish the job in the right dose, but, as I said, there was so little of the drug that it barely registered during the tests."

"Tex, maybe Nathan had a killer who subdued him with the etorphine. Thoughts?"

"But Debbie, Karl wasn't technically present when Nathan died. Karl had lost Nathan in the mist, and Mountain Rescue found him. Well, a search dog, to be precise." By this stage, Tex was lucky to get to the end of sentences, and Deborah wasn't taking too many breaths. "Yes, but who's telling us all of these stories? Karl Jackson was quoted in the Sydney Morning Herald about how he'd seen the Eastern Brown flashing past and how shocked he had been to find his camping partner dead. Karl doesn't have too much luck with camping partners, does he? Carlos? Nathan?" Debbie paused briefly.

"And then there's Karl's Uncle Charlie. I did some hunting while I was chasing the story for the Chronicle. Karl used to run with Bart McGoldrick, a Mountain Rescue bloke who'd helped recover the body of the first guy who'd fallen off the rock face. He gets close to a lot of death, does Karl Jackson. Tex, surely it's worth a closer look at this guy? Have I got this totally wrong? Tex...Tex ... are you there?"

Tex was trying to process a lot of information. "Yes, but you had a similar theory about Nathan. He seems to trigger death too. Ferris, the wee boy - I found out the kid's name - Peter Davidson, and then Charlie Jackson. Nathan had a motive for Ferris and Charlie. According to Karl, Charlie sexually abused him and, probably, Nathan too."

Debbie was beginning to shake a little with excitement, "Oh, that's horrific, but, to use your word, 'triggers', Karl had just as many, maybe more. Nathan? Was there a sibling grudge? A reason to kill his brother? Uncle Charlie, the boy, what did you say he was called? Peter Davidson? And now there's another one - Carlos Ferreira. Karl Jackson. Karl Jackson. Karl Jackson. Karl Jackson. Karl Jackson. Five deaths, and Karl was in the vicinity for four of them. The one we don't think he was close to was the Peter Ferris knifing - or was he?"

Tex and Debbie let another long silence dangle. "Tex, look, you're the detective here and a brilliant one, but, Oh God, I can't believe I'm questioning the great Tex Deacon, but are you one hundred percent certain it was Nathan walking towards the pontoon that morning? Look this isn't my job Tex, but I would do this as a journalist. Take out Nathan's suicide note from the equation, like it didn't exist and think again. You say that in your lecture Tex. Don't be afraid to start all over."

Tex had curled his lips back into his mouth. "Are you there Tex. Are you there?" Tex was there okay. His mind was spinning as he slalomed through the evidence. Tex had been so sure that Nathan was the Jackson family bad guy. In fact, Tex was still confident that Nathan was the killer. Or was he? Tex was wavering. Had he covered every base?

"Hi Debbie, yeah sorry, I'm here. You're right, it's worth another look. It still looks like Nathan is the man. Yes, Karl was beside this guy Carlos, but dozens of people get killed by snakebites every year in Australia. Yes, he was also with Nathan in the mountains, but it could all be a coincidence. Debbie, you might just be over thinking here and to get anywhere I'll have to get access to the Ferris evidence. Bracewell will take a lot of persuading. I mean, we haven't exactly got a smoking gun." Debbie put on her best persuasive voice, "Please Tex, please ask your Boss."

A short bark came from Tex, "Right, right, right. I'll go and see her. The next time you see me, I might have been sectioned. Please remember to bring me some grapes." Tex saw a flashing image of Thelma and Louise plummeting to their demise.

"Brilliant, Tex," said Deborah. "In the meantime, I'll collate my cuttings and ask the Sydney Morning Herald journalist to send me her original notes. There are, in total, three newspaper reports on the snake bite incident. To remind you, Carlos Ferreira was the deceased's name, in case you want to search it. Tex, I don't know if I'm right or wrong here, but we are certain of one thing. If the Jackson brothers are about, people die."

CHAPTER THIRTY

It was a morning for absolving your sins. The thunderclouds above Cumbria had blackened the skies. If passing evangelicals had suggested that this was the beginning of 'Revelation', and that the second coming was just minutes away, you might have believed them. The rumble was nuclear when it exploded, and the first crack of lightning was almost instantaneous. Tex Deacon was buried deep inside inadequate clothing and scurried and crouched at the same time, trying to make it to police headquarters before the egg-sized raindrops drenched his entire being. It had been a thirty-yard dash from his Audi, but Tex looked like he'd been through a carwash by the time he reached the main entrance.

"Come in," said the Chief Constable, "Good morning Tex. How are you?" said Bracewell while finishing off some notes on her yellow pad. "If you look up, you'll see exactly how I am," said Tex, talking through dripping lips. When Barbara finally raised her head, she saw a man weighed down by sagging garments that had been half a stone lighter when he'd put them on. Tex had a towel wrapped around his shoulders, one handed to him by the sympathetic desk sergeant.

"Tex, you see, when you go for your morning swim, you're supposed to take your clothes off first." Tex searched for his sense of humour but found that, like Lord Lucan, it had disappeared entirely. "Barbara, I got caught out by that flash storm," Bracewell smirked in the way that affectionate friends do, "I'm not really sure I needed that explanation." She looked at the water overflowing from Tex's squelching shoes. It was darkening her office carpet.

"Have a seat Poseidon, but bring over the wooden seat. I don't want my upholstery going the same way as the carpet." Tex, the miserable wretch, sat down. "So apart from being an hour away from double pneumonia, how are you?"

"Apart from being a bit wet, I'm fine, thanks. Well, more than fine. I'm grand. Very well indeed," Barbara's eyes narrowed.

171

"I'll bet you are Tex, but how are you? In yourself, I mean?" Tex knew that Bracewell was a living, breathing bull shit detector, and it was never a good idea to respond with some of your own.

"Well Chief, the work with the cadets is going to plan as far as I know. No complaints. They seem to enjoy it and, much to my amazement, so do I. I've no problem working with the students, in fact I think I'll focus on that post-retirement. Could be a nice wee earner. Bulk up the pension. I'm changing it up a bit next time. I'll do a question-and-answer session with them. I've given them a few days to prepare."

Barbara set her elbows on her buffed oak desk, which still carried the aroma of its morning polish. "Tex, I'm getting good reports from the senior staff at cadet training, and your lecture went down a storm. But you asked for this meeting, Tex, not me. I know you. You're not here for a wee catch-up. What's going on?"

Tex dripped constantly and could feel his clothes cooling against his skin, "As you say, Barbara, you know me probably better than anyone I suppose. You know I can't keep my nose out of the dirt. Just for myself, and to keep my senses sharp, I've been rummaging about," Tex put his hands up like a cornered criminal, "Nothing official and I haven't been into any case files. I've flicked through a few, but I haven't interfered."

Bracewell shook her head, a sardonic twist in her half smile. "What a shock, Tex, but I expressly told you to stay away from all that. Okay what have you been doing?"

Tex mumbled, feeling the red heat that embarrassment brings to the cheeks. "I was looking at the Peter Ferris file and then the updates to it following Nathan Jackson's suicide and admission. I also stumbled across some old newspaper cuttings."

"Stumbled?" said Bracewell. She knew all about Tex's love of subterfuge.

"Well yeah, kind of, look it's all linked to the Ferris/Jackson murder/suicide. I know that case is technically closed, but I think I've got the seed of a fresh lead. A reason, perhaps, to reopen the investigation."

Tex knew that's all he could say. If he'd told the Chief Constable where else he had been rummaging, Tex would have witnessed a human Krakatoa. He certainly wasn't going to hit her with his brace of Tex and Debbie/Cagney and Lacey theories. One: That Nathan had maybe killed more than one person. Two: That it might not have been Nathan at all and that the other twin was, in fact, a serial killer. These were theories that had no hard evidence, and he most certainly couldn't mention the secondment of a young newspaper reporter to do the trawling. This could be career oblivion, so Tex thought it best to tread with light, if wet, feet.

Bracewell was well-versed in the details of the Ferris/Jackson case. They didn't get many incidents like it that fell under the auspices of the Rimpton division. Bracewell remembered how the press and media had descended on that area of the Lake District. SKY news had sent in a helicopter, which broadcast magnificent live vistas of the mountain range. Nationally, it had been a one-day wonder on the fast-moving news cycle.

"Sorry Tex. You'll need a lot more than a few clippings to get me to re-open that case and, before you ask, no, you can't have the file. Maybe you are onto something, but if the clippings are all you have then it's not even worth a review. Sorry Tex, and anyway, you're not supposed to look at open or closed cases."

Tex rubbed his eyes with his fingertips, flicking droplets away, and moved to speak, but Bracewell wasn't finished. "Tex I've got the reports from the grief counsellor and the psychiatrist, David Braithwaite. The latter's brief concerns me, Tex. Braithwaite says you have clear indications of untreated Post Traumatic Stress Syndrome. Neither of us will ever forget that tortured paedophile, and you were first on the scene."

Tex shrugged, offering nothing else. "On top of the possible PTSD, there's the general work pressures and Susan's death. Tex. You need more time and probably a lot more therapy. I understand your desire to get back on the beat, but it's a no-go. I'll ignore your rummaging this time and put it down to frustration. Get some more rest, get back to Braithwaite, and focus on your work with the cadets."

Bracewell stood up and, without another word, guided a very damp Deacon towards the door.

PART THREE

CHAPTER THIRTY-ONE

The fell running scene was vibrant, and Karl Jackson was a decent mountain athlete. At the end of each season, he was usually in the top six in the age category awards, and this time Karl had managed to finish third in the over 35's section. The season consisted of a dozen races of varying lengths, from the short sprint-style bursts of around five miles to the longer endurance runs of up to twenty-two miles. Karl's physiology was more suited to longer distances, with the loping stride of an Ethiopian and the lung capacity of a Sherpa. He had a quirky style, as if on springs, which enabled him to ricochet from boulder to boulder. He skipped over rocks and appeared to levitate over boggy ground.

Patricia ran too, an elf-like figure who surfed over the broken ground. Patricia was a natural and was often up amongst the contenders in the competitive women's categories. Karl had always admired the women's athleticism and mental strength and was convinced they were the superior half of the species. A psychologist may have suggested that this stance had evolved from observing and admiring the remarkable resistance of his mother. In many ways, Valerie's courage had been an inspiration to Karl. He felt that his preference for men as targets was maybe a subconscious response to that. Perhaps, deep down, Karl just wanted to kill Harry over and over again. The problem was he could only kill Harry once.

Karl and Patricia were members of C.C.F.R.C, the Carlton Comets Fell Running Club. They were easy to spot in the mountains, their singlets a flash of scarlet, with "COMET" written in fluorescent yellow spiralling letters. The word "COMET" had a tail resembling a starburst.

The women had a thriving section with several members competitive at national level. The best of the women was Samantha Turkington, the wife of Richard. The husband, though, was no runner preferring to roam the hills with a rucksack on his back. Samantha had won the county championship several times. She was built like a racing snake, had phenomenal ability, and could glide up hills with gymnastic elasticity. Sam pressed the palms of her hands into her thighs to create a springboard effect and would bound up the higher slopes with amazing speed.

Karl used to irritate the men in the club when he started rattling out his theories, usually in the pub, while chomping through the post-race chicken nuggets. "Testosterone is the male curse. You lot should read more books on anthropology. It's heavily substantiated, you know, evolution is the reason for women's mental and physical durability."

Based on hard scientific research, Karl was sure this belief was why he was fascinated by the better female serial killers. He admired them hugely, for example, Irmgard Moller, a member of the Red Army who specialised in blowing up military facilities. Idoia Lopez Riano, known as 'The Tigress', a hit woman for ETA, the Basque Separatist organisation. Riano carried out an estimated 23 murders and, apparently, had a penchant for sleeping with her victims before killing them. She would document the psychedelic orgasms she had with men she knew she would kill. Karl found that amusing and arousing. Then there was Velma Barfield, who had poisoned six men. Lyda Southard, who had murdered her four husbands-both women used arsenic. A lot of women used poison, and maybe that fact also drew Karl to the mysteries of the fairer sex.

According to Karl's research papers on endurance, men, fuelled by testosterone, were inclined to burst away from the start line, even in very long 'Ultra' running races, and burn out far too quickly. Karl would hold court with the reluctant males in his pub audience, the women loved to hear this sexually charismatic man fighting their corner.

"You see, female fell runners are naturally inclined to settle into an early sustainable pace and stick with it. Women aren't weighed down as much by ego, which men have far too much of. Women also appear to have a better genetic capacity for running longer distances." Karl was unstoppable when he latched on to one of his favourite athletic topics. "The longer the race, the stronger women become. According to the anthropological arguments, womens pain threshold is higher, which is perfect for the demands of the fells."

But for Karl, the most fascinating paragraph from his wide reading on the subject was this one. "From an evolutionary standpoint, mans long-term survival is not important. However, the survival of women is essential for the rearing of children and nurturing of the young. The species' success depends on this. Men, in reality, are not much more than bags of sperm. They're disposable." Karl certainly agreed with the use of the word disposable. From his perspective, it justified, in one sense, the killings he carried out. The long-term survival of the men wasn't critical, and he was happy to assist on that front. Right now, Karl was running hot and had a particular bag of sperm on his mind. The one that belonged to the man he suspected of shagging his wife.

CHAPTER THIRTY-TWO

The annual fell runner's awards bash was in Longhampton at the Riverhill Hotel. Ghosts would have been afraid to haunt this place - the strange aura had been baked in. Yellowed walls were the calling card of a hundred years of tobacco smoke. The bar was set back from the grimy windows, far from the nearest dim strip light and you almost needed a torch to find it.

To re-paint the impossibly high ceilings, the owner, Jack Stoat, a crumpled man who looked older than Noah, would have needed to borrow Michael Angelo's scaffolding, so he hadn't bothered. The hotel looked like it had been vacuum-packed into its little slot between the shops on the High Street. One puff from the Big Bad Wolf might have tumbled the whole building but the function rooms were cheap to hire. Longhampton rested on the lower slopes of the western mountains, and the Riverhill was about to host an interesting event. If walls could talk the Riverhill would have had many tales to tell. These walls, though, would have had a smoker's cough.

Karl was here to collect a prize, but he also planned to uncover the affair he suspected his wife was having with Richard Turkington. Patricia may have strayed, but Karl didn't exactly fly with angel's wings either. In fact, he was generally excellent at anything serial, whether killing or sleeping around. Karl's thinking was typically nonchalant, though his view was that he had been acceptably faithful to Patricia. After all, it was just the occasional stress-relieving dabble. Karl thought that a little bit of drifting was good for his relationship as it released sexual tension, keeping him mentally and physically fresh for the rather gruelling marriage commitment.

Patricia never suspected Karl of infidelity. In keeping with the well-practised modus operandi elsewhere in his life, he had been meticulous with preparing and covering all of his affairs. Karl was much more vigilant than his wife. He didn't feel that he had many emotional weaknesses, but it surprised him how much his stomach wrenched when he saw Patricia moving into the airspace of another alpha male.

Karl and Patricia were both prize winners at the awards dinner. Karl won a bronze figurine of an Alpine Goat for third place overall in his category. There was the usual burst of ironic applause and jeering when he went up for his prize. Karl's habit when he won something was to perform a theatrical sweep with his right arm in the direction of his less than enthusiastic 'fan club'. Cries of 'Twat' and 'Wanker' were not uncommon, but it was put down to ribaldry and badinage. As the New Jersey Mafia put it in the Sopranos, "We're only breaking balls." Patricia won the over-30's category for the third year in a row. She collected £100 and her name was again engraved on the 'Mary Hunter Cup' plinth. As usual, Samantha Turkington cruised away with the over 40's category, picking up eight victories in the twelve-race series. Her husband Richard was there, but Karl had never liked him, finding him about as appealing as cold sick. At every opportunity, Karl would throw sneering and dismissive glances in Richard's general direction.

Richard Turkington's greying Beatle cut had a bald spot on top, giving him the appearance of a rock star monk. A fleshy roll wobbled over the top of his chinos. Turkington had clearly ignored the warning signs of middle age and had lived a pudgy existence, preferring a world of pints and puddings. Quite a contrast to the sleek, wire-framed fell runners. Surrounded by them at a function like this, Richard looked like Mr. Blobby.

Like many people in the area, Turkington loved the open expanses on his doorstep, although he rarely moved at a pace that forced fat to actually burn. The stress in his life, and there was plenty, was eased by his camping expeditions. No matter what Turkington was doing or wearing, you always got the impression that he had escaped from a display case at a top-of-the-range outlet. There was the sparkling pinky ring, his suits, which he purchased while on special visits to London, and his range of felt Fedoras. The leather on his shoes was so thick they could probably have taken a bullet and were as well polished as a Tom Cruise grin.

In the mountains, Turkington had all the gear. He never stopped talking about the latest top brand Gore-Tex jacket, designed to survive an Atlantic hurricane, and an Everest Expedition tent. He seemed either about to go to an exotic location or had just returned from one. It was always an extravagant trip somewhere like the Andes or the Himalayas. Turkington would return with volumes of boring photographs, each repeating the last. Mountain, snow, tent, mountain. Mountain, snow, tent, mountain. Unfortunately for any poor soul who found themselves cornered by Turkington, each photo was accompanied by a detailed description and an 'astonishing' story - which usually finished with him as the hero.

Richard said he'd made all of his money in pensions. Karl doubted that and used to fantasise about running his keys along the flanks of Richard's nausea-inducing cucumber green Lamborghini. Turkington could outshout a town crier, and dominate the conversations with his small coterie of fellow cash-rich misogynists. Gold plastic flashed as they ran through their, probably made-up, salacious stories. Turkington loved these lurid cabals.

Karl thought Richard was trashy, and that was before he suspected his wife of sleeping with this saggy sack of a man. *"The sort of dick head I would never tire of punching, stabbing, or poisoning."*

Richard and Samantha seemed to be well enough matched. He looked like he had exploded through an Oxford Street picture window, while Sam had a natural flamboyance and the build of Kylie Minogue, which had been honed through hundreds of miles splashing through mud and muck in the mountains, and she worshipped money. Samantha clearly thrived amongst the higher social strata. Her stunning transformations from fell running shoes, shorts and singlet to the high couture of the latest line in fashion were viewed as fabulous by some but tacky by others. You could have limbo danced under Samantha's high heels.

Patricia seemed to enjoy floating around the Turkingtons, now and again slouching far too close to Richard. Sam saw it happen but never reacted. Was Patricia hiding in plain sight? Certainly, at home, Karl's view was that Patricia talked about Turkington far too much.

Karl's well-tuned antenna was alerted at the awards dinner. The advantage of his persistent paranoia and jealousy. After the presentations, the runners and their partners mingled. Karl, from long range, saw Patricia whispering in Richard's ear, a hand on his shoulder. Her long hair flew back, and the accompanying laugh appeared to be exaggerated. Karl was hawk-like, observing and logging. He had no absolute proof, but there was enough in the body language of Richard and Patricia to trigger Karl's silent white rage.

CHAPTER THIRTY-THREE

A few days later, Karl clicked open the back of his wife's mobile phone. Struggling to focus on the motherboard through the magnifying glass, his fingers pinched around the magnetic clock maker's tweezers. It took him a few seconds to steady his hand, and then he inserted a microchip into the software. Karl most certainly didn't teach this kind of technology to his class. The microchip recorded and then transferred any phone calls and texts to a data bank on the computer in Karl's office. Initially, there was nothing. Karl regularly checked the file, but all he had were standard texts from Patricia to Kerry and numbing gossip that pinged between her and the chattering classes amongst her set of friends. There was the occasional text from wife to husband, but these were always curt and, unlike the others, emoji free. Karl was about to get back to his humdrum world of school scheduling when the live feed from Patricia's phone appeared on his computer screen in a pop-up box. It was from 'Dick'. A flame darted through Karl's belly as he expanded the pop-up to full screen:

DICK: Hi Pitty Pat. How are you? Miss you. Samantha is away all day Tuesday. How're you fixed?

Karl intensified his focus on the Toshiba laptop and waited. Time passed very slowly for Karl, and then, another message dinged into place.

PATRICIA J: Hey Dick Dastardly. I miss you too. Miss your kisses. Tuesday? God that's three days away! How can I wait that long? LOL. I'll make it work. Be in touch.

Karl couldn't believe that the lovers weren't conducting their clandestine relationship through burner phones. Very common, and common sense for those who had deviated away from the vows they'd made at the altar. "Big fucking mistake," Karl murmured. Another ding.

DICK: Great. I'll book a room at the Hilton Lancaster. One o'clock. Can't wait to consume you.

Accompanying this was another emoji. This one showed a wide-eyed wink from a man with a slurping tongue hanging out of his cartoon mouth. Karl felt a warm rush rising, "Consume you?" what kind of twat says that? Someone called Dick fucking Dastardly, that's who." PATRICIA: Oh God, Dick, don't. I love it when you consume me. You know how wet I get thinking about you. Why do you make me so horny?

The emoji this time was one of the Devil. At least Karl could resonate with that one. But Karl couldn't understand the attraction. Turkington was shapeless, like a sewer's fat berg, and he had no idea how Turkington could make anyone horny but, importantly, Karl had his evidence and closed the file. The messages would stack up automatically if he needed any more proof, but this was more than enough for him. Karl reminded himself to back up the messages to a memory stick later and then shut down his computer.

On Monday night, Karl and Patricia stood in the kitchen. Exchanges of words these days were generally brief and to the point. "How's your Tuesday looking, Karl? Are you still doing those one on ones with that Brewster kid? I'll bet he loves doing extra chemistry during the summer holidays." Karl had his head in the fridge, reaching for the Red Bull. "My holidays too remember, but it pays well. Bewster's parents have booked him in for five more sessions. He needs them. I'm hitting the hills for a run first, west probably, Yewbarrow, Red Pike and then circle back past Scoat Tarn to Wast Water. I'll shower at a caravan park and then go and see the boy. I'll not be home until five or five-thirty. Why do you ask Patricia?" Karl emerged from the cold, and the can hissed as he released the ring pull. "Oh, just wondering," Patricia replied, "I'm planning a long run in the hills too, maybe Nab Scar, Heron Pike and Great Rigg - some sort of loop. I really want to up my mileage this year."

Karl chucked his wife as laconic a glance as he could manage but inside the cogs were heating, darkness at work through the silence, "Up your mileage. You're certainly doing that sweetheart." Patricia noted the hint of a double entendre and then discarded the thought as her imagination.

CHAPTER THIRTY-FOUR

On Tuesday at lunchtime, Karl, having postponed the private lesson with Brewster, had parked his car well back from the Hilton on the outskirts of the town. Karl lay in the dense shrubbery at the perimeter of the grounds, prone, like a sniper, binoculars and camera ready. He was focused on the gate at the end of the runway straight asphalt entrance. Patricia's Red Honda Civic appeared blurred at first, but then Karl found focus. Through the glasses, he could see a wobbly image of the person he knew was his wife, the number plate was absolute confirmation.

"Is Dick stupid enough to arrive in that green Lamborghini?" Karl mumbled. There was no sign of Turkington. Karl watched his wife walk across the granite paving and up the glossed white steps into the hotel. Still no Turkington so Karl would have to wait. After an hour Karl felt the first patters and splashes and pulled up his hood. Before long, puddles had formed around him, and a buffeting northerly tugged at his waterproofs, but Karl wasn't moving until he had an answer. At four o'clock he thought he saw him and Karl, his body tight and arms stiff, raised the binoculars to his face and squinted. Richard Turkington came out of the hotel through its revolving doors.

"He must have arrived through the back," thought Karl as he moved with the dexterity of a squirrel and snatched his camera. There was a click-click whirr, then another, and then a volley. Karl had at least a dozen clear photos of 'Dick'. Fifteen minutes later Patricia walked out through the same exit, and Karl again pressed the burst mode button on his Minolta. He soon had his album of deceit.

Karl built a compendium of evidence. A part of him, deeply buried, was hoping this wasn't happening, but it was. To Karl, Patricia's transgressions were inexcusable. Karl knew that he was taking a serious risk as any actions taken now might put him back into the spotlight and draw the attention of DCI Deacon. As it stood, Karl was in a good place as Deacon had convinced himself that Nathan had killed Ferris, Uncle Charlie and, possibly, the boy on the river bank. In a sense, Karl had a clean slate, and fresh kills would most likely jeopardise that position. He'd already banked the considerable success of the Nutley framing. Karl's next move had to be the right one and yet again Karl had a lot of thinking to do before he even considered striking.

"Maybe I should just scare them? Leave my mark. Let them know what terror feels like. I must be patient." Karl kept himself in the loop. He went to the postseason social runs, listened to the chatter, and even eavesdropped on a few of Samantha Turkington's conversations. It was traditional for the runners to retire to a local pub, usually McArthurs, at the end of the town. Samantha had a small group of hill running buddies who would inevitably gather in the bar for a catch-up. After one of the social gallops, a fun five-mile team event called the 'Great Demon Scramble', Karl listened in to one of Samantha's fast-paced, high-pitched chin wags. She, and her botoxed cartel, were talking a lot but Karl was able to tune into the relevant stuff with the sonic senses of a bat. "Richard is heading off on one of his head-clearing camping trips at the end of the week. Thursday and Friday. He'll be back for the weekend, worst luck." Karl half heard the cackles that followed Samantha's limp quip. He was already crafting a plan. From before sunrise on Thursday Karl kept an eagle eye on Turkington's house, staking it out from a safe distance. Turkington's navy blue Range Rover scrunched its way down the drive. The gauche Lamborghini was unseen in the warehouse-sized garage. Parked beside it was a V8 Ferrari California.

Karl was in no rush and settled in like a birdwatcher, scanning Turkington's movements. Turkington made several trips from his mansion-sized house to the Range Rover and Karl watched his target load up the car. From his raised perch, Karl could see the stables, the guest cottage and a black blob that had to be a helipad.

When Turkington was all set, Karl scampered from his lookout to his own car, which he'd hidden off-road. It was now covered in bird droppings. Karl needed the binoculars again and waited for the Range Rover to nose out through the wrought iron electric gates.

Turkington's right turn told Karl he was heading west, probably for the lower car park in the shadow of 'Lucifer's Leap', a popular starting point for overnight campers. The frequent twists on the country road helped Jackson, who stayed two corners back.

Turkington turned left at a sign, 'Lucifer's Leap Car Park: Please Treat The Mountains With Respect.' Karl parked on the verge and, squatting on his haunches, moved behind the hawthorn hedge that was wrapped around the car park like a circus ring. It was just as Karl wanted it to be. Turkington's Range Rover was the only car in the car park. Jackson knew he didn't have to be patient any more. He covered the ground back to his own car fast and within a minute, Karl made the same left turn and reversed his VW between two white lines. Turkington was on his mobile phone, sitting in the driver's seat, and glanced at the vehicle manoeuvring close to the Range Rover. Karl was close enough to see Turkington's expression change from one of ease to horror. Hardly surprising that Richard wasn't too happy to see the husband of the woman he was having an affair with backing his Volkswagen Beetle into an adjacent space. Karl looked at Turkington whose tortured face betrayed a mind that was a blizzard of thoughts. Turkington felt his heart moving closer to his throat as Karl stepped out of the Beetle, but to Turkington's huge surprise, Karl carried a broad smile. Turkington's paranoia told him that Karl would be here to face him down.

Instead of the aggression Turkington expected, Karl stretched out his hand. Instead of the attack Turkington expected, maybe with a car jack, all he got was a lot of relaxed small talk. "Hello Richard. Great day for it. What are you up to?" Turkington wasn't sure whether to relax or cry.

"Hey Karl. Good to see you. I'm heading out for an overnight camp. You know, get away from the rat race. What about you?" Turkington wouldn't have been surprised if Karl had responded with, "Oh I'm here to kill you. I know you've been fucking my wife," but instead he heard the words. "I saw on the weather we might get the tail end of Hurricane Bertha. Amazing to have weather like that in England at this time of year, a tropical storm. Maybe all this chat about climate change is right. They're expecting quite a bit of damage to be done to the forests on the edge of the hills, but they don't expect the heavy winds until the weekend. Flat calm until then, apparently, but humid. Airstream from the tropics apparently." Turkington's heart rate dropped, and he even managed to force a smile in return. "Yes I'd checked the weather reports, Karl. I'm good to go and should be back here well before any bad stuff hits." Talk of cyclones had replaced the expected cyclonic rage. Turkington was unpacking the Range Rover as he talked. Karl managed to feign interest in Richards's Everest Expedition tent and his top of the range Ospreys rucksack.

"So many pockets on this design, bloody great they are," enthused Karl. "Jeez, look at the zips. Very durable they say, and great for big trips." Using his sleeve to cover his hand, Karl slipped a silicon-chipped tracker the size of a five-pence piece inside the rucksack. The tracker was lost amongst the clothes, camping equipment and supplies, but Turkington was still wary, "So what brings you out here, Karl?"

Karl's expression was one of faux shock. "What else would I be here for? I'm going for a run. Just wanted to go somewhere away from the old honey pot routes for a change. The gear is in the boot. Five or six miles, that'll do me." For many reasons, Turkington couldn't wait to get going, and after a few more meaningless exchanges he was leaving Karl head down, truffling about in the boot amongst the layers of his running gear.

Karl waited for a few hours, then he set off into the mountains, confident that he would find his human prey. He walked for five hours, keeping an eye on his GPS, which was linked to Richard's tracker. Turkington set up camp, and Karl highlighted the spot on his Garmin in the 'Way Marks' app. He then put up his own tent, making sure that it was perfectly placed with a mountain and a set of crags between them. He was securely hidden far enough away not to be noticed but close enough to receive a strong signal from Turkington's tracker. Karl took a pocket-sized monitor from his rucksack and electronically linked it to a small homemade quadcopter drone. He made sure everything was working properly, had some food and then slid into his sleeping bag. Karl slept well.

Karl was up before dawn the following day. He had to be in position before Turkington made a move. Then the sun rose, warm tentacles permeating a ghostly mist. It wouldn't take long for the heat to burn off a fog folding around creepy shapes, hugging the turf.

Richard sat beneath the flap of his tent watching the mist curling in strange spirals. He cooked breakfast, the gas fire hissing as he flipped the bacon. Turkington packed up fast. He had a long route planned, and the terrain was demanding on this side of the mountains with a lot of sphagnum moss and heather to negotiate. You had to be able to navigate well.

The day-hikers generally stayed away from here. There were very few paths, it was remote, and at this time of the day, the chances of anyone else walking around were very slim.

Turkington had been on the move for about fifteen minutes when he heard a monotonous hum. He looked up, trying to scan the sky but the fog snuggled around him, which meant that he couldn't see what was creating the buzz. Richard, however, knew from the noise what was above him: an approaching drone.

Karl was in his tent, watching his monitor and could just make out a grey-shaded figure on his black-and-white screen. He didn't need clear sight of his target as he had his GPS as well as the tracker, which was, of course, still nestling in Turkington's rucksack. Richard's reaction to the turbulence that disturbed his mountain peace was one of irritation. He had never liked this new-fangled drone culture, especially in the hills. He felt they were noise pollution and should be banned. Richard swore, cursing at the unseen owner.

Karl used the joystick to guide his drone towards Turkington, feeling the excitement build as he anticipated the euphoria that would follow. Karl's knowledge of technology and obsession with gadgetry gave him, as a killer, a wider range of options. He was thrilled with this design. Brushless motors were lighter on the battery. The drone had electronic speed control and super lightweight reinforced carbon fibre propellers. It had a GPS 4K camera and a USB key so Karl could save the filmed footage. The drone was also fitted with a modified syringe pump.

Turkington was by now just a little nervous, though he wasn't quite sure why. Instinct maybe. The trajectory of the drone dropped as it came closer and Richard could just make out its ghostly outline. Karl was controlling the drone's every movement and later he noted every detail in his journals.

"I guided the drone in and knew exactly where it had to be for maximum effect. I needed it to float about fifteen feet above the arsehole's head. There was no wind which was a massive bonus. There wasn't much that Turkington could do, although I did smirk when he got a tent pole out and started flapping at the drone, trying to swat it like a massive gnat. I was actually laughing so much that for a minute, I struggled to work the control panel. Anyway, it was all good. The important thing was that the drone was hovering in precisely the right spot. Timing was crucial here, and to be honest, I wasn't one hundred percent certain that the damn thing would work. Though it had all gone perfectly during my recce in the fields above the forest.

That gave me a bit of confidence. I released the button that pressed the syringe pump. I'd made the contents for the pump myself from the seeds of castor oil plants. Bloody hell, it was good to watch. I had that orgasmic ripple. Who needs sex? The chemistry teacher in me felt just a wee bit proud. A powerful spray of highly toxic ricin exploded around 'Dick Dastardly'. The flat calm helped a lot, and the ricin cloud floated down onto him. It only takes a dose of purified ricin powder the size of a few grains of table salt to kill a human. I went belt and braces and had ten times that amount in my hand-built pump. I'd hoped the toxic dust would get into his eyes to guarantee blind carnage. Turkington was enveloped in a cloud of ricin. What a feeling it was being able to watch all of this. Virtual multiple orgasms! Yee-Ha..!

The drone just hovered over him as he squirmed and choked, kneeling on the grass, clutching his throat. It's just a shame there was no sound on the camera. He started to vomit, and then there was diarrhoea. A hugely enjoyable show. The only slight problem was that the pictures on the six-inch screen were not quite sharp. God I wish

Patricia had been in my tent. How delicious it would have been to force her to watch the live show."

***

Symptoms of ricin poisoning set in fast. Victims can die of circulatory shock or organ failure and inhaled Ricin can cause fatal pulmonary oedema, respiratory failure or heart failure if you're vulnerable to it. It's a deeply unpleasant way to die, and Karl's camera had recorded the entire macabre scene. Richard Turkington's death was slow and agonising, and his body lay undiscovered for three days.

CHAPTER THIRTY-FIVE

Would it be third time lucky for Deborah? After a little tug of war, she managed to secure an invitation to Tex's house. Their phone conversation had included phrases like, "Are you sure this time?" "I suppose you want me to put my job on the line?" "Is this another one of your resolutions based on assumption?" Of course, all of those quotes came from Tex, while the phrases, "I've definitely got something more concrete to go on", "Can't you just trust me", and "I won't let you down" were all delivered by Debbie.

Debbie hoped to God that her info might lead to something substantial this time. She was still sure that her hunches, based on research, would end up being all, or at least part of, the truth. Debbie had a conviction that the Karl Jackson links to death were beyond mere coincidence. Debbie began talking as Tex's front door opened, "Tex, I'm mortified by what I put you through with the Chief Constable. Was it embarrassing?" Debbie talked as she slid past Tex. "Debbie, what have you done with your hair?" Debbie kept moving, "Oh I just fancied it short,"

"Short! You look like GI Jane," Tex wasn't being honest. He thought Debbie looked more like a young Sinead O'Connor and that the cut enhanced the symmetry of her face. It was the first time he'd noticed her true beauty. With his observation completed, Tex returned to business and said, speaking at pace, "The conversation with the Chief Constable was somewhere at the infinity end of the embarrassing scale." Deborah knew deep down that she shouldn't have gone to Tex with such lightweight material, and maybe Tex shouldn't have listened to her.

"Your persistence is to be admired Debbie and now here you are, at it again." Like an excited terrier, she went straight for his trouser leg.

"Tex, I've been doing some more research, and I just can't shake Karl Jackson out of my head. He used to be the Science Editor of the Longhampton College newsletter,"

Tex held his hand up. "Let me guess. At the Chronicle, you have a globally linked access widget to all of the universe's registered college newsletters." Even Tex was surprised by the thickness of his sarcasm, and as soon as he spoke, he regretted it. "Sorry Debbie, I apologise, that was flippant and rude. What have you got?"

Debbie accepted a cup of coffee, and they both picked a chocolate biscuit off a plate, but neither spoke. There was a short, who speaks next, kind of silence, and by the time Tex next drew breath the chocolate had melted onto his fingers.

"We do have access to all kinds of print sources, Tex, but I was locked out of this system. If you want to look at it you'll have to find a way to get into it yourself. And yes, it was a college newsletter, or quarterly to be precise. All I could see was the feature's title. The article was called "An Evil Way to Die - The Enthusiasts Guide to a Toxic Death" by Karl Jackson (Science Editor). The subtext underneath read, 'The Longhampton guide to the deadliest poisons on the planet'... It's toxins again, Tex, and yes, I know he was studying chemistry, but it looks like an obsession. Anyway, I'm not giving up. It's up to you if you want to try to get into the system and read it."

Debbie had by now calmed down from her unchained typhoon mode to a much more restrained version. Debbie didn't know it, but this was what Tex really loved to do. Beaver into the soft corners of a potential suspect's life, because you never know what would turn up. Everyone had a history, and if you were a killer you might drop a hint or two somewhere along the line. If you knew what you were looking for you could find indications of character or mindset and maybe signs of a disturbance in personality. Tex sat still for a moment and Debbie watched him drift into an almost catatonic state. His eyes appeared to be fixed on a spot on the lounge curtains. He remembered the hard yards he'd walked in the past and the lessons he had learned. Tex repeated those learnings out loud without removing his gaze from the thermally lined peacock blue drapes. He had a rapt audience of one.

"Psychopaths usually flash their hazard lights early. Harming animals, for example. Let's take arson in childhood. Setting gorse ablaze, even on a reasonably regular basis, doesn't make anyone a certifiable lunatic, but it should probably warrant some time in a Young Offenders Centre. But then it doesn't guarantee that the culprit will turn into a career criminal either. If the gorse fire habit escalates into something more extreme, like the burning down of warehouses, then it's worth taking note. This kind of thing can quickly become a hobby for a burgeoning psychopath."

Debbie listened open-mouthed and wide-eyed. Still looking into the mid-distance, Tex said, "You were there, Debbie. That night at the Robert Peel lecture. The question Karl Jackson asked; do you remember the content of it? That stuff he brought up about the hunter and the hunted. If Karl is a serial killer, what nerve to go to the lecture in the first place and, I suppose, even more of a nerve to ask a question. But then psychopathic types specialise in nerve, amongst other things. Was Jackson baiting me, Debbie?"

Tex turned from the apparently hypnotic fascination of the drapes and looked at Debbie. By now, she too was a victim of the curse of the melting chocolate. "Maybe, Tex, maybe."

CHAPTER THIRTY-SIX

When Debbie left, Tex sat back in his old armchair, looked at the ceiling, and pondered the future. He knew it was time to do some serious thinking and maybe break some rules.

Sometimes it was the only way to get results. Tex knew that home life had not been good for the Jackson boys. The formative years of the troubled early adulthood were rich pastures for a fertile mind. If that mind happened to belong to someone with an antisocial personality disorder, then it was a good idea to stay on full alert.

Tex got up and poured himself a Bushmills, threw in a few ice cubes, and rattled them with a swirl as he thought. *"I'll have to do some ducking and diving. This is a dangerous play, and it could end with Bracewell first flogging me and then dragging me naked behind a police horse through the lanes and byways of Cumbria."*

Tex was, of course, temporarily banned from using the police computer to access case files. Yes, he was allowed to build his lectures on it via the cadet training school application on the desktop, but nothing more. Tex found it incredibly frustrating using the keys on the computer for cadet training, while knowing he was a slippery finger or two away from sourcing the more interesting side of 'Big Blue'. That's what the coppers called the force's computer network. Tex still had his access code, and Debbie couldn't get past a security lock on the college's own files. Tex thought this particular lock was what they called a 'soft block', probably a low-level General Data Protection Regulation filter. For perfectly viable reasons, like data breaches and ransoms from hackers, educational facilities and many other bodies put these blocks in place. Tex's slippery fingers twitched.

For Tex, with his little code, it wouldn't be a problem so with a, "Fuck it, it's too late now" exhalation, Tex found those digits working as if by magic, and soon, Bingo! Tex went to the Longhampton College website. On the right-hand side was a section that included information about the newsletter. Every front page was there, going back decades and hundreds of articles. Fortunately, the contributors were listed alphabetically. Tex scrolled through to the science section and a number of 'Longhampton Life' feature pieces penned by Karl Jackson. He was listed as the Science Editor and Tex could open several of Jackson's features, but they seemed full of harmless enough student content.

There was one on the college's version of 'Robot Wars' and Karl's involvement. Karl had developed an effective machine and his hand-built 'Doomsday Destroyer' had lost narrowly in the final. There was a photograph of Karl holding something aloft. It looked to Tex like a mass of twisted metal and the caption said it was the runner-up trophy. And there was that smile that Debbie had said would make a career heterosexual think twice.

Tex rolled his finger over the mouse and found the article Debbie had told him about, but he couldn't open it because it appeared at least one level up from a soft block. Tex smiled, "Time to deploy 'Hacker Sacker'. That was the nickname of the badass software the force used to get past more difficult opponents. The police version of Robot Wars and Tex was in.

As Debbie had said, the piece was titled, 'An Evil Way To Die'. To be honest it looked like some more fairly standard student fare. They do like to be shock jocks, after all. Mischievous science students wrote stuff like this all the time, but Deacon reckoned that the nature of the feature was weighted with more ominous tones. Deacon read the article several times, carefully ingesting the content. He thought he was supposed to find bits of it funny, but Tex didn't laugh once:

'An Evil Way To Die - The Enthusiasts' Guide to a Toxic Death' by Karl Jackson

Paracelsus (Swiss Physician and Alchemist) 1493 - 1541 "All things are poison, and nothing is without poison: the dose alone makes a thing poison."

Do you remember Rosa Klebb from the James Bond movie, "From Russia With Love"? Lotta Lenya played the role of a high-ranking Colonel from Russian Intelligence. Klebb, Number 3 in SPECTRE, was the assassin who used a knife in her shoe in an attempt to kill Bond. The poison on the tip of her "Brogue Blade" was tetrodotoxin. Bond doesn't die. He blocks the attack with a chair. What a pity. I liked Klebb.

Tetrodotoxin: A substance you can source in various places. For example, in the Blue Ringed Octopus which changes colour in spectacular fashion when threatened. It bites (I didn't know octopus had teeth!), and an adult carries enough venom to kill up to twenty-five people.

Tetrodotoxin exists in nearly every organ and gland in the body of the octopus. Surely that would make sex deadly? Tetrodotoxin can also be found in certain species of Brazilian frogs and the Puffer Fish.

Approximately 50 Japanese natives die each year after eating what appears to be a nice harmless fillet. The Puffer fish is a delicacy in the Far East, but you have to be careful who's doing your cooking. Make sure it isn't Ms Klebb! You need to know what you're doing, as a small piece of this fish can kill you if it's not prepared in the right way. Tetrodotoxin is one of the most poisonous toxins on earth. Eat this fish, and you'll have your chips!

Batrachotoxin: This comes from the skin of the aptly named Golden Poison Frog. Native Indians collect them in Western Columbia. The frog is tethered over a fire and the poison sweats out. Humans call it a sun bed. The average frog carries enough of the toxin to kill two Bull Elephants. The Indians then use the toxin in their darts. So be afraid if you're on holiday in Columbia and you feel a sharp pain in your buttock. Heart failure is minutes away.

VX: This is a nerve agent and is, perhaps, in terms of effectiveness, one of the top three toxins in the world. It interrupts nerve messages. Muscles contract wildly, and victims die from asphyxiation. VX was made by both sides during the Cold War and featured in the Hollywood movie, "The Rock" which starred Sean Connery, Nicola Cage, and Ed Harris. A group of rogue marines threaten to launch rockets filled with VX nerve gas over San Francisco.

Cage plays an FBI Chemist. VX has a sense of humour! The nerve agent was once accidentally sprayed in Utah in the USA and was responsible for the death of 4,000 sheep. BAAAAD luck. See what I did there?

Ricin: This was used to kill Bulgarian dissident Georgi Markov. In September 1978, he was patiently waiting for a bus at Waterloo Bridge in London when he felt something being jabbed into the back of his thigh. Markov spun around to find a man bending down to pick up an umbrella. He'd been shot with a tiny platinum-iridium alloy sphere. This sphere had been drilled, and inside was enough ricin to kill him. The evidence suggested that a micro air gun had been concealed in the brolly. You could see Rosa Klebb using this method on a wet day! Ricin has also been sent by mail to several US politicians, including President Barack Obama.

Ricin comes from the seeds of the castor oil plant. One or two seeds hold enough ricin to kill a child, and the ricin in eight seeds is enough to kill an adult. The actual castor oil is an excellent moisturiser, anti-inflammatory and laxative. If you saw a tipped umbrella coming your way, you wouldn't need a laxative. A castor oil plant's danger is in the seed extract. A glycoprotein from that source interferes with protein synthesis and causes cell death.

Amongst poisons, ricin might be the gold standard. Your nervous system fails and you die in extreme pain. If you're in a garden centre and you see a madman carrying a castor oil plant...run!

Deacon was mesmerised by what he was reading and disturbed by Jackson's heavily salted sense of humour, "*Bloody hell, this is a killer's compendium for murder. If you were deranged enough and knew how to handle these poisons, you could cause chaos. All you need is a demented chemist.*" The article continued:

Saxitoxin: Another poison from the sea. It comes from shellfish, which live in the same ecoculture as a particular species of algae blooms. Another similar toxin is Maitotoxin. This comes from a type of marine plankton. It rapidly increases the flow of calcium ions, and you have a fatal cardiac arrest. I once heard Sir David Attenborough talking about "the heart-stopping beauty of the ocean", but I don't think he meant that!

Botulinum: Many scientists believe that this is the most toxic substance known to man. One nanogram per kilogramme can kill a human being. It was first found in 18th-century Bavaria in a poorly cooked sausage. The motto is beware German barbecues! At the lethal dose, Botulinum causes the fatal locking of muscle. At a clinical level, a much lower dose is used in beauty salons in Botox injections, which does the same kind of thing as the death dose but obviously doesn't kill you. It just flattens out your wrinkly skin. Take too much, and you can be paralysed by vanity.

Amatoxin: From the death cap family of mushrooms. Destroys your liver and kidneys. This can take days. You remain conscious and in excruciating pain. This one is for someone you really don't like.

Anthrax: Deadly when inhaled. A popular biological weapon. It feels like the flu at the start, and your respiratory system collapses.

Sarin: A viciously effective nerve gas. Hundreds of times more toxic than cyanide. Foaming at the mouth is one of the more unpleasant symptoms. Sarin was banned as a war agent in 1997. Famously used in 1995 on the Tokyo subway by the Aum Shinrikyo cult. This spiritual group left punctured bags full of nerve agent on central train lines. Thirteen people were killed, and thousands were injured. The leader of the group, the charismatic Asahara, was caught and executed. ZanNen Na, as they say. (Japanese for "Too bad")

Cyanide: Present in nature and can be easily manufactured. This is your friend if you fancy seizures, cardiac arrest and death within minutes.

Strychnine: There are more toxic poisons. You need the right dose. Used as a pesticide. This is a poison with style! Causes a horrific death. Every muscle in your body spasms violently until you die from exhaustion. What a jolly way to go!

Rosary Pea: I wanted to get this one in so you could enjoy a one to one with The Holy Spirit. The humble Rosary Pea. Yes you've guessed it. They are used in rosary beads but rub them and pray. Don't eat them. Chew just one of these peas and you will definitely get your audience with God. It acts a bit like ricin and causes organ failure.

I hope you've enjoyed this cut-out and keep guide to some of the best toxins known to man. They can be useful in an emergency, but don't tell anyone I told you, right?

by KARL JACKSON, SCIENCE EDITOR.

Tex placed his right index finger beneath his nose, gently rubbed his top lip, and, simultaneously, shook his head. As was his habit, he muffled the words out loud, "The boy was obsessed. Debbie's right. He loves his poisons. The more grisly the outcome, the more he likes them." Tex was getting a lot closer to Debbie's wavelength now, sixth senses intertwined. Maybe, on occasion, hunches were good after all.

While he was on 'Big Blue', and the office was quiet, Tex worked his way through any more information on Karl Jackson that he could find. The public really did have no idea how much information was stored on almost every member of society. It was very Big Brother; and Tex was sniffing for hints of the demonic in Jackson.

There were records of reasonably successful schooldays, through school reports, and a note on a short early teenage stint in the army cadets. As a standalone Jackson's time with the cadets didn't look that interesting, but if you looked at the shadows between the lines, the hints were there. There was a brief interview at the outset, and Jackson had done well. He came across as charismatic and capable. One of the officers in attendance had actually written, "Possible long-term leadership material." Jackson had filled in a form at the end of his stint with the cadets, and it read well, but there was definitely a positive spin.

As Karl had written in the 'Additional Notes' section, "It was an enjoyable and successful six months. I really appreciated the chance to learn more field craft, navigation skills and first aid. The adventure training was gruelling but a lot of fun. I felt I showed aptitude when it came to making decisions under pressure and planning and organising tasks. I worked effectively as a team player. We took part in kayaking, abseiling and mountain biking challenges in the mountains. It was a proud moment for me when I was awarded my Army Proficiency Certificate at the passing out parade."

Positive spin indeed. The truth was a little different. Tex Deacon cross-checked all of the details with cadet records. Karl had struggled to get past the basic physical but they let him in; however, he wasn't there for long. Karl had been ejected within the first fortnight for "Insubordination towards a superior". It appeared that Jackson had

---

forged his report. In the main, the 'Additional Notes' segment had been cut and pasted from comments from other candidates on the Army Cadets official website. Though to be fair, if he was a multiple killer, Karl Jackson actually was very good when it came to "Making decisions under pressure and planning and organising tasks".

Tex chased up Debbie's info about the gap year. He reckoned that Karl had been chastened by his failure with the cadets and wanted time out. Tex requested and received details of Karl's successful visa application from Australian Immigration. The Assistant Chief Customs Officer told Tex he would check the records and get back to him if anything interesting came up. Tex was sure that all he'd get from Australian Customs, or their police for that matter, was confirmation of an accident involving Carlos Ferreira, and that's exactly what came back. He kept digging and found that Jackson had come home and completed his tertiary education. Karl was not a star student, but he always seemed to do just enough to work his way through.

Tex surmised that Karl must have been a very impressive teacher to have made it to Head of Department, or maybe he just used lashings of charm. Karl had plenty of that. Tex logged off, sat back from the computer, tilted his head back and talked to the ceiling. "Karl Jackson has been very smart so far with no obvious signs of a slip-up. But today, we have made a little progress."

CHAPTER THIRTY-SEVEN

Richard and Patricia had conducted a mostly successful and private affair. The only person who suspected a thing was Karl, who now had all the information he needed. Patricia also knew only too well that Karl was the one man in particular from whom the adulterous couple needed to hide their secret.

Initially, Richard's death was extremely difficult for Patricia to deal with. Karl, on the other hand, was seething over his wife's disloyalty, while simultaneously feeling an orgasmic delight at the success of his covert mission to the lover's hotel. At the Jacksons' house Karl had a wonderful time inflicting slow torture on his wife. Karl wanted his silently and stoically grieving wife to hurt as much as possible. He wasn't sure if the current suffering would be the only penance for Patricia, or if he would take additional remedial action. In the meantime, psychological torture would do.

"Awful news about Richard Turkington," Karl feigned, leaning against the kitchen worktop, "That Turkington fella, never liked the guy, something very sleazy about him. Fat insignificant kind of bloke, you know, weak personality. Extravagant, arrogant, wallowed in his own self-importance. I wonder where all the money came from? Pensions? Unlikely. What was he up to? Maybe that's why he's dead? Do you think he was murdered? Crossed the line somewhere with the wrong sort. Probably deserved it. Bit of an arsehole, wasn't he?"

Patrica had her back to Karl, yellow gloves retrieving plates from the bubbles. She was doing her best to bind her emotions, "Stop being so unkind, Karl, the man is dead, and he was okay. At least he socialised, unlike you." Patricia's eyes were moist, and a lip quivered but she made sure she stayed facing the window. Too many words and her voice might have cracked. She felt she could publicly show concern following the death of her lover, but not too much anguish. A certain level of mourning was fine. After all, she knew Richard through Samantha, and the fell running world, but the truth and depth of her despair gnawed at her, causing relentless pain. Patricia had fallen in love with Richard. Karl stayed physically very close to his wife through all this, knowing very well that she was trapping a vast range of emotions inside. He wanted to savour Patricia's pain as she was forced to bottle her true feelings. Patricia was exploding inside. She had been planning on leaving Karl and Richard had been shuffling funds into an offshore account. For many months, the two lovers had been scheming about a life elsewhere.

Karl moved closer, put a hand on his wife's shoulder and spun her round - the bubbles from her rubber gloves threw a spatter pattern across Karl's shirt. Karl stared into eyes that were a mist of pain, the laser effect felt like physical force to Patricia and she instinctively recoiled. "You were friendly with Richard, weren't you? I noticed how relaxed you looked in his company at the awards night. I mean, if you want to talk about his death, that's fine, I'm here for you, I can be compassionate, and it's such a tragedy for Samantha too. I'm not an animal, Patricia, I have emotions."

By this stage, due to his far too smug manner, Patricia was suspecting that Karl knew a little more than he was giving away. Inside she was in complete turmoil. Had Karl discovered the affair? If so, was she now in danger? Patricia had long feared Karl's potential, and she'd heard that phrase "I'm not an animal" many times before, usually before a seismic outburst. Patricia knew she had to play the game and assume that Karl didn't know the truth. "I'm fine, Karl. It's just such a shock. Not just for me but for everyone around here. So many people were close to Richard and Samantha. The fell running scene is such a small community. I mean, it's a tragedy." Patricia's true feelings were being held in her very own panic room.

For several years, Karl's treatment of Patricia had been appalling. He had never hit her but the mental torment Karl put her through was coercive. He lied to Patricia regularly, while demanding full and detailed explanations of Patricia's every movement. Patricia felt all-consuming claustrophobia and whatever was left of the relationship crumbled a little more with every passing day. Patricia, obviously, didn't know that Karl had bugged Richard's phone, but if she'd found out it wouldn't have come as a surprise. Karl lashed out verbally in the house, screaming at Patricia if she made the smallest mistake, like arriving home from work five minutes late or presenting a slightly tepid meal. Karl wasn't too happy if the bathroom towels were marginally out of alignment.

"For Christ's sake try and make life bearable for me," was Karl's common cry. It hadn't always been this way. When Karl was wooing Patricia, the other half of the narcissist came out to play and he smothered her with love and gifts. Within a few weeks of meeting his soon-to-be wife, Karl had announced to her that they were soul mates. The love bombing phase.

Patricia thought that the relationship was developing too fast but, like a raft on white water, she was carried away. "I've met my other half, " Karl had whispered those words to Patricia in the second week of their courtship. Karl devoured Patricia in a very unhealthy way, but she had never received attention like this. Patricia didn't see the red flags because she didn't want to. Patricia ignored her intuition. If only she'd listened to her inner angel. The initial phase was intense, and they soon became a young married couple. Patricia was nineteen, and Karl was twenty. Kerry was born within a year of the wedding day.

Patricia's personality was very close to being the polar opposite of Karl's. She was a marvellously empathetic woman with an athletic figure, blonde hair and Icelandic blue eyes. She had a soft nature and a subtle sense of humour. Patricia was the girl that all the other girls came to in a crisis. She always seemed to understand the pain of others and pick appropriate soothing words.

At the outset, when Patricia said she wanted to meet his friends, Karl deflected, "Oh darling, there's plenty of time for that. For now, I just want one on one time with you. I can't believe how lucky I am to have met a woman like you. Patricia, this was meant to be. You're a diamond, I'm a diamond, and we can shine together." Karl, of course, couldn't hear the crassness of lines that he thought were high-quality romantic poetry, but neither could Patricia, who had been hooked into an abusive future.

During the rare times they were in company, Patricia seemed to be spending far too much time defending his behaviours. He was forever trying to outsmart her tight group of friends to prove his intellectual superiority. Patricia, pre-Karl, had a vibrant social life and a network of confidantes. But Karl started to weaken the bridges between her and her friends in a premeditated process of isolation. Karl verbalised his brainwashing, demeaning and gaslighting tactics:

"That friend of yours, Andrea, I've heard she says many negative things about you behind your back."

"I know you're training hard, but do you think you've put a few pounds on your hips? Maybe you should back off the chocolate. You're addicted to it, aren't you?"

"Why did you put my car keys in the bedroom? I definitely left them on the hall table. Stop moving my things around. Do you even know you're doing it?"

"As usual Patricia you are overreacting, you do this all the time, the smallest thing and you're off. I'm doing my best for the family here. Ease off."

"Everyone agrees with me. You've changed Patricia. Something's wrong. Is it paranoia or depression? Maybe something else. I think you should see your doctor."

"You've always been a little off the wall, a little crazy. It was one of the things that attracted me to you, but lately you've gone off the scale. I can never predict your behaviour, which puts a lot of pressure on Kerry and me."

Patricia became convinced that the relationship was dissolving because of her and wondered if she was good enough for him. Karl slowly and insidiously wore Patricia down. The blame game intensified and, thoroughly confused, Patricia began to second guess her every move. Before long, all of her decisions were made with Karl's potential reaction in mind. The marriage was a tsunami of subterfuge and Patricia felt like she was in a strait-jacket. Over the years Patricia developed a serious codeine addiction, as it was the only way she could dull the emotional pain. By this stage, Patricia didn't care about her husband's increasing absences and the pathetic porous excuses he made. This was probably why Patricia began to drift towards Richard. Patricia wasn't initially attracted to him, but she noticed a compassionate side that was wholly absent in her husband. Now, with Richard dead, Patricia was in a terrifying emotional limbo.

Karl's kills were like a magnesium flame. He'd lit so many in the chemistry labs of the school to show off to his students. A powerful ignition, intense heat and bright light followed by a cooling-off period. To Karl, killing Richard was like wiping up a toxic spill. Karl loved the line from Michael Corleone in 'The Godfather', "It's not personal, it's strictly business."

Karl knew he was taking a big, if calculated risk when he murdered Turkington. He knew that the autopsy would most likely reveal the presence of ricin. There are several ways to detect the toxin. By testing for clinical specimens in body fluids. Some laboratories, with particularly sensitive equipment, can pick it up in urine samples. A week after the discovery of Richard Turkington's body the result of the autopsy came through. There had been ricin in his system and it was a possible cause of death although, according to the pathologist it could have been a cardiac arrest that actually finished him. Turkington had blockages in two of the main arteries in his heart.

The body was found in a very remote spot many miles from the nearest road. Initial inspections of the scene failed to uncover any supplementary forensic evidence. Karl was sure that there was no one smart enough to be able to unravel the mystery.

Karl had been drawn to the ricin poisoning idea from the famous 'Umbrella Murder' of Georgi Markov. Great invention, perfect result, and no one got caught. In the Markov case, the ricin had apparently been injected into his thigh via a pinhead sized drilled pellet in a modified brolly. They never found the Bulgarian's murderer. Closer to home, the launch of a man hunt for Turkington's murderer was guaranteed, and Karl's job now was to remain outside the bubble of suspicion. The fact that Richard and Patricia had managed to keep their relationship vacuum sealed could play to Karl's advantage.

Apart from him, not one other soul had concrete evidence. Patricia could of course reveal the affair to the police and implicate him but Karl had considered that. The evidence would be circumstantial, with nothing to link him directly to the crime. He was banking on his own dexterity, average police work and his very good friend-luck. Karl reckoned that this kill would probably make him a suspect eventually, but he was still confident that he'd be able to negotiate any hurdles. Karl had a clear view of the various problems on the horizon.

"I know her too well. Patricia will surely suspect me of some form of involvement. What's she thinking? Did I hire a contract killer? Do it myself? Her head will be burning with it all, but I'll be able to deal with anything when the time comes. At the very least, I might have to threaten her to keep her quiet or, if she doesn't play ball, make it clear to Patricia that she'll face the same fate as "Dastardly Dick".

On the day of the murder, Karl had flown the drone back to his nearby tent and diligently dismantled it. He hiked to the body and, wearing latex gloves, carefully removed the tracker from the bottom of the rucksack. Karl had disposed of all evidence with great care. The metalwork, including the camera, had ended up in the jaws of a car crusher. The syringe pump and the camping equipment had been burned at the top end of a forest fifteen miles from the murder site. Karl was confident that he'd covered the critical bases and was sure that he could sail the potential of an incoming storm.

CHAPTER THIRTY-EIGHT

There'd been a soggy conclusion, in more ways than one, the last time Tex had been to see his Chief Constable. Bracewell had been unmoved by his batch of unconvincing information pointing up his suspicion about Karl Jackson - the man who wouldn't go away. From Barbara Bracewell's perspective, Tex Deacon wouldn't go away either, but here they were again.

"At least you're dry this time Tex. How was the pneumonia? Course of antibiotics?" Bracewell and Deacon had always enjoyed their gentle sparring. The Chief Constable had been thinking a little more deeply about Tex's immediate future since he'd last appeared at her office. The day when he looked like a washed-up haddock.

"You know something Tex, it's probably better to give you a proper police job to do, just to end these regular pleadings in my office. To be fair, the reports back from the training college on your fledgling teaching skills have been impeccable. Tex... the grief? Elsewhere in the report the experts say you're still a long way from processing Susan's death, but then maybe you never will, which, I think, is understandable." Bracewell inhaled a huge puff of air that reminded Tex of the last actions of a pole vaulter before a run-up, and then she spoke again. "I've looked closely at that folder you have on Karl Jackson. If you could get a conviction based on workload your man would probably get the electric chair. But unfortunately, paper mountains don't win cases. There's nothing of massive evidential importance in there, but you are beginning to paint a picture."

The Chief Constable had made up her mind, and she was short and pointed in classic Bracewell fashion. "Tex, there's a fresh case that I want you to look at. I'm integrating you into it, but you won't lead it. You'll be part of the team so I can ease you back in, which will give me a chance to keep a close eye on progress. In my opinion, it's the best way forward." Tex could feel excitement tingle in his guts when Bracewell broke the news, and then anxiety. He had quite enjoyed the covert approach while working as Deborah Pilkington's hard-boiled wingman. There was much less direct pressure, but now he was being edged closer to the front line. Mentally, would he be able to handle it? He wasn't sure.

CHAPTER THIRTY-NINE

Tex, of course, already knew all about the Richard Turkington case, as it was the talk of the county and Tex was about to be placed in its crosshairs. When the Chief Constable confirmed it Tex was both delirious and horrified. He couldn't wait to immerse himself in his favourite subject - murder. At the same time, the demons on his shoulder were telling him that he wouldn't be able to cope. Bracewell had shown incredible, if slightly unjustified faith but she and Tex went back a long way and a lot of trust had been built. Tex, officially, went to work. At the moment all the investigating team had was a dead body and the ricin. Murder? The chances were very high indeed. After all it was hard to see how the presence of ricin could be accidental or self-inflicted. Any leads apart from what was found at the scene? No.

Tex contacted Debbie, "I'm out of mothballs. Nervous and excited, and it's the Turkington case. I'm on the team but not leading it. Thanks for all the input and enthusiasm so far." Debbie's response of, "Bloody Hell, really? That's Mother fuckin' great news Texy boy," caught Tex by surprise, but then a deficit of enthusiasm wasn't part of the Pilkington gene pool. "Can we meet?" said Tex, "Somewhere close and very soon."

Half an hour later, the unlikely duo were sitting against the back wall of a deserted cafe that had grease on everything, including the salt cellar. The inside of the un-imaginatively named 'High Street Halt' was permanently submerged in the smell of fried food. The coffee looked like a liquid cow pat and didn't taste much better. "Debbie, I'm already thinking of Karl Jackson as a possible suspect, a person of interest." Debbie sipped carelessly, causing a mild singe to her bottom lip. "Because of what I told you about him? Have I unleashed the tiger?" There was a twinkle, Tex thought he sensed a hint of flirtation but quickly dismissed it.

"Yes Debbie, that was the start of it. You've been fantastic, laid the bedrock and my detective juices might have evaporated completely without you. Now - the Turkington case - we have Jackson's favourite things here, namely the mountains and a toxin. Combine those with Karl, and the smell of death often follows. That's a paraphrase of one of your quotes, isn't it?"

The police had leaked bits and pieces of information from the Turkington case into the public domain to accelerate the pace of their inquiry. Flyers had been posted in the locale and on them was a hotline number to phone for anyone who had spotted suspicious activity or seen Turkington, or anyone else in the vicinity of the murder site.

After another door knock from Tex, "Honestly, Barbara, this will be the last time," the Chief Constable bent a little further and agreed to Tex's request to be allowed to do the initial interviews. Barbara knew Tex's trusted investigation formula, which always started with the family. That's how he had nailed the Black Bridge Lodge Assassin.

Tex began to chisel into the background of Richard Turkington and started with the heartbroken wife, Samantha. Tex drove up the winding drive to Turkington's palatial residence, which was nestled in the mountain foothills. Gothic turrets enhanced the incongruous look on the gates and at each corner of the swimming pool. The garage could have doubled as a hangar for light aeroplanes. Samantha opened the front door to Tex's rap. Her heavily made-up eyes were damp and smudged with mascara.

"The last time I saw Richard was at breakfast on Thursday morning," Samantha sobbed, the tears softening the tissues she used to mop up the sliding morass of make-up.

"He was going for a two-day camping trip. Richard was in good form and excited to get away to the mountains for some solitary respite. He loved camping on his own, and Richard needed some peace and quiet. He'd been so busy and had just returned from a business trip to Africa." Tex watched Samantha closely. Her grief seemed genuine, but she was still a suspect at this stage. No one had been ruled out.

Tex pushed his face forward like a man placing his head into a guillotine's slot, "Was your husband having an affair?" Samantha looked shocked, "An affair? Good God no." She flapped away the suggestion with insouciant flamboyance, "Richard didn't like sex."

The house was a little too 'bling' for Deacon's tastes, with an ostentatious crystal chandelier hanging in a hallway wide enough for a game of tennis. The staircase looked like it had been plucked straight from the Titanic. The bannisters were gaudy and Samantha proudly proclaimed that the colour was 'Crushed Peruvian Gold'. Tex thought that the lampshades might have been made of pure silk. Richard and Samantha hadn't spared on the interior design and this alerted Deacon right away. He didn't think that Turkingtons declared income would be able to fund a house like this. The Lamborghini was one of four vehicles. The Turkington's were well known for their fancy Caribbean breaks, and Samantha was usually found flouncing around in the latest designer outfits. Her sparkling diamond jewellery simply hardened Tex's concerns. He fired up a number of subsidiary teams, including one from the financial fraud department. Had Turkington made any excess money illegally?

Tex scanned the expanse of what was one of several drawing rooms. "Samantha, are you certain that this all came from a career selling pension funds? We are trained to be suspicious, and, yes, all of his income could well have been above board, but we'd like to do a deep clean just to be sure."

Samantha didn't appear to be too happy but she reluctantly agreed to a specific search. Turkington might have been clean but Tex was taking no chances. The Russians used ricin and at this point Tex had no idea what Turkington had been up to. He suspected Turkington would have used burner phones for any ad hoc criminal contact but chances were he'd have secreted some information elsewhere. In particular Tex wanted to have a look at any computers in the house and officers conducted a thorough hunt while Samantha fussed about. She was very concerned about any damage they might do to the ivory shag pile. One of the search team brought Tex to an office that was smaller than any of the five bathrooms in the house. "Boss. We've found this trunk. It was double padlocked." Tex bent down and looked into a tiny, built-in triangular cupboard which nestled below a small purpose-built mezzanine. "What have we got?" said Tex. The officer replied, "Two computers inside the trunk, Boss."

It took the team three days to wade through the hard drives. As Tex mused with a smile, the contents were revealing and probably explained how Samantha could afford the silk lampshades. Turkington, as a businessman, had become embroiled in something a little more exotic than pension funds. The evidence was damning, and Richard hadn't done much to hide it, except to lock the trunk. Dodgy Richard Turkington was up to his gunnels in money laundering. There were two memory sticks stacked with incriminating information and details of a Cayman Islands bank account. They were all linked to a source in Nigeria and Turkington's flight ticket stubs confirmed that Nigeria had been his recent African destination.

After several weeks of thorough enquiry and good old-fashioned dogged police work, Tex and the rest of the team had all they needed. Turkington had been entangled in an intricate 'Nigerian Prince' scam and a follow up 'Phantom Lawyer' scam. His job had been to clean the cash, which he had done through hundreds of false pension funds. There were also dozens of children's ISA's set up in the names of kids who had never been born. Turkington, and his accomplices, had often conned the same person twice. The African gang had probably made millions, with Turkington taking a significant cut. His lodgements were located in the bank in the Cayman Islands.

Nigerian Prince or 'foreign money exchange' scams start with an email from supposed 'Royalty'. The fraudsters lure you in by offering a share of a huge investment opportunity or a fortune they can't get out of the country without your help. Then they ask you either for your bank account number, so they can transfer the money to you for safekeeping or for a small advance payment to help cover expenses. According to social psychologists, these scams are so effective because they present victims with a 'perfect storm of temptations'. These scams feed on people's greed. The scammers are also good at luring victims into a supposed personal relationship before the sting occurs, building a sense of trust. Nigerian Prince scams sit alongside Ponzi and Pyramid schemes as the most successful of their type.

Richard Turkington would also chase victims of the 'Nigerian Prince' scams while pretending to be a lawyer who could help them get their money back. How cruel was that? A double sting. A 'Scum Scam' as Tex referred to it. It turned out that Turkington had actually made phone calls in person to victims using his burner phones. Tex wasn't impressed with the character of this so-called reputable citizen.

"A despicable slimy individual. I wonder, had he upset his African contacts? It looks highly probable." Because of the ricin, Tex was also thinking Karl Jackson, but maybe this was just another red herring swimming around inside his head. Turkington wouldn't be the first man to be murdered for betraying criminal gangs. Tex knew that falling out with these often vicious and vengeful people wasn't a pathway to a long and happy health. Proving that Turkington had been killed by an operative hired by one of these gangs would be tough to nail down.

However, the use of ricin fitted the profile. It had been used before in Nigerian Prince scams when money had been syphoned away. The hit man theory would also explain the cleanliness of the murder scene, which was often part of the raison d'être of these professional assassins. Tex felt he was on the right route to solving the case. As far as he was concerned it was all knitting nicely together.

Rumours about the direction of the investigation were soon leaking around the area. The news that ricin had killed Turkington was already out there, but now stories of scams and contract killers were echoing around Cumbria and beyond. On top of all that, there was also the chitter-chatter about an affair, and the names of several local women were whispered by the rumour mongers. A mountain wildfire of gossip had broken out but Tex still had an itch and that itch was Karl Jackson. He knew that if he didn't scratch it, Debbie most certainly would.

CHAPTER FORTY

Debbie sat on her bed, a variety of limbs sticking out from under the duvet as an antidote to the sticky air that fluttered at the curtains. She'd had another night of patchy sleep, partly due to the humidity and partly due to the dogfight of emotions that were now a constant partner. The murders and the murderer, Debbie thought of nothing else. She rested against the mauve pillows, hands clasped around a mug, and watched the steam rise from her second turbo fuelled coffee. The sun was climbing from its overnight resting place, a million shafts of light glinting above the horizon. Almost as many questions, answers, theories and philosophies ran through Debbie's head like rabid rats. Her mobile rang. It was the now familiar 'seashore' tingle that she'd allocated to Tex's number. "Tex, yes, yes, what is it?" Debbie had splashed coffee on the sheets in her mad grasp for the phone. "Hi Debbie. Look sorry, I know it's early but..." The line crackled and broke up. "Tex, Tex, shit it's a crap line. Are you there?"

"Debbie, yep, bad reception here. I'm on the road. I'll be at yours in twenty minutes to pick you up. We're going to the murder scene. We'll be hiking out. Wear boots."

Debbie threw a cascade of clothes onto the floor. She hadn't been into the mountains for a long time, but she found enough appropriate clothing to do the job. She dressed in a frenzy and fell over once while hopping in an attempt to put on a sock. She was waiting on the kerbside, fresh coffee in her flask and a croissant in her hand, when Tex drove round the corner. Debbie couldn't remember ever being as excited as she was now, "A murder scene? Me?"

Bonnie and Clyde reviewed the case, as they knew it, during the drive and, amongst many other aspects, talked about the rumours of an affair. Debbie was hyper knowing it wasn't a cool look in front of the DCI, but she couldn't help it.

"A married woman, that's what our source said. It's all the talk at the Chronicle. An anonymous call that came straight through to the news desk. They're trying to find a way to use the story, even though it's just rumour. It would give us another angle, but Thorpecroft isn't having it now. He might change his mind but he says there's not enough evidence. The story only works for him if we can name Turkington's lover. Jim doesn't fancy a libel case on his hands." Tex glanced at Debbie, noticing that the words were tumbling out of her mouth much faster than usual.

"I don't know, Debbie. If that lover story makes the paper, I'm unsure if it helps us or hinders us. If he hasn't fled the country, it could flush out the killer, or it could put this lover, if she exists, in danger. If the girl is married, there's going to be a pissed-off husband knocking around somewhere, who might be dangerous too."

It was an hour's journey to the 'Lucifer's Leap' car park. "What are we looking for?" said Debbie. "I have no idea," said Tex, "But there's a good chance that something will come up. Anything that might link in with a contract killing, that's a decent starting point. Just scan, Debbie, stay focused, you'll miss clues if you're not. They're like synergies - you don't see them unless you are specifically looking out for them."

They were in the hills by nine o'clock and the morning mist had yet to burn off. Tex had an eight-figure grid reference for the spot where Turkington's body had been found. The Garmin E-Trex 10 would get them there. Tex had reckoned on a two-hour hike and even though they contoured the steeper ground it was still hard going.

Bog cotton covered huge areas of saturated ground. Tex and Debbie were well away from any worn tracks so progress was slow. They had peat hags, long tangled meadow grass, and innumerable tussocks to go up and over. Debbie was fine; relatively speaking, she was young and fit, but by the time the E-Trex displayed the relevant grid reference, Tex didn't have a dry pore on his body. Inactivity since Susan's death had taken its toll. Tex looked at the flat patch of grass, yellowed where the body had begun its process of decomposure, "Well?" said Debbie. Tex was silent. Debbie watched the experienced detective suck in every detail of the spectacular scenery, then, eventually, he spoke.

"Time of death was 'early morning'. There was no wind that day, and a major high-pressure system was in place. The weather was coming in from the sea. Perfect conditions, at this time of year, for fog. Those conditions were confirmed by locals who said there'd been morning mist every day since the high pressure got locked over England. From the autopsy, we know Turkington had inhaled ricin, but how was it delivered? It had to be done from a distance.

First, if someone had hiked in to kill Turkington, the victim would have picked up the noise of something or someone approaching. You can hear if a weasel moves on quiet open terrain, in long grass like this. Second, the killer couldn't have burst a bag of the toxin in front of him because that would have killed them both. Did he wear a mask? Breathing equipment?

Cumbersome and a mask would probably steam up. The killer, I suspect, would be far too clever to allow himself to be that close to a victim while carrying a lethal toxin. Too much could go wrong. The mist gave some sort of cover but I can't see how any killer could have done it face to face." Tex looked at Debbie, "It's Shoeshine Johnny we need." Debbie looked back with a look of perfectly sculpted confusion on her face.

"Who the hell is Shoeshine Johnny?" she said.

"Oh yeah," said Tex, "You're a bit young to know him I suppose, but you can find clips online. The old 'Police Squad' TV series with Leslie Neilson. When he couldn't crack a case, his character Detective Lieutenant Frank Dreben, would go to get his shoes polished at Johnny's streetside pitch, pay him a few dollars, and ask him. Johnny always had the crucial piece of evidence that cracked the case. Very funny and always made me laugh. We need Johnny now."

Tex's throaty rumble resembled a giggle but he was soon refocused. Debbie wasn't sure if she should speak, as Tex was clearly formulating his synopsis, but she did.

"Just for fun, let's assume Karl Jackson did it. He was Head of Technology at Rimpton Hollway as well as Chemistry. Could he have built something like a buggy?" Debbie wondered if this was the most stupid thing she had ever said and baulked as the suggestion left her lips.

"Over this ground? Some buggy. It would have had to be like a moon lander, and a silent moon lander at that," said Tex, "And there's the delivery of the poison. Technical to say the least."

Tex spread his arms and did a full and measured pirouette, "This is a remote wide open expanse. I can't see a hiding place, can you? Even if we work out the delivery method, it mightn't get us too far. The killer, or killers, would surely have destroyed whatever that device or method was."

Debbie was thinking so hard now that she was sure her temples were actually pulsating. "A drone?" Tex turned his head, "You're not short of ideas Debbie." Tex stared at the ground and then did another 360 spin. "Could have been, but to kill, it had to be a cloud of ricin around Turkington. But, a possibility, a drone. I like that."

The pair just stood there. Debbie heard a distant animal rustling past through the meadow grass. The rising humidity further dampened her skin. They found themselves saying, almost in unison, "How did the killer do it?"

More silence. "Tex, how did we get to the murder scene?" It was rhetorical, "With an eight-figure grid reference. Tex, if the killer hadn't followed Turkington, could he or she have used something like our Garmin E-Trex to locate him?"

Tex shook his head, "Not a Garmin. They don't work in that way. Great for us today - it took us to a marked spot. Excellent for that kind of thing." He folded his left index finger, put it to his mouth and bit into the flesh around the knuckle. The mild pain helped to trigger a thought. "A tracker maybe. Yes that would work but there was nothing like that on Turkington's body or amongst his equipment."

Debbie looked at Tex, "So if it was a tracker, and the ricin had somehow been delivered from a distance, the killer must have come back to get it." Tex was in tandem with his young sleuth, "Yes. Definitely. But where was it? In a pocket? No. Too easy for Turkington to accidentally find. The rucksack? That's the best bet, but this killer's kill was so clean. No DNA. He, or she, would have worn gloves."

As Tex again stared at the ground, beads of sweat gathered on his forehead, forming globules, and then plopped onto the turf, lightly colouring the yellow grass. They looked at each other, thinking the same thing. Sweat. "If we could find evidence of that," said Tex, "The victim died covered in sweat, there was lots of dried salt on his skin, clothing and equipment. If face to face, the killer would probably have walked in to remain covert. Hard to do that without sweating and if the killer had retrieved the tracker, he or she, would probably have walked in too. Perspiration - plenty of DNA in that."

Tex took in another deep pull of air, "Remember our Omerta Debbie. You can't write a word about this until I give you the say-so. And you can stop thinking about your headline right now." Debbie threw a frustrated grin back at Tex, "HEATWAVE COULD PROVIDE CRUCIAL CLUE IN RICIN MYSTERY - that sort of thing, Tex?"

"Yes, Debbie, that sort of thing. Not one word in your paper about any of this. Not yet." Tex couldn't have been crueller if he'd strapped an alcoholic to a bed and dripped whiskey on his belly. Inside Debbie, every strand of DNA was screaming the words "Print Or Be Damned!" but she fully understood that the wrong leak at this critical stage might compromise the whole investigation.

CHAPTER FORTY-ONE

Karl, yet again, couldn't believe his good fortune. He didn't think he was merely lucky, he was sure he was blessed by the Almighty himself . Karl knew that, once more, he could get away with murder; all he had to do now was keep Patricia quiet. His wife, emotionally speaking, was on the very cusp of snapping. She had been grieving for the man she was preparing to break up her marriage for. That in itself was enough to drive her close to a breakdown. Now the pain had intensified, and, due to his crueller than normal behaviour, she suspected that her husband knew about the affair.

How could Patricia cope with the dramatic revelation that Richard Turkington, a relentless and ruthless scammer and money launderer, may have been murdered by a contract killer? Or was it her husband? Psychologically Patricia found herself spiralling. Yet again, she had fallen in love with an illusion, and Patricia was totally exposed and vulnerable. All she wanted to do was curl up and scream. She decided to take a firm grip on the situation or as firm as she could manage in the circumstances. She had to talk to someone, but there was only one person Patricia felt she could confide in; her son Kerry. On trembling legs, Patricia climbed the stairs to his bedroom. There was a cursory knock, and Kerry spun round on the stool at his computer and watched his Mum walk in, "Mum you are as white as a ghost. Are you okay?" Kerry had noted how fast she had gone downhill since they'd found the body of Turkington.

"Kerry, I need your help, but you need to know something first and... I'm so so sorry." The sight of his Mum in such a crumpled state of emotional collapse made Kerry feel sick. They held each other. Kerry felt his Mother shaking on his shoulder, holding back tears.

"Kerry, I was having an affair with Richard, and he was going to leave Samantha. I think your Father had suspicions, and he's been almost too nonchalant since Richard's death. That scares me Kerry. I'm going to the police tomorrow morning."

Kerry pushed back, his arms like ramrods, gripping his Mother's shoulders. "Mum, is that a good idea? I mean, there are all sorts of stories racing about. Fraud, hit men, God knows what else. You want to officially implicate Dad? The police will be onto him straight away, and then, if they don't arrest him and put him away, you'll have to deal with all of the fallout from that. To me, that's a terrifying thought."

Patricia was the colour of a corpse. "I've thought of that. When your Dad goes for his run, I'll pack, go to the police and then drive to my Mother's in Scotland. I'm hoping the police can give me some protection until this is sorted out. Our marriage is over anyway, and this horror seals all that."

Kerry was trying to work out how the police might see this. "Mum, from what the news has been saying, the hit man synopsis looks plausible. You must have seen it. The police have put it out there that the fraud and the hit man are their main line of enquiry. The police might view your romance as nothing more than a coincidence and a distraction."

Patricia knew that her son was just trying to ease her fears, but Patricia's nervous system was saying something else. She felt as if a nest of vipers had crawled inside her guts. "Or they might not, Kerry. I have to tell them. If I don't I might be accused of withholding evidence, and, most importantly, if your Dad has killed, I want him caught." Patricia's rationale was that revelations about her tryst with Richard would at least put Karl into firmer focus. "Your Dad might be the killer. Christ, no one knows him better than me, we've been married for over twenty years. I think he's capable of it, and I don't feel safe." Patricia told Kerry about Karl's snide remark at the fell running awards about how well she and Richard were getting along. "Kerry, Karl is a very jealous man."

Kerry knew all about his Dad's knowledge of the mountains and chemicals. There were pointers, that was for sure. "Okay Mum. It's the police. We'll go together. First thing."

CHAPTER FORTY-TWO

Unfortunately for Patricia, Karl was waiting to pounce just when his wife was about to reach out for salvation. Patricia's recent behaviour had been strange - twitchy and guarded - and Karl wasn't prepared to waste any more time. He waited for his wife to fall into a fitful sleep. Nathan had felt the stinging prick of a Karl micro syringe, and he had placed one in his reading glasses case in the drawer beside his bed. The syringe pump was four centimetres long and one centimetre in diameter. Karl was about to use a procedure first adopted by the S.A.S. In the killing fields, they deployed several ingenious strategies. This particular practice was designed to kill silently and quickly without leaving a trace.

As dawn approached, and with slick movement, Karl injected the chemical fentanyl into Patricia's eardrum. His wife swatted at the irritating presence in the way you would flick at a mosquito. Patricia didn't wake, and Karl hoped she never would again. This method was virtually foolproof because even a thorough autopsy from an experienced forensic pathologist was very unlikely to uncover a pinprick to an eardrum. Fentanyl was a rising popular recreational drug, and addicts overdosed on it regularly. Karl knew that, if you were like Patricia, a codeine addict, fentanyl was the natural progression. An overdose was quite common in codeine addicts who weren't used to the additional strength of fentanyl.

Getting hold of the fentanyl hadn't been too difficult. Using his chemistry skills, Karl had made his own ricin from the seeds of Castor Oil Plants. Not many killers bought their murder weapons in the house plant section at the garden centre. Karl was nothing if not resourceful. This time all Karl needed were the right contacts and the post office. Acquiring fentanyl was much easier than getting cyanide.

***

Karl knew some people from one of the pharmaceutical laboratories in Beijing. He had met them at a chemistry conference in China

224

several years ago. Karl had listened intently when they told him about the growing mail-order drugs trade. Again the excitement was clear in Karl's records:

"It's incredible really. It's a billion-dollar industry. I found out during the winter. Teams sent in by Asia's cyber security network had raided jungle camps in Burma close to the Chinese border. They found 990 gallons of fentanyl. A synthetic version of it. It's an opioid painkiller fifty times as powerful as heroin and hundreds of times stronger than codeine. Getting hold of the amount of fentanyl I needed to kill someone was surprisingly straightforward. I didn't even need to use the Dark Web this time to get my hands on it. My deals were made on encrypted messaging services. They send the packages by Royal Mail. I actually read a feature about it in The Sunday Times. Remarkably one of the production centres was based in a state-run prison. Can you believe that? In prison. They say you can get anything you want in prison. Fentanyl has great street names like China Death, Dance Fever, Goodfella and Apache."

Karl waited for his wife's breathing to become shallow, and now he was confident that Patricia was drifting towards death. Of course, Karl had to leave before Patricia died. It would have been difficult to explain why he'd left his breathless and lifeless wife in bed. He knew that a defence of, "I just thought she was in a deep sleep," wouldn't cut it in a police interview room. With Patricia's breath now a mere whisper, Karl threw on his running gear and left the house to head for the hills. Patricia was always up by seven, and at half past, Kerry, who was cramming in some extra exam revision, shouted across the landing,

"You okay Mum, get up Mum. We'll have to leave soon. Can you stomach breakfast?" The minutes passed with no sound of his mother stirring.

Kerry went to Patricia's room where she was now in a semi-coma. Kerry shook Patricia and noticed, as he rolled his mum onto her back, that her lips had a light blue tint. Patricia's breath was now imperceptible. Kerry listened for a heartbeat, but it was very slow. He dashed for the phone, and an ambulance was at the Jackson home within fifteen minutes. Kerry's calls to his Dad's mobile rang out in the house; he'd left it beside the marital bed. Kerry sat beside his Mother on the short journey to the Royal Burlington Hospital. Kerry waited in A+E, his figure hunched, knuckles white, and feet tap dancing on the disinfected white linoleum.

Eventually, a doctor came over.

"Are you Kerry, the son?" Kerry looked up through scarlet eyes and nodded while holding his breath. "Kerry we got to her just in time. We did a blood test, and it was fentanyl. We administered naloxone, an antidote that blocks opioid receptors. We reversed the effects of the drug. She's going to be fine."

Kerry blasted out a sharp rush of breath and then inhaled just as fast. The tears came quickly as Kerry clutched his head. "Can I see her? Can I sit beside her bed?" Kerry hyperventilated between each word. He was allowed into the ward and held his Mum's hand, rubbing his fingers over hers. Eventually Patricia roused from her disorientated daze.

"Mum, Mum. Thank God you're okay. Can you hear me? Can you talk?" Patricia's head moved on the starched pillow case, and she offered the weakest of smiles, "Mum, why did you do it? Why did you overdose?" Kerry whispered, "We had a plan. We were going to the police. The Doctor told me you took an overdose." Patricia looked at Kerry through bleary eyes. She was slurring in a barely audible whisper. "Kerry, trust me, I didn't take an overdose."

Kerry was listening, but he had his misgivings, as he too knew about his mum's codeine problem. Patrica's hiding places had been poorly chosen. Kerry once found a stash of his Mum's tablets in a plastic bag in the downstairs toilet cistern, and he knew from his old science classes that fentanyl was often the next step up for a codeine addict. Codeine is converted into morphine in the bloodstream, a perfect emotional balm for an abused woman suffering from acute anxiety and in fear for her life.

When at home, Kerry had developed the capacity to shapeshift. There was the lounging student, but he could explode from that emotional cocoon. When Dad was about he threw a protective cloak around his Mother and, metaphorically, would prowl, panther-esque, ready to spring. Kerry had heard a lot of the coercive emotional abuse his Dad handed out to his wife and rarely reacted, but he knew that he would respond very differently if he ever saw Karl lift a hand. Kerry had witnessed, over the years, the stress Karl's cruelty inflicted on Patricia, so he could understand her seeking solace in someone else's arms. One thing just didn't sit with Kerry though. Why tell him all about her decision to go to the police and then, a few hours later, do this? If not an overdose, then how did this happen? Kerry was pretty sure that he knew the answer.

CHAPTER FORTY-THREE

Tex phoned Lexington Dawson in forensics, "Lex, Tex." They both enjoyed this careworn repartee, "It's been a while Tex," said Lex, "Yep buddy, I'm sure you'd heard. Bracewell stood me down, you know, after Susan."

"Yeah Tex, I'd heard. I've also heard that the cadets are having a ball and loving your lectures. Are you going to tell them some juicy stories from the good old days?"

"Good old days!" said Tex, "Yeah, the good old days of multiple murders." Lex laughed. They'd always enjoyed a relationship laced with jet-black humour. "Well what can I do for you Tex?" Lex and Tex went back decades, and Lex had led the forensics in a bundle of Tex's cases. This meant, of course, that he knew Tex very well, and knew he was quite capable of manipulating to get what he wanted. "Lex, the Turkington murder. Have you finished the forensics?" Lex clicked his tongue, "Yes Tex, late yesterday, in fact. But, I know you buddy, when you say, 'Have you finished the forensics' it's usually your way of telling me that, in your opinion, we haven't."

"Ah yes," said Tex, "Well, I just want to check something." Lex Dawson's reply was guarded. "Tex, you know this place. Nothing stays quiet for long. I know you're edging in on the Turkington case, and it's great to have you back, but I also know you're supposed to be on light assisting duties. I hope you're not overstepping and heading off script here Tex. If Bracewell finds out, we'll both be in the shit."

"Not off script as such," said Tex. Lex was arching his eyebrows, "Lex, I just want to ask you what you'd found at the murder site, DNA-wise. I'll be getting your report in a day or two anyway. Anything out of the ordinary?"

There was no overstepping with that request, "Nothing Tex. All of the DNA we found was Turkington's. After the usual thorough murder scene and body check, we paid specific attention to his equipment." Tex spoke, "Sweat?" "Yes there was sweat, Tex, quite a lot of it, and it all belonged to the victim."

Tex hated doubting his old pal, but Lex was used to it, resigned even. "Lex, I'm looking for the DNA from what might be one bead of sweat. How hard would that be to find?"

"You're on another of your 'Mission Impossible' crusades, Tex. One drop of sweat? Turkington's rucksack was nylon construction, honeycomb and crosshatch. One drop would evaporate and dissipate fast. There was so much sweat from Turkington that it had left salt tide marks in multiple places."

"I have a theory Lex. If Turkington has been contract killed, or killed by anyone else, I think they must have used a tracker," Tex persisted, "I think the killer will have retrieved that tracker - on a hot morning." The deep breath from Lex sounded like exasperation, "We'd have to start the fluids all over again Tex. A specific area? The rucksack?"

"Yes, the rucksack, Lex. Webbing, buckles, hip belt, harness... and inside."

"Tex, did you get clearance from Bracewell to contact me?" Lex knew fine well that Tex hadn't, but if the killer's DNA was anywhere at the murder scene, Tex's old buddy wanted to find it. "Okay Tex, I'm with you. Glad I hadn't filed my report. I'll get the boys onto it."

CHAPTER FORTY-FOUR

The Lake District was getting itself another mountain, which was the fast-growing mound of information piling high on DCI Deacon's desk. More circumstantial evidence about Karl Jackson. Soon they'd have so much stuff they'd have to give this stack a name, 'Karl's Cornice'? In the past challenging climbs had never been a problem for Tex. Catching serial killers was high-altitude work for a detective, and Tex had murderers like The Black Bridge Lodge Assassin, Colin Nedbank and Gary Bloomberg amongst his collection of peaks. Tex didn't know it, but the Arnold Nutley case was the climbing equivalent of a fatal slip on the summit ridge.

Tex's colleagues had long badgered him about writing a book. A 'Life and Times' kind of publication, a memoir in some guise or other. He had been presented with, and helped solve, some of the biggest murder cases in the country. It was the investigations involving serial killers that Deacon's fellow detectives knew would make the best copy - true crime sold well.

***

Tex's problems were threefold. Firstly he didn't know if he could write well enough, and yes, he could draw up official case reports, but that was written in the cold, straightforward language of police speak. Tex had read the memoirs of others, with their flowery descriptions and clever metaphors. In conversation, Tex was usually economical with his syllables. A straight-to-the-point blunt-nosed detective.

Secondly, Tex hadn't retired yet. He thought this book should wait for another fifteen years or so until he was sitting in a villa somewhere, alternating looks out to sea with untidy scrawls of gnarly best-selling prose. Tex wasn't a sun-kissed veranda kind of guy; instead, he visualised himself in the clichéd setting of a remote mountain cabin, though bizarrely, the thought of that made Tex nervous. He was swilling an amber nightcap, ice-clinking with every spin, and thinking about himself alone in some isolated retreat.

"*Vengeful felons, out on parole, coming after me,*" Tex stretched out a frame that needed a little loosening and suddenly felt old when he looked at his pensioners slippers, "*On my own in the woods, stalked at night, during a storm.*" Tex was smiling but without conviction. "*Jeez, it's happened to detectives before. I could end up as a grisly chapter in someone else's tale. The one's killers write from their cells. Maybe I'd need to find a panic room to write the bloody thing.*" Tex knew well that there were a few nasty individuals out there with powerful vendettas who would risk a lot to see him dead.

The memoirs could wait, Tex preferred to stay in the moment for now. He was dealing with the Turkington file and already knew that he was well past the light touch approach that Bracewell had insisted on. The cover notes for the case said simply, "Isolated body found in Lake District. Probable Cause of Death - Heart Failure accelerated by ricin inhalation."

As far as writing his own memoirs were concerned, Tex did have a head start. This is where he had something in common with Karl Jackson - scrupulous documentation. Tex had kept rough records of his game-changing murder hunts, the cases that Tex had found most difficult to crack and where he had learned the most. These were also the cases that haunted him, the ones where he had burrowed a little too deeply into the minds of evil men. In a trunk in the garage Tex had three box-style folders. On the front of each was a name printed in large bold type. 'Black Bridge Lodge' 'Arnold Nutley' 'Colin Nedbank' 'Gary Bloomberg.' If Tex wrote a book, these men would definitely be in it. These were the most heinous characters he'd ever encountered. Under the box folders there was a plastic binder with a self-adhesive label on the front and written on it, in faded lettering, was the name Matt Barrington. This was the man who had killed Tex Deacon's father.

***

Nutley, Nedbank and Bloomberg had all killed multiple times and terrorised a certain well-defined group of people, like student couples and rent boys. Deacon's triple challenge had come after the 'Black

Bridge Lodge Assassin' case. For Tex, that investigation had gone from the murder site to prison cell with relatively few hitches. His profile of the killer had been spot on, and it didn't need a machete to find the path to his door. The Black Bridge case and the crimes of Nutley, Nedbank and Bloomberg were the biggest, toughest, most gruelling jobs of Tex Deacon's career. Up to now.

Nutley, who was, of course, in reality, Karl Jackson, had been called 'The Jester' because of his signature; the leaving of pathetic Christmas cracker standard jokes, written in lipstick on the bodies of his victims. Nedbank was the 'Sundown Slaughterman' and was on the loose for over a decade. To be accurate, Nedbank didn't always kill at sundown. However, he did slaughter somewhere in the window between gathering darkness and the sun disappearing.

The papers wanted a nickname, so they came up with that. Gary Bloomberg acquired the gruesome tag 'The Backdoor Bloodsucker'. He always entered the homes of victims through their back garden or porch. He loved nothing more than biting a post-mortem chunk out of the corpse. All of his murders seemed to be burglaries gone wrong, but they turned out to be much more than that. Tex rolled his eyes at the media's habit of attaching snappy denominations to each killer. The almost inevitable alliteration annoyed him, but he could do nothing about it. Those were the habits of the media; anyway, Tex was prepared to tolerate such minor irritations. Generally, he enjoyed a good relationship with the press and fully understood and utilised the give and take. Tex was always good for a tip-off, but he knew how to work the scribes to his advantage. In the Turkington case Tex knew that his hardest job might be keeping Debbie on message.

Most members of the murder squad were squeamish regarding the press hacks and struggled to tolerate them, never mind indulge them. Some detectives were paranoid about sensitive details getting out, but Tex saw it differently. Critical leads needed to stay in-house, but Tex was a clever tactician outside those parameters. He used the fourth estate as an engine to drive his investigations, often dropping carefully chosen snippets of information into the mainstream outlets.

In the view of Tex, the police were far too anal when it came to the media. Tex saw it as free advertising and he sometimes actively encouraged rumour in the broader community. Several times, in big cases, he'd obtained significant breakthroughs from behind the hand of a whispering gossip. If the worst of it was reading cringe-worthy headlines like "More Black Comedy From The Jester," then Tex could cope.

CHAPTER FORTY-FIVE

Tex wanted to focus fully on the intricacies of the Turkington case, but, in tandem, he had to stay in step with the wishes of the Chief Constable. Barbara Bracewell had insisted that Tex continue to see the police psychologist David Braithwaite, and there were the cadet lectures to be accommodated too. Tex had a busy morning ahead. There was a cadets class on the itinerary at eleven o'clock, but first, at nine am, there was another session with Braithwaite. Tex sat opposite him, feeling very much like the Mafia boss Tony Soprano in the scenes with his psychiatrist Jennifer Melfi. Tony's sessions with Melfi ran through all six series of 'The Sopranos' and were a central block of the narrative. Sometimes Tex felt like an actor playing a role in his own twisting plot.

"Tex it's good to see you again. How have you been?" After a quick purse of the lips, Tex replied, "Okay I suppose. I'm feeling pretty good, and as you probably know, the Chief Constable has allowed me to assist on a murder case."

"I'd heard that Tex, in fact, it's in your notes." Braithwaite patted the brown folder that sat on his knee. "From the evidence of your last session here, I think we both know that you still have quite a bit of work to do until you are back to something approaching full mental fitness." Tex gave a slightly despairing nod and drummed his fingers on the arm of his leather chair. "Tex, we know that you're here, mainly, to talk through how the death of your wife Susan has affected you and see if we can ease the pain. But is there anything else you need to deal with Tex? I knew your father, DCI Bradley Deacon. It was a very sad day for the force when he was murdered. I remember it well. In fact I worked on the mental health of a few of his colleagues. How did the murder affect you?" Tex was shocked to learn that his dad's death was suddenly part of his therapy.

"Affect me?" said Tex, raising his voice, "It inspired me. My Father's passing made me doubly determined to do the job I do now." Braithwaite was running his finger across a page from the folder and talked as he traced, "You were nineteen when Bradley was killed, a highly impressionable age, just when you were crossing the final barrier from boyhood to manhood."

"I've never been asked to talk about Dad before, Dr. Braithwaite. I just sort of mourned him and got on with life, but I did want to make him proud."

"I get that, Tex, but I wonder whether you have buried anything from those days. Things that you might talk about now to help you make progress?"

Tex looked at the carpet, "Maybe. As you say, I was nineteen and I wanted to avenge my Father's death, you know, catch his killer. To be honest, I wanted to kill my Father's murderer, but I didn't get the opportunity. I think you know the story Dr. Braithwaite?"

"I do, Tex, I do, and I really think that we need to look into your feelings at the time and what mental blocks you may, or may not, have put in place as protection. There might be some levels of denial to work through. That's not for today, Tex, but this whole area needs careful consideration and probably serious analysis."

Tex sighed loudly, clenched his teeth, and stared out of the window while his fingers formed into fists. The memories flooded back. Bradley Deacon's killer, Matt Barrington, had himself been murdered in prison, where he was serving a life sentence, choked in the laundry room by a fellow inmate with a grudge. Barrington had stolen four of his assailant's cigarettes and was killed with a rolled hand towel jammed into his throat. Four years previously, Barrington had shot Tex's dad in the face.

**

Tex had worshipped his policeman father, a determined detective admired for his meticulous approach to his work and high success rate. Bradley's reputation fuelled his young son's adolescent enthusiasm and desire to follow his old man into the force. Tex's Dad was well known for his ability to find patterns, and Tex loved it when his Dad handed down the nuggets that had helped him catch the criminals. "Son, killers are inclined to use a series of templates.

Multiple murderers often adhere to a particular modus operandi. They usually stick to a preferred style but nevertheless, expect the unexpected. They can tweak and twist a method as they gain experience." Tex had used quotes from those wondrous discussions with his father in the 'Sir Robert Peel Lecture', and he kept the story of his Dad's life - and death - in one of the files he kept in the trunk in the garage.

∗∗∗

"Dad was my hero. I worshipped him. I had always wanted to be a policeman just like him. Dad was forty-five when he died. He had set up a sting. One of his men had infiltrated a gang of low-key mobsters. They had been importing ketamine using small fishing boats to ferry the narcotics up the coastline. The drugs had been stored in a small abandoned warehouse about half a mile back from the pier. It had previously been used to gut fish and, apparently, smelt like it. Dad had placed a stooge in the gang, he'd been embedded for five months, and now they had all sorts of proof. Incriminating material was recorded by wire and hidden camera, so there was a stack of hard-core physical evidence. This was the night when the rest of the team would move in." Tex's handwriting was full of slants and squirls. It had a beauty that made it look like the work of a calligrapher.

"Dad's six-man detail surrounded the seaside storehouse that was piled high with ketamine. There were four drug traffickers and Dad's informer inside the building. In traditional style, they kicked down the door and burst in and three of the four were quickly subdued. Matt Barrington was the gang leader, a man with a long criminal record, and he was where Dad expected him to be, at the rear wall of the warehouse. Barrington sprinted out the back door but Dad was waiting. He had this exit covered and, weapon already drawn, shouted the usual commands, but Barrington kept on coming. They say Dad could or probably should have shot Barrington, but instead he chose to rugby tackle the gang's top man. Dad wanted the arrest, but Barrington slipped free and pulled out a nine-millimetre Glock. He fired two bullets

236

at Dad from point-blank range. One entered just below Dad's right eye socket and the second in the centre of his forehead."

The murder of his Father shattered Tex but, in his dad's honour, the devastated teenager was determined to follow him into the force. Tex had a mission to be relentless and thorough, just like his dad. Tex thought that criminal convictions would ease his pain, but they never did.

However, it was Bradley's death that served as the trip switch that triggered Tex's obsessive nature, and when he rummaged about in his old trunk, he could see why his colleagues were sure Tex had a book in him.

CHAPTER FORTY-SIX

The session with David Braithwaite left Tex with a lot to ponder. Deep down, he knew that his dad's murder and Susan's death had, in combination, a devastating effect on his mental health. It was only now that the true damage was becoming apparent, but thoughts about the next meeting with Braithwaite had to be parked. Next on the schedule was another of the cadet lectures, but Tex, with the recall of his teenage trauma still whirling in his head, was glad that he'd decided to make this cadet session a simple Q+A. He didn't have the energy to do anything else.

As always, there was a full turnout for Tex's classes. The morning sun broke through the windows in shards and danced with the dust that clouded the air in the police academy's classroom. "Good morning all," said Tex, "I'm going to do something a little different today. I've noticed that you're a nosy bunch, so I'm going to unleash the curtain twitcher that exists inside every budding police officer." This got a laugh from the crew of cadets, a gathering of hugely enthusiastic boys and girls who were high on ambition but still low on knowledge.

Tex hoped that might change on this warm summer morning. "It's an open house," said Tex, spreading his arms like a TV evangelist, "This is question time, and I'll answer anything you want to know. No holds barred, just hit me with the best you've got; drain my brain." A flurry of rising hands accompanied another team guffaw. Tex picked out a girl in the middle of the room, one he'd previously noted to be extremely conscientious and keen to learn.

"DCI Deacon, you've built your reputation, it seems, on capturing serial killers. Could you talk us through your most challenging case and tell us, specifically, what techniques you used to catch the killer?" Tex looked at his audience, and their expressions suggested that this was the question most of them would have asked. The class sat back, and Tex launched into his flow.

"Okay. Well there was Colin Nedbank, 'The Sundown Slaughterman.' Nedbank picked up rent boys and murdered them. He was a fairly standard serial killer in many ways, but in other ways, he wasn't. Nedbank was a classic kerb crawler who did his deal through an open car window, and the boy got in. The boys' bodies were found on various patches of waste ground spread over quite a large area. Each boy had been killed the same way, strangulation. They were always found fully clothed and face down. Their heads had been driven, after death, into the dirt. Five boys were murdered over a five-year period. Nedbank's patterns were regulated, so it had to be the same person who killed all of the boys. The police put a watch on recognised rent boy pick-up areas using plainclothes officers and unmarked cars. During the hunt for information they spoke to sex trade workers of all ages and sexes."

The complete silence in the classroom told Tex that he had the cadets' total attention. "One of the problems for the case detectives was that Nedbank didn't kill often enough. The murders took place a year apart, each one on the same date. It was a long wait each time, with not much to go on. The detectives on the case were very sure that their target didn't pay for one rentboy a year. The opinion was that he was a regular customer who only KILLED once a year. The police had discreetly interviewed dozens of rent boy clients, and this turned out to be hugely embarrassing for quite a few local businessmen and the Mayor, who resigned in disgrace."

The cadets, as a collective, sniggered and then quickly realised that their reaction was inappropriate and returned to their focused state.

"The police logged the number plates of over a hundred cars, but all they had, despite countless hours of reconnaissance, was a blank. The original team kept bumping into dead ends, so I was eventually called in to assist. I thoroughly studied the large corkboard murder wall in a stuffy anteroom at police headquarters. I can still remember the smell, a bit like the contents of a full laundry basket. The wall was covered in maps, photos of the victims and a web of thin string linking events together. My view was that the killer was probably a man who hated his own sexuality. The driving of the head of the victim into the ground was a sign of self-disgust. I was pretty sure that they had a closet homosexual on their hands. In some cases strangulation indicates a killer's internal battle. He stares at the victim's face as he kills them. A mirror image? Maybe, metaphorically speaking, the killer is killing himself?"

The cadets who weren't open-mouthed were making copious notes.

"A question we needed the answer to was why were the police unable to match a particular car to the killers? The sex trade workers were inclined to remember the vehicles of most of their regular tricks. After many hours of questioning those on the streets, the investigating team concluded that each murdered boy had been lifted in a different car. So what was happening there? I thought there were two possible options. One: The obvious solution. The killer changes his car on a very regular basis. Two: He works in a job that gives him access to different cars. Our man can take these cars without arousing any suspicion as it will be a regular occurrence in his job. I also said to the original team chasing the killer that it was likely that they'd already interviewed him and dismissed him as a suspect.

I also suspected that the kill date was the anniversary of the birth or death of someone who had hurt the killer, simple as that. And the pickup and dump sites? This man used several areas when he was cruising. He would have had an intricate knowledge of the area so the killer would have known the network of streets very well. He would have walked them regularly, probably over the years, as well as driven them."

Tex looked around the classroom, studying the expressions on the faces of his students. "How's it going folks? Learning anything? Will I keep going?" There was a communal nod, not a word was spoken, so Tex went on.

"We learnt so much when we eventually caught Nedbank. In his case, he did have a very sound knowledge of the network of dark side streets. As a boy, he had spent a lot of time in the area, flitting between smoky snooker halls. Murderers often thoroughly understand the geography and topography of their killing fields. We finally arrested Nedbank at work, sitting at his desk in a crisp, shiny suit. Nedbank was a car salesman and he often took home one of the second-hand vehicles from the showroom. After each kill, close to the scene, Nedbank conducted a rudimentary clean of the car. The next morning it was given a deep steam by the unsuspecting staff back at the showroom to prepare the car for the next customer, and this helped to remove any remaining DNA. It must have been nice to have other people to wash away incriminating forensics. Under caution during his interviews, the killer revealed that he murdered on the date of his father's death to 'celebrate his departure'. Nedbank, as a fifteen-year-old, had come out to his dad, who didn't take it well. Nedbank's father went berserk and beat the boy. Nedbank despised his father and lived a life of self-hate in his own personal hell. He was appalled by his own homosexuality and felt even more guilty about his attraction to teenage boys. Nedbank had indeed been interviewed during earlier routine inquiries into the murders but had been dismissed as a suspect.

In his straight life, Nedbank was married with children and came across to everyone as an upstanding and honourable family man. We'd nailed him, but it took a lot of graft and gruelling detective work to get our man and put him away." Tex looked around the room again at his goggle-eyed bunch of apprentices, "Would you like a break, or shall we crack on?" There was an almost unified chorus of, "Crack on," so Tex invited another question. A young man, with heavy eyebrows and a bright smile asked, "The serial killers, male or female, are all psychopaths, it seems, and they need to be caught and jailed for as long as possible. That's obvious, but can you change them? Can they be cured?"

Tex nodded with vigour, "That's a very good question. The mechanics of the mind of a psychopath have always fascinated me. First of all, how do they become killers? There's the nature or nurture argument. Are killers born, or is the desire to kill precipitated by abuse in early life or by other childhood factors? Early in my career as a detective, I came across a series of controversial experiments conducted on psychopaths at the Waypoint Centre for Mental Health Care in Ontario, Canada. I was drawn to it by a documentary which focused on the 'Secrets of Oak Ridge', which turned out to be invaluable homework. Oak Ridge was a forensic mental health division that housed several serial killers. There they used various controversial therapies, including psychoactive pharmaceuticals and LSD. At the time, it was seen as a 'positive form of treatment' and a 'promising advance in the field.' The goal was to make the killers safer for parole, but all that the therapy and hallucinogenic treatment did was make them better psychopaths. One of the inmates, Peter Woodcock, killed a man almost immediately after release. As Woodcock said, 'I did learn how to manipulate better and keep my more outrageous feelings under wraps.' None of this surprised me really because, even by that stage, I'd read too many research documents on psychopaths. My opinion? Lock them up and keep them locked up."

Tex addressed the room once more, "Right guys, I think we've time for one more question. What have you got?"

A female cadet sitting beside the window had locked onto Tex throughout, apparently without blinking. In fact, Tex hadn't noticed any part of her body move at all during his address. "So when you catch these killers, you have to convict them. You have all this evidence, presumably, but how difficult is it to go from arrest to jail?"

"Good one, again," said Tex, "Loving the questions, and yes, we have to go through court, don't we? That can be a minefield, and you often deal with difficult people. Notably, the defence counsel, who often know that their client is guilty, but they'll snarl like dogs anyway. I've found that rather callous and cruel in so many ways, especially for the killer's victims. One court battle stands out, and it was a hell of a fight. Gary Bloomberg was the accused and was represented by the law firm, 'Montague, Fortescue and Trapp'. To me, they sounded rather Pythonesque, and I referred to them simply, as M,F + T. Before or since I have never encountered so many appeals and adjournments. This man Bloomberg - 'The Backdoor Bloodsucker' - was a cannibal who killed seven male and female fashion models.

A spree killer who murdered all seven over a five-week period. He had a facial disfigurement and was employed by a model agency. He killed out of jealousy and then consumed chunks of his victims so that he could 'become them' as Bloomberg, memorably, told us in court. The evidence was absolutely cast iron, but the defence counsel crafted a spurious defence and even applied for bail. The murder squad couldn't believe that one, as Bloomberg had been charged with butchering seven people. His legal team seriously believed that the judge would let him walk the streets. When I was in the witness box giving evidence, I often had my fists clenched below the level of the wooden railing.

The style of cross-examination was irritating and arrogant, but the defence lawyer, a pompous prick called Jasper Montague, the 'M' in 'M,F+T' delivered a master class in smugness which was shattered, in a dramatic turn, when Bloomberg admitted his guilt. I was delighted on two fronts. First, that the killer was going to prison for life and second, that, hopefully, I'd never have to deal with M,F+T again. Especially 'M' - my 'M' stood for Mother - but it was only the first half of the nickname I'd given him! When the case was closed, I made a silent salutation, praying that I would never have to deal with 'M' for the rest of my life."

Tex threw a clown-like theatrical grin in the cadets' direction. "I just couldn't stand the guy and his methods. When cross-examining me, Montague said that the evidence had been 'meticulously created by utilising otherwise effective forensic techniques to frame my client'. Really Jasper? Bloomberg literally ripped the flesh from his victims, sinking his teeth into them and, with considerable savagery, wrenched out a mouthful of bloody flesh. Bloomberg didn't leave any useable teeth imprints until the seventh murder. Then the forensic team recovered an impression of a canine. This critical piece of evidence helped us get over the line. We'd also discovered chloroform in his house, which was used to disable the victims and the knife he used to kill them. There was more evidence, but Montague kept on squealing. Thankfully the jury, with their verdict, gave him and his client a massive kick in the nuts." The cadets were smiling, and they'd been enthralled. When Tex said, "That's it class, see you next week," they burst into spontaneous applause. Tex's experience with the cadets was certainly proof to him that he had a gift for storytelling and a strong spine for his memoirs, but were the best chapters still to come?

CHAPTER FORTY-SEVEN

Tex walked from the cadet's class to the canteen for a quiet lunch and a refreshing cup of builder's brew tea. At around the same time, Kerry Jackson phoned police headquarters to report his mother's revelation that she had been having an affair with Richard Turkington. He was put through to the office set aside for the Turkington investigation, and the desk officer instinctively rang Tex on his mobile. Tex took the call and listened while he sipped his tea.

***

An hour later, Tex led Kerry Jackson to a gloomy interview room at the station. It hadn't been used for a while, and the standard recording equipment, required elsewhere, had been removed. Rusted bars pressed against a wire glass window. On the narrow sill sat three polystyrene cups with ancient cigarette butts lying marooned at their base, wallowing in cold black liquid.

A bleak, watery and dusty light crept into the room. Curling, badly worn and dark patterned lino covered the floor. On the right-hand side of the room, resting against the grey flaking paint of a breeze block wall, was a dangerously lop-sided wooden table. It was covered in different coloured ballpoint streaks, multiple unidentified stains and dried spills. Many souls had opened up here, some admitting guilt and others vehemently denying it. This was the perfect spot, far from the madding crowd. It gave Tex the privacy he needed.

To Kerry, the room looked like some sort of cockroach paradise. He stared at the camera that hung, somewhat precariously, from the corner of the chipped ceiling. It was clear to see that the wiring had been disconnected, but the mere presence of the camera added to the intimidating atmosphere. Kerry's senses were contorted, but Tex was well used to this dimension.

"Sit down Kerry," Deacon's voice had a soft tone, with a matter-of-fact delivery that was without threat. "Why do you need to see me

Kerry? Is it just a chat you want? I imagine you're concerned about your mum. That was a close call last night. I've just received the toxicology diagnosis from the hospital - it was fentanyl. It wouldn't have taken much more of it to kill her. The doctor who looked after Patricia says the incident has the hallmarks of a suicide attempt."

Kerry sat like an ice statue on his chair, inhaled deeply and then released slowly.

"That's what I thought, and maybe it was, but I spoke to Mum, and she says it wasn't." Tex was used to denial from people who had attempted to kill themselves. In some, it was a natural response.

Kerry went on, his eyes staring at the scratchings on the table, "I thought it was a suicide attempt too. I mean, Mum has suffered from stress for a long time. She was hooked on codeine. It hasn't been easy for her or for any of us in the house. She'd been in an awful state recently, much worse than normal, and I couldn't really work out why."

Kerry stretched his hands behind his head and pulled in a huge breath. He then let it out with the force of a jet engine, "Detective Deacon. Mum told me that she'd been having an affair with Richard Turkington. She had been in love with him, and my Dad possibly knew about it."

Tex pinched his nostrils together and then wiped his lips. Suddenly the Turkington death had another thread, but as it stood, the resolution of the inquiry wouldn't be his responsibility alone. Tex had been asked to prepare a file for the Foreign Office due to the possibility of an overseas dimension to the murder. This wasn't necessarily bad news as there were now two teams working on the killing, with each coming from slightly different perspectives.

The Foreign Office focused on the contract killer angle, and those guys were top-class specialists. The team Tex was supposed to be on the fringe of was looking at the local possibilities.

Now though, with Kerry's revelation, Tex suspected that the probe into the Turkington case was about to speed like a bullet towards Karl Jackson. Again, Bracewell wouldn't be too happy if she found out about his informal chat with Kerry, despite the call from the desk officer, but experience had told him that sometimes boundaries had to be pushed.

"Okay… Kerry," said Tex, emphasising the two words. "Right. An affair. Your dad MIGHT have known about it?"

Kerry wished he knew more, "Mum's not certain. She didn't tell him, but there isn't much that Mum does that dad doesn't know about. He's like a stalker. He's totally paranoid about her." Kerry tumbled out some more, "This explains to me why Mum had been so emotional lately, much worse than usual. It all makes sense now. Mum was so unhappy with my Dad. She used to go on all the time about being stuck in exactly the same trap my Gran had been jammed in for decades. My Dad's mum, Valerie, was brutalised by my grandad Harry. Now here was my Mum being brutalised by Harry's son. Mum had long conversations with Valerie. She would go to her when her relationship with Dad got out of hand. Valerie understood. My Granddad and my Dad were so similar."

Any semblance of nerves had long since disappeared, and Kerry went on, "I should have done more to help my Mum. Stuck in a crap marriage. I never blamed her for wanting out. Now this Turkington man is dead, probably murdered. To the untrained observer, like me, it would certainly explain why Mum might attempt to kill herself."

"Yes," replied Tex, "To the untrained. I met your grandmother after Nathan's death. Tidying some rough edges really. Valerie came in to look at the CCTV taken at the Ferris killing. It wasn't easy for her to watch her son on that tape, but she did confirm that it was Nathan. He had that limp and dropped foot."

"Yes", said Kerry, "I know about the accident."

"Lucky to survive the fall," said Tex, who knew he'd have to have a second, and more detailed conversation with Karl Jackson, but first he had work to do. As it stood, Tex had a bunch of hunches and a gathering pile of mostly thin circumstantial evidence. When he got back to his house, Tex phoned Debbie, asked her to come over, and poured himself a double shot. As usual he splashed in some ice and sat down to once again review the file on Richard Turkington.

CHAPTER FORTY-EIGHT

Debbie was at Tex's place in twenty minutes, and Tex was talking as he opened the front door. "I've spoken to Kerry. He told me he thought his mum and Turkington were having an affair. He's not so sure if it was a suicide attempt by Patricia. Looks like there are a lot of layers to this case. It's about finding them all and making some sense of the mess."

Tex sensed a tingle of excitement which was a feeling absent in recent years. He laughed and turned to Debbie, "I thought my instincts had been mummified long ago. Maybe they're back-and I think it's your fault."

Tex and Debbie worked their way through anything and everything. As far as Tex was concerned, the local school teacher was very much a suspect in the Turkington death, if still, officially, a peripheral one. Tex's discovery of the Nigerian and Lawyer Scams continued to make the 'killer for hire' hypothesis most probable.

Tex didn't even know for sure if Karl knew about his wife's affair. But if he did? Tex scrubbed his fingers through his hair as he pondered the possibilities, and, of course, he hadn't forgotten the contribution of his young partner. "To be honest, Debbie, I doubted a lot of the stuff you came up with, but it did keep me thinking. Bloody hell, I say it all the time - it's one of my mantras. I said it in my Robert Peel lecture - expect the unexpected." Now Tex needed to focus fully. "Sorry Deborah. I need to give this my complete attention. On my own." Debbie understood but pleaded, "Please ring me if anything changes."

CHAPTER FORTY-NINE

Tex drove to the office, pulled out the Nathan Jackson/Peter Ferris file, found a quiet corner, ands immersed himself in the folder. He wasn't quite sure what he was looking for. Tex was thinking out loud, "Karl, Nathan, Peter Ferris. Nathan kills Ferris. Nathan was racked with guilt. Goes hiking with Karl. Nathan gets lost (or gets lost on purpose) and commits suicide. Leaves pre-prepared note. No Ferris body, but missing presumed dead. It is straightforward isn't it? Nathan has killed Ferris. Valerie looks at the CCTV from the boatyard. Sees the limp, pours a river of tears, and confirms that it's Nathan. Case wrapped up."

Tex paused abruptly. His throat tightened as he ran thoughts through his mind. *"Case wrapped up on the ASSUMPTION that this was a murder/suicide. Jeez Tex, your first law - no assumptions, but what am I doing here? Trying to re-master the Nathan Jackson case to make it look like something else, just because Karl Jackson was now on the edge of the Richard Turkington murder? You can't match things up like that Tex, just because it might suit a certain conspiracy. It's about eliminating Karl Jackson from this, not implicating him. Isn't it? Tex, it's about fact not fabrication."*

Tex was now ruminating hard as he continued to flick through the Nathan Jackson folder. A mini disc in a small plastic bag was stapled to the top of page eight. Below it, a report on the contents of the boatyard CCTV. Tex muttered. "That was the piece of evidence that did it for me. Nathan was pinpointed at the scene." Tex slipped the disc into the player and watched the footage. The images were ghostly as they'd been filmed on low-grade tape in poor light fifteen minutes before dawn.

Tex was still deep in thought, *"Minutes later, Peter Ferris would be murdered. The killer then driven to suicide, and Karl loses his brother."* Tex zoomed in on the CCTV, but all that did was increase the pixelation, blurring the images further. *"In a court of law, if we tried to suggest that it was Karl, the defence would have a field day. I can hear them, some prat like Jasper Montague going through his full range of gloating prose. If Valerie insisted that it was Nathan, due to the dropped foot, it would be a massive advantage for the defence."*

Tex needed a fresh pair of eyes, so he made a call to Debbie. "I'm in the office, but meet me at my house. Sorry to have you racing all over Cumbria, but I want you to look at something." Debbie was exhilarated, feeling that she was now becoming more fully immersed in the police work. Tex slipped the boatyard CCTV disc into his coat pocket and left the station.

At home, when Tex answered the door, he was met with a sheet of rain that looked like a tumbling mass of ball bearings. Debbie shook the remnants from yet another summer storm off her umbrella. Hot tea was a good antidote on days like this, and soon Tex and Debbie were sitting in front of his DVD player. "Have a look at this Debbie. I've watched it so many times my head is close to blowing up." Debbie shuffled Tex out of his seat. Play, re-wind, fast forward, close up, zoom. Debbie took her time, her concentration absolute.

"I've just one thing to add, Tex. Let's say it's Nathan, and let's say, for the sake of argument, that when he killed Ferris, Nathan, at that stage, hadn't decided - one hundred percent - to take his own life?"

Tex stuck out his bottom lip, like a child who's just been nicked stealing chocolate from the fridge. "So that's the new premise Tex, okay?" Tex nodded, and Debbie went on, "Then why is Nathan not wearing anything on his head? He would have worn something like a peaked cap if he wanted to get away with it. Nathan would have been well aware of the presence of CCTV.

It had been there when the young boy had died at the lake and Nathan knew the boatyard like the back of his hand. Let's imagine, for a moment, that this is Karl. If this is part of a blackmail of Nathan then, naturally, he'd want us to think it was his twin....so no hat. Do you get me?" Tex replied in a flash, "Yes Debbie, I do." Debbie and Tex were now thinking in parallel. Tex jumped in, "And the limp - the dropped foot is idiosyncratic - but if Karl had watched Nathan doing it for so many years, then maybe he could have replicated it?

But as evidence, it's flimsy at best. Defence will scream 'prove it' so loudly you'd be able to hear them on the summit of Helvellyn."

They viewed the footage over and over and over again. Nathan or Karl? "Debbie, there's nothing to place Karl at the pontoon. We have nothing on him unless we can place him there on the morning Ferris was murdered."

This proved to Tex precisely how deeply he'd been distracted by Susan's illness. The usually obsessive Deacon had left an angle uncovered, maybe because it didn't slot into his internal visualisation of it. On the final page of the Nathan Jackson report was Tex Deacon's profile of Peter Ferris's potential killer. Of course this had been written as guidance before Nathan's body was found. Tex had typed on official Police Department stationary.

"Killer will have a detailed knowledge of the area. Probably knows the lake from childhood. In all likelihood born in the neighbourhood. Probably has a grudge against Peter Ferris. Could have worked with him in some capacity." Tex shook his head in self-admonishment, "The profile fits Nathan all right, but of course, the first half of it fits Karl too."

***

There was no proof of anything, just conjecture, but this added yet another perspective. Tex had to get back to the office and once again promised to keep Debbie in the loop as he headed out of the door.

Back at police HQ Tex again used his police computer access code and typed "Jackson"; "Death"; "Killing" and "Murder" on the keyboard. Dozens of pieces of information, going back decades, popped up. With painstaking precision, Tex scrolled through them all. He stopped at many, and several stood out, including an article on the accidental death of Charlie Jackson. It jumped at Tex, because it was an article Debbie had written. He did a speed read. "Yesterday morning Keswick Mountain Rescue discovered the body of Charlie Jackson at the base of what the locals call 'Baby Beelzebub'… A police investigation revealed that Jackson had placed a sling as a top rope… The sling had apparently slipped up and over the granite spike…

This incident was a carbon copy of one that had occurred in exactly the same place several years previously?" Tex's thoughts were caught in a centrifuge and spinning with possibilities, like the clothes on a whirligig flapping in a gale, "Christ, what a day."

CHAPTER FIFTY

Patricia was conscious but still in hospital, where the police had placed a light protection detail on the advice of DCI Deacon, who didn't want to take any chances with the health of a woman who might have been the victim of an attempted murder. Kerry had called his father and spoke with sarcasm riddling every word, "Dad, are you, or are you not pleased to hear that Mum is alive." Karl had shot back, "Of course I'm pleased, it's a huge relief. Why wouldn't it be?" Patricia's husband was banking on his wife being too afraid to tell anyone why she thought fentanyl was in her system. Patricia had been told that she'd soon be released from her ward, but Kerry wanted to talk to her first and drove to the hospital to be at her bedside. "Mum, what are we going to do?" Patricia was propped up on two pillows in her single room and the colour had returned to her face. "I can't go home, that's for sure. Have you told anyone about my suspicions?" Kerry, who was sitting on a small plastic chair, scraped its metal legs across the floor to get closer to his mum. "Yes, DCI Deacon, who's working on the Turkington case, knows that you suspect that Karl is aware of your affair, and I told him that you said you hadn't taken the fentanyl. He's looking into it, but he said that the information would be kept secure for your safety until they can back it up with facts."

Patricia wriggled slightly under the bedcover, "Okay, good. I'm supposed to be getting out tomorrow, and I'm going straight to Mum and Dad's in Scotland. I'll phone your dad and simply say that I want to recover with my parents in the peace and quiet of the Scottish Highlands. Do you think DCI Deacon would provide me with any protection there? I think your dad has tried to kill me once, and I'd expect him to try again."

Kerry was in total agreement with his mum's decision but not certain what his own next move should be. "Mum, should I make myself scarce too?" Patricia thought for a few seconds, "I would say no because your dad doesn't suspect you of doing anything as far as we know. Act normal is my gut thinking, but maybe you should get some advice from your contact DCI Deacon."

CHAPTER FIFTY-ONE

The following day the latest edition of the twice-weekly Rimpton Chronicle came out, and a copy was on Debbie's desk. The first word at the top of the front page was in red capital letters, "SHOCK: Ricin Poisoning Suspected in Turkington Death." It might have been the biggest story The Rimpton Chronicle had ever run, and the name Debbie Pilkington was on the byline. Tex, in his official press release, had been very happy to confirm the presence of ricin as he was looking for further leads and information.

Tex was waiting in the reception area of the Chronicle, holding a fresh copy of the just printed newspaper. A cheap plastic fan whirred away and moved just enough air to disturb a few page corners. Debbie's head appeared around a door, the hinge pleaded for oil by making a single squeak. Debbie slid coins into the vending machine, which, after she kicked it lightly at the base, produced cups of lukewarm dishwater, which was supposed to be coffee. They walked to the back of the building for peace and quiet and stood beside a rusted bicycle rack. "Debbie, more and more of those puzzle pieces you threw at me in that first frenetic phone call are beginning to make sense. The Charlie incident, I've double-checked with Mountain Rescue, and it's not that I doubted you, but I needed some official quotes."

Deborah felt a little rush of adrenalin as she listened to Tex, "I spoke to Robbie Benson, the most senior member of their crew. He was prepared to go on the record this time. He confirmed that a few years ago, a guy called Bob Crabtree died the same way when his sling came off the same spike and down he came. Robbie said there were a few rumours about Bob and some dodgy deals. He appeared to have been living on the edge of crime, but was he murdered? No proof. Robbie told me that 'Baby Beelzebub' is an extremely popular spot for rock climbers. From Crabtree's death to Charlie Jackson's, a span of several years, hundreds of climbers had used that very spit of rock and that precise method to climb the cliffs, but no one had died. Maybe, yes, maybe, by the law of averages, it was quite possible someone might die again but murdered? Maybe Charlie Jackson was that someone? Nathan? Karl? Was one the killer? And let's remember Karl had a much better knowledge of the mountains, and rock climbing, than his brother."

Debbie took a sip of what had been advertised as a cappuccino. "I've heard the rescue guys say that if you want to commit a murder, the mountains are the perfect place." Neither of them knew that those were exactly the same words Bart McGoldrick had proferred to Karl Jackson. Tex had absorbed every word that Robbie said and listened very carefully to Benson's account of their re-enactment of the Bob Crabtree fall.

"Debbie, I floated the name of Charlie's nephew, Karl. Robbie knew him, they all did. One of their number, Bart, was a member of the same fell running club and he and Karl had sometimes trained together." Tex and Debbie both knew that they were still scratching for solid ground but the landscape was altering.

An ocean of concerns still gnawed away at Tex and he was overwhelmed by a frenzy of educated speculation. He knew there were more people he had to talk to. Deacon had worked on this kind of case before, in fact many times. Killings within a family setting are relatively common and when a murder is committed family members are often the first reference point. Husbands killing wives, mothers smothering their own children, there was a long list of crimes in this category.

Tex would never forget the 'Black Bridge Lodge Assassin' case where his killer had been a warped version of 'Bad Grandpa.' Tex also remembered how he'd solved it, and wondered how Lex was progressing with the forensics review of the rucksack. "But there aren't too many instances like this when someone works his way slowly through his nearest and dearest over a period of years."

Debbie looked around for a bin for her paper cup and then showed Tex why she was the writer in this partnership. "Has Karl Jackson taken a chainsaw to his family tree?" Tex smiled, "Good line Debbie. Maybe you'll be able to use it in the Chronicle sometime soon."

CHAPTER FIFTY-TWO

Armed with Kerry's background information, Tex had a call to Valerie's house next on his list. His previous contact with Valerie had been quite brief. That had been the day when she viewed the CCTV, but now he needed to drill deeper.

The following morning Deacon was at the Jackson's family house. When Tex looked at it, he felt the word tatty scream back. The soft look of rot had settled into the window frames, and the chimney needed re-pointing. He visualised the returning beast, Harry Jackson, as a weaving drunk driving home with retribution on his mind. The building had a sparse gravel path around it, and grass borders and huge hedges of Leyland Cypress surrounded that. *"A kind of natural soundproofing,"* Tex thought, *"There's space between the properties here. And what do they say? In space, no one can hear you scream. It would be difficult to hear the cries of the beaten."*

Valerie opened a door that needed several coats of paint. She was welcoming but cautious. Valerie was in her early sixties but still retained a natural beauty. The Italian genetics were clear to see, she had lustrous black hair and emerald green eyes. However, there was a catish mistrust about Valerie's demeanour - maybe those eyes had seen a little too much. "Good morning, Mrs. Jackson," A thin-lipped smile was on Tex's face. Valerie had her arms folded protectively and took a deep breath before uttering a rather strange remark.

"There's not a lot I can tell you about Harry except that, thankfully, he's dead." Tex wasn't quite sure why Valerie began with a direct verbal assault on her deceased husband. Maybe it was an automatic reflex.

Tex forced a smile towards the petite widow. He tried to reassure her, "Valerie, can I call you Valerie?" She nodded, and Tex continued. "Kerry has told me a little about your ex-husband. If he's telling the truth, it doesn't sound as if this house was a very happy place."

Valerie spat out a few stinging words, "He was a brutal bastard that man, and a drunk. I felt nothing but relief when he died." The wrinkles crinkled around Valerie's eyes. She gripped a tea towel and, for a second, Tex feared her knuckles might break through the parchment-tight skin on her pipe cleaner fingers. Deacon continued, "Kerry said that no one was safe from Harry's attacks but that you were the main target?"

Thanks to Kerry, Tex knew about Valerie's resilience but had to strain hard to hear her. Valerie was quiet, but each word overflowed with venom. "I could handle it Detective Deacon, or rather I got used to it. My concern was for the boys. He was vicious with them too, but Harry got weaker and fatter as the years passed. The drink really got to him, and towards the end he was rarely sober, but they got stronger and began to stand up to him. I sometimes wondered if the boys might gang up together and kill him. I wouldn't have blamed them if they had. A heart attack in a hospital bed was an easy end for Harry. You see he deserved a drawn-out, more miserable death."

Valerie sat down on the high straight-backed wooden chair at the edge of the Formica covered island breakfast bar. She was becoming more emotional, "I might have helped them get rid of him. My God, Detective Deacon, this house was a hell hole. We lived in terror, and I think it damaged Karl and Nathan terribly. Nathan was such a loner, even from a very young age. He hardly left his room. We spent our lives on eggshells. The shouting and the threats and the beatings and the terror of anticipation. We didn't know what Harry was capable of, but we were all frightened that one day he might punch one of us too hard. I've really struggled to cope, Detective Deacon. I feel so much guilt about Nathan's suicide. I spin it around and around hour after hour and day after day. Could I have done more for him?"

By now, Valerie was distressed, but Tex pushed on and got to the point. He knew he had to. "Valerie, what exactly was the nature of Nathan's relationship with Peter Ferris? Nathan's note made it very clear that he held a grudge against his Probation Officer."

Valerie shot a sharp defensive glance towards the detective, "Nathan was upset with Peter Ferris, and we talked about it a lot. Ferris was so patronising. He was supposed to be there as support, and Nathan was angry with Ferris, but angrier with Harry. Maybe

Nathan thought the ball of fury that roared inside him would burn out with Ferris's death. I don't think it did Detective Deacon. Then the guilt kicked in, and Nathan killed himself. That's what I think anyway."

Valerie stood up, turned and peered, unseeing, through the kitchen window, "As kids and teenagers, Nathan's anger was nothing compared to his brother's - Karl could really explode. Yes, they might have been twins, but there was no comparison in that respect. Karl could be as terrifying as his Father, and there were days in here when it wouldn't have surprised me if Karl had tried to kill Harry. Karl was braver too. He used to mimic his father in front of him. It was like watching an horrific pantomime. Karl would copy his Father's every pathetic drunken movement, and Harry would become madder and madder as Karl, while retreating, loped and lunged around, throwing air punches. Karl would sometimes laugh, even when Harry was hitting him, repeating his Dad's curses back to him. Harry would end up totally enraged at his…" Valerie searched for a phrase and changed tack, "Karl was Harry's mini-me."

Tex jolted. His mind was flipping like a Cirque du Soleil acrobat. A thousand cockroaches crawled through his belly. Tex was stitching thoughts into a pattern, "Karl Jackson, the master mimic."

CHAPTER FIFTY-THREE

Tex had made an appointment with the records department of the Royal Burlington Hospital. Files spilled from the dozens of rows of packed shelves. They rose precipitously behind the office clerk's desk. "DCI Deacon," Tex flashed his warrant card, "I'm here to see Harry Jackson's medical notes."

The clerk answered in the affirmative, "Yes I already have the file here." Tex was staggered that the clerk had managed to find it so quickly. "It looks haphazard," said the clerk rather proudly while spinning on his chair, "But you get used to the system, and it's all on the computer."

The file Deacon needed was a relatively thin one. "Harry Jackson" was written in black capital letters on the beige cover. The clerk looked over his half glasses, "I'll have to read it to you. Medical protocol. What do you need to know?" Tex knew this was a long shot, but sometimes, long shots became leads in his business. "Could you confirm the time and cause of death, please, and there's something else. Did he have any visitors? Maybe you don't keep a record of these things?"

The clerk replied almost before Tex had finished his sentence, "Let me see. Only family members were let into CCU, and yes we do keep a log of their names. They have to sign in at the CCU nurse's station. Okay, let me go through this."

Deacon's mouth dried as the clerk turned over the page, "Harry Jackson died of natural causes from complications following a cardiac arrest at 0200 in the morning. His last visitor, in fact, his only visitor, was with him the previous night between 2100 and 2200. The signature is illegible… but the name is printed alongside-Karl Jackson."

**

Tex, in his own internal filing system, was piling up the bodies. As he drove away from the hospital, Tex ran everything he had learned through his head. His memory whirred as he revisited Karl's 'Science Editor' article in the college newsletter. Karl's knowledge of the lake, the mountains, the boatyard CCTV, and much more. Tex created a mental profile, trying to put the Karl he was getting to know out of his head and instead concentrate on the raw evidence.

"The killer likes using drugs and toxins. Ricin in the Turkington case. Fentanyl for Patricia. Our killer will have access to chemicals, or at least he knows exactly how they work and where to get them. The murderer may work in a laboratory with a job description like a forensic scientist," Tex sighed, *"Or a chemistry teacher."* His thought process gathered pace. *"A motive for the murder of Richard Turkington and attempted murder of Patricia Jackson is there. Revenge/Jealousy. Turkington, Nathan Jackson and Charlie Jackson all died in the nearby mountains. Our man is probably a local, but not any local, this one would have serious knowledge of those mountains as well as a better than average understanding of mountain craft - and he would be a good navigator. Ferris died at the lake which, of course, is near the Jackson's family home. Motive for the Ferris killing? Unknown, but maybe the slaughter was a set up to make Nathan look like a murderer? Is that a step too far? Was Nathan's death suicide or did the man who killed Ferris kill Nathan too? Motive for Nathan's murder if it was Karl? Unknown, but perhaps some sort of family dispute? On the Harry Jackson death. Karl Jackson was in the right place at the right time not long before his father died. Valerie gave us enough to suggest that Karl had plenty of reasons to kill his father.*

Revenge again and revenge killings are usually borne out of hatred and anger and according to Valerie, Karl Jackson had plenty of both. The medical records say heart failure, but hearts can fail in many ways."

It was time for Deacon to talk to Karl again. Tex couldn't conduct a formal interview, he'd need Bracewell's clearance for that. He could go to Barbara again with his cuddly bunny face in place, but reckoned he'd get the tarantula version of Bracewell in response. Tex also knew that under these circumstances, anything said between him and Jackson wouldn't be admissible in court, but that wasn't the reason for the chat. Tex wanted to flush the killer out. He wanted to talk to Karl back at Jackson's house, and he wanted Karl to feel as comfortable as possible. For Tex, the key to this case would be forcing Karl into a mistake to test the edges of Jackson's arrogance. Tex phoned Debbie.

"Be Socratic," said Debbie, "Make sure he can't escape from anything with a one-word answer." Tex felt well-armed.

CHAPTER FIFTY-FOUR

Tex blamed his potential misinterpretation of the Nathan Jackson case on a general malaise, generated by Susan's death, but now Tex had his energy back. This was like the good old days when Tex had been the detective others had gone to when they hit a brick wall. He wasn't by qualification a specialist profiler, but his reputation had been enhanced by successfully hunting down several serial killers. Blue sky thinking was the modern idiom for DCI Deacon's left-field approach, but sometimes he burrowed too deeply into their minds.

Deacon got behind the eyes of a killer and worried that, someday, he'd never come back. Despite what he knew, Karl Jackson felt chilled on the morning of what was to be his second meeting with Tex Deacon, mainly because of the supreme confidence he felt in situations like these. He'd thought it through, *"Patricia is alive, yes, but it's still being seen as a suicide attempt, isn't it? I'm sure she'd try to explain the overdose away, probably by accusing me, but why would anyone believe a codeine addict? And if anyone believed Patricia, why hadn't I been questioned or arrested? Patricia's Doctor had been attempting to wean her off the codeine, so if her bleating led to a court case, the Doctor would be called to the witness stand. How could Patricia prove that someone else had forced her to take fentanyl? It would be her word, and the Doctor's, against mine."* The more Karl spun his version of the probabilities around in his head, the more certain he was that he was in the clear.

Yes, Karl was devastated by Patricia's survival, but he still managed a laugh when he thought about an ironic parallel of his own creation. Patricia hadn't been the first female to receive his specialist attention. Rebecca, a lover, had become a little irritated when Karl inevitably became bored. Rebecca's unwelcome harassment had started with a barrage of threatening texts. These were all on the mobile phone he kept behind the false wall in his office. Ignoring Rebecca didn't do the trick, and soon she was parking outside the house. The sight of her brooding where Patricia might see her was enough to ignite Karl.

He decided that he needed to reconnect, dip into his narcissistic resources, and as if by magic, the passion for Rebecca was reborn. Karl had seen the 'error of his ways' and was determined to 'make it up to her'.

The antique romantic clichés worked.

Karl wanted all that came with extramarital activity, but he didn't want to leave his wife. Karl would say to Rebecca that, while he wanted to, he couldn't destroy his marriage and hurt Patricia and Kerry. His script was as worn as a miller's stone, and he knew it by rote. One of Karl's killer lines was, "I have to finish our relationship because I love you too much." He always felt nauseous when his silver tongue slithered that line out. Karl worked hard to remove Rebecca from his life without harm, but she was persistent.

Rebecca was partial to chocolate and for their staged reunion, Karl bought champagne and some rather moist chocolate cupcakes. The ingredients were what you would expect: Dark chocolate, butter, flour, muscovado and golden caster sugar, cocoa powder, eggs… and strychnine. The final ingredient was the only one that didn't make you fat. Karl had referred to the excellent work of Christiana Edmunds, a Victorian lady who was called 'The Chocolate Cream Killer'. She injected strychnine into confectionery, which was good, but was caught and died in Broadmoor, which was not so good.

Karl made sure he knew which bun was which, but unfortunately, and rather importantly, he didn't inject quite enough strychnine. Rebecca suffered from severe spasms but nothing more, and it was put down to acute food poisoning. Karl the Chemist had hoped for 'asphyxiation by paralysis of the neural pathways', which was the usual cause of death from an overdose of strychnine. It was a favourite of Agatha Christie's in her whodunits. While Rebecca recovered alone at home, Karl worked on the final detachment. The relationship with Rebecca continued for a while and then fizzled out, and Patricia didn't uncover it. Karl saw it as a mission failure but also as part of his learning curve.

There was a knock at Karl's front door. Like before, DCI Tex Deacon stood on the welcome mat below the doorstep, his eyes level with Karl's chest. A full summer sun blast hit Jackson's body and silhouetted him against the dark hallway behind. The effect made Karl look like some biblical superhero, maybe Jesus himself. It made Tex feel inferior, but only for a moment. Karl certainly looked like a man who might have superpowers. Tex hoped it was a trick of the light.

Karl was fairly certain that if Tex had built up the required mass of evidence, he wouldn't have turned up like this, knocking politely like a Jehovah's Witness. Karl mused to himself as he invited the DCI into his home. *"They'd have hit the house with a S.W.A.T team. They'd be swinging off the chimneys. I'd have been mugged by a horde of screaming, helmeted officers and read my rights."* This rather sedate scenario, which existed outside Jackson's imagination, had started with Karl Jackson asking Tex Deacon if he'd like a cup of tea. Karl had convinced himself of his own thoroughness, but he also knew there were plot holes. If Karl was the only person who knew what they were, he was safe.

***

Tex nestled into Karl Jackson's sofa. The cushions had the consistency of blancmange and immediately put a strain on the detective's bulging disc. This was exactly where Tex had sat when he had commiserated with Karl after the death of Nathan. Now though, the DCI was seeing Karl through a different lens. Tex's eyes darted, looking for any indication of a method of attack in case he triggered Karl. Jackson strolled from the kitchen carrying a tea tray and a gentle funnel of steam rose from a spout beside digestives, laid out like toppled dominos. Tex wondered if there was poison in anything on the tray. Digestives dunked in Novichok weren't part of the Tex Deacon nutrition plan. He was a long way from the hermetically sealed safety of a police interview room, and the smell of lavender potpourri confirmed it. Tex could feel the hard edge of his own small can of pepper spray pressing into the small of his back. Karl Jackson eased himself into his favourite chair.

"So Detective Deacon, what can I do for you?" Tex responded, despite being slightly ruffled by a nervous rasp in his throat, "I'm here to talk to you about a couple of things Mr. Jackson. The murder of Richard Turkington is already in the public domain, and I'm hoping that you might be able to fill in some detail. I'll get to that in a moment but first, let's discuss Patricia's fentanyl overdose. Is there anything you'd like to say about that?"

Karl smirked the Karl smirk, "The great DCI Deacon, at my house of all places, without a caution or back-up. Do you suspect me of anything?" Tex opened his right hand, but didn't get a chance to open his mouth because Karl hadn't completed his diatribe, "Well you might do, but if you had incontrovertible evidence, I'd be at the station, and you certainly wouldn't be on your own. I could check you for a wire, but I know the rules of engagement in a situation like this. Are you even here officially DCI Deacon?"

Tex moved quickly past Jackson's attempted block, "Let's stick to the subject matter please. Now, your wife Patricia, is there anything you have to say about her fentanyl overdose?" "DCI Deacon, it was a bit of a shock. Very distressing for me. Obviously, I'm incredibly relieved that Patricia is okay. I phoned the hospital shortly after her admission, and they told me that it wouldn't have taken much more fentanyl to," Karl slipped in a dramatic pause, "Finish her off." Another pause, Karl went on, "Look, Patricia was addicted to opioids, and obviously, I know a lot about them. I'm a chemistry teacher as you know." Karl was motoring, purring like a Porsche on an autobahn. "Patricia was taking a lot of codeine, and fentanyl is a natural step up from that. It's a street drug. A few of the boys at my school have talked about it. Would you believe it, small-time dealers have approached them. Apparently, it's not that difficult to get hold of. Maybe your men should be posted on the school gates." He sniggered. Karl's prose was flowing.

As Tex moved, the pepper spray can dragged, creasing a cushion, "Mr. Jackson. Your wife says she didn't take an overdose." Karl responded instantly, "Well she would say that wouldn't she? Addicts are in denial. The last thing she would do is admit to it. Like an alcoholic," he added as a mark of punctuation. "She's probably embarrassed that she's still alive. Embarrassed that she's made a suicide attempt that didn't work." Tex had observed how the timbre of Jackson's voice had risen and how he only referred to Patricia as 'she'.

"Mr. Jackson, Patricia told your son Kerry that she'd been having an affair with Richard Turkington." Karl, without hesitation, launched himself into a display of hammed outrage. Jackson bluffed and blustered, flapping about like a penguin trying to discover the secret of flight. The unconvincing exhibition of theatrics lasted several minutes. Too much Widow Twanky panto stuff suggested a lie to a man with DCI Deacon's knowledge.

"Mr. Jackson. Patricia suspects that you knew about the affair." Karl's inner thespian appeared again and he feigned surprise. Tex waited and then threw in his own pre-prepared scenery eating line. "And of course, the fentanyl, Mr. Jackson. Drugs being your area of expertise, maybe I should suspect you of attempted murder." This set in motion paroxysm number three. Jackson was on his feet again, moving in all directions, looking like a child playing on an invisible bouncy castle. Tex watched as dispassionately as he could. When he'd settled again Jackson spoke pointedly, "Detective Deacon, I hope for your sake, that you have evidence. That's quite an accusation."

Instead of feeling pressured, Karl was emboldened by the faceoff with Tex Deacon. He wondered if that was the best the detective had. After all, accusations didn't lead to convictions, but Tex was being a beagle here, trying to flush the grouse from the moor. He let the atmosphere in the room settle. "I want to talk to you about your brother Nathan and Peter Ferris." Tex arrowed in and waited a few seconds before continuing. "And there's one other thing. The mysterious death of your Uncle Charlie."

Tex watched Karl carefully but there was nothing to see apart from a barely perceptible knee twitch. Tex continued, "It's interesting isn't it? Nathan Jackson, Peter Ferris, Charlie Jackson and Richard Turkington. Here I am, wondering if the man I'm looking at might have had reason to kill all four. Did you Karl? Maybe you killed even more?" Tex's gambit had been carefully calculated. He wanted to agitate Karl, and maybe, in that state, Jackson would make a mistake, maybe not now, not here, but sometime soon. To Tex Deacon's surprise, Karl burst out laughing, rolling back his head. Karl 'The Greatest Showman' had some more amateur dramatics for his one-man audience. "What?" Karl boomed, "Kill them?" The laugh had turned into a sarcastic rat-a-tat growl from the back of his throat.

"Remember Detective Deacon, I was with Nathan. I reported him missing. You know I'm still devastated at the loss of my brother. This is insulting, and what about the note? Nathan's hatred of Ferris? If me and Nathan hadn't got split up, maybe he wouldn't have killed himself that night? Maybe Nathan would have talked to me and I might have been able to help him, to soothe him. Do you have any idea how difficult that is to live with?" Karl tried, unsuccessfully, to force a tear. Instead, he looked away and shook his head, "You've some nerve Detective. You heartless bastard."

Tex locked onto a frothing Karl, "Mr. Jackson, Nathan was your twin brother. Let's talk about the CCTV of Nathan at the boatyard. In theory that could have been you. How long did it take you to master Nathan's limp?"

Jackson continued with his spitting verbals, "There you go again Detective Deacon. Throwing out bogus nonsense. You're good at fiction, aren't you? All make-believe crap. If you could back that up, we wouldn't be sitting here having tea and bikkies, would we?"

Tex was now even happier that he hadn't imbibed in the tea and bikkies, and he glanced at the digestives wondering again if some of them had been impregnated with something fatal. Tex remained stoic and continued, "Let's move on to Charlie Jackson. I've spoken to mountain rescue and a local journalist. Both have their suspicions about his death. You have told me yourself that you didn't like Charlie. Karl, what was your true relationship with your Uncle?" Jackson pulled a strangely comic expression, open-mouthed, jigging his head from side to side. Briefly, he looked like the Joker from Batman. Karl's bludgeoning tones reached a crescendo, "My Uncle?

Bloody Hell. Are you telling me I killed Uncle Charlie now? You're some boy, Detective Deacon."

Karl climaxed the latest tirade with a patronising scowl. He had planned for days like this. Tex may have been expecting a series of Jackson cover stories, but Karl didn't think he needed any. Karl clung to his supposition that Deacon, in all probability, didn't have anything other than sketchy bits and pieces, all circumstantial. Tex had taken the diatribe with a monk's calm and continued, "Let's get back to the Turkington saga." Jackson listened intently, a hard edge to his expression, "If your wife is right that you knew about her affair, then there's a motive. Murder a cheating wife, murder her lover. It's hardly rare." Karl, externally, remained unruffled. Tex thrust again and flashed a blindsiding spike, "Karl, did you love your father?" For the first time during the heated exchange, Karl hesitated. In his eyes, he held pure contempt. "What has he got to do with it? You're a crazy man." Jackson's face changed colour for the first time in their exchange, going from butter to blazing.

"Next you'll be telling me I shot Liberty Valance. What are you going to do? Go through my entire family? My Great Great Grandfather died in suspicious circumstances. Maybe I killed him and then hid in mum's womb beside Nathan. We had the labrador put down, or did I poison Casper the mutt? Karl the 'Dog Slayer'? Is that me? Are you just making this up as you go along Detective Deacon?"

Tex asked his question again, "Did you love your father?" Pumped blue veins appeared at Karl's temples. "Love him? I hated the bastard. Evil, hateful, child-beating, wife-beating bastard. But kill him? Ridiculous nonsense. My Dad died from heart failure Deacon. In the hospital, and that's exactly what it says on the death certificate."

Tex kept going, "I'm aware of that Karl, of course, I am, but you were Harry Jackson's one and only visitor. You were the last person to see him alive. Four hours before he died. We have that on record."

Jackson roared again. This time it sounded less like a laugh and more like a werewolf's howl. "So, hang on a minute, what do they call those mercy killers? 'Angels of Death'?" So I'm the 'Angel of Death' now and 'The Dog Slayer' and what else? No let me guess, Detective Deacon. 'Fentanyl Phantom', 'Rock Face Ripper', 'Campsite Killer'. You guys love to give murderers big juicy dramatic nicknames. Splash it all over the papers. It's concocted nonsense. If there's a madman in this room, Deacon, it's you."

The meeting had played out just fine for Karl Jackson, and suddenly he was ice cold again. "Detective Deacon. You used the word 'if' too often. That's a very big word isn't it? If... If... If. Are you hanging your hopes on that? Use the word 'if' in a court of law, and the judge will run you out of the chambers, and I'll piss myself while he does it."

Tex stuck to his tactic, "Mr. Jackson, three of the deaths occurred in local mountainous terrain, and you are a man who possesses considerable mountain craft. A killer with such skills would be at a distinct advantage. And the ricin, and the fentanyl. Maybe I should be hunting for a deranged chemistry teacher. Do you know any Karl? Peter Ferris died beside a lake, the very same lake where you spent many childhood days. I have it on good authority that you hated your father, and I mean really hated him. An investigator wouldn't need much imagination to link you to all of those deaths."

Karl dug in. "Imagination might be all you have, Detective Deacon. And unless you come up with anything better than fantasy, I'd appreciate it if you left me in peace. I will be contacting my lawyer. This is harassment, and I'd appreciate it if you got out of my house DCI Deacon." Tex rose quickly from the too-soft sofa and felt a nip in his back. He hid a wince, "Very happy to go, Mr. Jackson, but I suspect we'll see each other again - very soon."

***

Catching Karl was going to be tough. Tex knew that he might need at least one piece of gotcha evidence to nail him. Threads eventually come together to make rope, would Tex gather enough threads? Damning forensics would be a huge bonus, and he was still waiting on DNA from the rucksack. At least Jackson now knew that Deacon was aware that he'd been close to Harry not long before he died. As for the boatyard, Tex hoped he was rolling doubt towards Karl there too. Tex still had a big problem with the CCTV footage. The black and white video looked like it had been filmed through a misted bathroom window. The CCTV showed a seven-second clip of a man of Nathan's height, build and stuttered gait. Tex still had no idea why Karl would want to kill his brother. He was up to the axles in mud, hoping the killer would help pull him out.

CHAPTER FIFTY-FIVE

Tex walked from Jackson's house, feeling a lava-like heat in his veins. The street outside was quiet. The poplars that lined the road framed the emptiness. It was as if the residents had been told that the bubonic plague was in the area and had packed up and left in a hurry. Tex climbed into his car. His nervous system felt like it had been plugged into an electric fence, and his attempt to find first gear was met with a crunching grate. The car bucked and then lurched away. L plates wouldn't have looked out of place, and Tex wondered if his style of approach with Jackson the previous day had made him appear like a learner detective too.

The glorious green of Cumbria flashed past, but Tex saw none of it as he sped home, trying to stabilise his emotions. He tried deep breaths and chanted a mantra he'd learned at a transformational meditation seminar. The force had paid for that, it was part of a sponsored mental health programme for officers, but Tex was struggling to locate his Yin and Yang. The adrenalin was still ripping through his system when he called Debbie on the hands-free, and when she answered, the normally phlegmatic Deacon was straight into rapid fire.

"I have to admit, Jackson is one cool son of a bitch. I shouldn't allow myself to be impressed by a sociopath, but the way he handled the situation was incredible. Debbie, I felt like I was appearing as an extra in someone else's drama, with Jackson very much the male lead. It was a strange feeling. Jackson was the one being questioned, but somehow he seemed to control the whole show."

"I can't wait to meet him," said Debbie, "Do you think he'll let me interview him when he's eventually banged up?" There was almost a giggle, "I can already see my name on the front page of the nationals, 'DEBBIE PILKINGTON EXCLUSIVE' So, come on Tex, how did he react, I want detail."

Tex replied, "Well, his side of it sounded scripted, but it was all delivered with flamboyance, and he had a plausible explanation for everything. He never once hesitated. I can visualize Karl winning an Oscar and only thanking himself. I don't really have anything that drives us any further forward, and there was something about Jackson's swashbuckling confidence that was very disturbing. On the one hand, he was convincing, though not once did he sound authentic, but Jeez, this is going to be tough. Catching Jackson? Greased seaweed is easier to get hold of. He dodges bullets better than Keanu Reeves in 'The Matrix'!

When the call ended, Tex took a deep breath. A scudding greyness filled the horizon beyond his windscreen. Irregular splats became a steady stream, and Tex switched on the wipers. His thinking, again, was mostly fermentation without too many hard facts. He was about as confident as a vodka sozzled tightrope walker taking his first step across the Grand Canyon. Tex focused on the white line that blurred into the distance, amazed that he could drive a car when in this mental state.

Tex began to settle - the last thing he needed right now was something that might fracture his slowly rebalancing equilibrium. Just as his inner calm was beginning to return, his mobile rang. Tex didn't even look at the name that had popped up on his dashboard in case the identity of the caller meant bad news. "Leave me alone please, ten minutes peace. That's all I ask."

The mobile was slotted between the arms of a plastic holder suckered to the window screen. *"I'll let it go to voicemail,"* he thought, which would be on the sixth ring. On the fourth, his resistance cracked, and Tex glanced across. The grimace was immediate, and Tex let out a long mewling bellow, not unlike the sound made by abattoir cattle when they sense there's a bolt coming. Tex's voice exploded with anguish, "Oh bloody hell noooooo. Anyone but him. That fucking tosspot twat of a wanker."

Tex surprised himself at the variety of language. Tex preferred to avoid profanity, but here it was fully justified. The identifying moniker, "Montague - Lawyer" was on the phone screen. Tex could have let the phone ring out, but that would only have delayed the inevitable. His thumb pressed the connection button on his steering column. Tex was determined to get the upper hand fast. "Montague. Is this a great day for you? Let me guess. Karl Jackson has phoned you."

He hadn't been charged, but Tex had accused Jackson of murder. In this fairly remote corner of England, 'Montague, Fortescue and Trapp' was the most likely initial contact point for someone like Jackson. Tex was ready for what was coming next. When Jasper Montague made important statements, he had the most irritating habit of inhaling through his saliva. He sounded like he was sucking the last remnants of a milkshake through a straw.

"That's right Detective Deacon. Mr. Jackson approached us, and the partners knew straight away that I was the man for the job." The arrogant smugness had started already. Tex may have been hands-free, but he would rather have had his hands on Montague's throat.

"DCI Deacon, I've already begun my research. Mr. Jackson called me just after you left his house, a second visit, I believe? You ranted on about all sorts of heinous crimes, is that right? Shouldn't you have been doing that under caution at the station? Gone crazy horse, have you DCI Deacon?"

Montague waited for a response. All he could hear was nasal breathing and the low rumble of the car engine. He barrelled on. "I've already been digging into my fabulous little black book of contacts. I hear that you are assisting with that dreadful Richard Turkington crime but that it's 'light duties', that's the actual quote Detective Deacon. I've heard a lot more too. Please accept my condolences regarding your wife. I really do hope that the treatment programme works well for you."

Tex visualised the strangulation and Montague's eyes popping and bursting while, at the same time he pondered why anyone would want to call their son Jasper. Tex wondered if Jasper liked being called Jasper. Tex doubted it. Montague went on.

"You are harassing my client Mr. Deacon, without full authority. Legally speaking, your conversation with Mr. Jackson at his house overstepped several legal boundaries. If you have enough evidence Mr. Deacon then arrest him. The very FACT that you didn't suggests to me that you have no proof at all. Is it all circumstantial Mr. Deacon? - as my client strongly suspects."

In terms of getting a conviction, Tex knew that any evidence he did have was about as safe as a circular firing squad. Montague had many phenomenally annoying habits. Saliva sucking was the worst, but he had others. For example every time he said the word fact he shouted it. Montague had done this literally hundreds of times during the Gary Bloomberg trial. Another thing about Montague that piqued Tex was his dress sense. Somehow his sartorial tastes seemed to parallel his posh name and Tory boy accent. Every day of the Bloomberg trial, Montague wore a different waistcoat, often with a paisley design and a different coloured bow tie. Tex used to imagine it spinning wildly, tightening as it went, and choking him to death.

"Detective Deacon. Unless you can produce a warrant, I suggest you stay well away from my client. If you continue to torment Mr. Jackson with false and unsubstantiated accusations, we will be very quick to press charges against the police for harassment. And it won't look good for you, will it? Setting off on your own like Miss Marple."

Good old Jasper, *"Not the kind of man I'd get tired of punching,"* thought Tex, who picked his moment to interject. "Press charges? At the moment, we have no intention of pressing charges. You are getting ahead of yourself Mr. Montague. Yes, I talked to Karl Jackson at his house, on my own, and yes, it was twice. All we've had are a couple of relaxing chats in his lounge. The last time we almost got to the brandy and mints." Tex liked that line, and his blood was warming nicely. "Would you prefer it if we brought him into HQ? You remember the Bloomberg case. Those long overnights at the station. I imagine you enjoyed those, didn't you? Sitting on that plastic chair, bum sweating. Did it feel like an eternity? Sipping lukewarm police station pish and trying to defend a cannibalistic serial killer. Guilty, wasn't he? Very, very guilty in the end. Slaughtered seven people in cold blood. Do you ever lose sleep over that Jasper? How did it feel trying to get a man like Bloomberg off? Imagine him back on the streets, and you responsible for it. Just as well we had a cast iron case wasn't it."

Tex hadn't noticed, but his voice level had risen exponentially as he delivered his monologue.

Montague's turbo jets had been gently cooled, "Everyone knows you played dirty tricks in the Bloomberg case, Deacon. Charge Mr. Jackson if you wish but be sure that your evidence is overwhelming. You and I both know that you have nothing right now. In the meantime, I'll emphasise my advice: Leave my client alone." And Jasper was gone, his voice replaced by a flat hum. Tex reflected on the Bloomberg trial and Montague's role in it. The 'dirty tricks' he had referred to weren't dirty tricks at all. Montague hated the fact that brilliant police work had undone his defence of Bloomberg. The final piece of evidence needed to nail a guilty verdict was actually found during the trial. Even though the Bloomberg case was in court, Tex's team kept on digging. They knew that Bloomberg had used a series of aliases and had a number of forged identity documents, but his movements, and any transactions, had been hard to trace, but the investigation team had discovered that, under one of his false names, Bloomberg had rented a remote lock up garage.

They were several weeks into the murder trial when the lock-up was identified. The rental matched to a Bloomberg alias. Tex spoke with supreme confidence from the witness box, his eyes never once leaving Montague's.

"In the lock-up was a freezer and in the freezer was a small box. Inside the box, there were a number of flesh medallions. Bite size mementoes taken from each victim, with bites that match Bloomberg's canine impression. We now have enough evidence and DNA here to convict him a dozen times."

***

After the Bloomberg verdict, Montague was seething, and Tex knew Jasper would love nothing more than another opportunity to get one over on his old foe. Bloomberg was in a high-security hospital for the criminally insane and now Tex was trying to hunt down another man who he wanted to see rot in jail.

Following his terse phone call with Jasper and his rasping saliva, Tex reflected on his second Jackson house visit. *"What do I make of Karl's vaudevillian excitability? Maybe an indicator of many things. Perhaps Karl verges on psychosis, the tantrums indicate an unstable personality? Maybe he is, quite simply, a purebred psychopath? Or were the outbursts the reaction of an angry, innocent man furious at being accused of something he didn't do?"*

Tex doubted the final option, but he needed more, and now, after the bruising spar with Montague, Tex knew he had to be put onto the case in a bona fide, hardcore, official capacity.

CHAPTER FIFTY-SIX

Tex hastily arranged a meeting with the Chief Constable, and now, a day after his metaphorical gunfight with Jasper, Tex was minutes away from his very own High Noon. He sat, once again, outside Barbara Bracewell's office. Only three of the legs on the chair made the floor at any one time. It was the epitome of cheap, and Tex's back was becoming sticky against the green plastic. He felt like the schoolboy who had stolen lunch money from the other kid's pockets. What would he get? Three strokes of the cane? When it flickered, a buzzer accompanied the red light. This was his invitation to enter, and, feeling like one of Pavlov's dogs, Tex followed the instructions. The silver plate on the door needed a buff, but you could still clearly see the engraved name, "Chief Constable Barbara Bracewell."

Now in her late forties, Bracewell had kept the athletic figure of her youth. The features had picked up a line or two, but her face had retained its freshness. Plenty of men in the building reserved a spot for her in their fantasies. As Tex walked in, Bracewell had her head down, writing up a report. As he sat down, she slid her newly acquired reading glasses onto the tip of her nose. "Tex, Tex, Tex. Montague, Fortescue and Trapp?" The Chief Constable pinched the skin between her eyes, "The great Jasper Montague, Tex. Have you awakened the beast?" Tex moved to speak, but Barbara put her hand up, like a traffic cop, "I was going to ring you but thought this would be better done in person." Tex wondered if he was going to get those strokes of the cane, "Montague called me late yesterday and told me you were at the house of Karl Jackson, having tea and biscuits. I was hoping you had dropped in for some extracurricular chemistry lessons, but Jasper said no, instead, you'd popped over, without my say so, by the way, and accused him of a number of murders." Bracewell's voice ended that sentence several octaves higher than it had been at the start.

"Yes, sorry Barbara, I know it's not admissible, but that's not important," Bracewell interjected, "Tex, yes, you are on the Turkington case and yes, Jackson's potential involvement is a viable lead to chase, but you know that you are not officially allowed to go that deep. I put you backstage for a good reason, but no, the mighty DCI Deacon ploughs on outside the remit afforded to him by the Chief Constable and does his own thing. And as for talking to Jackson off tape!"

Tex was the very definition of sheepish. If he'd been holding a bowler hat, he would have rolled the rim around with his fingers, "I'm waiting on some DNA. If it comes back the way I think it will, it puts Jackson at, or near, the scene of Turkington's death."

"DNA of what?" said Bracewell, "Sweat," said Tex, " I'm hoping it'll be Karl Jackson's sweat." Barbara looked hard at Tex and spoke, "I was told that the Turkington forensic file was complete but hadn't been typed up. If there had been any errant DNA Lex would have told me. This has gone through Lex hasn't it?"

"Yep," said Tex, "But he's doing me a favour." "Yet another favour," said Bracewell, dribbling sarcasm.

"Okay, another favour. Barbara, I've been hunting from, as you say, 'backstage' and I've found out, through his son, that Jackson's wife Patricia was having an affair with Turkington. Gives Jackson a motive and also, I'm not sure that her attempted suicide wasn't attempted murder. The ricin that killed Turkington had to be delivered to the site. Karl, the technology teacher, might have been able to create a delivery method."

"Hold on Tex. I'm across the forensics here." said Barbara, but Tex interrupted, "I think Turkington must have had a tracker on him somewhere, but there was no tracker when the body was found. The killer would have retrieved it. Hot morning in August. It might be one bead of sweat, but that's all I need. Lex is having another look before closing the report." Bracewell pulled at her bottom lip with a finger and thumb, "Good stuff Tex. Good stuff. Jackson DNA would certainly move this investigation on. Would give us the green light to bring him in, but sounds like a long shot to me"

"Lex is the best, and he knows exactly what I'm looking for."

The only sound in the room was Bracewell tapping digits on her desk, "But you still went way beyond your remit Tex. This is you in recovery, not chasing a crazed killer around like some mad lone wolf."

"Yes, lone wolf. About that. As we're having a truth session, there is one more thing. I'm not exactly a lone wolf." Bracewell was wide-eyed and shaking her head at the same time, "I've had a helper. A young journalist from the Rimpton Chronicle, Deborah Pilkington."

Tex wondered if he should just bend over the Chief Constable's desk right now and take his lashing. "A young journalist?" Bracewell threw her head back and slumped against the high back leather chair, "Mother of God."

"Barbara," said Tex, now doing his best wounded Bambi impression, "She's good. I needed someone. I know, my bad, my very bad, but I feel so much better now, you know, getting my teeth into a case. I'm good to go, Barbara, good to go."

Bracewell was being defeated in this little battle, but her instinct told her that, in the long run, it might be a battle worth losing. She could see Tex was moving forward, even though she was sure the word 'hunch' would have been used if Tex had been totally honest. Whether it was Deacon's lateral thinking, or a combination of his and Debbie's, progress was being made, and it was the human side of Barbara Bracewell that made her such a superb Chief Constable.

"All right Tex - go ahead. Officially. But I'm not happy about this girl Deborah Pilkington. A local hack helping us with a murder inquiry?"

"Trust me, Barbara, please. Debbie is well aware of the rules, I know I can trust her."

"Okay, but I'm very tempted to finish this meeting with the words, 'against my better fucking judgement'. Just make sure I don't regret this Tex."

CHAPTER FIFTY-SEVEN

Feeling relieved to have regained his professional freedom, Tex was sitting alone at the Victorian mahogany writing table in his front room. A low wattage glow from his desk light dusted across scattered notes. There was an A4 pad with scribblings and various other hieroglyphics in Tex's long scrawl, networked across the paper. "Were the killings linked? Looks likely, or were they carried out as individual whims. That would be unusual?'"

His crumpled shirt was clamped in place by a pair of bright blue Clitheroe FC braces, and he slurped at a tasteless dark liquid. In the morning, it was a simple hot beverage and not alcoholic. The tick of the clock was Tex's only companion, and he ruminated in silence. *"The kills. Sometimes close together, like Nathan and Peter Ferris. For others, like Harry Jackson and Charlie Jackson and Richard Turkington, there were gaps - some longer than others."* Tex had learned so much while accumulating convictions, 'Murder Sobriety' – common enough in a serial killer - they could sometimes go on the wagon. Satiated for a while or had no reason to kill. *"This is no 'calendar killer' when there was a regulated time frame between murders. Modus operandi? Toxins and drugs were used to dispose of Richard Turkington and to poison Patricia Jackson. Etorphine Hydrochloride and liquid Valium in the case of Nathan. Was his death suicide or something else? If suicide where did Nathan get the Etorphine? Peter Ferris had been butchered with a single knife wound to the heart. Clinical. Charlie's death was either an accident or, as Mountain Rescue suspected, the sling had been deliberately slipped off the crag. Harry? Still in the weeds with that one. Body exhumation? Not exactly possible. He's been cremated. There's nothing neat and tidy here. Is it my imagination, or instinct that is weaving pieces into place?"* Tex was still worried that he was falling into a habit of putting his sixth sense ahead of hard fact.

He pushed his lead pencil across a web of criss-crossed lines on the paper. The page looked like a game of cat's cradle with arrows connected to various names. Four of the victims Harry, Nathan,

Charlie, and Patricia. Three dead, one alive, and all had been related to Karl.

Tex jumped when the landline jangled. Very few people had his home number, and even fewer called at this time of night. "Hello, Tex Deacon here. Who's that?" He felt a pump against his ribs and then a voice.

"Tex, it's Lex. I knew you'd want to know straight away. The late shift guys at the lab have just processed that DNA." Involuntarily Tex squeezed the phone to his head as if the action might hurry up the information.

"Tex, there IS someone else's DNA on the rucksack, but as you guessed, there wasn't very much of it. One bead of sweat. It was on the main plastic clasp. The jellyfish pattern under the microscope suggested that it had dropped from a height. Maybe a foot, possibly two feet. But it's there Tex. I'll finish up the report tomorrow morning first thing. Up to you to find a match buddy. I've looked. There's nothing on the database." Tex closed his eyes and answered his old buddy, "Lex you are my man. I think I might love you. Just one more thing. Do you have any tyre tracks near where you found Turkington's Range Rover?"

"Obviously not in the car park at Lucifer's, Tex, it's all tarmac, but, yes on the verge outside it. When the spaces are full, especially at weekend's, walkers and hikers park on the road. There were innumerable tyre tracks on the soft shoulder, most of them a mush of mud, but there were a few fresh ones. We have the photographs. But I'd need a tyre make to give us any chance of making a match." Tex knew where he'd be first thing in the morning, at Jackson's. Except this time, he'd have uniformed company on his third visit to Karl's house.

CHAPTER FIFTY-EIGHT

It would be a curtain-twitching kind of morning on Karl Jackson's road. It was another stuffy day, and the very act of movement brought perspiration. Tex was first there and parked his car on the pavement close to Jackson's house, hiding it on the blind side of the poplars. He'd tipped off Debbie and Kerry to keep them in the loop, as he'd promised. When Jackson opened his front door, he saw Tex up close and personal alongside his VW Beetle. The pain in Tex's knees reminded him that his body didn't like positions like this anymore, but he needed to be able to read the numbers and letters. Deacon had just made a note, 'Michelin 235/45 R18' when he heard Jackson's voice.

"Having fun over there DCI Deacon. You're not invited this time. You're trespassing on private property." Tex hauled himself up with a pain-filled groan and placed his butt on the egg-shaped bonnet. He could feel two lines of sweat between his blue braces and white shirt. "Did you know that Ted Bundy drove a yellow VW Beetle?" Tex didn't wait for an answer. "Yes, I know this is private property, but I've a few friends arriving to plead my case in a minute." At that moment, a police car appeared from behind the tightly planted poplars and pulled into the driveway.

"What's going on Deacon?"

"Oh come on Karl, you know what a detective says at moments like this, it's in all the crime movies. We need to ask you a few questions down at the station." Karl snapped back, "I'm going to call my lawyer right now."

"Go ahead Karl, and when you're on to Montague, let him know that we'll be doing a standard DNA test, and right now, we're getting a print from your Beetle's front left forward and rear tyres. We can arrest you if you want, I'm sure the neighbours would have a field day seeing the well-respected chemistry teacher being taken away in handcuffs."

"Arrest me for what?" Karl sneered. "Suspicion of murder, Mr Jackson. Will you be coming voluntarily?" The look of hate on Karl's face seared into the bones of DCI Deacon.

CHAPTER FIFTY-NINE

DCI Deacon led Karl Jackson into the police station. Tex was fascinated by the man he hoped to bring down. Jackson projected a personna, a block of ice inside a suit of skin, but, for the first time, Tex glimpsed signs of Jackson's cold soul beginning to defrost. "You can't take a DNA test without my permission," Karl said with a raised vibrato voice. He didn't look frightened, far from it, but now there were wrinkles of concern etched across his hard and handsome face. Tex moved within the boundaries of Jackson's personal space, "I can, Mr. Jackson. I can take your DNA whenever I want. I don't need your permission and we're going to do it right now. If you've any complaints, you can take it up with your lawyer." There was a layer of frustration now in the voice of Jackson, "I phoned his office," said Karl, "Montague's in court, he can't get here until three o'clock. I want you to take me home until he's free." There was a child-like pleading in Jackson's voice and Tex, for the first time in his dealings with him, felt that he held the power.

"Oh we wouldn't dream of putting you through all that Mr. Jackson," said Tex, "We've got some excellent accommodation here. You can enjoy the pleasures of one of our hospitality suites. It's got a mini-bar – in fact, it's got several mini-bars – they're all on the window."

A constable took Jackson away to do his DNA test and Tex immediately phoned his buddy in forensics, Lex Dawson. "Lex, Tex." Lex smiled at the other end of the line, "What do you want, Tex?"

"I need a big favour, Lex. We've got Jackson's DNA. How quickly can you process it for me? I can have Jackson's sample with you in twenty minutes. See if it matches with the sweat."

"No pressure, Tex, just the usual from you! Do it now, and if you can't do it now, do it faster." The warmth between the two men was clear, and Tex needed his friend now. "Tex, I'll fast-track it, but that'll probably take four hours, at the very best, three and a half. I'll start as soon as I get the sample into my hands."

It was late afternoon when Jasper Montague eventually turned up, looking drained after losing a close call in a fraud case. Jackson was taken from Cell Four to an airless and windowless interview room. The walls had been roughly rollered, the shade dark granite. Karl Jackson reckoned that the colour had been chosen on purpose to enhance the mood of misery.

There were four men in the room. Jackson and Montague on one side of a desk that looked like it had been rescued from a dump, and on the other side DCI Deacon, and Stan 'The Man' Hansen, another Detective from the Turkington case. Cameras hung like vultures, one in each corner. Many years ago, the solitary air conditioning vent had given up supplying cold comfort and now chugged out a tepid flow through grimy slats. This promised to be steamy in more ways than one.

Tex hoped that Montague would suffer heat stroke or something equally unpleasant. Jasper was beautifully tooled in a suit so sharp that it could have cut your throat. The ensemble completed with the usual waistcoat and bow tie. Tex wore beach shorts and sandals. It wasn't a fashionable look, as it was matched with a short-sleeved white shirt and braces, but a lot more practical. Jackson had left his house in a hurry, helped by a couple of officers, and was still wearing the jogging bottoms and black polo shirt he'd eaten his breakfast in. Hansen looked official and sported the classic hard-nosed detective 'uniform' of rolled up sleeves and open-necked shirt, with a roughly loosened tie. A four-day shadowed stubble completed the cliché.

***

There was a click and then a voice, "This is a recording of an interview with Karl Jackson in the presence of his lawyer Jasper Montague and DCI's Deacon and Hansen."

"Mr. Jackson," said Tex, "Let's start with the death of Peter Ferris. Your Mum confirmed that it was your twin Nathan in the CCTV. The unmistakable limp, but she also said that you are a remarkable mimic. Karl, do you do impressions of Nathan's disability?"

Before every answer, Montague suggested to Jackson that he say nothing, but Karl generally batted that advice away. "Impressions of Nathan's limp?" Karl was laughing as he said, "What are you saying DCI Deacon?"

"As I said Mr. Jackson, just a few questions to help us tidy things up. The man on the CCTV wasn't wearing a hat. No attempt to cover up his identity. Do you find that strange?"

"No I don't. It was Nathan at the pontoon, he got his revenge, and I don't blame him. He was planning suicide, so I imagine he didn't care if he was identified or not," Jackson, once again, smirked that smirk, but Tex noticed that there was a hint of nervousness to it.

Montague stepped in, "I can't see where this line of questioning is getting any of us. You are just going over old ground, and that's a closed case." Tex looked at Montague and fantasised about driving his nose bone into his brain.

"I could go through a number of incidents that ended with the unfortunate climax of a funeral, and, with Peter Ferris, Nathan Jackson, and Richard Turkington in particular, the evidence is pointing us in a certain direction. We do know that your client was in the vicinity, or right up close, for at least two of those deaths."

"Oh God," said Jackson, who would have leant back and balanced on the back legs of his chair if it hadn't been bolted to the floor. "Here we go again with the stuck record."

"Karl, Richard Turkingon. We have reason to believe that your wife Patricia was having an affair with Turkington. Did you know about that?" Tex sucked his lips together, and Jackson folded his arms. Tex continued. "When your wife got out of hospital, she went to Scotland to be with her parents. It'll help her with recovery, and we think it's a good idea. We'll be keeping an eye on her, just in case."

Karl cast an insouciant glance at Tex and shrugged his shoulders. Tex changed tack, "Mr. Jackson, tracks from the front left and rear right tyres of your VW Beetle were found on the verge close to Lucifer's car park, where we found Turkington's Range Rover. Quite fresh those tracks."

Karl's arms stayed rigid across his body. Saying nothing but certainly listening. A knock on the door opened just far enough for a constable to poke his head into the small space. Tex got up and walked over to the officer, who whispered, "Phone call DCI Deacon. It's very important, you have to take it." Tex looked round at Jackson, ensuring that Karl knew this intervention was all about him.

"Pause the recording please. I'll be a couple of minutes." And Tex was right, two minutes later he was sitting again at the desk in the interview room. The recording recommenced, and Tex leant forward on his elbows, sliding himself close to Jackson's face.

"Can you explain something, Karl... please? Why does your DNA match the DNA we found on Turkington's rucksack? For your information it was a sample taken at the murder site. The DNA was taken from sweat, your sweat Mr. Jackson."

This news hit Montague with a sting and he twisted in his seat, but before he could say anything, Jackson pumped out his arm, imitating a rugby player's hand off, his palm halting an inch short of his lawyer's face.

"I'll speak. Yes I was there. I met Richard in the car park. We were the only one's there. I was going for a run. I love the heat at this time of year. I had sweat on my brow just putting my gear on. It's a great feeling getting a good sweat up, you know you're working hard. And yes I talked to him, and no I didn't know he was having an affair with my wife, so thanks for the breaking news. Turkington had a new Ospreys rucksack. Best make in my opinion. It was in his boot. I popped my head in for a look at it, as mountain nerds like us do."

Montague remained muted. Karl's eyes were pinpricks, like a demon's. "And I parked the Beetle up the road because I needed a pee. Wasn't going to urinate in the car park, I didn't know it was empty until I drove into it after I'd relieved myself."

Tex had to admire Jackson's unbreakable confidence, but, just like the second visit to Karl's house the experienced detective knew what he was trying to achieve. All he wanted to do was make Jackson aware that they were slowly putting bricks in the wall.

By now everyone in the room had dark stains spreading out from their armpits. Shirts were sticking to the backs of all those present. The humidity had seeped over all four men in the interview room. Something ran from Karl's forehead and then followed a path down his nose - the path of least resistance. Then it stopped, hanging from the top of his right nostril. The water tension broke, and a bead of sweat splashed on the table. Karl and Tex watched it and then looked at each other with unblinking eyes. Both wondered if that one tiny piece of DNA would eventually become significant.

Karl watched the bead slowly disappear into the wooden table. He was deep in thought, *"I must destroy the journals. I can't take chances. They're a life's work, but they've got to go – immediately."*

CHAPTER SIXTY

Kerry was at home again, trying to complete his psychology project, which was due to be submitted soon. Not surprisingly, he was finding it hard to concentrate as it isn't every day that your dad is called in for police questioning. In this case, the stool pigeon was the suspect's son, which is rarer still. Kerry was taking a calculated risk by deciding to stay in the house. As long as Karl didn't find out that he was the man who'd revealed that his Mum was having an affair with Richard Turkington, he reckoned he was safe. Kerry felt it was a risk he had to take.

A police car dropped Karl outside the front of the house, and he shouted up the stairs as soon as he crossed the threshold into the hallway, "Kerry, Kerry." A muffled response came from Kerry's bedroom, "I'm doing my psychology stuff Dad." Karl kept on shouting, "Can you believe it? The police had me in for questioning. They suspect me of all sorts of things. An absolute joke, with no evidence of any consequence at all. There's a guy, DCI Deacon, he's a complete idiot – arrogant and overconfident. Traits I hate in a man." Fortunately for Kerry, his dad didn't appear to know where some of this apparently insignificant evidence had come from. The police had sworn to Kerry that his information about his dad would be treated with one hundred percent discretion, and it looked like they'd kept their word. Kerry was not in the least bit surprised by his Father's flippant demeanour, despite the fact that he'd just been questioned about the killing of a man who was having an affair with his wife.

Kerry had shifted from his bedroom and was moving fast down the stairs as he spoke, trying to look surprised and shocked, "What exactly did the police want Dad?"

"Oh it was the usual bullshit," said Karl. Kerry was now face to face with his father. "Kerry, I'd met Turkington in the car park at the start of his camping trip, and they wanted to know if I'd spotted anything suspicious," then Karl did a strange thing, well strange for

290

him. He put his arm around Kerry. Straight away, Kerry suspected this had little to do with the usual emotions exchanged between father and son. Goose pimples ran over and through him and Kerry felt very scared indeed.

"Kerry, would you believe it? They asked me if I knew that Patricia was having an affair with Turkington? I mean, your Mum with that prick? And Kerry, if it was true, how could the police have possibly found out?" Karl pulled Kerry tight with a muscular squeeze, grasping his son's shoulder with a wrestler's strength. It felt like a threat to Kerry, and his skin picked up a layer of ice. Kerry stiffened, waiting for his dad's next move, but Karl simply let his son go and strode towards the kitchen. "Cup of tea son? I think we could both do with one."

Kerry sat on the bottom stair and listened to the noise of a tap being turned and water powering into a kettle. The immediate panic had passed, but thoughts raced through Kerry's head. *"What do the police really know? Do they have any evidence of Mum's apparent fentanyl poisoning? Maybe the police are holding it back from me. Did Dad try to kill Mum and murder Turkington? Deacon must have something more to hang on Dad apart from the affair, or they wouldn't have brought him in, would they?"* Kerry's brain was a maelstrom. He got up and walked slowly into the kitchen. Karl pressed the boil button on the kettle, "Kerry, did you know that your Mum has gone to Scotland to recover from her suicide attempt? The police told me." Kerry said, "Yes Dad, Mum phoned me this morning, and I was going to tell you. She's done that before Dad, though under different circumstances, I wouldn't worry about it."

Kerry was choosing every word carefully. "Why didn't she tell me, son - her husband? Funny isn't it don't you think?" Kerry answered as fast as the question came. "Dad, you and Mum have hardly been on speaking terms lately. Your relationship, from this end, appears to have been very strained. I'm sure Mum was just avoiding an inquisition. She's tired and simply wants to rest with no hassle." Kerry didn't want to annoy or alert the tea maker. After all he might have been sharing the kitchen with a killer.

CHAPTER SIXTY-ONE

Back at the office, Tex was writing up some notes from the interview with Jackson when his phone rang. "Hello, DCI Deacon."

"Ah, Detective Deacon, excellent, the man I want. This is Dr.Pullman from the Royal Burlington Hospital. Patricia Jackson was my patient. I gave her the fentanyl antidote. I think I have some information here that might be of some use."

Tex leant forward and pressed the phone tight to his head, "Go on Dr. Pullman."

" Of course, Detective Deacon. It's a funny one. Something I haven't seen before. I'd given Patricia antibiotics to treat some puffy inflammation but it's in a rather interesting spot. There was a tiny residue of fentanyl around the sensitive tissue of the eardrum which may have caused the infection we found. But there's a little necrosis there too. I'm running some more tests. I'll keep you posted."

Every muscle in the gut of DCI Deacon tensed, "Dr. Pullman could you give me an educated guess? Do you have any idea how that residue might have got there?"

"Hard to say at this stage, Detective, but if you pushed me, I'd say a dirty needle caused the inflammation. We've seen this with heroin addicts. But, as I say, we've more tests to run." Tex's throat was dry, and he rasped out a few words, "Dr. Pullman, this could be very important indeed. If you don't mind, I'll send down a forensic team to assist you. This might well become critical police evidence."

Tex had seen this before. Administering poisons this way was popular, especially in the Eastern Bloc. He'd heard that the S.A.S. used this method too. "Would you testify in court Dr. Pullman."

"Of course," he replied, "We've documented the finding of fentanyl. We've stored the test tube that contains the swab samples. It would certainly be my medical opinion that the fentanyl was delivered to the infected area by injection."

CHAPTER SIXTY-TWO

The following morning, another hot one, Karl Jackson left for the Rimpton Hollway school. The trees were beginning to carry the amber shades that came when autumn began to roll onto the horizon. Karl was going in for the first of two 'Baker Days' - training sessions for teachers when the kids are off. School would officially start immediately afterwards. Kerry couldn't believe how relaxed his father appeared to be. His dad actually whistled as he walked to his VW Beetle, briefcase swinging in his hand.

On the other hand, Kerry was consumed by anxiety and didn't feel much like whistling. When he was like this, he often tinkered with his bike, which was in the concrete outhouse. This was his father's home time playground. His fascination for gadgetry kept him occupied for hours on end and gave the rest of the family respite from the resident tyrant. The outhouse sat on its own beside the garage, but there were no cobwebs here, no rusting piles of garden equipment. You would have been sorely disappointed if you'd hoped to find a dust-shrouded barbecue. This outhouse was pristine, and a slightly surgical smell replaced the usual mustiness of places like this.

Every single item had its own throne. Karl had a tool or drill for every occasion, and each one had its own special resting place, either in neatly arranged perspex boxes or hanging from shining steel bolts on the wall. The floor had been painted metallic red, which looked like fresh blood, and the walls were such a radiant white you almost needed to shield your eyes.

The bikes were on large silver butcher's hooks high on the wall. Kerry thought that a cycle around the lake might release some pressure and ease the onset of what felt like the start of a migraine. As Kerry moved towards the hooks, his attention was drawn to something on the floor. This was unusual as Karl was paranoid about spotlessness.

"Is that a seed? It looks like a ....crushed husk or something."

Kerry put it into the zip pocket of his tracksuit bottoms and felt a sizzle run up his spine, "Is this something or nothing?" Kerry was hyper-vigilant and decided to hunt, knowing the risks. Incurring the wrath of his father was a dangerous thing to do. Karl would know if anything had been disturbed, and Kerry knew that his rummaging had to be delicate. With fear beginning to ripple, Kerry was heating slowly, like a frog in a pot. He had no idea what he was looking for or what he might find. Kerry scanned the outhouse, and his eyes were drawn to a small metal filing cabinet in the corner of the back wall. It was covered by a tarpaulin, and only a few inches of the gunmetal grey peeked from beneath the canvas. Kerry gently removed the tarp and pulled out the myriad of tiny drawers one by one. The contents of every single one were arranged like a surgeon's instruments.

Kerry was about to abandon his search of the cabinet when he saw the corner of something brown, right at the back of the bottom drawer, and buried under layers of perspex boxes full of various screws, nails and other hardware sundries. It was an envelope. Kerry carefully slid it out from its hiding place and opened it, feeling sweat running down his neck. He pulled out about forty photographs, all very similar and shot on a long lens. Photos of Richard Turkington and Patricia Jackson. They weren't together, but it looked like they were arriving at, and leaving, the same hotel. Kerry knew he'd be making another call to DCI Deacon very soon to tell him what he had found. It would be up to the detective to organise a fast-tracked search warrant. Kerry was about to put the photos back and replace the envelope when he spotted something else. A small plastic zip lock bag with a folded yellow post-it note inside.

Kerry slid back the blue zip and unfolded the post-it, taking great care not to damage or crease it. He stared at a puzzling combination of seven symbols, numbers and letters, both capital and lowercase. Underneath it was a number: 372. Kerry pulled out his phone, took a photograph of the post-it and then, for safety, typed the number and the code into his reminders app. Then he carefully replaced the zip lock bag and left the outhouse.

CHAPTER SIXTY-THREE

Tex was at police HQ and trying to make sense of the lattice-style patterns in his head. He looked at the 'murder wall' which covered a significant expanse on the far side of the room. *"Another safety pin, another string. Are they going to end up in knots or tied in a neat bow?"* Tex got in touch with the research department of the Drugs Squad. They didn't need too many details to start a trail, and these guys loved nothing more than a rabbit hole, the more labyrinthine the better. Tex revealed his suspicions about Karl Jackson. Tex was confident that a well-known and respected Head of Department at the town's main secondary school would not have bought opioids directly from a local street pusher. So if Karl had bought fentanyl, where did he get it? Tex was still considering the implications of the Pullman revelations when his mobile vibrated. It was Kerry, sounding manic.

"Mr.Deacon, Mr.Deacon, I've been in Dad's man cave, our outhouse. I think I've found something…or some things. There's what looks like a husk, but it could be from the garden. Then other stuff. In a drawer. There's a strange code. Maybe it says something. Can you crack codes? You know, MI5, do they do that? And there were photos of Mum and Turkington arriving at and leaving the same hotel. Can you get a search warrant?"

Tex processed words that had been fired like paintballs, "Right Kerry. You need to do something for me. Go get those photos and bring them, the number, the code and the husk. Walk to that children's playground near your house. I'll have an unmarked car there to pick you up. We'll get you over here. Well done son, well done."

CHAPTER SIXTY-FOUR

In the incident office, Tex examined the code and the photos on Kerry's phone. Kerry had put the husk into a sandwich bag. Tex brought it to Steve Nevin in forensics - he knew that Nevin was the perfect man for a job like this. He was a particularly nerdy operative, thin as a cracker, with old-style national health glasses. He reminded Tex of Stephen Merchant. Nevin rolled the husk along the folds of his latex glove, treating it like a rare butterfly. He knew straight away what it was.

"It's a seed from a Castor Oil Plant." Tex and Nevin both knew what that meant - ricin. Tex walked at pace back to the office. Kerry liked the expression on the detective's face as he walked through the door. Kerry bolted to his feet. Tex negotiated the office door and talked as he walked. "It's a husk from the seed of a Castor Oil plant. If you knew what you were doing and you had enough of them, you could make ricin. You don't happen to know a criminally insane chemistry teacher do you?"

Kerry sat down again, wondering if his legs might give way. "Look Kerry. Castor Oil is a very common house plant. Any family member could, for example, have picked up the husk on the tread of a shoe. Do you have a Castor Oil Plant in the house?"

Kerry tried to relax, "Don't know. There are plants in the house, but identifying shrubs isn't my thing." Tex went on, the pace of his voice measured, "My gut feeling is to keep things quiet at the moment, but I've more to build on now." Tex filled Kerry in on the conversation he'd had with Dr. Pullman. Kerry was very glad that he'd sat down because he was dizzy now and felt the tears coming.

"Kerry, we have evidence of the potential of ricin production, yes, it's one husk, but it helps us to put a foot on the next rung of the ladder. We might have a fentanyl injection site. The means to make ricin was in your dad's man cave, and we have proof of the presence of fentanyl in the eardrum of his cheating wife." Tex was building a body of work with Kerry and Debbie's help.

CHAPTER SIXTY-FIVE

The next morning Karl, in a fresh and crisp white shirt, with a paisley patterned tie, left the house early for Rimpton Hollway for his second Baker Day. From Kerry's west-facing bedroom, he could hear the soft crunch of gravel as his father reversed the VW Beetle towards the open wooden gates. He'd lost count of the number of times that sound had triggered a feeling of relief. Kerry was still in bed and dozing when the doorbell rang.

Wearily he got up, pulled on his dressing gown and, cursing, stumbled barefoot down the stairs. The postman stood on the porch, a silhouette against the rising sun, "Recorded Delivery. Are you Mr. K. Jackson?" Kerry blinked, wakened fast, and his thinking sharpened. "Yes. I'm Mr. K. Jackson. Thank you very much." Kerry scribbled an illegible signature on the postman's pad and scuttled into the kitchen. Using the kettle, he steamed away the glue from the flap. Inside the envelope was a small, flat, purple felt bag with a silver tie string holding it closed. Sitting on top was a sheet of headed white card with gold lettering and an address printed on top. "Norton Commercials, Security Specialists, 27 Churchill Heights, Birkhamster." with, "Mr. K. Jackson" embossed in red. Kerry read the card, "Dear Mr. Jackson. Sorry to hear that you lost your keys. Please find, as requested, your spare set. For security reasons, we have changed the lock." Kerry looked in the bag, where he saw three tiny brass keys on a ring.

Within minutes Kerry had Tex on the phone. "You wait there Kerry. I'll pick you up. Wear a suit and tie. We're going straight to Norton's Commercials. Bring ID, but your driving licence or passport, not your student card."

***

Tex picked up a couple of things and was in the car in two minutes. He turned the key in the ignition and waited for bluetooth to connect.

Then he phoned Debbie. Now things were moving almost as fast as Tex's monologues, "There's an infection in Patricia's eardrum, and there's fentanyl there. It might have been injected, maybe with a dirty needle. Karl's son Kerry found a crushed husk and a code in their garage. He's also in possession of a set of keys. Quick explanation: with enough of those husks, you can make ricin. The code is a mystery at the moment, but I have my suspicions. I'll be at your house in fifteen minutes. Then we'll get Karl's boy, Kerry." Debbie had read the phrase 'fast-paced inquiry' in crime thriller novels, and now she was in the middle of one.

Tex noted that the normally fashionably dressed journalist was in what was, relatively speaking, her slops. Pumps, jeans and a Metallica tee shirt. She looked like a refugee from the Glastonbury festival. Debbie's list of questions came at Tex like a tsunami. Clearly, she'd gone from bed to battle mode in about a minute and a half. "Tex, what does this mean?" ... "Are we getting closer to catching Karl?" ... "Are we going to the school to arrest him?" The questions were all stitched together as one, like the segments of a centipede. Tex listened patiently while looking out for Kerry's pick-up spot. He saw him standing on the kerb when he rounded the corner into Rimpton Grove. Kerry jumped into the back seat, and Debbie turned and offered her hand. When their eyes met, they both felt a small churn of heat in the belly, and, for a few seconds, they simultaneously lost the power of speech, so Tex spoke. "Kerry, this is Debbie Pilkington. She writes for the Rimpton Chronicle. Don't worry Debbie's not here to write a story. Well not yet, but trust me Kerry, without her persistence, we wouldn't be where we are now."

Kerry had been over-excited waiting for the car, but now that he'd met Debbie, that excitement had intensified and a tingling warmth was heading south. Kerry was trying to stay calm but burbled as Deacon drove.

"What do you think we are going to find?"

Tex stayed focused on the road ahead, "I have absolutely no idea Kerry but it could be critical. We can't miss a chance like this. You know my catchphrase, 'It could be nothing and it could be everything.' Find out what you can about Norton Commercials."

Kerry Googled the company on his phone. They specialised in high security safety deposit boxes. Kerry imagined rows of them full of diamonds and gold bars. What would be in Dad's? The chatter in the car had stopped by the time they reached Birkhamster. The Sat Nav took them into Churchill Heights. The Norton Commercials site sat back from the roadside on a broad mound surrounded by an expanse of grassland and well-tended flowerbeds. From a distance, the building looked like it was made completely of glass. Tex parked up, and the intrepid trio took a few minutes to settle themselves. Then Tex handed a nervous and nauseous Kerry the briefcase he had thrown into the back seat.

"It's important to stay calm," said Tex, as he looked at the pale and sweating Kerry, whose face had turned waxy, like cheap margarine. He had a dread in his gut and an acidic burn in his gullet.

"Easy for you to say," said Kerry.

"I know Kerry, I know. We'll be here, waiting. It shouldn't take long." Debbie wanted to give Kerry a hug.

"Deep breaths Kerry," said Tex, "It's important that you hold your nerve, and yes, I know that's difficult. There should only be one moment of real tension. When they check your identification. Then go to the box, open it and take the contents. Simple."

Tex knew very well that they shouldn't be doing this. He didn't have a warrant, and, yet again, the detective was breaking protocols, but he reckoned the risk was worth it. Almost any risk was worth it if it led to the scalp of Karl Jackson.

At the front desk of Norton Commercials, the staff checked Kerry's identification. The very serious clerk, who had the look and demeanour of a KGB agent, didn't help Kerry's sense of trepidation. Kerry was sure that he smelt of fear and wondered how much attention the clerk would pay to the name? The KGB agent looked at Kerry's embossed card and his passport while Kerry's brain screamed, *"If he checks for Dad's Christian name we're all fucked."* "Nice to see you Mr.Jackson. Could you open the briefcase please? Purely for standard security reasons." Kerry now knew how drug mules felt. The empty case passed muster, and within minutes Kerry was standing in front of safety deposit box number 372. The room was heavily protected with cameras and lined with large cream ceramic tiles. The boxes were set against three of the walls in groups of eight. Against the opposite wall were a wide expensive looking mahogany desk and an upholstered green leather chair. Customers had complete privacy, they were only allowed in one at a time.

Kerry slowly rubbed his hands on his thighs, drying the dampness on his fingers and then took the silver keys out of the felt bag. He couldn't stop thinking of the cameras as he opened the security door. Kerry swallowed hard, there was another door, another layer to the security, and there was no lock.

On the second door, there was a pad, and on the pad were letters and symbols and numbers. Kerry's heart sank and then jumped. Was this the code he had on his phone? Kerry prayed to some imaginary friend while opening the reminders app on his phone and then, with care, typed the code onto the pad.

Kerry typed in a capital K, the seventh and final symbol of the code. He heard a soft buzz as a bolt slid sideways. This released the door, which popped open, and Kerry was into the inner sanctum. Inside Box 372 there was a transparent plastic folder stuffed with cash. Beside it, a cardboard box file and Kerry removed it, hands shaking. He wondered if the cameras would pick up his tremble. The silence in the room remained unbroken. Kerry took the file to the mahogany table, and the nausea returned. It crossed his mind that throwing up over critical evidence mightn't be a great move. Kerry pulled out the file's contents.

There was a CD, an A4 size manilla envelope, and nine thin journals with seven red covers and two black covers. On the front of each journal, a name was spelt out very neatly in large capital letters.

On the red journals: HARRY JACKSON, CHARLIE JACKSON, NATHAN JACKSON, PETER FERRIS, RICHARD TURKINGTON, CARLOS FERREIRA, STEPHEN CRAWFORD. On the black journals: PATRICIA JACKSON, REBECCA JOHNSON. On the

CD, there was a label, *"Turkington: Drone Footage"*. On the manila envelope were the words, *"Even the best need inspiration."*

Kerry opened a journal and immediately recognised his dad's handwriting. He flicked through the pages absorbing the horror in every one. Kerry slumped forward as the magnitude of the discovery hit him. He wanted to wail and scream, but Kerry knew that he had to hold himself together, especially in front of the CCTV. Kerry took several long deep breaths, trying hard not to hyperventilate.

The realisation hit Kerry hard. His dad had killed family, a social worker, some random Brazilian, Mum's lover, some kid called Crawford and attempted to murder Mum and a girl called Rebecca. "Mum survived. Is that why she's in a black journal? And who's Rebecca Johnson?" Eventually, when the shock had subsided a fraction, Kerry gathered up the journals, CD, and manilla envelope and put them into the thin cardboard file, which he slipped into the briefcase.

Retaining composure as he walked past the security desk was difficult, "Mr. Jackson. Everything okay? Did you get what you wanted?" The man from the KGB smiled, but with his mouth only. "Yes thank you. All good." Kerry kept moving. He wanted to run but kept the pace slow, taking long, slow, deep breaths. Tex and Debbie watched Kerry walk through the automatic sliding doors of Norton Commercials. Tex leaned forward in the driver's seat to get a better view. A thin moss of droplets coated the windows and Tex rubbed a porthole through the condensation.

A very pale Kerry was doing a poor job of looking nonplussed. He stumbled with every second or third step and fought the urge to take off like Usain Bolt. Kerry couldn't get to Tex and Debbie fast enough. When he climbed into the back seat, Kerry let out an involuntary rasp, like a death rattle. He was waving the briefcase, "Bloody Hell, Tex. My Dad is a serial killer. It's all in here. Everything."

CHAPTER SIXTY-SIX

On the drive back from Norton Commercials, Kerry cradled his head, rocked back and forth and sobbed. Kerry's overwhelming despair was the only noise. Debbie and Tex watched the road, neither of them knowing what to say. The mountains were on their horizon, a massive, bleak and beautiful graveyard. Deacon's mobile buzzed, "Kerry, sorry, can I take this? I'll let it go to voicemail if you want," Kerry didn't shift from his hunched and emotional pose, "No Tex, go for it," Tex pressed blue-tooth - it was the drug division.

"Detective Deacon, are you ready for this?" It was Steve Nevin, the very useful nerd from the dungeons of the drug department. His favourite radio programme was 'The Shipping Forecast'. Nevin enjoyed his moment, "Your boy Karl Jackson has been a naughty boy. Going back quite a long time. Payments made through encrypted transactions, and there's a recent one. Synthetic fentanyl from Asian syndicates based in China. One of the sources was a state-subsidised company, and the drugs were redirected through a Mexican cartel, so they wouldn't have come cheap. Dangerous people to deal with too. There's an impressive distribution chain, and your man was all over it. You'll be interested in this as well. Your bloke has been at this over a long period. We've traced strychnine and cyanide purchases through the Dark Web. The cyanide was drug muled into Amsterdam."

Kerry heard it all and shook his head aggressively, as if the violent movement might make this all go away. They went through a Starbucks drive-through. Still not the world's best coffee, but definitely better than the pond overflow served in the incident room. All the equipment they'd need was in that office.

***

Tex spoke to Hansen, who guaranteed them peace and quiet. When they got back, Tex opened the briefcase and took the CD out of its flimsy plastic case. The CD player was on a desk beside a squiggle-covered whiteboard with a head and shoulders photo of Nathan Jackson beside it. A drawing pin had been pushed through Nathan's chest to hold a piece of string in place.

Tex pressed play, and the audience of three was hypnotised. It quickly became apparent to a man of his experience that the CD was drone footage, but there was nothing much to see. The pictures were fuzzy - was it fog? It was like looking out of an aeroplane window while it flew through clouds. It was a short silent movie, black and white, and reminded Tex of the boatyard CCTV. Then the mist began to clear, and they could see shadows of mountain summits flitting in and out of view. After that, the pictures became clearer, and more and more distressing. Through the gloom, you could just make out a man who looked very much like Richard Turkington. He was squinting right into the camera lens, and as the drone closed to within arm's length of Turkington, there was the almost comical sight of the victim flapping at it with what looked like a walking stick or a tent pole.

Then a puff of dust engulfed the stick waver, who clutched his throat with both hands. His tongue shot out, and he dropped onto his knees into the purple heather. Eventually, he collapsed onto his face, writhed for a while, and then stopped moving. Tex and Debbie watched the CD over and over. Kerry sat in one of the few soft chairs in the room and focused on the ceiling, as if he'd just been rescued from the desert and was expecting water to pour from a crack in the roof.

An hour passed by when they turned their attention to Karl Jackson's journals. Kerry had recovered a little from his apparently parched state, "Kerry?" said Tex, "I'll understand if you don't want to read these."

"This is about family Tex, I want to see them,"

To say they were disturbing was an understatement, and Tex, Debbie, and Kerry were engrossed. Debbie knew she'd be able to fill the entire Rimpton Chronicle with this, and she was already thinking of a full-colour supplement.

Karl Jackson's red journals signified success, and black represented failure. Karl had, in detail, recorded the thinking behind and the method used in each kill. Jackson had even ranked them giving marks out of ten. The murder of Nathan was top with nine, while Harry Jackson, and Richard Turkington were awarded a posthumous eight. Carlos Ferreira, the Brazilian boy from the Blue Mountains, was a seven on the disturbed Karl Jackson scale, as was his Uncle Charlie. Stephen Davidson was the young boy's name, and he only managed a six. Tex reckoned that this was Karl's first kill. He certainly hoped this series of horrors didn't go back before that. The failures, Patricia Jackson and Rebecca Johnson, didn't warrant a score at all. The words, with one exception, were written in blue ink, and the sentences were formed in a punchy staccato style. All of the covers were highlighted, in capital letters, by the name of the victim. Written on the first one:

STEPHEN DAVIDSON.

Inside, instead of the usual neatly organised script, there was a torn-out page from a red-lined exercise book. This had been stapled onto the host journal, and on the page, in fading pencil, was the immature and spidery writing of a child: "*Kicked Stephen down the river bank today. It was fun to watch.*" And that was that - just one line.

Elsewhere, it was the craftwork of a more mature hand, the hand of evil. Tex, Kerry, and Debbie picked up journals and sat in a triangle around the table. They took turns reading excerpts of the contents. Tex cleared his throat, "*CARLOS FERREIRA: Everything went to plan. The Eastern Brown stayed sedated in my backpack for just long enough. Carlos fell asleep in the tent, and I slipped the snake into his sleeping bag. I slept well, and by morning, Carlos was dead.*"

Tex looked at Kerry, who was next to read: "*HARRY JACKSON: Success. Pressing the syringe was such a thrill knowing that a lethal toxic poison was flowing into the body of the man I loathed so much. It was such a shame I had to leave before he died. I would have loved to watch his final pathetic gasp.*"

The men looked at Debbie, who took her turn: "*CHARLIE JACKSON: Putting rubber around the handle of the chisel proved to be a masterstroke. No marks were left on the rock. The best bit was just after I had prised the webbing from the rock spike. On the far side of the cliffs, I could hear the sound of screaming as Uncle Charlie fell. I think I heard a dull thud, but I may have imagined that. The bastard deserved it.*"

Tex picked up from Debbie: "*PETER FERRIS: This was a means to an end. Felt nothing killing this one. I just needed a dead body and a motive to let me get at Nathan. My concerns were blood spatter and Ferris's yell when I slipped in the knife. That could have attracted a distant early walker. Thankfully Ferris died pathetically and quietly with a constipated grunt.*"

Kerry, of course, had already flicked briefly through the journals while in Norton Commercials. But he felt very weird reading out loud the method his Dad had used to murder his own brother and Kerry's deceased uncle:

"*NATHAN JACKSON: The combo of etorphine and valium isn't a very exciting murder weapon. Quiet death. Overall this was complicated. It was hard work having to knit together the Ferris kill and Nathan's 'suicide'. Fortunately, I managed the situation very well.*

Because there were so many moving parts, this was probably my most satisfying project to date." Kerry repeated the words, 'satisfying project to date' with horror in his voice.

It was Debbie's turn again: "*RICHARD TURKINGTON: A brilliantly perceived plan. The drone worked a treat. I was concerned that the pump syringe might not release. It was a difficult design, and there were obstacles between me and Turkington, but the GPS and the electronics behaved beautifully. The homemade ricin was a raging success. Due to the nature of my methods, I am rarely able to watch, in real-time, the death of my targets. The decision to fit a camera to the drone was inspired. Being able to watch the footage over and over was such a treat.*"

The two black-bound journals had the women's names on them. Written in jagged, angry looking red letters, on the bottom right-hand side of each cover, was the word: FAIL. By now, Kerry had returned to the haven of his soft seat, and was again focused on the peeling paint on the ceiling. Tex half expected to see Stephen King sitting in the corner of the room, taking notes.

"*REBECCA JOHNSON: This girl had begun to irritate me. Unbelievably, when I told her it was over, she threatened to go to Patricia. Rebecca had the nerve to stalk me. Her survival was a huge disappointment. I don't think I'll use strychnine again. I need to find something more powerful and effective.*"

PATRICIA JACKSON: The fentanyl was surprisingly easy to get hold of. The SAS killing fields method of ear drum injection is creative, but not foolproof."

Kerry, with the glazed eyes of a heroin addict, was thumbing through the pages inside the manilla envelope. He stopped when a phrase smashed into his senses, like a baseball bat, "I think these are Dad's heroes. How sick is this? Bloody hell."

Tex and Debbie watched the serial killer's son. They were compassionate and silent, listening to Kerry's choking voice as the magnitude of the discoveries seeped into his bones. "I think Dad has copied these from biographies on the internet. Quite a bunch they are." Kerry read verbatim from the profile.

"*Charles 'Carl' Panzram claimed to have committed 21 murders. He often described his murders in graphic detail, "His brains were coming out of his ears when I left him, and he will never be any deader." Panzram said that he had contemplated mass killings and other acts of mayhem, such as poisoning a city's water supply with arsenic. Panzram was eventually sentenced to death, but death penalty opponents and human rights activists tried to intervene. Panzram wrote, "The only thanks you and your kind will ever get from me for your efforts on my behalf is that I wish you all had one neck and that I had my hands on it.*"

Kerry was losing strength, emotionally and physically, but persevered.

"Christiana Edmunds. The 'Chocolate Cream Killer,' who carried out a series of poisonings in Brighton during the early 1870s. Edmunds purchased confectionery from a local shop and laced them with strychnine. Edmunds sent parcels of chocolates to prominent personalities, and also sent parcels to herself, claiming that she, too, was a victim of the poisoner." "Hiding in plain sight," said Kerry, whose barely audible voice was a muddied mess. He was looking nowhere in particular, his right foot making a repetitive, dull slap on the worn floorboards. Tex reached over and slid the envelope across the table. He took over the reading of this most unholy of documents.

"Donald Harvey was a prolific American serial killer and hospital orderly who claimed to have murdered 87 people. Harvey said he started out killing to 'ease the pain' of patients by smothering them with their pillows. He mostly killed cardiac sufferers."

Deacon instantly thought of Harry, and his nervous system shuddered. *"Harvey used many methods to kill his victims, miscellaneous poisons; morphine; turning off ventilators; insertion of a coat hanger into a catheter, causing an abdominal puncture and peritonitis. The majority of Harvey's crimes took place at the Marymount Hospital. Harvey did not limit his victims to helpless hospital patients. When he suspected his lover and roommate Carl of infidelity, he poisoned his food with arsenic."*

Deacon's delight at the discovery of the damning evidence was tempered by grim realisation. It seemed to have been a dream of Karl Jackson's to join the pantheon of the 'greats' in his field. Kerry had moved to the low sofa bed beside the door and was sobbing again, his knees pulled to his chest. Debbie, however, was leaning forward, her fingers wrapped around her cheekbones, chin cradled in her palms.

"This has been quite a day, quite a day," she looked at Tex and then at the page, encouraging him to read on.

"Donald Ewen Cameron was a Scottish-born psychiatrist who served as President of the World Psychiatric Association. Cameron was viscerally criticised for his role in the development of psychological and

medical torture techniques. Some of this work took place in the context of the Project MKUltra program, which focused on mind control and psychoactive poisons."

Tex noticed a loose page that was still in the envelope. It wasn't a profile. It looked more like a leaflet, with a photograph of a shrub on one side and the information on the other.

"The castor oil plant from which ricin is derived is a common ornamental plant and can be grown at home. The United States investigated ricin for its military potential during World War One. At that time, it was being considered for use either as a toxic dust or as a coating for bullets and shrapnel. The Soviet Union also weaponized ricin. The KGB used ricin outside the Soviet bloc, most famously in the Georgi Markov assassination. In 1978, the Bulgarian dissident was assassinated by secret police who stabbed him with a modified umbrella. They used compressed gas to fire a tiny pellet into Markov's leg. It was contaminated with ricin."

Kerry sat up at the mention of the word ricin. He appeared, for now, to be back on Planet Earth. DCI Deacon leant back, bending the plastic chair and held court, "Kerry. It looks like your father has written his own life sentence."

CHAPTER SIXTY-SEVEN

The following morning Debbie was back in the day job at the Rimpton Chronicle, wondering how she could ever replicate the adrenalin rush of the previous day at Norton with Tex and Kerry. Writing a story on missed bin collections didn't exactly consume her with enthusiasm. Elsewhere, Tex was in the car with Kerry alongside him. The contents retrieved from the security box had been bagged up, marked as evidence, and put into the hands of the investigation team. The men drove to the grounds of the school at Rimpton Hollway. Kerry's head was still melting, but, fortunately, he wouldn't be needed for now.

Inside the Rimpton Hollway School, the chemistry and technology teacher Mr. Jackson had just started the post-lunch class with the senior students. After the two Baker days, this was the first day proper of the new term. The sun streamed through the half-open venetian blinds, casting spikes of light across the desks. The room was pungent, as it always was when the classroom was full of teenage boys. Jackson had his back to his pupils, writing formulas on a whiteboard. Karl's shining brown shoes stood flat on a small platform. He was immaculate as always, wearing crease-less charcoal trousers and a cobalt shirt. The classroom door, which had a central window, opened through the middle of the back wall. Tex Deacon walked in unnoticed. He watched Karl's back for a few seconds, and listened to the squeak of his pen tip on the whiteboard. Then Tex made an exaggerated throat clearance. The boys turned as one connected herd, and the teacher spun on the heels of his brogues. The two protagonists locked eyes. Not a word was spoken. From behind him, Tex pulled a red journal and held it up so that Karl could read the words on the front.

HARRY JACKSON

CHAPTER SIXTY-EIGHT

After several months in custody, the trial of Karl Jackson began. The schoolteacher was charged with seven murders and two attempted murders. Rebecca Johnson came forward two days after news of the arrest of Karl Jackson had been released and told police of her suspicion that she too may have been poisoned. She told the police, "I had an on/off affair with Karl. I had a period of about nine days when I suffered from stomach cramps and agonising spasms. I didn't report it at the time simply because I thought it was extreme food poisoning. I took Imodium and electrolytes, and that was it. Eventually, the problem went away."

Being able to put Rebecca and Patricia on the stand, two alleged survivors of Karl Jackson's murderous intent, gave the prosecution an advantage. Dr.Pullman had already agreed to give evidence of Patricia's suspicious infection. The Drug Squad's successful dig into Jackson's dark web manoeuvres added another crucial layer.

The story of the alleged serial killing teacher from a sleepy, picturesque mountain village in the shadows of the mountains of the Lake District attracted international attention. There were plenty of photos in the press and on television of Jackson at school prize-giving ceremonies and in mountain fell races. The hyenas of the media loved the fact that the accused was a fit, swarthy and good-looking athlete. They published multiple action photos of Jackson with arms and legs akimbo as he searched for balance on the wet rock. The journalists didn't hold back on their portrayal of the killer as a bit of a sex symbol, and one tabloid even compared him to Ted Bundy. Jackson was described as a 'popular rural teacher' with a 'dark side' who lived a 'bizarre and murderous double life.' There were dramatic splash headlines like, 'The Rampage of the Rimpton Psycho.'

Under those were multiple columns of sensationalist copy with 'See pages 5,6,7 and 8 for more.' The spreads inside carried details and photographs of all of the victims. Journalists scrambled to find an appropriate and descriptive epithet for the suspected murderer, 'The

Chemical Killer'; 'Mountain Murder Madman.' One of the red tops went, simply, for 'Killer Karl'. At The Rimpton Chronicle, Deborah Pilkington's by line was printed below day after day of front page leads. Not long into the trial Tex noted a short piece of copy inserted into the bottom right of the newspaper's cover - the headline was 'Norton Commercial withdraw security company's contract'. That made Tex smile. Debbie was also writing features for the national press under the heading 'Special Report'. Tex controlled the content to make sure that the case wasn't compromised, which frustrated Debbie, but she understood.

The case itself lasted eleven weeks and received frenzied attention. Every day the public gallery was jammed and outside, underneath the Union Jack that flew from the courthouse roof, hundreds more milled around. A vast bank of TV crews curved around the building, with reporters relentlessly chirping their reports to various distant outposts. Any time someone arrived at, or left the courthouse, they would be besieged, quickly surrounded by a hive of yelping journalists. Karl Jackson came and went in a secure police van. Photographers would morph into basketball players and slam dunk at the windows of the vehicle, firing off a firework display of flashes.

The damning evidence, as expected, was the collection of notebooks which contained reflections on each kill and attempted murder. The newspapers called them the 'Journals of Death.' The prosecution brought in a calligraphy expert. When comparisons were put up on the large courtroom screen, it was abundantly clear that it was the handwriting of Karl Jackson, with the letters and words punctuated with dramatic swirls and sweeps.

***

At this trial, unlike the Gary Bloomberg case, there had been a very noticeable lack of smugness from Jasper Montague. He only had one real get-out in his limited repertoire. Montague persuaded the judge to discuss his argument that the journals and the rest of the contents of the safety deposit box should be dismissed as evidence. Montague approached the bench with prosecution lawyer Duncan Thurgood and spoke directly to the judge, The Honourable Mr. Justice Delamont. "Your honour, we are here to uphold the rule of law and the proper administration of justice. Some evidence, in this case, has been covertly obtained. This was privileged material and personal data belonging exclusively to the defendant. These documents were acquired illegally and therefore should be declared inadmissible."

Judge Delamont was having none of it, "I suspect that you are banking on my powers of discretion working in favour of your client, Mr. Montague. Yes the contents of the safety deposit box were obtained through a technically criminal act. As you know, Mr. Montague, there is no absolute prohibition of covertly secured evidence. That's if it is particularly relevant to the case, and here I think you'll agree it's particularly relevant. This court will allow the presentation of all material facts. You are overruled Mr. Montague." Jasper felt like he'd just been attacked by a psychotic octopus in hobnail boots.

Thurgood and DCI Deacon were immensely relieved. They were much more hopeful now that the flamboyance of Montague's approach and his wardrobe full of paisley waistcoats and colourful bow ties wouldn't save Karl Jackson.

Apart from Jackson's forthcoming appearance in the dock, there was another showpiece moment. Montague and DCI Deacon coming face to face in a court of law. Montague may have been one of the earth's most obnoxious humans, but when on form, he could be good. Tex took the oath and Montague sauntered, lounge lizard style, towards the DCI. Tex was ready for Jasper's passive-sarcastic approach.

"Detective Chief Inspector Deacon. I'm going to make this easy for you. All I need are yes or no answers because this, ultimately, is a yes or no case." Tex began to chew the tiniest corner of his bottom lip. "DCI Deacon, can you one demonstrate beyond all reasonable doubt that my client, Karl Jackson, murdered Stephen Davidson?"

Tex's reply? "No."

DCI Deacon, can you demonstrate beyond all reasonable doubt that my client, Karl Jackson, murdered Carlos Ferreira?

"No."

Jasper Montague asked the same question several times more, and, of course, Deacon's reply changed to "Yes" for the deaths he felt he could prove as murder. Montague also covered the fact that Deacon had been working without official consent for part of the investigation. Tex knew that he had to play a waiting game. However, the cross-examination from the despised Jasper hadn't been easy. Tex resented being silenced, and the chew of Tex's lip had become a gnaw by the end of his cross-examination. He could taste blood.

The Jackson defence was the bizarre assertion that the journals in the security box were written with a book in mind. Montague announced, with some triumph, "The killings were all in the public domain. My client made some notes about them. Is it a criminal offence to write fiction? If it is, we need to get out there now and arrest John Grisham."

After much mewling from Montague, Tex expanded on his evidence, and, despite a few, "Objection your honour," pleas from Montague, which were all declined, Tex painted a picture of Jackson's arrest.

"By the time I entered Karl Jackson's classroom, our response team had already surrounded the school. Jackson looked at the journal I was holding and froze for about three seconds. Then he charged straight at me. I braced myself, however, the man we were about to arrest for multiple murders wasn't interested in me. This was all about self-preservation. Jackson was desperate to make it to his only possible route of escape, the door behind me. I left the physical stuff to the armed officers who, by now, were in the corridor. Jackson put up a good fight, and it was a decent struggle, but quite quickly,, Jackson was overpowered. Strangely, I thought, he didn't scream, shout, or even utter a word. He was a much more subdued figure than the uber-confident man I had encountered before."

Montague intervened, "But this is all natural human instinct from my client. A threatening detective enters his place of work, what would I or you do? I'll tell you DCI Deacon, we'd make a run for it. It's natural preservation to try and get away from the fear -

313

fight or flight DCI Deacon - Mr. Jackson chose both. After all his amygdala was fully fired up."

Tex continued with an expressionless gaze, and without breaking stride, it was as if he hadn't heard a word Montague had said. "In terms of evidence, even at that early stage, we were very confident of securing a conviction. The journals were the central plank. Also significant were the remains of the castor oil plant seed husk that Kerry Jackson had found on the outhouse floor. The Jackson's had never possessed a Castor Oil House plant. The forensic evidence and the superb work by the drugs squad gave us that important critical mass." Montague was in again, but louder this time, "I'm still waiting for your gotcha piece of evidence DCI Deacon. This is all either circumstantial, spurious or explainable."

Again Tex calmly allowed the interruption and went on as if Jasper was a ghost in the room. "In the journals, Karl Jackson had described in enthusiastic detail how he had killed or attempted to kill each victim. The method he used to murder his own brother was particularly vile. In the outhouse, we found the tools and machinery necessary to make the drone and the electronics to fly it. The manilla envelope included biographies that read like tributes. Jackson worships at least four serial killers."

Jackson denied all charges and throughout treated the court with arrogant contempt. In the dock, Karl took an interesting tangent. Through promptings from Jasper Montague, Karl went for the crime fiction novel defence. It was all they had. "It's unique, at least," Tex whispered to Duncan Thurgood, who smiled and raised his eyes. Jackson set off in full theatrical mode, something Tex had witnessed first-hand during his visits to Jackson's house.

"It's going to be a blockbuster, a New York Times best seller. Every incident can be easily explained, and everyone here knows that. Each death cut me deeply. They were friends and family, I knew them all in some shape or form. I think my documenting of the tragedies was my way of dealing with it all. Call it cathartic."

***

The Jackson, Montague defence of the case was simple, "All of the so-called evidence is either coincidental or circumstantial." They hoped they would be able to manipulate the jury with that attack strategy and clever verbal dexterity. Jackson did his best, but his performance was generally unconvincing, like the desperate attempts of a rim block to fragrance a chemical toilet. At times Jackson became almost vaudevillian in style. There were occasions when some members of the jury appeared to be submerging laughs behind cupped hands.

This was like a Woody Allen movie - but less well-written. It wouldn't have been a huge surprise if Karl had cried out, "The killer is behind you," with the packed courtroom harmonising a reply of, "Oh no he isn't."

"So what is the truth?" said Karl, appealing directly to the jury from the dock, "The boy on the river bank, Stephen Davidson: Accident. Slipped down the bank. Carlos Ferreira: Carlos had been bitten by a snake: Accident. Harry Jackson: Natural Causes. Charlie Jackson: Accident. Nathan Jackson: Suicide. Peter Ferris: Murdered by Nathan. Richard Turkington: Murdered by an as-yet-to-be-named Contract Killer. Patricia Jackson: Overdose. Rebecca Johnson: Lies from her, a vengeful ex-lover. She even said she thought it was food poisoning. The contents of my safe, nothing more than research for my New York Times bestseller thriller. Show me a crime writer who hasn't got a vivid imagination."

Duncan Thurgood asked Jackson why he thought his version of the deaths could possibly be believable. Jackson was ready for that, and when Jackson started, he was almost impossible to stop. "There's a true story about a guy, Jim Cochrane, who played for a football club, go check it out; it was Bransfort Town FC. He was accused of the murders of several members of the team. The police had an old black-and-white photo of the side. The accused - a teenager in a men's squad - was sitting at the extreme left end of the bottom row. The Captain was holding a trophy, 'The North-West Amateur League Cup'. Shift twenty years on from the photo being taken, and our alleged murderer was the only one left alive. The rest had died, a few from natural causes, but many of them suspiciously, in Bransford and other villages, towns and cities around the country. A detective had been tipped off about a possible link between the deaths, and off he went, determined to find 'the killer.' So what did the police know? That the supposed killer had never been picked in the starting lineup for any major match. Which was true. Cochrane was always a substitute."

Thurgood achieved the almost impossible by interrupting and appealing to the Judge. "Where in heaven's name is this getting us to Your Honour?" "I get your point, Mr. Thurgood, but I'll allow Mr. Jackson to finish his story. It may not be relevant, but at least it's entertaining." There was a ripple of quiet laughter from sections of the court.

Karl continued, "The police said that this 'crazed and seriously mentally disturbed psychopath' murdered purely through a fit of anger that grew through envy and jealousy. Cochrane had been teased about his lack of ability and had decided to get his revenge, slowly working through those who had relentlessly bullied him. Jim's paranoia told him that the team had a vendetta against him, but what had really happened? The other players had died in various ways, some were a little suspicious yes, but nothing untoward was ever found. Just like my case the police had forced pieces that didn't fit into their imaginary jigsaw. Cochrane, by now a broken man, was eventually released. He'd killed no-one."

Tex watched on, remembering that he'd also been guilty of making at least one imaginary jigsaw in this case. The prosecution still had key men to call. Lex went through the forensics from the Turkington murder site, but, of course, there was no proof that Jackson's bead of sweat had been dropped on the rucksack clasp at the kill site. However, Lex asserted that the sweat "must have fallen from a height due to the splash outline". Karl noted that several members of the jury looked at each other at that moment. Jackson had a cover story for that, which was the truth - he had met Turkington at 'Lucifers' car park.

Thurgood questioned Daniel Triskin from the drugs squad, who told the court that Jackson had paid for illegal substances through surreptitious methods via suspect foreign accounts. Dr. Pullman was called to give evidence about Patricia's infection and the tiny quantity of fentanyl found in her eardrum, which, in his professional opinion, had been delivered by injection.

Another key moment came when the CD footage, collected from Jackson's security locker, was played on the court's big screen. The defence struggled to explain away why Jackson had in his possession rushes of a man who was about to be murdered. When the fog cleared to reveal a startled and panicking Turkington, there were gasps from the jury. Montague did, of course, attempt to make sense of the CD content, "Many companies use drone footage commercially." "Filming from drones has become a popular hobby." Montague focused on the 'hobby' defence and the 'fluke moment' when it just happened to appear above Turkington just before he died, but this defence was all rather flaccid.

On Wednesday of the trial's eleventh week, the prosecution and defence read their closing arguments. Montague's address to the court was brief and delivered with saggy resignation.

***

Legally, Jasper and his client were dead meat and must have felt like the dinosaurs did just before the asteroid hit the Earth.

On a Monday morning at three minutes past eleven Judge Delamont received the judgement from the jury and rose to his feet, "Karl Jackson. You have been found guilty of the murders of Stephen Davidson, Carlos Ferreira, Harry Jackson, Peter Ferris, Nathan Jackson, Charlie Jackson, and Richard Turkington, as well as the attempted murder of Patricia Jackson. The case of Rebecca Johnson shall remain on file. You are hereby sentenced to the maximum term under this jurisdiction… Forty years in prison without parole."

Like the day in the classroom, Karl Jackson didn't say a word, and sat upright with the accelerated blink rate of his eyelids, the only inference of extra tension. Debbie was sitting in the press gallery, scribbling at pace, and once more, her story would lead the front page.

Jackson moved his head and stared with fury at the judge and jury, a look of flint-edged hate on his face, but, again, said nothing. The killer scanned the court and found his nemesis DCI Theodore Deacon. For a few seconds, their eyes met. Then Karl Jackson was taken down.

CHAPTER SIXTY-NINE

A category 'A' prison was the only place for Karl Jackson, who'd been designated as 'Highly Dangerous', and he was sent to HMP Wakefield in West Yorkshire. The prison was also known as Monster Mansion, but this particular monster quickly became an exemplary resident. Some of the prison officers were sucked in by his charisma. Jackson was polite and helpful, and within a couple of weeks, albeit with two guards present, he was allowed to do a little ad hoc teaching with a few of his fellow long-term inmates. Plenty of prisoners study behind bars. Some never had the opportunity to gain an education while encased in the hurly-burly bubble of their own criminal world. For others, it was something to do to alleviate the long days, weeks, months and years of boredom. The lucky ones had a release date and wanted to build a skill set that they could take into the outside world. 'Fat Jake' Muscroft fell into this category.

Jake was a 'Peaky Blinder' kind of character, and he was coming to the end of a twenty-one-year sentence for a gangland-linked manslaughter. Muscroft and Jackson quickly developed a decent friendship. Karl, who had an agenda, of course, was rather sceptical about the nature of Jake's conviction and would quiz him about the killing, whispering out of earshot of the guards, "How is repeated pounding to the head with a breeze block interpreted as manslaughter?"

Jake would laugh in response. He had a year to go on his sentence and was now being allowed sporadic days at home. The 'resettlement overnight release scheme' helped inmates prepare for life after prison. Karl wondered what Jake might do with his basic chemistry and technology education. Maybe build a dungeon and keep a stock of sulphuric acid, so he could dissolve the body after his next so-called manslaughter.

DCI Deacon kept tabs on the progress of the latest killer he'd helped to convict. This was standard for Tex. He'd done the same with Thomas Jacobsen (The Black Lodge Assassin), Colin Nedbank,

Gary Bloomberg and Arnold Nutley. Karl could have had Nutley released by admitting to those additional murders - but he didn't - psychopaths love to keep some of their secrets, if they can. It gives them a feeling of power.

Tex received regular reports on all of the serial killers he had put away. Deacon liked to remind over-enthusiastic psychologists that psychopaths couldn't be fixed. He referred them to the Canadian Oak Ridge Experiment results, which backed up Tex's argument. Tex was, by now, well into writing his memoirs, 'The Hunter and the Hunted.' He had been procrastinating about writing the book, and it was Debbie who convinced him to do it, and she even came up with the title. The main spine of the book were Tex's taped and written profiles compiled during interviews with killers, and now he had Jackson's journals too.

Two of the convicted men, Nedbank and Bloomberg, had agreed to follow up conversations. This had become a more regular procedure in policing and during these discussions Tex learned so much about these people and why they did what they did. Information gained from DCI Deacon's face-to-face recorded sessions helped the authorities to spot psychopaths early, leading to quicker arrests and fewer murders. Before conviction, killers, including Karl Jackson, usually stressed innocence. Once inside, with little chance of parole, some were prepared to talk about their crimes. There was gold dust to be gained from the minds of the guilty.

***

Psychopaths love to boost their vast egos. Bloomberg, in particular, enjoyed burying himself in the malevolent fissures of his mind. He even showed Tex, using gruesome actions, how he'd removed, with his teeth, the flesh medallions from the corpses of his victims. Some psychopaths get a huge kick out of reciting their crimes. It allows them to relive the moments that brought them so much pleasure. Tex always recoiled when serial killers delved into the details. They could deliver a description of the most horrific specifics in the same matter-of-fact way they'd describe a visit to the prison library.

Tex wanted to talk to Karl Jackson in prison and conduct a series of interviews. He was fascinated to see if Jackson would, even this early, let him into the inner workings of his unhinged mind, and, as Debbie kept reminding him, the memoirs wouldn't be complete without that conversation. Tex had to clear it first with the Chief Constable. Barbara Bracewell felt delight, relief and justification when Jackson was convicted because the faith she'd put in Tex had paid off, but here was Tex again, pushing those boundaries.

"Tex, can I remind you of the moment when Gary Bloomberg lunged at you to prove that he could actually do the flesh medallion trick. That prison officer had to move like Muhammad Ali to prevent you from, quite literally, becoming lunch." Bracewell did have a weakness though. She was a sucker for Tex's 'little boy lost' persuasiveness. The Chief Constable gave his request the all clear as did the prison service who were getting used to these follow ups. In the modern era everyone knew the value of profiling.

Tex only needed to tick one more box. He needed Jackson's agreement, but wasn't surprised when the consent came back. Tex had a great feel for the way that psychopath's thought, and the date for an initial meeting was set. Deacon had eight weeks to prepare, and he started counting down the days. Tex hoped the killer of seven would be in a boastful if not repentant mood.

CHAPTER SEVENTY

Karl Jackson had managed to acquire an extra blanket for his segregated cell at Wakefield. The charm was still working with some, but the prison governor, Charles Dagnall, wasn't taking risks with this relentless sociopath. Jackson's food was always delivered, pre-chopped, on paper plates with soft wood cutlery. He didn't want this relentless killer to use his technology skills to make weapons. In the canteen, there was no fraternisation with fellow prisoners. Maybe Dagnall thought Jackson could fashion deadly poisons out of mashed potatoes and parsnips. Jackson was also segregated for his daily exercise, so his only proper human contact was during his heavily guarded teaching sessions. Dagnall agreed to those, "Well, if he can do some good in here, we'll let him."

When a prisoner walked into Wakefield prison, he entered hell. It had the look of a Russian Gulag, and was as welcoming to a man as an oil slick was to a seabird. This grouchy gargoyle of a building would have been the perfect setting for a poltergeist B movie. The chatter of incarcerated men reverberated constantly, the evil retained by a long arched ceiling. Dark souls lived in dark cells, contrasted by the cream walls on the parallel raised walkways outside the steel doors. Wakefield had hosted some of England's most notorious criminals.

The guest list included Dr. Death: Harold Shipman, the Soham child killer Ian Huntley, and Levi Bellfield, who had a penchant for butchering teenage girls.

***

Karl did his teaching classes in his cell, with those two armed guards standing like gate posts nearby. 'Fat Jake', in particular, was voracious for knowledge, and Karl gave him full focus during their chemistry and technology lessons. Jackson got as close as he could to Fat Jake, befriending his fellow killer.

Jackson knew that Jake's day release scheme could work to his advantage. Jake was allowed to keep his exercise book for further home study. The guards sometimes flicked through it, but they were only cursory glances. On the outside, as well as being an expert with breeze blocks, 'Fat Jake' had specialised in money laundering and fraud. He knew his way around a computer. Karl built two codes into the chemical equations in Jake's book. One was the access to his Dark Web account, and the second was for a certain substance. During a teaching session Jackson whispered instructions to his star pupil.

"Access to the dark web is the easy bit. An unmarked package will arrive and will not raise suspicion. I've done this exact process myself. There'll be bubble wrap inside. Remove the duct tape and wrapping with extreme care. I can't stress that enough… extreme care." "What's in the package?" was a fair question from the obese prisoner. Jake, of course, like all of the inmates, knew exactly what had led to Jackson's incarceration.

"Could this stuff kill me?"

"No," Karl insisted, "You'll be one hundred percent protected, if you are careful when unpacking it. Inside the bubble wrap sleeve, you'll find a tiny, transparent, hard silicone rubber pearl, with a viscous amber liquid inside."

Fat Jake followed Jackson's instructions, and when the time came to return from his latest day release, Jake lifted a layer of fat that hung from his morbidly obese two hundred-and-eighty-pound frame, and found a sweaty crevice. The pearl was the size of an average ball bearing, and Jake pushed it deep into a slab of flab. 'Fat Jake' had been through enough internal and external body searches to know that he'd have no problem getting Karl's micro-sized gift back into the prison.

CHAPTER SEVENTY-ONE

There was one proviso Jackson had laid down before he would talk on the record. He wanted five minutes in private with Tex Deacon to go through what Jackson described as 'the parameters'. Jackson insisted that there'd be no recording of any kind during this brief encounter, and Tex guaranteed it.

***

Jackson sat on the edge of a springless mattress supported by wooden slats. His wrists were handcuffed close together, which made him look like he was holding a small bird. Jackson's ankles were chained to the legs of the bed, which allowed him about six inches of wriggle room. A prison officer flicked the latch on the viewing window, pushed an eyeball towards it, and then clanked a key into the lock. Its turn created a small symphony of echoes. Jackson was wearing the uniform of a maximum security prisoner. A baggy green and yellow boiler suit. Two armed officers entered the cell and did a final sweep, making sure to check Jackson's cupped hands for anything - perhaps a razor blade.

Steel bars separated Jackson's holding cell from the one next door. Charles Dagnall, who had given the final green light for the meeting, was taking no chances. Tex appeared at the doorway of the sister cell, flanked by two officers who were holding weapons. Jackson looked at his nemesis, but the man with the mask was, for once, unable to disguise a sneer.

The agreement had been for a private meeting, and this was respected. The two cell doors were shut and locked, with an officer present at each viewing window, always watching, and primed to move fast if required. Then the smile that Debbie found so attractive lit Jackson's face. Tex wondered how Jackson would react if he told him that two of the people who helped catch him, Debbie and Kerry, were dating.

Jackson was on the front foot straight away but spoke so quietly Tex could barely hear him. "Well, well. Detective Chief Inspector Tex Deacon. As I live and breathe. Here to see the smartest killer he ever captured. Isn't that right Detective Deacon? The Genius Killer? You said it yourself."

The cells had a natural chill, and Tex was surprised to feel sweat prickling on his spine. "Karl. You said you had parameters. I respect that. You'll be giving me your time." Tex knew that he had to play Jackson's game. The serial killer rocked his head from side to side, "Oh, I've plenty of time - thanks to you."

Tex got to the point, "What do you want Karl?" Jackson pouted his lips, "There's one thing they won't allow me to do in here, but it's a problem you can solve. They won't let me talk to Kerry. Honestly, I don't know if Kerry wants to talk to me. The prison services just refuse me any contact with my son at all, in person, by letter, or anything, and they won't tell me why. Here's how you can make me happy."

Jackson's chains jangled as he strained to lean forward, "I want you to get a letter from me to Kerry, that's all, and here's what we'll do. At the end of our big interview, we'll shake hands. I'll have a one-page letter, folded tightly, in a small plastic bag at the cuff of my boiler suit.

You take it and give it to Kerry. I'll tell you anything you need to know in the interview - full disclosure."

Tex knew that, once again, he'd be stampeding all over protocol, but he looked at Jackson, waited for what seemed like a very long time, and nodded. Tex was desperate for the interviews, and Karl had banked on DCI Deacon's maverick tendencies.

CHAPTER SEVENTY-TWO

DCI Deacon sat in front of one of two doors on opposing walls of a bright white room in Wakefield prison. The high wattage in the ceiling strips flooded a centrally placed angular wooden seat. It looked like an electric chair without the wiring. Tex had seen this kind of set up many times. The feng shui in this room was designed for interrogation.

A shaft of sunlight sliced through a single pillar box window and cut like a sword across the interview chair. The gunboat grey steel door opposite Tex swung open. Karl Jackson stood still for a moment, eyed the detective, and was then shuffled towards his seat. He was heavily shackled as before and clanked as he moved. Even Tex was surprised by the size of the protection team as six armed officers filed in one by one. The man at the front, who had held Jackson by the elbow on the way in, used the leg irons to clip Jackson to bolts attached to the base of the chair. Unless he had concealed a welding torch, there was zero chance of the killer escaping. Once the other five officers had formed a semi-circle, the lead man removed Jackson's wrist chains. Jackson flexed his wrists, hands and fingers. He was sitting roughly ten feet from Tex, who opened his mouth to ask his first question but didn't get a chance to make a noise.

Jackson was off, "What was that closing line in Scooby-Doo? "I'd have gotten away with it if it wasn't for those meddling kids." You didn't do it on your own did you Tex? The Superman Detective needed a lot of help. What happened to your cape Tex? Did you get a rip in it? Swallow some kryptonite?

My boy Kerry has got a big future, and I'm very proud of him, you know. And your journalist friend Deborah - pretty little thing. I watched her in the press gallery in Court. I think we could have had a good time together. Anything going on between you and Debbie? Your wife is dead, isn't she? Agonising death I heard. Did you groom Debbie? Well, did you? You can tell me. I won't say a word." Jackson sniggered.

Tex didn't react to the baiting and chose to remain silent. "Is that why you made so many mistakes Tex? Did the death of your wife affect your decision-making? I never let the death of others affect my decision-making. In fact, the very thought of the death of others improved mine. Things like grief are signs of weakness Tex, and that's why people like me are superior. When you told me you thought Nathan was a multiple killer in that first interview in my house, I nearly pissed myself. You're no genius Tex, that's for sure."

Tex stayed on message, "Seven dead, could have been two more. Karl, what kind of man does that?"

"What kind of man? The kind of man who knows when he's been betrayed. Every single one of them deserved what they got. I'll qualify that slightly. Peter Ferris maybe didn't deserve it, well, not from me. You could say I was doing it for Nathan. Doing him a favour. My brother hated him. Maybe he would have killed Ferris sometime anyway. Sorting out Ferris was nothing more than part of a plan. Carlos? He was too popular. It was costing me money, and anyway, killing Carlos was great practice. My Dad? Any one of the family would have been justified in killing that bastard. Uncle Charlie? All paedophiles should die."

Tex was now getting exactly what he'd come for.

"Nathan? He snitched on me. You don't squeal on your twin brother. Turkington was having an affair with my wife, I'd plenty of justification there, didn't I? It should have been nine. Patricia? She was cheating on me, and I was punishing her. Turkington was fucking my wife. What would you have done? Rebecca was stupid. I gave her an opportunity to get out of my life, and she chose to hang around. What did she expect? It - Should - Have - Been - Nine, ten if I'd had a chance." Jackson looked cold and hard into Tex's eyes, "Ten would have been a lovely round number. Wouldn't it, Tex?"

The expression on Tex's face didn't change, and neither did his tone, "You've missed one of the seven out. The boy. He was only seven Karl. Stephen Davidson."

Jackson's response was a laugh, "I was young too. I was just mucking about. The way kids do. If he'd made it back to the bank, I might have pulled him out. Do you know anything about the human brain Tex? At that age, the prefrontal cortex is very poorly developed. It's the part of the brain that manages impulse control. It helps you to predict the consequences of your actions. My prefrontal hadn't fully formed, it's an evolutionary glitch, so God's fault if you believe in a creator. Are you religious Tex? Design flaw. Davidson's death? Go blame God."

Tex was finding it difficult, but he stayed cool and composed, "Emotionally, Karl how does it feel to be a serial murderer?"

Another laugh from Jackson, "Emotionally? That's funny. Emotions and mind states are dangerous, so I don't bother with those apart from the fun ones like revenge. And you said murderer. Nonsense. I didn't murder anyone. Not in the way Bundy did or John Wayne Gacy, Ed Kemper, Dahmer or Shipman. Lust killers, greed killers. My kills were not murders in that sense Deacon, I simply dealt with people who deserved to be dispatched. That's a different philosophy and we all have our philosophies don't we Tex? You talked about yours at that lecture. Feeling Stoic today are you, Tex? And one more thing. You didn't catch me. I got sloppy and you and your acolytes got lucky."

To Tex, it was no surprise to hear Karl Jackson justify everything. People like him weren't very good at accepting blame. All he wanted to do was boast about his exceptional ingenuity and the quality of his execution. The tightly regulated two-hour window allowed by the prison service for this first interview was passing fast. Karl, in terms of background, had helped Tex immeasurably. This would make for a fascinating start to the central chapter in his memoirs. Tex had one more question for Jackson that had been bugging him. "Karl, why didn't you destroy your journals and notebooks?" Jackson looked at Deacon for a long time, considering whether he should speak or not. Eventually the serial killer spoke in a low monotone, "I should have, shouldn't I? ...but I lost the fucking keys."

***

A buzzer went. Time was up. There wasn't a molecule of honour or remorse in Karl Jackson, but Tex was a man of his word, and when Jackson stuck out his right hand Tex looked at the senior guard, "Can I shake his hand? The prisoner didn't have to do this interview. The information has been very helpful to me and very helpful to the authorities." The six officers snatched quick looks at each other. The senior man spoke, "Up to you Detective Chief Inspector. We've got you covered." Jackson's leg irons were just loose enough to allow him to stand up. Tex took two steps forward and stretched his right hand to meet the serial killer's.

The grip was loose, allowing room for Jackson to slip the palm-sized, folded and sealed plastic bag down his wrist and into the hand of Tex Deacon. The transfer was completed in a few seconds. Tex put his hands behind his back as if to hitch his belt, and slipped the letter into his pants. Jackson, without a backward glance, was led away. Guards gripped Karl's biceps and turned the killer towards the door. The ankle chains clinked like bling jewelry and a hard smirk played across his lips.

The amber liquid inside the transparent silicone pearl Fat Jake had smuggled in was VX. An odourless nerve agent developed for chemical warfare. It had been illegally stockpiled in Asia. Tex had actually read about it in Karl's college newsletter, "An Evil Way To Die - The Enthusiasts Guide to a Toxic Death." As Karl had recorded, it was "One of the top three toxins in the world." The globally banned VX was a poison used to assassinate Kim Jong-nam, the half-brother of North Korean dictator Kim Jong-un. Two assassins approached Jong-nam at Kuala Lumpur Airport, and a minute globule of VX was smeared on his face with a cloth. He was dead within minutes. When absorbed through the skin it doesn't take very much VX to kill. The amount of liquid you'd find in an average teardrop contains approximately 2,500 fatal doses.

***

In the dead of night, Karl Jackson, with a blanket wrapped around his face, had used a folded sheet as a makeshift glove. It was the nearest Karl could get to a hazmat suit with the fabrics available in a prison cell. This was not the time for him to lose his genius. Karl had a pin to pierce the pearl and knew he had an hour between prison officer cell checks. He ground down some lead from a tiny pencil and made a thin paste from the minute droplets he'd squeezed from the pearl. Jackson wrote a short note with the paste and slipped the impregnated sheet of prison notepaper into an envelope. On the page, the chemistry teacher had written. "DON'T OPEN MY MAIL"

The End

ABOUT THE AUTHOR

Mark Robson is a sports journalist and broadcaster with over forty years of experience working for many channels including SKY Sports, the BBC, UTV, ITV, Eurosport, BT, Premier Sports, Setanta, Eirsport and NEP. His focus now is on rugby commentary and he works mainly on international matches which go to a global audience through the 'World Feed'. Mark has commentated on four Rugby World Cups, two football World Cups, and the Olympics in Sydney 2000.

Fell running has been a passion for Mark, he has run over a hundred races and competed in many navigation-focused Mourne Mountain Marathons. Mark has also run several 50-mile Ultra races (very slowly he says) and they include the Addo Elephant Safari Park Ultra in the Zuurberg mountains in South Africa and the Grand Raid des Pyrenees. Mark has hiked in the Andes, the Blue Mountains, the Picos de Europa, the Alps and many other ranges around the globe, so no surprise then that quite a bit of 'The Genius Killer' is set in the mountains. In this case, the magnificent peaks of the Lake District.

PLEASE REVIEW

Dear reader,

Thank you for taking the time to read my book. As a first time author, I would really appreciate if you could tell others about it if you think it is something they would enjoy to read. Also if you could leave a review of the book on Goodreads or if you purchased the book online, if you could leave an honest review there.

This matters because most potential readers first judge a book by what others have to say. Thanking you in advance.

Mark

Printed in Great Britain
by Amazon

31621421R00192